1976

Modern Chinese

Modern Chinese Stories

SELECTED AND EDITED BY

W. J. F. JENNER

Translated by W. J. F. Jenner and Gladys Yang

OXFORD UNIVERSITY PRESS

LONDON   OXFORD   NEW YORK

Oxford University Press

LONDON OXFORD NEW YORK
GLASGOW TORONTO MELBOURNE WELLINGTON
CAPE TOWN IBADAN NAIROBI DAR ES SALAAM LUSAKA ADDIS ABABA
DELHI BOMBAY CALCUTTA MADRAS KARACHI LAHORE DACCA
KUALA LUMPUR SINGAPORE HONG KONG TOKYO

ISBN 0 19 281087 1

Selection, introductions, and translations by W. J. F. Jenner
of stories by Gao Yuanxun, Guo Tongde, Rou Shi, Guo
Moruo, Mao Dun, Lao She, Ye Zi, Zhang Tianyi, Ai
Wu, Zhao Shuli, Gao Langting, Sun Li, He Guyan, Fang
Shumin, Wang Xingyuan, © Oxford University Press 1970

First published as an Oxford University Press paperback 1970
Reprinted 1972

The translations by Gladys Yang of three stories by Lu Xun
and of the two modern storytellers' stories are from publications
of the Foreign Languages Press, Peking.

*Printed in Great Britain by Richard Clay (The Chaucer Press), Ltd.,
Bungay, Suffolk*

CONTENTS

INTRODUCTION

Although a number of anthologies of modern Chinese stories were published in the West in the 1930s and 1940s, and although many have been brought out in translation by the Foreign Languages Press, Peking, over the years, contemporary Chinese writing has so far failed to make any serious impact in parts of the world formed by very different historical and cultural forces. This is not very surprising. In their formal and technical qualities the stories of nearly all modern Chinese writers except Lu Xun have little to offer to those in search of literary novelty and brilliance. The main aims of this collection are to illustrate life and to enable the reader to see some Chinese views of the world.

In the fifty years covered by the collection the Chinese people have gone from a feudal, medieval society, predominantly rural and backward in character, through the agonies of famine, disaster, civil war, and literally murderous exploitation, to evolve a revolution of prolonged intensity that has already lasted for several decades, profoundly changing the lives of all who were involved. A quarter of humanity has been drawn into struggles on every scale from the global war against fascism to the conflicts inside an individual's mind on whether to handle some problem in his own or the general interest.

Most of these struggles have been set in the countryside, where the overwhelming majority of the population live. The traditional order there was one that some writers portrayed as idyllic, though a sombre picture of oppression and want was both more common in literature and nearer to the truth. The landlord, the official, the tax-collector, the money-lender, and the press-ganger (these functions could be combined), together with the natural disasters of drought and flood, made the peasant's livelihood precarious at best and all too frequently impossible. Though death from starvation was common, writers, not usually threatened with the same fate themselves, rarely found it worth dealing with. Although many of the peasantry resigned themselves to their lot, there were always sparks of resistance. Thus the villagers of northern Anhwei province preserved the memories of the Nian rebel heroes who had fought against the Qing rulers in the nineteenth century. When the traditions of peasant war were brought up to date and given a reasonable basis in ideology and organization by the Communist Party from 1927 onwards, the old order was first rocked to its foundations and then toppled.

It would be hard to exaggerate how deeply the villages have been changed by the long and still incomplete revolutionary process. Peasants, previously unprepared and ill-equipped to make complicated political decisions, took over the running of their own villages in a few parts of the country during the stormy years of civil war in the 1930s, in much larger areas during the war against the Japanese invasion (1937–45), or through the land reform completed almost everywhere by 1953. In this last movement the economic, social, and political power of the landlords was destroyed not so much by administrative decree and Party directive as by the mass action of the peasants. The position of women, one of the most fundamental injustices of the old society, was radically changed now that they owned land and property and had begun to take their rightful part in political life. The difference between the heroines of 'Slaves' Mother' and 'The Moon on a Frosty Morning' is one that could be paralleled millions of times over in real life. Because the revolution has freed them from even more shackles than their menfolk, they have often been its strongest supporters.

Within a few years of the redistribution of land by the peasants through land reform, private farming came virtually to an end. In the middle 1950s the aptly named high tide of socialism brought the peasants into collective agriculture. The co-ops and the communes that soon succeeded them involved far more than economic reorganization. The family unit ceased to be the sole focus of loyalties when people learned to work together for the common good, which was not always easy. The people's communes had to overcome natural as well as human obstacles to development, and the strains were most critical in the lean years around 1961. It is from the trials of collective agriculture that most of the best novels and short stories in contemporary China have come. The raw material has certainly been rich enough.

As so many of China's writers have been city dwellers, much of their work has been on urban themes. This collection has tended to include rather few of such stories. This is because in the first part of the period covered far too many of them were written by, about, and for schoolteachers and students on themes familiar enough to Western readers and without any outstanding merit. Such work has, besides, been well represented in earlier anthologies. In more recent decades stories on such themes have tended to be sugary, while inhibitions about discussing factory problems with the same frankness used for rural subjects has meant that stories by and about factory workers have not generally been up to the standard of their peasant counterparts. It may be that the Cultural Revolution will open the way for more serious treatment of urban problems in literature.

War and army life have featured strongly throughout the fifty years. In the earlier decades most wars fought in China—and they can be counted by the hundred between 1911 and 1936 alone—were struggles between war-lords for power and plunder. Like the barons of feudal Europe at their worst, and with much more murderous weapons, they caused untold suffering to their soldiers and the peasantry alike. Writers naturally had little to say in favour of such wars; the wretchedness of soldiers and their victims was a common theme in their work.

Other wars met with different responses. Guo Moruo and Mao Dun, for example, were among many writers who made active propaganda for the Northern Expedition of 1926, when, during the heyday of the Communist–Kuomintang alliance, the revolutionary armies with peasant, worker, and student support swept away war-lord power in parts of south China. This was also a war against imperialism, as is illustrated by Guo Moruo's sketch 'Double Performance'. When the Northern Expedition was turned into a massacre of the left by Chiang Kai-shek the next year, most writers became anti-army again. The epic campaigns of the Red Army over the next decade were too far from the cities and under too strict a censorship to be the subject of much literature at the time, though the remarkable Ye Zi did refer to them and some of their veterans wrote about them later, as did Gao Langting in 'Huaiyiwan'.

The comparative easing of censorship and the surge of patriotism in the first years of the war against the savage Japanese invasion gave war literature the chance to develop in the Kuomintang-ruled areas of China. In those parts of the countryside where the Communists led the guerrilla struggle against Japan, the urgent needs of the war effort and the revolution made the demand that literature should educate and inspire the ordinary peasants, soldiers, and cadres a pressing one, while the growth of mass literacy ensured such writing a readership that would not otherwise have existed. Such literature was naturally concerned not so much with the sufferings of war as with its achievements, and since then writing on military subjects has dwelt on the heroism of soldiers and civilians as well as, more recently, the deep political dedication of the men of the People's Liberation Army. Such writing is popular: in a country where armed force was necessary to overthrow an extremely violent old order and is still needed to protect the revolution, outright anti-war sentiment is not to be expected, and is besides not published.

Right through to the 1960s writers have normally come from a fairly small part of the population. In recent years there have been a number of workers, peasants, and soldiers taking up pens and writing brushes, but the bulk of published work has come from those who earn their living through words—journalists, teachers, office workers, and professional novelists, for example. From the 1920s to the 1940s the short story was almost exclusively an urban middle-class product, even when dealing with rural themes. The readership was small, making it difficult even for a successful writer to sell more than a few thousand copies of a book. The rewards were so low that to be a full-time professional writer, to say nothing of a rich one, was a near impossibility. It was not until the 1950s, with the rapid growth of literacy, that royalties and fees enabled some authors to live well, in some cases after political changes had brought their writing careers virtually to an end. Although royalty arrangements were later adjusted to prevent a writer from making a fortune with a best-seller, some members of the Writers' Union received a monthly grant that often separated them from the working people with whom they were supposed to identify. One result of the Cultural Revolution may be to make it more difficult for writers to be a race apart; another will be to encourage amateurs. In the short term the flow of published work has been reduced to a trickle.

No discussion of Chinese literature, past or present, can go far without considering politics. In antiquity even lyric poetry or a ghost story could be used to carry a deliberate political message; the Confucian philosophies were more political than religious; and the execution of writers hostile to the Kuomintang regime in 1931 was but the continuation of a tradition over two thousand years old. If the advocates of art for art's sake met with suspicion in feudal times, the harsh realities of modern China have made them appear to be deliberately attempting to weaken the leftist tendencies that have had so strong an influence even among the middle-class writers. That art should be propaganda is usually taken for granted; the arguments are over propaganda for what.

The modern short story in China has been part of the pattern of revolution and counter-revolution since its birth. The journals, some published in exile, in which young intellectuals learnt how to write in an approximation of the language of ordinary speech instead of the dead, difficult, and sterile classical style, carried stories side by side with political attacks on the old order. Before the 1920s the mere attempt to write seriously in the vernacular was a form of rebellion. One name stood out above all others in the short story— that of Lu Xun. Others, such as Chen Duxiu and Hu Shi, theorized, but Lu Xun alone among the leaders of the new literature movement wrote stories still worth reading. His art, though not at first

Marxist, was always consciously political. It was also consciously art.

The anti-imperialist demonstrations from 4 May 1919 onwards, that were sparked off by the refusal of the Western powers to treat China as an equal, sovereign power, also marked the beginning of a literary movement that flourished in the following decade. This movement, largely confined to urban intellectuals, was deeply influenced both ideologically and formally by the Europe and Japan of the bourgeois revolution and by Russia, whose Tsarist past and Soviet present were often closer to the realities facing Chinese writers and the hopes in their minds than were Western Europe or North America. Its strong points were a demand for change, rejection of the feudal culture that had oppressed China, and a willingness to experiment with new ideas. Its weakness, both in art and life, was inadequate contact with ordinary people. The writers generally spoke only for themselves and their own small class in a language that was too alien for those who were not intellectuals.

There is little to be gained from studying the details of the disputes between the ever-changing literary-political groups that flourished in Shanghai and elsewhere in the 1920s and 1930s. Apart from a few ultra-rightists on one side, and a larger number of dedicated revolutionaries who did more than just talk on the other, the continuing tone was one of dissatisfaction with the state of China and of a greater interest in foreign rather than in Chinese literary forms. Many of the writers of short stories were also translators, and while this broadened horizons in many useful ways, it also helped to distract some from looking hard enough at their own country and its literature.

When some of the members of these groups of the 1930s became leading figures in the literary establishment first in Yenan, the Communist headquarters during the war against Japan, and after 1949 throughout the country, their creative careers tended to end while at the same time they gained political influence that they had never enjoyed before. A series of struggles against various older writers has been portrayed as a clash between the advocates of authority and those of freedom. A more basic issue was the role of the bourgeois intellectual in the People's Republic; appeals for freedom appeared to those who did not share their privileges to be demands for more power. They did not have the popular prestige that writers enjoy in some other countries because their art and literature was still too alien. These struggles came to a head in the Cultural Revolution with the final ousting of 1930s writers from positions of power. It remains to be seen whether professional writers will emerge again.

The clearest and most authoritative Communist directives on art and literature were given by Mao Tse-tung at Yenan in 1942. Writers were urged to think in terms of which side they were on, for whom they were writing, and how best to serve their interests. It was no good being theoretically in favour of serving the people if your work used forms, grammar, and vocabulary that they did not understand. The weapons of satire and ruthless exposure were to be kept strictly for use against the enemy. Foreign forms, like those of China's own feudal past, could only be used if they were adapted to the needs and tastes of the masses. Politics had to be in command.

By these criteria the short stories of earlier years had not done very well. Their writers had been too busy learning the techniques of the European story to pay much attention to the living and very popular art of the storyteller except in an occasional and academic way. In rejecting the stifling aspects of the traditional culture they also ignored the oral forms that meant most to the ordinary man, and while these writers usually sympathized with the sufferings of the people, they rarely bridged the gulf that separated them. It is one of Lu Xun's many strong points that he did recognize and regret this, as he showed in 'My Old Home'.

In these respects the literature of the liberated areas during the war against Japan and the Third Revolutionary Civil War (1946–9) showed a way forward. Zhao Shuli and others drew on the ballads and story-telling of rural entertainers to bring the short story back into touch with Chinese traditions while changing the contents to meet the needs of the new situation. Even if, as has been said recently in China, Zhao Shuli was not able to make the jump from resisting feudalism and foreign imperialism to supporting socialism, his contribution at that time was a considerable one. Even more significant was the unprecedented surge of amateur writing by men and women who would have been illiterate but for the revolution.

Although the Yenan Talks were regularly proclaimed as the guideline for art and literature during the first decade and a half of the People's Republic, Mao Tse-tung himself and others were increasingly dissatisfied with the political soundness of much of what was produced. The debates on literature and class struggle grew into the storms of the Cultural Revolution, whose constructive literary results have yet to be seen. Very little creative writing has been published since 1966.

If so political a discussion of the short story seems odd to the Western reader it should remind him of how wide is the gulf between the mood of revolutionary China and that of a society in which style and technique are far more important than content. That which seems familiar and acceptable to Western eyes may become alien and irrelevant or even repulsive out of its own context. Similarly, the Westerner tends to wish that contemporary Chinese fiction had a little more room for the exploration of individual character, and that didacticism was subtler.

In the fifty years covered here the story has moved from the coastal cities back into the countryside; foreign styles have been absorbed into the Chinese literary form and have influenced the traditional short story; and only in the past decade or two has this new Chinese story been produced. There is still plenty of room for further development, and this is likely to take it still further away from Western ideas of what short stories should be like. The Chinese revolution is, after all, creating a very different sort of society.

In making this collection I have tried to follow criteria that are often incompatible—those of my own background and those of the Chinese revolution. Readers may decide which stories were chosen on which grounds. On the whole, the problems of choosing stories from the earlier decades were not so great, since one was dealing with what was in some ways an extension of Western literature, at any rate in form and approach. For the later twenty years, in which the short story has been much more Chinese in both style and spirit, it has been difficult to find stories that are faithful to the popular, enthusiastic, and intensely political writing of a revolution but which will not seem too foreign to the reader.

This selection makes no pretence at representing anything more significant than the editor's tastes. There has been no attempt to include all the well-known names. It is only fair to the authors whose work is included to explain that nobody asked their leave to do so. The translations of the stories by Lu Xun and of the latter pair of storytellers' tales are from the work of Gladys Yang, whose great contribution towards making Chinese literature available in English, though known to a few, has yet to receive the general recognition it deserves. The other translations and the introductory notes to all the stories are mine. I am indebted to others who have helped in many ways, particularly Miss Judith Osborne of the Oxford University Press, who removed much stylistic awkwardness from the typescript; I alone am responsible for mistakes.

W. J. F. J.

Leeds 1969

A NOTE ON PRONUNCIATION

Apart from very well-known names of places, people, and institutions I have used the Hanyu Pinyin system of romanizing Chinese in this book. This is the one adopted by the Chinese Government and taught in Chinese schools; it is gaining ground as the standard method for writing Chinese words in roman letters. I have omitted the tone-marks. The author's name in Wade-Giles spelling, where this differs from Hanyu Pinyin, has been added in brackets at the head of each story.

Full and systematic explanations of the phonetics of standard Chinese and how they are represented by Hanyu Pinyin can be found in a number of the more recent manuals of the language; the serious student is advised to consult one. A fairly good idea of what the names of the characters in the stories sound like can be got by pronouncing the letters more or less as one would expect. Some of the trickier sounds are these:

a	as in 'father', never as in 'late'.
ao	rhymes more or less with 'now'.
c	is 'ts'. Thus *cang* is read *tsang*.
chi	is roughly 'chuff' without the 'uff'.
ci	is roughly 'rats' without the 'ra'.
g	is always hard, as in 'get'.
i	is 'ee' after all consonants except c, ch, s, z, and zh, when it is a buzzing of the vocal cords with the teeth nearly together and the lips relaxed. Before another vowel it is a 'y' passed lightly over.
o	as in standard English 'hot', never as in 'moat'.
ou	nearly rhymes with English 'go'.
q	is 'ch' and is always followed by a closed vowel.
qi	is a lighter version of 'chee' in 'cheese'.
qu	can be approximated by saying 'chew' in a Scottish accent.
si	is roughly 'sud' without 'ud'.
u	is like French 'u' when it follows j, q, and x or is written 'ü'. Otherwise it is a lighter version of English 'oo'.
x	is written in some romanizations 'hs', which gives an idea of what it sounds like—a cross between 'h' and 's'.
zh	is roughly English 'j'.

W. J. F. J.

TWO NIAN STORIES

The living fiction of modern China, as of earlier periods, has generally been the storyteller's tale. Its more sophisticated professional practitioners can be traced back to the tea-house entertainers of Hangchow and other cities nearly a millennium ago and still flourish in the towns; while every village has its tellers of tales on themes old or new.

The two stories that follow were collected at the beginning of the 1960s, probably in north-west Anhwei, the area where the great Nian (otherwise spelt Nien) rebellion with which they deal grew up about a century ago. Apart from their fresh and vigorous style, that stands in contrast to much westernized writing in China, they are of value for the impression they give of what the Nian rebellion and its leaders mean to the descendants of its participants. The picture is of course rather different from the dry and hostile one that historians have compiled from nineteenth-century official sources. Liu Eryuan, for example, the hero of the first story, is little more than a name in more orthodox accounts; and the battle reports of the campaign in which the Mongol general Senggelinqin (the Seng of the second story) was defeated and killed after being led a dance round several provinces by the brilliant Nian cavalrymen do not report his failures in quite such vivid terms as the second story.

Such stories help us to understand more of the traditions of armed insurrection and guerrilla war that the Communist-led Eighth Route and New Fourth Armies revived in the former Nian areas during the struggle against Japan, showing as they do that although defeated the Nians were not forgotten, becoming instead legendary figures. It is impossible to know about the evolution of these stories over the past hundred years or to guess how and to what extent they have been edited for publication.

Gao Yuanxun 高元勋
[Kao Yüan-hsün]

Liu Eryuan

All the older folk have heard of Liu Eryuan. His real name was Liu Yuyuan, and his childhood name Dog Liu. 'Old Liu Eryuan' was a nickname he was given later.

He came from Tengxian in Shantung. When he was seven his father was thrown into prison because of a quarrel with a landlord, and died there. As Dog Liu's family had no land, and he and his brother were too young to be of any help, they all depended on his mother for food and clothing. She had been widowed at twenty-eight and by the time she had brought up the pair of them her tears would have filled a couple of gourd water scoops.

In the twenty-sixth year of Daoguang [1846] the county of Tengxian had a very poor harvest. That year the rich were laying off their labourers and storing up their grain, while the poor had to sell their land and leave as famine refugees. It goes without saying that in Dog Liu's family they could not even get husks or wild plants to eat.

'We'd better go away too, mother,' said Dog Liu one day.

'All the crows in the world are black,' said his mother, 'and life is as hard for the poor wherever you go. Where could we go that would be better?'

'Everyone says it's better to go a thousand miles south than one brick's width north. Let's go south. It's our only chance of surviving—I can't let you stay here and starve.'

After a great deal of persuasion his mother finally agreed.

'Very well then. As long as you two boys are willing to work and won't let my old bones be scattered about far from home, we'll do as you say.'

The two boys loaded a wheelbarrow with their battered belongings, put their mother on top, and went to the town of Yimenji with one of them pushing while the other pulled.

They put up a matting shed by the river bend at Four Bridges there, and settled down.

How true it is that nobody cares about a poor man. They lived there for the best part of a year without anyone taking any interest in them at all. Just imagine what sort of a life it was for the three of them. Their mother took in washing and the two youngsters gathered firewood or went begging with sticks in their hands. Sometimes they ate and sometimes they didn't, but they managed to keep going.

As Dog Liu was now a young man of seventeen his mother searched high and low until she found a kind-hearted person to put in a word for him and get him a job as a farm labourer for the rich landlord Deng. A few months later, when the autumn wheat harvest was in, Deng fired him with the excuse that there was less work to do in the winter and that he ate too much.

Dog Liu was furious. 'The rich are vicious,' he thought. 'They eat the donkey that used to turn the millstone for them.'

'Never mind, son, forget it,' his mother kept saying, 'and keep your mouth shut. Remember how your father died.'

Dog Liu went on thinking about the whole business.

'When a man is poor his belly doesn't do well.' It was true that Liu was a big eater—he could down a dozen or so half-pound steamed loaves in a single meal. He was so strong that he could tuck a three-hundredweight sack under his arm and walk off with it. Once the landlord Zhao, who lived at the west end of Yimenji, had a *chun* tree over three spans thick cut down. 'If you can carry that away, Dog Liu,' he said, 'you can have it.' Dog Liu braced himself and, believe it or not, grabbed it in his arms and carried it home without stopping.

Liu was never able to get another job as a long-term hired hand because the landlords all thought he ate too much. He was only able to get temporary jobs in the busy seasons of spring and autumn, and in winter and summer he had to manage by selling green vegetables, melons, and fruit.

At last he caught the eye of Ma Laowu, the ganger at the Yimenji waterfront. One day Ma Laowu said to Liu's mother, 'Don't let Dog Liu go on messing about like this. I can find him a job.'

'What sort of a job could he possibly get?' his mother replied.

'He's so stupid, there's nobody who would do him a favour, and he hasn't any capital.'

'I'll guarantee him for working on the waterfront.'

'You're too kind, uncle,' she said. Then she told Dog Liu to kotow to him.

'I'll be working for my keep, so why should I kotow to him.'

' "If you're poor you're three generations junior to the rich," so don't be silly,' she said. 'Do as your mother tells you, there's a good boy.'

So Liu became a dock labourer. When he went to the dock to start work the next day, the book-keeper told him to register.

'What's your name?' he asked.

'When I was six,' Liu thought, 'my father gave me a proper sort of name but, though I'm in my twenties now, I've never used it. Well, today I can.' So he replied, 'My name is Liu Yuyuan.'

'Nonsense. Someone like you can't have a fancy name.'

'Why ever not?' asked Liu in astonishment. 'My father gave it to me.'

'Rubbish. Dockers are low people and they can only have low names.'

'I knew that there were rich and poor,' thought Liu, 'but I never realized before that people could be divided into high and low.' He started getting very angry, but he checked himself when he remembered that the poor were weak. Low he would just have to be. Swallowing his anger he said, 'My name is Dog Liu.'

The dockers who were standing there found him amusing but sympathized with him at the same time. One of them said to him, 'Liu Yuyuan, Liu Yuyuan, you really are a yokel. Why didn't you ever find out that people like us aren't allowed to use fancy names?'

From then on they often called him Yokel, and from then on also he had a regular job.

After over two years as a docker Dog Liu had grown a lot wiser, learnt some skills, and become stronger than ever. The others could only lift one two-hundredweight bag of salt at a time, but he could manage two or three. He had a violent temper, but not with everyone. He was honest, straightforward, and hard-working. All his work-mates liked and respected him.

One day Ma Laowu came to Liu's home with two strings of cash just when he was eating. Ma Laowu came in grinning and said to Mrs. Liu, 'How are you, Mrs. Liu?'

Never having been spoken to like this before, she hurriedly put down her bowl, pulled up a straw cushion for Ma Laowu to sit on, and asked him, 'How do you find the time to come here, uncle?'

'I wanted to see you. Do you have enough rice porridge to fill your bowls these days?'

'Yes, all thanks to your help, uncle.'

'Good. As long as you remember who did you the favour that's all right. Times might get harder again. Here'—he handed her the two strings of cash—'take this money.'

'What?' she said in astonishment. 'I couldn't possibly take all that money from you for no good reason at all, uncle.'

'Ma Laowu,' put in Dog Liu, sure that something was wrong, 'say whatever it is you have to say. We don't want your money.'

'Yuyuan,' said Ma Laowu with an ingratiating giggle, 'what I'm getting at is this: up to now I've deducted twenty per cent of your wages. But my expenses are rising these days, so I want to raise the deduction to twenty-five per cent. I'd like you to put in a word for the idea among your mates. That'll do the trick. Of course, when I make the twenty-five per cent deduction I'll leave yours at the old level.'

When he heard this Liu leapt eighty feet into the air, he was so angry. 'Damn you bloody rich,' he cursed, 'you vicious lot. You take twenty per cent of our wages without lifting a finger all day and you're still not satisfied. Do you want to squeeze every last drop of blood out of the poor?' In his fury he tossed the two strings of cash right out of the door and told Ma Laowu to get out.

As Liu was so influential among the dockers Ma Laowu was really scared of him. He didn't even dare to sigh. He went outside, picked up the money, and scurried off with his tail between his legs.

The incident gave Dog Liu's mother a terrible fright. 'Dog,' she said, 'you'll get yourself killed.'

'Don't be afraid, mother. What if I do get killed?'

Although Ma Laowu ran away that time it was not the end of the matter. If a ganger wanted to pick a quarrel with a docker it was as easy to get his hands on him as to put out someone's eye with a drill.

Once Old Liu Eryuan, as he was now known, was out on official business with twenty or so other dockers carrying salt for a government salt shop. After they had been shifting the salt right through until nightfall the salt official checked and insisted that they were two sacks short. 'You paupers have been stealing government salt,' he snapped, 'so I'm sending you to the magistrate's office. You'll have to make the salt up too.' The dockers realized that he was deliberately trying to put pressure on them and tried to argue with him, their eyes blazing. Liu, unable to hold back his temper, gave the official a piece of his mind: 'I've been working for nothing all day, my lad, and I haven't dropped a pennyworth of it, and now you're trying to rake the stuff in for yourself.'

'As you've come forward,' said the official, 'you must be the ringleader in the salt-stealing.'

'That's right,' said Liu, who was angrier than ever. 'Go ahead and do something about it.'

'Tie the wretch up.' No sooner had these words left the official's mouth than four or five thugs came out of the salt shop and tied Liu up.

This was too much for the dockers, who rushed on the thugs like a pack of twenty tigers and beat them up till they fled. Liu grabbed a carrying-pole. The salt official must have been destined to die young: at a single blow from the pole blood came gushing out and his head went flying. That was the end of a much hated man.

This fight involving the twenty or so of them was the start of something much bigger. Ma Laowu had only intended that the official should extort some money from them to avenge himself, so when the incident turned into something so serious he was panic-stricken. He rushed to the sergeant in charge of the local military post and gasped, 'It's terrible, sir, Liu Eryuan and twenty odd dockers have risen in rebellion. They've smashed up the salt shop and killed the official. I beg you to take the necessary precautions at once.'

No sooner had the sergeant heard this news than he mustered fifty men, each wielding a huge gleaming sword. They headed for the salt shop as fast as they could go, arresting or cutting down every docker they came across. When they reached the salt shop they found the twenty or so dockers distributing the salt to the poor. This made the sergeant so angry that he ordered two of them to be killed as an example. Those of the poor and defenceless people who did not run away fast enough were caught and cut in half by the soldiers.

The sight drove the dockers into a fury. Liu Eryuan roared in a voice like a clap of thunder, 'Let's get 'em even if we have to die for it.'

'Yes!'

'Kill the misbegotten devils,' shouted the common people, angry too.

They all swept round the fifty soldiers like a flood-tide. Liu Eryuan, who was so big and so strong, shot forward like an arrow, grabbed one of the soldiers, took the sword from his hand, and killed him with it. In the twinkling of an eye the street in Yimenji was a river of blood. More and more of the common people joined in with hooks, spades, and carrying poles till the soldiers were wailing like ghosts and howling like wolves.

The sergeant was by now petrified with fear as, one by one, his men were killed till only a few remained. Ma Laowu was already dead. The sergeant had to charge wildly around till he was able to break out and, instead of going back to his barracks, he fled from Yimenji to the town of Bozhou.

The dockers were all beside themselves with joy. 'With you as our leader,' they said to Old Liu Eryuan, 'we'll fight.'

This was how Old Liu Eryuan rose in rebellion at Yimenji. Later he led a force of over a hundred thousand men to join Old Zhang Loxing.[1]

(*As collected and edited by the Guoyang County Nian Story Team.*)

[1] The most famous early leader of the Nian rebels, Zhang Loxing (Chang Lo-hsing, 1811–63) called the Nian bands together in 1855 at Zhihe to form a unified rebel organization.

Guo Tongde 郭同德
[Kuo T'ung-te]

The Flagpoles

Zhang Zongyu, the Prince of Liang,[1] and Ren Huabang, the Prince of Lu,[2] were taking it in turns to lead the fiendish Qing troops by the nose, fighting round and round in circles. One day they would be in Honan province and the next in Shantung. Their tactics were like a game of tag in which the Qing troops were able to catch sight of them but could never get hold of them. The evil Seng was furious. 'That old wretch Zeng Guofan[3] was able to beat the Taipings,' he thought, 'so why shouldn't I, a full prince of the Great Qing, be up to smashing a few lousy Nians?' He was far too angry to think of any way of dealing with the mobile tactics of the Princes of Liang and Lu.

The more the evil Seng thought about it the greater his fury became; his eyes were blood red, he swore at everybody, and he was always pulling his sword out. 'Heroes,' he shouted throughout the day, 'listen to me. If you don't catch up with the Nians in another three days I'll cut off your heads, you dogs.'

So the evil Seng and his Qing troops rode on and on after them, and as the days dragged by the men were so tired that they ached in every limb and the horses were so worn out that

---

[1] One of the later Nian leaders. A native of north-western Anhwei, he became a brilliant exponent of mobile cavalry warfare, defeating Senggelinqin's Mongol cavalry and killing their commander in 1865. His own end after being encircled by Qing troops in 1868 is not clear. His title, like Ren Huabang's, was a purely honorific one conferred by the Taiping Heavenly Kingdom, one of the other great rebellions with which the Nian co-operated.

[2] Another Nian commander closely associated with Zhang Zongyu. He was killed in 1867.

[3] Zeng Guofan (Tseng Kuo-fan, 1811–72), whose official career is a symbol of the crushing of rebellions and the defence of the Confucian-feudal order, took the Taiping capital at Nanking in 1864.

their coats were falling out. Over a month more went by, and still they had made no contact with the Nians.

One day they reached the town of Zhuxianzhen in Honan. Seng was so exhausted that he gave the order to pitch camp and rest. He had just sat down on his camp stool and poured himself a cup of wine when a cavalry scout came running in.

'Your Highness, the Yellow Banner Nian Zhang Zongyu's flag is flying by the pine wood ahead of us.'

'Hoho, we've got 'em.' The evil Seng dashed his cup to the ground, leapt on his horse, put his telescope first to his left eye and then to his right to search the horizon, and found that there was indeed a flagpole beside the pine wood. At the top of the pole fluttered a yellow flag with the name Zhang on it.

Seng put down his telescope, and said with a cackle, 'Did you think you'd get out of my clutches, you dirty Nians? Heroes, to the wood and after them.'

The Qing troops, who were so tired that they were lying stretched out on the ground gasping for breath, had no inclination to be after them at all.

When the evil Seng saw this he pulled out his sword and started to curse them at the top of his voice: 'What do you draw your pay for, you dogs? Be after them or I'll behead the whole damn lot of you.'

The evil Seng led the charge to the flagpole, roaring, 'The Nians are in the wood. Surround them. Don't let a single one get away.'

The Qing cavalry rushed the wood, but after a long search they did not find even the hair of a Nian.

Seng's face turned green, then white, and in his rage his goatee beard curled right up. 'Damn them and curse them, they did this deliberately to stop us resting and getting a meal.' As he said this he drew his sword with a great swish and took a hack at the middle of the Nian flagpole. There was a loud crack as the flagpole, made of bamboo as thick as a rice-bowl, broke in two. Then with a roar thousands and thousands of hornets poured out from inside the bamboo pole; they blotted out the sky as they swarmed towards the evil Seng. In the twinkling of an eye he was so covered with stings that he looked like a ball of puffed rice stuck together.

'Damn you, you slaves,' howled Seng for all he was worth, 'up and at 'em, up and at 'em.'

The colonel in charge of his escort just gazed at him in stupefaction, not knowing what to do.

'Get them off,' shouted Seng, 'get them off.'

The colonel had no idea what he was meant to get off, but as he could see that Seng was scratching his head he grabbed the strap of his own hat and pulled it off. Then, when he noticed that Seng was dancing around because his feet had been stung, he hurried to tug off his own boots, after which he knelt helplessly on the ground.

The evil Seng's horse had also been stung so badly that it was bucking about. Seng was thrown to the ground, where he rolled around still shouting, 'Strip me and kill them. . . .'

Only then did the colonel of the guard realize what he was meant to do. He scrambled to his feet with his hat and boots in his hands and started flailing out at the hornets all over Seng's head and body. This didn't drive them away. The only result was that Seng yelled and cursed him, 'Damn you, slave, get my jacket off and hit them.'

The colonel at last understood what he was really meant to do. Tearing off Seng's jacket he hit him and hit him until the hornets were finally driven away.

Seng's face was as swollen as a judge's, his hands were so lumpy that they looked like a pair of toads, and he could not see out of his eyes. He was moaning and groaning with no sign of stopping.

As the saying goes, when the scar heals you forget the pain. It certainly applied to the evil Seng. Within a few days he had recovered from the stings and was after the Nians again, pursuing them harder than ever. Before he had just been following orders, but now he was doing it for all he was worth. Even when half of the horses were dead from exhaustion he did not care. The chase had to go on.

One day they reached the county of Dingtao in Shantung province, and they still had not caught up with the Nians. The evil Seng was absolutely exhausted, so tired that he could not even hold his horse's reins. He had just put a halter round the animal's neck and was on the point of having a meal, when in rushed a scout to report, 'Your Highness, the flag of Ren Huabang, the Blue Banner Nian, is flying by the grassland in front of us.'

Seng leapt on to his horse, looked through his telescope, and saw that there really was a tall flagpole by the grassland. At the top of it flew a blue flag with the word Ren on it.

Seng may have been angry before, but now he exploded. 'Damn you, Ren Huabang, you and your blue Nians are trying this trick on me now. After them, my heroes.'

The Qing troops rushed into the grassland and turned the area upside down. They didn't find even the shadow of a Nian.

As Seng gnashed his teeth in fury, looking at the tall Nian flagpole, he suddenly burst out in a rage and started swearing. 'Damn the bloody Nians. Do they think they can gobble me up? They've got no more chance of doing that than a tiger has of eating grasshoppers with comfort. I'm not fool enough to fall for that trick a second time.' So turning round he shouted, 'Heroes, make me a burning brand and pile dry grass round the bottom of the flagpole.'

They soon had a big pile of grass round the base of the pole. Seng took the brand from one of his guards, cackled, 'I'm going to have the pleasure of burning you myself,' and thrust the brand into the grass. The dry grass lit easily and was soon burning away; the flames licked closer and closer to the flagpole, which was made of bamboo the thickness of a rice-bowl. In a few instants the flames turned it first brown, then black, and finally red before it split open with a popping noise. Suddenly there was a tremendous roar followed by a series of explosions all over the grassland that threw the sandy soil into the air and blacked out the sky for a moment. Thousands of the evil Seng's soldiers and horses had indeed found a place to sleep.

Seng was really quite lucky, because the moment he heard the bang he had realized something was wrong and clutched the colonel. The blast lifted the pair of them high in the air, and when they came down Seng used the colonel to cushion his fall. Although Seng wasn't killed he was badly wounded.

Where did the gunpowder come from that blew up when Seng set fire to the flagpole? It was part of the flagpole tactic used by the Princes of Liang and Lu in their mobile warfare. First the Prince of Liang had rigged up the hornet flagpole in the Zhuxianzhen pine wood when he had exhausted Seng by leading him round and round in circles in Honan. When the trick worked the Prince of Liang went away with his horsemen, leaving the Prince of Lu to take over leading the evil Seng by the nose. When he felt that Seng was exhausted again he used the gunpowder flagpole tactic at Dingtao. The inside of the bamboo was filled with a fuse of gunpowder, which was led in bamboo tubes to packets of the stuff under the grass. When the flagpole was set on fire the fuses lit and set off all the other explosions.

Lu Xun 鲁迅
[Lu Hsün]

THREE STORIES

The importance of Lu Xun extends far beyond the modern short story, to the development of which he made such great contributions. An intellectual, deeply read in the cultures of traditional China and the modern West, his literary and scholarly reputation was firmly established before he started to move to the revolutionary left in the 1920s. His scourging criticism of the evils he saw about him and his healthy contempt for new and old style hypocrisy were an inspiration to students and intellectuals, many of whom found in him a teacher they could respect both politically and for his literary and academic achievement. When Lu Xun rejected the old culture he did so as a scholar of great distinction, not as a young hot-head; and when he turned to Marxism in his later years it was after decades of thought and study.

He was born in Shaoxing ('Luzhen' in the stories that follow), in 1881; his family was a declining official one, which meant that much of his childhood was spent in genteel poverty. Shaoxing and the nearby countryside, where he was brought up, provided the material for many of his short stories, including the three in this collection. He studied in a naval academy and then a school of mining in Nanking before going to Tokyo in 1902 to learn the Japanese he would need for the medical training he was to start at Sendai in 1904. In the middle of his medical course he realized that he could be more use to China as a writer, curing her mental problems, than as a physician. The next three years were spent studying European literature and publishing in Japan. In 1909 he returned to China, where he supported himself as a teacher and educational official in various places until the late 1920s, from when until his death from tuberculosis on 19 October 1936 he supported himself by his writings. Like many other writers of the time he is better known by his chief pen-name, Lu Xun, than his original name, Zhou Shuren.

In the first years after his return from Japan he had tended to withdraw from the real world into scholarly pursuits; the publication of his first short story, 'A Madman's Diary', a cry from the heart against the stifling old society, marked his return to the world of political writing and activity. At first stories were his main weapon. He wrote them not to entertain but to shock and enlighten. Later he relied chiefly on short, barbed essays attacking reaction and praising the brave men and women who opposed it. He had to use allusive and indirect methods of writing to avoid censorship, and his last years were spent in constant danger from Kuomintang murder squads. His spirit of prickly independence made him react against the crude attempts of leading Communists active in Shanghai cultural circles to make him adopt some of their political lines; but his commitment to the revolutionary cause was much stronger than his dislike of the individuals who purported to represent it.

Lu Xun has towered over Chinese literature since his death as he did in life. Even though the times have changed his stylistic economy and, more important, his unyielding integrity are still very relevant in China and elsewhere.

The first of these three stories, 'Kong Yiji', shows how decrepit and moribund the traditional Confucian culture was, and it does this far more effectively and economically than a long polemical article might have done. 'My Old Home' starts from nostalgia for the lost understanding that he and his peasant friend Runtu had enjoyed in childhood and looks forward to a time when the barriers that separate them now will have disappeared. 'The New-Year Sacrifice' is one of the best of the many stories about the wretched lot of women that were written in the 1920s.

Gladys Yang and her husband have translated much of Lu Xun's work for the Foreign Languages Press, Peking, including four volumes of *Selected Works*, his *Old Tales Retold*, and his *Brief History of Chinese Fiction*.

Kong Yiji

The layout of Luzhen's taverns is unique. In each, facing you as you enter, is a bar in the shape of a carpenter's square where hot water is kept ready for warming rice wine. When men come off work at midday and in the evening they spend four coppers on a bowl of wine—or so they did twenty years ago; now it costs ten—and drink this warm, standing by the bar, taking it easy. Another copper will buy a plate of salted bamboo shoots or peas flavoured with aniseed to go with the wine, while a dozen will buy a meat dish; but most of the customers here belong to the short-coated class, few of whom can afford this. As for those in long gowns, they go into the inner room to order wine and dishes and sit drinking at their leisure.

At the age of twelve I started work as a pot-boy in the Prosperity Tavern at the edge of the town. The boss put me to work in the outer room, saying that I looked too much of a fool to serve long-gowned customers. The short-coated customers there were easier to deal with, it is true, but among them were quite a few pernickety ones who insisted on watching for themselves while the yellow wine was ladled from the keg, looked for water at the bottom of the wine-pot, and personally inspected the pot's immersion into the hot water. Under such strict surveillance, diluting the wine was very hard indeed. Thus it did not take my boss many days to decide that this job too was beyond me. Luckily I had been recommended by somebody influential, so he could not sack me. Instead I was transferred to the dull task of simply warming wine.

After that I stood all day behind the bar attending to my duties. Although I gave satisfaction at this post, I found it somewhat boring and monotonous. Our boss was a grim-faced man, nor were the customers much pleasanter, which made the atmosphere a gloomy one. The only times when there was any laughter were when Kong Yiji came to the tavern. That is why I remember him.

Kong Yiji was the only long-gowned customer who used to drink his wine standing. A big, pallid man whose wrinkled face often bore scars, he had a large, unkempt, and grizzled beard. And although he wore a long gown, it was dirty and tattered. It had not, by the look of it, been washed or mended for ten years or more. He used so many archaisms in his speech that half of it was barely intelligible. And as his surname was Kong, he was given the nickname Kong Yiji, from *Kong, yi, ji*, the first three characters in the old-fashioned children's copy-book.

Whenever he came in, everyone there would look at him and chuckle. And someone was sure to call out:

'Kong Yiji! What are those fresh scars on your face?'

Ignoring this, he would lay nine coppers on the bar and order two bowls of heated wine with a dish of aniseed-peas. Then someone else would bawl:

'You must have been stealing again!'

'Why sully a man's good name for no reason at all?' Kong Yiji would ask, raising his eyebrows.

'Good name? Why, the day before yesterday you were trussed up and beaten for stealing books from the He family. I saw you!'

At that Kong Yiji would flush, the veins on his forehead standing out as he protested, 'Taking books can't be counted as stealing. . . . Taking books . . . for a scholar . . . can't be counted as stealing.' Then followed such quotations from the classics as 'A gentleman keeps his integrity even in poverty,' together with a spate of archaisms which soon had everybody roaring with laughter, making the whole tavern ring with their voices.

From the gossip that I heard, it seemed that Kong Yiji had studied the classics but never passed the official examinations and, not knowing any way to make a living, he had grown steadily poorer until he was almost reduced to beggary. Luckily he was a good calligrapher and could find enough copying work to fill his rice-bowl. But unfortunately he had his failings too: laziness and a love of tippling. So after a few days he would disappear, taking with him books, paper, brushes, and inkstone. And after this had happened several times, people stopped employing him as a copyist. Then all he could do was resort to occasional pilfering. In our tavern, though, he was a model customer who never failed to pay up. Sometimes, it is true, when he had no ready money, his name would be chalked up on our tally-board; but in less than a month he invariably settled the bill, and the name Kong Yiji would be wiped off the board again.

After Kong Yiji had drunk half a bowl of wine, his flushed cheeks would stop burning. But then someone would ask:

'Kong Yiji, can you really read?'

When he glanced back as if such a question were not worth

answering, they would continue: 'How is it you never passed even the lowest official examination?'

At once a grey tinge would overspread Kong Yiji's dejected, discomfited face, and he would mumble more of those unintelligible archaisms. Then everyone there would laugh heartily again, making the whole tavern ring with their voices.

At such times I could join in the laughter with no danger of a dressing-down from my boss. In fact he always put such questions to Kong Yiji himself, to raise a laugh. Knowing that it was no use talking to the men, Kong Yiji would chat with us boys. Once he asked me:

'Have you had any schooling?'

When I nodded curtly he said, 'Well then, I'll test you. How do you write the *hui*[1] in aniseed-peas?'

Who did this beggar think he was, testing me? I turned away and ignored him. After waiting for some time he said earnestly:

'You can't write it, eh? I'll show you. Mind you remember. You ought to remember such characters, because you'll need them to write up your accounts when you have a shop of your own.'

It seemed to me that I was still very far from having a shop of my own; in addition to which, our boss never entered aniseed-peas in his account-book. Half amused and half exasperated, I drawled: 'I don't need you to show me. Isn't it the *hui* written with the element for grass?'

Kong Yiji's face lit up. Tapping two long finger-nails on the bar, he nodded. 'Quite correct!' he said. 'There are four different ways of writing *hui*. Do you know them?'

But my patience exhausted, I scowled and moved away. Kong Yiji had dipped his finger in wine to trace the characters on the bar. When he saw my utter indifference, his face fell and he sighed.

Sometimes children in the neighbourhood, hearing laughter, came in to join in the fun and surrounded Kong Yiji. Then he would give them aniseed-peas, one apiece. After eating the peas the children would still hang round, their eyes fixed on the dish. Growing flustered, he would cover it with his hand and bend-

---

[1] *hui*—A Chinese character meaning 'aniseed'.

ing forward from the waist would say: 'There aren't many left, not many at all.' Straightening up to look at the peas again, he would shake his head and reiterate: 'Not many, I do assure you. Not many, nay, not many at all.' Then the children would scamper off shouting with laughter.

That was how Kong Yiji contributed to our enjoyment, but we got along all right without him too.

One day, shortly before the Mid-Autumn Festival I think it was, my boss who was slowly making out his accounts took down the tally-board. 'Kong Yiji hasn't shown up for a long time,' he remarked suddenly. 'He still owes nineteen coppers.' That made me realize how long it was since we had seen him.

'How could he?' rejoined one of the customers. 'His legs were broken in that last beating up.'

'Ah!' said my boss.

'He'd been stealing again. This time he was fool enough to steal from Mr. Ding, the provincial-grade scholar. As if anybody could get away with that!'

'So what happened?'

'What happened? First he wrote a confession, then he was beaten. The beating lasted nearly all night, and they broke both his legs.'

'And then?'

'Well, his legs were broken.'

'Yes, but after?'

'After? . . . Who knows? He may be dead.'

My boss asked no further questions but went on slowly making up his accounts.

After the Mid-Autumn Festival the wind grew daily colder as winter approached, and even though I spent all my time by the stove I had to wear a padded jacket. One afternoon, when the tavern was deserted, as I sat with my eyes closed I heard the words:

'Warm a bowl of wine.'

It was said in a low but familiar voice. I opened my eyes. There was no one to be seen. I stood up to look out. There below the bar, facing the door, sat Kong Yiji. His face was thin and grimy—he looked a wreck. He had on a ragged lined jacket, and was squatting cross-legged on a mat which was

attached to his shoulders by a straw rope. When he saw me he
repeated:

'Warm a bowl of wine.'

At this point my boss leaned over the bar to ask: 'Is that
Kong Yiji? You still owe nineteen coppers.'

'That . . . I'll settle next time.' He looked up dejectedly.
'Here's cash. Give me some good wine.'

My boss, just as in the past, chuckled and said:

'Kong Yiji, you've been stealing again!'

But instead of a stout denial, the answer simply was:

'Don't joke with me.'

'Joke? How did your legs get broken if you hadn't been
stealing?'

'I fell,' whispered Kong Yiji. 'Broke them in a fall.' His eyes
pleaded with the boss to let the matter drop. By now several
people had gathered round, and they all laughed with the boss.
I warmed the wine, carried it over, and set it on the threshold.
He produced four coppers from his ragged coat pocket, and as
he placed them in my hand I saw that his own hands were
covered with mud—he must have crawled there on them.
Presently he finished the wine and, to the accompaniment of
taunts and laughter, slowly pushed himself off with his hands.

A long time went by after that without our seeing Kong Yiji
again. At the end of the year, when the boss took down the
tally-board he said: 'Kong Yiji still owes nineteen coppers.'
At the Dragon-Boat Festival the next year he said the same
thing again. But when the Mid-Autumn Festival arrived he
was silent on the subject, and another New Year came round
without our seeing any more of Kong Yiji.

Nor have I ever seen him since—no doubt Kong Yiji really
is dead.

March 1919

My Old Home

Braving the bitter cold, I travelled back some seven hundred miles to my old home that I had left more than twenty years earlier.

It was late winter. As we approached the day became overcast and a cold wind howled through the cabin of our boat, while through the chinks in its bamboo covering could be seen sprawled far and near under the sombre yellow sky a few lonely, desolate villages, devoid of any sign of life. My heart sank.

Surely this was not the old home that had been so often in my thoughts during the past twenty years?

The home I remembered was completely different. It was far, far better. But if I was asked to recall its beauty or explain its charm, my memory failed and I had no words to describe it. And now I was back it was a disappointment. I promptly rationalized to myself that home had always been like this, and while it might not have improved it was probably not as depressing as I imagined either. It was only my mood that had changed, because I was coming back to the country this time with no illusions.

My sole object in making this journey was to say good-bye. The old house occupied by our clan for so many years had been sold to another family and was to change hands before the end of the year. That was why I had to get there before New Year's Day to bid a final farewell to the familiar house and leave my old home, taking my family far away to the town where I was working.

I reached home early the next morning. The ragged blades of withered grass trembling in the wind on the roof made it very clear why this old house had to change hands. It was unusually quiet, no doubt because several branches of our clan had already moved away. By the time I reached home my mother was at the door to welcome me, and my seven-year-old nephew Honger rushed out after her.

A good deal of sadness and distress underlay mother's

happiness at seeing me. She made me sit down to rest and have some tea, without mentioning the move. Honger, who had never seen me before, stood as far away as he could, staring.

In the end, though, we had to talk about the removal. I explained that I had rented lodgings elsewhere and had bought a few pieces of furniture, but that we would have to sell all that was in the house to buy other things that were needed. Mother approved and told me that most of the heavy luggage was packed, while about half the heavy furniture had been sold, though it was hard to get people to pay up.

'You must rest for a day or two before calling on relatives, and then we can go,' said mother.

'Yes, of course.'

'Then there's Runtu. Each time he comes he asks after you and says how much he'd like to see you again. I told him when you were likely to be back. He may be here any time.'

At this point a strange picture flashed into my mind: a golden moon hung in a deep blue sky over a seashore planted as far as the eye could see with jade-green water-melons. A boy of ten or eleven, wearing a silver necklet and grasping a steel pitchfork, was thrusting with all his might at a *cha* which dodged the blow and darted away through his legs.

This boy was Runtu. He had been little more than ten when I first met him thirty years previously, and since at that time my father was still alive and the family comfortably off, I was quite the young gentleman. That year it was our family's turn to take charge of a big ancestral sacrifice, an important one because it came round only once in every thirty years. A sacrifice was offered in the first month to the ancestral images, and the host of offerings, the costliness of the sacrificial vessels, and the crowd of worshippers made it necessary to guard against theft. Our family had only one part-time servant. (In our district we divide servants into three classes: full-timers, who work all the year for one family; dailies, who are hired by the day; and extras, who farm their own land and work for a particular family only during the New Year and other festivals or when rents are being collected.) Since there was so much to be done, our servant told my father that he would fetch his son Runtu to keep an eye on the sacrificial vessels.

When my father gave his consent I was overjoyed; I had long since heard of Runtu and knew that he was about my own age, born in the intercalary month. There were only four elements in his horoscope—that of earth was missing—so his father called him Runtu (Intercalary Earth). He could trap small birds.

I started counting the days until the New Year, for the New Year would bring Runtu. At last the year drew to a close, and one day mother told me that Runtu had come. I flew to see him at once. He was in the kitchen. His round face was ruddy under a small felt cap, and his gleaming silver necklet showed that his doting father had made a vow to the gods to safeguard his life, using this necklet to keep the boy from harm. He was shy of everybody but myself, and when no one else was about he would talk to me, so that within a few hours we were firm friends.

I forget what we talked about, but I do remember that Runtu was in high spirits because of all the new things he had seen since coming to town.

The next day I wanted him to catch some birds.

'Not now,' he said. 'You can only do it after a heavy snowfall. On our sands, when it has been snowing, I sweep a patch of ground clear, prop up a big flat bamboo basket on a short stick, and scatter husks of grain beneath it; then when I see birds coming to eat, I pull the string tied to the stick from a good distance and the birds are caught under the tray. All sorts of birds: wild pheasants, woodcocks, wood-pigeons, bluebacks. . . .'

I started looking forward eagerly to snow.

'It's cold just now,' said Runtu later, 'but you must come and visit us in summer. In the day-time we'll go and pick up shells by the sea, green ones, red ones, "scare-devil" shells and "Buddha's-hands". And you can come with us in the evening, when dad and I go to mind the water melons.'

'To look out for thieves?'

'No. If passers-by pick a melon to quench their thirst, folk down our way don't count that as stealing. What we have to watch out for are badgers, hedgehogs, and *cha*. When you hear a crunching in the moonlight, that's a *cha* biting into a melon. Then you take your pitchfork, creep over, and. . . .'

I had no idea what this creature called *cha* was—I am not much clearer now for that matter—but I visualized it as something like a small dog, only very much fiercer.

'Don't they bite?'

'You have a pitchfork. You creep across and when you see it—wham! But it's so cunning it will rush straight at you and slip through your legs. Its fur is as slippery as oil. . . .'

All these curious facts had been unknown to me: that by the sea were shells all the colours of the rainbow; and that water melons, which I had simply thought of as sold by the greengrocer, had such dangerous pasts.

'On our beach, when the tide comes in, you can see whole shoals of jumping fish with two legs like frogs. . . .'

Runtu's mind was an inexhaustible repository of wonders, all unknown to my usual friends. Poor, benighted creatures; while Runtu was by the sea they, like me, could see nothing but the square of blue sky above the high courtyard wall.

Unfortunately at the end of that month Runtu had to go home. I burst into tears and he took refuge in the kitchen, sobbing and refusing to emerge until finally his father carried him off. Later his father brought me a packet of shells and some beautiful feathers from him, and I sent him presents once or twice, but we never met again.

Now, as soon as mother mentioned him, these childhood memories flashed into vivid life, and I seemed to see my beautiful old home. So I answered:

'Fine! And Runtu—how is he?'

'Runtu? . . . He's in a bad way too.' Mother looked out of the window. 'Here are those people again. They pretend they've come to buy furniture, but really it's just to pick up whatever's going. I must go and keep an eye on them.'

Mother got up and left the room. Several women's voices could be heard outside as I called Honger over and started talking to him, asking whether he could write and whether he was glad to be leaving.

'Will we be going in a train?'

'Yes, we'll be going in a train.'

'And a boat?'

'A boat first, yes. . . .'

'Well! Look at you! With such a long moustache.' Without warning a strange voice was shrilling in my ears.

Looking up with a start I saw a woman of fifty or thereabouts with thin lips and prominent cheekbones standing in front of me, her arms akimbo. She was not wearing a skirt over her trousers and looked for all the world like a pair of compasses in a box of geometrical instruments as she stood there with her legs apart.

I was flabbergasted.

'Don't you recognize me? Me that held you in my arms!'

I felt even more flabbergasted. Luckily mother came in at this point to explain:

'He's been away so long, he's forgotten everyone. You ought to remember,' she said to me, 'this is Mrs. Yang from across the road. . . . She has a beancurd shop.'

Then it came back to me. When I was a child there had indeed been a Mrs. Yang who used to sit all day long in the beancurd shop across the road and was generally known as the Beancurd Beauty. But she had powdered herself in those days, and her cheek-bones had not been so prominent, nor her lips so thin. Moreover, since she remained seated all the time, I had never noticed this resemblance to a pair of compasses. People said that thanks to her the beancurd shop did excellent business. But she had made so little impression on me, no doubt on account of my tender age, that later I had forgotten her completely. However, the Pair of Compasses was thoroughly indignant and eyed me as scornfully as if I were a Frenchman who had never heard of Napoleon, or an American who had never heard of Washington. With a caustic smile she said:

'Forgotten, had you? Of course, you're very high and mighty. . . .'

'Not at all. . . . I. . . .' I rose nervously to my feet.

'Then you listen to me, Master Xun. You are rich now, and this rickety old furniture is too heavy to move, so you can't possibly want it. Better let me take it away. Humble folk like us can do with it.'

'I'm not rich at all. I've got to sell these to raise money. . . .'

'Oh, come, you've been made intendant of a circuit, and you still say you're not rich? You have three concubines now and always go out in a big sedan-chair with eight bearers, and you still say you're not rich? No, you can't fool me.'

Knowing there was nothing to be said, I stood there in silence.

'Really, the more money people have the more miserly they get, and the more miserly they are the more money they get....' Muttering to herself, the Pair of Compasses turned away indignantly and walked slowly off, casually tucking a pair of mother's gloves into the waist of her trousers as she left.

After this a number of relatives in the neighbourhood came to call. In the intervals between entertaining them I snatched the chance to do some packing, and so three or four days passed.

One very cold day as I was sitting drinking tea after lunch I heard someone come in and turned to see who it was. The sight of the new arrival quite staggered me. I scrambled to my feet to meet him.

The newcomer was Runtu. But although I recognized him at a glance, this was not the Runtu I remembered. He was twice the size he had been, his face once so round and ruddy was sallow now and heavily lined, while the rims of his eyes were swollen and red like those of his father before him, or indeed like those of most peasants who work by the sea and are exposed all day to the wind from the ocean. In his shabby felt cap and thinly padded jacket he was shivering from head to foot. In his hands were a paper package and a long pipe, but his hands were not the plump red hands I remembered either—they were rough, clumsy, and chapped, like the bark of a pine-tree.

I had no idea how to express my delight, and could only say: 'Well, Brother Runtu—so it's you. . . .'

I had a whole string of things then I wanted to talk about: woodcocks, jumping fish, shells, *cha*. . . . But I felt too tongue-tied to put into words the thoughts milling about in my mind.

He stood there, happiness and distress on his face. Though his lips moved, not a sound came from them. At last, straightening up respectfully, he addressed me clearly:

'Master! . . .'

A shiver ran through me as I realized what a tragically thick barrier had grown up between us. Yet I could not say anything.

He turned away to say:

'Shuisheng, kotow to the master.' With that he pulled forward the boy who had been hiding behind him. This was the Runtu of twenty years before, only slightly paler and thinner, and with no silver necklet.

'This is my fifth,' he said. 'He's seen so little of the world, he's shy and awkward.'

Mother and Honger, who no doubt had heard our voices, came downstairs now to join us.

'Your letter came some time ago, ma'am,' said Runtu. 'I was mighty glad to know that the master would be back. . . .'

'What's come over you? Why so polite?' asked mother gaily. 'Didn't you once play together? You'd better go on calling him Brother Xun.'

'You're too good, ma'am. . . . That would never do. I was only a nipper then and didn't know about these things.' While speaking Runtu motioned Shuisheng to come forward and bow, but the child was too shy and stuck close to his father.

'So he's Shuisheng? Your fifth?' asked mother. 'You can't blame him for feeling shy with all us strangers. Honger had better take him out to play.'

When Honger heard this he walked over to Shuisheng, who went out quite cheerfully with him. Mother urged Runtu to sit down, and after a little hesitation he did so. Then, leaning his long pipe against the table, he handed me the paper package saying:

'In winter there's nothing worth bringing, but we dried these few beans ourselves, sir. . '

When I asked how things were with him, he shook his head.

'Very bad. Even my sixth lends a hand, but there's never enough to eat . . . never any peace. . . . Everything costs money, you don't know where you are . . . and the harvest's been poor. You grow a crop, but when you take it to market there are so many different taxes to pay that you lose out; but it'll go off if you don't sell it. . . .'

Though he kept on shaking his head, not one of the wrinkles on his lined face moved, as if he were made of stone. Unable to put his wretchedness into words, he lapsed into a profound silence and, after a pause, picked up his pipe and began to smoke in silence.

Mother, who questioned him, learned that he had to go back the next day as there was work to be done; and since he had had no lunch she told him to go to the kitchen and fry himself some rice.

After he had gone out, we both sighed over his plight. He had so many mouths to feed, but crops failures, taxes, soldiers, bandits, officials, and the local gentry had bled him as dry as a wooden dummy. Mother said we should offer him his choice of all the things we would not be taking away.

That afternoon he made his choice: two long tables, four chairs, an incense-burner and candlesticks, and a balance. He also asked for all our ashes. (In our parts we burn straw in the kitchen, and the ashes are a fertilizer for sandy soil.) He would come for them with a boat, he said, after we had left.

That night we chatted again, not of anything serious, and the next morning he took Shuisheng home.

Nine days later it was time for us to leave. Runtu arrived in the morning, without Shuisheng, having just brought a four-year-old girl to mind his boat. We were too busy all day to have time to talk. We had quite a few visitors too, some to see us off, some to collect things, some to do both. It was getting on for evening when we boarded our boat, and by that time a clean sweep had been made of everything large or small in the old house, no matter how worn or shabby.

Our boat set off. And the green hills on both banks turned a deep blue in the dusk as they receded towards the stern of the junk.

Honger and I were sitting by the cabin window looking out at the hazy landscape, when suddenly he asked:

'When will we be coming back, uncle?'

'Coming back? Why think of coming back before you've even left?'

'Well, Shuisheng invited me to his home. . . .' He thought this over anxiously, his black eyes wide open.

Mother and I were both rather disconcerted, and so Runtu's name came up again. Mother told me that Mrs. Yang from the beancurd shop had come over every day ever since our family had started packing up, and the day before in the ash-heap she had unearthed a dozen bowls and plates, which after some discussion she insisted must have been buried there by Runtu, so that he could take them home when he came to collect the ashes. Mrs. Yang was so pleased with herself after this discovery that she flew off taking the dog-teaser with her. (The dog-teaser, used by poultry-keepers in our parts, is a barred container for food into which hens can stretch their necks while dogs can only watch in impotent fury.) And it was a marvel, considering how tiny her feet were, how fast the woman could run.

As we left the old house farther and farther behind, the hills and rivers of my old home too were gradually lost in the distance; but I felt no regret. What did depress me thoroughly, however, was the feeling that a high, invisible wall was cutting me off from my fellows. The vision of that small hero with the silver necklet among the water-melons which had once been as clear as the day had now suddenly blurred, and this distressed me still more.

Mother and Honger were asleep.

I lay down, listening to the water rippling beneath the boat, and knew that I was going along the way destined for me. I thought: Although there is such a barrier between Runtu and myself, the children are still close, for Honger was thinking of Shuisheng just now. I hope they will not be like us, that they will not let a barrier grow up between them. But I would not like them either, because they want to be close, to lead a wretched, treadmill existence like mine, nor a wretched, stupefied existence like Runtu's, nor yet the wretched, dissipated existence of some others. They should have a new life, a life that we have never known.

Suddenly the thought of hope made me afraid. When Runtu had asked for the incense-burner and candlesticks, I had laughed up my sleeve to think that he was still worshipping idols and could never put them out of his mind. Yet what I now called hope was no more than an idol I had created myself. The only difference was that the object of his desire was close at hand, while mine was very remote.

As I dozed, a stretch of jade-green seashore spread itself

before my eyes, and in the deep blue sky above hung a round, golden moon. Hope could neither be said to exist, I thought, nor not to exist. It was like roads crossing the earth. For the earth, of course, had no roads to begin with; but when many men pass one way, a road is made.

January 1921

The New-Year Sacrifice

The end of the year by the old calendar does really seem a more natural end to the year for, to say nothing of the villages and towns, the very sky seems to proclaim the New Year's approach. Intermittent flashes from pallid, lowering evening clouds are followed by the rumble of crackers bidding farewell to the Hearth God and, before the deafening reports of the bigger bangs close at hand have died away, the air is filled with faint whiffs of gunpowder. On one such night I returned to Luzhen, my home town. I call it my home town, but as I had not made my home there for some time I put up at the house of a certain Fourth Mr. Lu, whom I am obliged to address as Fourth Uncle since he belongs to the generation before mine in our clan. A former Imperial College licentiate who believes in Neo-Confucianism, he seemed very little changed, just slightly older, but without any beard as yet. Having exchanged some polite remarks upon meeting he observed that I was fatter, and having observed that I was fatter launched into a violent attack on the revolutionaries. I did not take this personally, however, as the object of his attack was Kang Youwei. Still, conversation proved so difficult that I shortly found myself alone in the study.

I rose late the next day and went out after lunch to see relatives and friends, spending the following day in the same way. They were all very little changed, just slightly older; but every family was busy preparing for the New-Year Sacrifice. This is the great end-of-year ceremony in Luzhen, during which a

reverent and splendid welcome is given to the God of Fortune
so that he will send good luck for the coming year. Chickens
and geese are killed, pork is bought, and everything is scrubbed
and scoured until all the women's arms—some still in twisted
silver bracelets—turn red in the water. After the meat is cooked
chopsticks are thrust into it at random, and when this 'offering'
is set out at dawn, incense and candles are lit and the God of
Fortune is respectfully invited to come and partake of it. The
worshippers are confined to men and, of course, after worshipping they go on letting off firecrackers as before. This is done
every year, in every household—so long as it can afford the
offering and crackers—and naturally this year was no excep-
tion.

The sky became overcast and in the afternoon it was filled
with a flurry of snowflakes, some as large as plum-blossom
petals, which merged with the smoke and the bustling atmosphere to make the small town a welter of confusion. By the time
I had returned to my uncle's study, the roof of the house was
already white with snow which made the room brighter than
usual, highlighting the red stone rubbing that hung on the wall
of the big character 'Longevity' as written by the Taoist saint
Chen Tuan. One of a pair of scrolls had fallen down and was
lying loosely rolled upon the long table. The other, still in its
place, bore the inscription 'Understanding of principles brings
peace of mind.' I strolled over to the table beneath the window
to turn over the books on it, but only found an apparently incomplete set of *The Kang Hsi Dictionary*, the *Selected Writings of
Neo-Confucian Philosophers*, and *Commentaries on the Four Books*.[1]
Whatever happened I must leave the next day, I decided.

Besides, the thought of my meeting with Xiang Lin's Wife
the previous day was preying on my mind. It had happened in
the afternoon. On my way back from calling on a friend in the
eastern part of the town, I had met her by the river and knew
from the fixed look in her eyes that she was going to accost me.
Of all the people I had seen during this visit to Luzhen, none
had changed so much as she had. Her hair, streaked with grey

---

[1] A selection of books suggesting that their owner was a dreary and third-
rate advocate of Neo-Confucianism.

five years before, was now completely white, making her appear much older than her early forties. Her sallow, weather-beaten face that looked as if it had been carved out of wood was fearfully wasted and had lost the grief-stricken expression it had borne before. The only sign of life about her was the occasional flicker of her eyes. In one hand she had a wicker basket containing a chipped, empty bowl; in the other, a bamboo pole, taller than herself, that was split at one end. She had clearly become a beggar pure and simple.

I stopped, waiting for her to come and ask for money.

'So you're back?' were her first words.

'Yes.'

'That's good. You are a scholar who's travelled and seen the world. There's something I want to ask you.' A sudden gleam lit up her lacklustre eyes.

This was so unexpected that surprise rooted me to the spot.

'It's this.' She drew two paces nearer and lowered her voice, as if letting me into a secret. 'Do dead people turn into ghosts or not?'

My flesh crept. The way she had fixed me with her eyes made a shiver run down my spine, and I felt far more nervous than when a surprise test is sprung on you at school and the teacher insists on standing over you. Personally, I had never bothered myself in the least about whether spirits existed or not; but what was the best answer to give her now? I hesitated for a moment, reflecting that the people here still believed in spirits, but she seemed to have her doubts, or rather hopes—she hoped for life after death and dreaded it at the same time. Why increase the sufferings of someone with one foot in the grave? For her sake, I thought, I'd better say there was.

'Quite possibly, I'd say,' I told her falteringly.

'That means there must be a hell too?'

'What, hell?' I faltered, very taken aback. 'Hell? Logically speaking, there should be too—but not necessarily. Who cares anyway? . . .'

'Then will all the members of a family meet again after death?'

'Well, as to whether they'll meet again or not. . . .' I realized now what an utter fool I was. All my hesitation and manoeuv-

ring had been no match for her three questions. Promptly taking
fright, I decided to recant. 'In that case . . . actually, I'm not
sure. . . . In fact, I'm not sure whether there are ghosts or not
either.'

To avoid any further questions I beat a hasty retreat to my
uncle's house, feeling thoroughly disconcerted. I may have
given her a dangerous answer, I was thinking. Of course, she
may just be feeling lonely because everybody else is celebrating
now, but could she have had something else in mind? Some
premonition? If she had had some other idea, and something
happens as a result, then my answer will be partly responsible. . . . Then I laughed at myself for worrying so over a
chance meeting when it could have no serious significance. No
wonder certain educationists called me neurotic. Besides, I had
distinctly declared, 'I'm not sure,' contradicting the whole of
my answer. This meant that even if something did happen, it
would have nothing at all to do with me.

'I'm not sure' is a most useful phrase.

Bold inexperienced youngsters often take it upon themselves
to solve problems or choose doctors for other people, and if by
any chance things turn out badly they may well be held to
blame; but by concluding their advice with this expression of
doubt they achieve blissful immunity from reproach. The
necessity for such a phrase was brought home to me still more
forcibly now, since it was indispensable even in speaking with a
beggar woman.

However, I remained uneasy, and even after a night's rest
my mind dwelt on it with a certain sense of foreboding. The
oppressive snowy weather and the gloomy study increased my
uneasiness. I had better leave the next day and go back to the
city. A large dish of shark's fin clear soup at the Xingfu Restaur-
ant used to cost only a dollar. I wondered if this cheap delicacy
had risen in price or not. Though my good companions of the
old days had scattered, that shark's fin must still be sampled
even if I were on my own. Whatever happened I would leave
the next day, I decided.

Since, in my experience, things I hoped would not happen
and felt should not happen invariably did occur all the same,
I was much afraid this would prove another such case. And,

sure enough, the situation soon took a strange turn. Towards evening I heard what sounded like a discussion in the inner room, but the conversation ended before long and my uncle walked away observing loudly: 'What a moment to choose! Now of all times! Isn't that proof enough she was a bad lot?'

My initial astonishment gave way to a deep uneasiness; I felt that this had something to do with me. I looked out of the door, but no one was there. I waited impatiently till their servant came in before dinner to brew tea. Then at last I had a chance to make some inquiries.

'Who was Mr. Lu so angry with just now?' I asked.

'Why, Xiang Lin's Wife, of course,' was the curt reply.

'Xiang Lin's Wife? Why?' I pressed.

'She's gone.'

'Dead?' My heart missed a beat. I started and must have changed colour. But since the servant kept his head lowered, all this escaped him. I pulled myself together enough to ask:

'When did she die?'

'When? Last night or today—I'm not sure.'

'How did she die?'

'How? Of poverty of course.' After this stolid answer he withdrew, still without having raised his head to look at me.

My agitation was only short-lived, however. For now that my premonition had come to pass, I no longer had to comfort myself with my own 'I'm not sure', or his 'dying of poverty', and my heart was growing lighter. Only from time to time did I still feel a little guilty. Dinner was served, and my uncle sternly kept me company. Tempted as I was to ask about Xiang Lin's Wife, I knew that, although he had read that 'ghosts and spirits are manifestations of the dual forces of Nature', he was still so superstitious that on the eve of the New-Year Sacrifice it would be unthinkable to mention anything like death or illness. In case of necessity one should use veiled allusions, but since this was unfortunately beyond me I had to bite back the questions which kept rising to the tip of my tongue. And my uncle's stern expression suddenly made me suspect that he looked on me too as a bad lot who had chosen this moment, now of all times, to come and trouble him. To set his mind at rest as quickly as I could, I told him at once of my plan to leave

Luzhen the next day and go back to the city. He did not press
me to stay, and at last the uncomfortable meal came to an end.

Winter days are short, and because it was snowing darkness
had already enveloped the whole town. All was stir and commotion in the lighted houses, but outside was remarkably
quiet. And the snowflakes hissing down on the thick snowdrifts
intensified one's sense of loneliness. Seated alone in the amber
light of the vegetable-oil lamp I reflected that this wretched
woman, abandoned in the dust like a worn-out toy of which its
owners have tired, had once left her own imprint in the dust,
and those who enjoyed life must have wondered at her for
wishing to live on; but now at last she had been swept away
by death. Whether spirits existed or not I did not know; but in
this world of ours the end of a futile existence, the removal of
someone whom others are tired of seeing, was just as well both
for them and for the individual concerned. Occupied with these
reflections, I listened quietly to the hissing of the snow outside;
until little by little I felt more relaxed.

But the fragments of her life that I had seen or heard about
before combined now to form a whole.

She was not from Luzhen. Early one winter, when my uncle's
family wanted a new maid, Old Mrs. Wei the go-between
brought her along. She had a white mourning band round her
hair and was wearing a black skirt, blue jacket, and pale green
bodice. Her age was about twenty-six, and though her face
was sallow her cheeks were red. Old Mrs. Wei introduced her
as Xiang Lin's Wife, a neighbour of her mother's family who
wanted to go out to work now that her husband had died. My
uncle frowned at this, and my aunt knew that he disapproved of
taking on a widow. She looked just the person for them,
though, with her big strong hands and feet; and, judging by
her downcast eyes and silence, she was a good worker who would
know her place. So my aunt ignored my uncle's frown and kept
her. During her trial period she worked from morning till night
as if she found resting irksome, and proved strong enough to do
the work of a man; so on the third day she was taken on for
five hundred cash a month.

Everybody called her Xiang Lin's Wife and no one asked her

own name, but since she had been introduced by someone from Wei Village as a neighbour, her surname was presumably also Wei. She said little, only answering briefly when asked a question. Thus it took them a dozen days or so to find out that she had a strict mother-in-law at home and a brother-in-law of about ten, just old enough to cut wood. Her husband, who had died that spring, had been a woodcutter too, and had been ten years younger than she was. This little was all they could learn.

Time passed quickly. She went on working as hard as ever, not caring what she ate, never sparing herself. It was generally agreed that the Lu family's maid actually got through more work than a hard-working man. At the end of the year, she swept and mopped the floors, killed the chickens and geese, and sat up to boil the sacrificial meat, all single-handed, so that they did not need to hire extra help. And she for her part was quite contented. Little by little the trace of a smile appeared at the corners of her mouth, while her face became whiter and plumper.

Just after the New Year she came back from washing rice by the river most upset because in the distance, pacing up and down on the opposite bank, she had seen a man who looked like her husband's cousin—very likely he had come in search of her. When my aunt in alarm pressed her for more information, she said nothing. As soon as my uncle knew of this he frowned.

'That's bad,' he observed. 'She must have run away.'

Before very long this inference was confirmed.

About a fortnight later, just as this incident was beginning to be forgotten, Old Mrs. Wei suddenly brought along a woman in her thirties whom she introduced as Xiang Lin's mother. Although this woman looked like the hill-dweller she was, she behaved with great self-possession and had a ready tongue in her head. After the usual civilities she apologized for coming to take her daughter-in-law away, explaining that early spring was a busy time and they were short-handed at home with only old people and children around.

'If her mother-in-law wants her back, there's nothing more to be said,' was my uncle's comment.

Thereupon her wages were reckoned up. They came to 1,750 cash, all of which she had left in the keeping of her mistress without spending any of it. My aunt gave the entire sum to Xiang Lin's mother, who took her daughter-in-law's clothes as well, expressed her thanks, and left. By this time it was noon.

'Oh, the rice! Didn't Xiang Lin's Wife go to wash the rice?' exclaimed my aunt some time later. It was hunger, no doubt, that reminded her of lunch.

A general search started then for the rice basket. My aunt searched the kitchen, then the hall, then the bedroom; but not a sign of the basket was to be seen. My uncle could not find it outside either, until he went right down to the riverside. Then he saw it set down fair and square on the bank, some vegetables beside it.

Some people on the bank told him that a boat with a white awning had moored there that morning but, since the awning covered the boat completely, they had no idea who was inside and had paid no special attention to begin with. But when Xiang Lin's Wife had arrived and knelt down to wash rice, two men who looked as if they came from the hills had jumped off the boat and seized her. Between them they dragged her on board. She wept and shouted at first but soon fell silent, no doubt because she was gagged. Then along came two women, a stranger and Old Mrs. Wei. It was difficult to see clearly into the boat, but she seemed to be lying, tied up, on the planking.

'Disgraceful! Still. . . .' said my uncle.

That day my aunt cooked the midday meal herself, and their son Aniu lit the fire.

After lunch Old Mrs. Wei came back.

'Disgraceful!' said my uncle.

'What's the meaning of this? How dare you show your face here again?' My aunt, who was washing up, started fuming as soon as she saw her. 'First you recommend her, then help them carry her off, causing such a shocking commotion. What will people think? Are you trying to make fools of us?'

'Aiya, I was completely taken in! I've come specially to clear this up. How was I to know she'd left home without permission from her mother-in-law when she asked me to find her work? I'm sorry, Mr. and Mrs. Lu. I'm growing so stupid and careless in my old age, I've let my patrons down. It's lucky for me you're such kind, generous people, never hard on those below you. I promise to make it up to you by finding someone good this time.'

'Still, . . .' said my uncle.

That concluded the business of Xiang Lin's Wife, and before long she was forgotten.

My aunt was the only one who still spoke of Xiang Lin's Wife. This was because most of the maids taken on afterwards turned out to be lazy or greedy, or both, none of them giving satisfaction. At such times she would say to herself, I wonder what's become of her now?—implying that she would like to have her back. But by the next New Year she too had given up hope.

The first month was nearing its end when Old Mrs. Wei called on my aunt to wish her a happy New Year. Already tipsy, she explained that the reason for her coming so late was that she had been visiting her family in Wei Village for a few days. The conversation, naturally, soon touched on Xiang Lin's Wife.

'Xiang Lin's Wife?' cried Old Mrs. Wei cheerfully. 'She's in luck now. When her mother-in-law dragged her home, she'd promised her to the sixth son of the Zhang family in Zhang Village. So a few days later they put her in the bridal chair and carried her off.'

'Gracious! What a mother-in-law!' exclaimed my aunt.

'Aiya, madam, you really talk like a great lady! This is nothing to poor folk like us who live up in the hills. That young brother-in-law of hers still had no wife. If they didn't marry her off, where would the money have come from to get him one? Her mother-in-law is a clever, capable woman, a fine manager; so she married her off into the mountains. If she'd given her to a family in the same village, she wouldn't have made so much; but as very few girls are willing to take a husband high up in the mountains, she got eighty thousand cash. Now the second son has a wife, who cost only fifty thousand; and after paying for the wedding she's still over ten thousand in hand. Wouldn't you call her a fine manager? . . .'

'But was Xiang Lin's Wife willing?'

'It wasn't a question of willing or not. Of course any woman would make a row about it. All they had to do was tie her up, shove her into the chair, carry her to the man's house, put on the bridal head-dress, make her bow in the hall, lock the two of them into their room—and that was that. But Xiang Lin's Wife is quite a character. I heard that she made a terrible scene. It was working for a scholar's family, everyone said, that made her different from other people. We go-betweens see life, madam. Some widows sob and shout when they remarry; some threaten to kill themselves; some refuse to bow to heaven and earth after they've been carried to the man's house; some even smash the wedding candlesticks. But Xiang Lin's Wife was different. They said she screamed and cursed all the way to Zhang Village, so that she was completely hoarse by the time they got there. When they dragged her out of the chair, no matter how the two chair-bearers and her brother-in-law held her, they couldn't make her go through with the ceremony. The moment they were off guard and had loosened their grip— gracious Buddha!—she bashed her head on a corner of the table, gashing it so badly that the blood spurted out. Even though they smeared on two handfuls of incense ashes and tied it up with two pieces of red cloth, they couldn't stop the bleeding. It took three or four of them to shut her up finally with the man in the bridal chamber, but even then she went on cursing. A shocking business, it was!' Shaking her head, she lowered her eyes and fell silent.

'And what then?' asked my aunt.

'They said that the next day she didn't get up.' Old Mrs. Wei raised her eyes.

'And after?'

'After? She got up. At the end of the year she had a baby, a boy, who was one this New Year. These few days when I was at home, some people back from a visit to Zhang Village said they'd seen her and her son, and both mother and child are plump. There's no mother-in-law over her, her man is a strong fellow who can earn a living, and the house belongs to them. Oh, yes, she's in luck all right.'

After this even my aunt gave up talking of Xiang Lin's Wife.

But one autumn, after two New Years had passed since this good news of Xiang Lin's Wife, she once more crossed the threshold of my uncle's house, placing her round bulb-shaped basket on the table and her small bedding-roll under the eaves. As before, she had a white mourning band round her hair and was wearing a black skirt, blue jacket, and pale green bodice. Her face was sallow, her cheeks no longer red; and her downcast eyes, stained with tears, had lost their brightness. Just as before, it was Old Mrs. Wei who brought her to my aunt.

'It was really a bolt from the blue,' she explained compassionately. 'Her husband was a strong young fellow; who'd have thought that typhoid fever would carry him off? He'd taken a turn for the better, but then he ate some cold rice and got worse again. Luckily she had the boy and she can work—she's able to chop wood, pick tea, or raise silkworms—so she could have managed on her own. But who'd have thought that the child, too, would be carried off by a wolf? It was nearly the end of spring, yet a wolf came to the village—who could have guessed that? Now she's all on her own. Her brother-in-law's taken over the house and turned her out. So she's no way to turn for help except to her former mistress. Luckily this time there's nobody to stop her and you happen to be needing someone, madam. That's why I've brought her here. I think someone used to your ways is much better than a new hand. . . .'

'I was really too stupid for words. . . ,' put in Xiang Lin's Wife, raising her lacklustre eyes. 'All I knew was that when it snowed and the wild beasts up in the hills had nothing to eat, they might come to the villages. I didn't know that in spring they might come too. I got up at dawn and opened the door, filled a small basket with beans and told our Amao to sit on the doorstep and shell them. He was such a good boy; he always did as he was told and out he went. Then I went to the back to chop wood and wash the rice, and when the rice was in the pan I wanted to boil the beans. I called Amao, but there was no answer. When I went out to look there were beans all over the ground but no Amao. He never went to the neighbours' houses to play; and, sure enough, though I asked everywhere he wasn't there. I got so worried, I begged people to help me find him. Not until that afternoon, after searching high and low, did they try the gully. There they saw one of his little shoes caught on a bramble. "That's bad," they said. "A wolf must have got him." And sure enough, further on, there he was lying in the wolf's den, all his innards eaten away, still clutching that little basket tight in his hand. . . .' At this point she broke down and could not go on.

My aunt had been undecided at first, but the rims of her eyes were rather red by the time Xiang Lin's Wife broke off. After a moment's thought she told her to take her things to the servants' quarters. Old Mrs. Wei heaved a sigh, as if a great weight had been lifted from her mind; and Xiang Lin's Wife, looking more relaxed than when first she came, went off quietly to put away her bedding without having to be told the way. So she started work again as a maid in Luzhen.

She was still known as Xiang Lin's Wife.

But now she was a very different woman. She had not worked there more than two or three days before her mistress realized that she was not as quick as before. Her memory was much worse too, while her face, like a death-mask, never showed the least trace of a smile. Already my aunt was expressing herself as far from satisfied. Though my uncle had frowned as before when she first arrived, they always had such trouble finding servants that he raised no serious objections, simply warning his wife on the quiet that while such people might seem very pathetic they exerted a bad moral influence. She could work for them but must have nothing to do with ancestral sacrifices. They would have to prepare all the dishes themselves. Otherwise they would be unclean and the ancestors would not accept them.

The most important events in my uncle's household were ancestral sacrifices, and formerly these had kept Xiang Lin's Wife very busy, but now she had virtually nothing to do. As soon as the table had been placed in the centre of the hall and a cloth put on it, she started setting out the winecups and chopsticks in the way she still remembered.

'Put those down, Xiang Lin's Wife,' cried my aunt. 'Leave that to me.'

She drew back sheepishly then and went for the candlesticks.

'Put those down, Xiang Lin's Wife,' cried my aunt again. 'I'll fetch them.'

After walking round in circles several times without finding anything to do, she moved doubtfully away. All she did that day was to sit by the stove and feed the fire.

The townspeople still called her Xiang Lin's Wife, but in quite a different tone from before; and although they still talked to her, their manner was colder. Quite impervious to this, staring straight in front of her, she would tell everybody the story which night or day was never out of her mind.

'I was really too stupid for words,' she would say. 'All I knew was that when it snowed and the wild beasts up in the hills had nothing to eat, they might come to the villages. I didn't know that in spring they might come too. I got up at dawn and opened the door, filled a small basket with beans and told our Amao to sit on the doorstep and shell them. He was such a good boy; he always did as he was told, and out he went. Then I went to the back to chop wood and wash the rice, and when the rice was in the pan I wanted to boil the beans. I called Amao, but there was no answer. When I went out to look, there were beans all over the ground but no Amao. He never went to the neighbours' houses to play; and, sure enough, though I asked everywhere he wasn't there. I got so worried, I begged people to help me find him. Not until that afternoon, after searching high and low, did they try the gully. There they saw one of his little shoes caught on a bramble. "That's bad," they said. "A wolf must have got him." And sure enough, further on, there he was lying in the wolf's den, all his innards eaten away, still clutching that little basket tight in his hand. . . .' At this point her voice would be choked with tears.

This story was so effective that men hearing it often stopped smiling and walked blankly away, while the women not only seemed to forgive her but wiped the contemptuous expression off their faces and added their tears to hers. Indeed, some old women who had not heard her in the street sought her out specially to hear her sad tale. And when she broke down, they too shed the tears which had gathered in their eyes, after which they sighed and went away satisfied, exchanging eager comments.

As for her, she asked nothing better than to tell her sad story over and over again, often gathering three or four hearers around her. But before long everybody knew it so well that no trace of a tear could be seen even in the eyes of the most kindly, Buddha-fearing old ladies. In the end, practically the whole town could recite it by heart and were bored and exasperated to hear it repeated.

'I was really too stupid for words,' she would begin.

'Yes. All you knew was that in snowy weather, when the wild beasts in the mountains had nothing to eat, they might come down to the villages.' Cutting short her recital abruptly, they walked away.

She would stand there open-mouthed, staring after them stupidly, and then wander off as if she too were bored of the story. But she still tried hopefully to lead up from other topics such as small baskets, beans, and other people's children to the story of her Amao. At the sight of a child of two or three she would say, 'Ah, if my Amao were alive he'd be just that size. . . .'

Children would take fright at the look in her eyes and clutch the hem of their mothers' clothes to tug them away. Left by herself again, she would eventually walk blankly away. In the end everybody knew what she was like. If a child were present they would ask with a spurious smile: 'If your Amao were alive, Xiang Lin's Wife, wouldn't he be just that size?'

She may not have realized that her tragedy, after being generally savoured for so many days, had long since grown so stale that it now aroused only revulsion and disgust. But she seemed to sense the mockery in their smiles, and the fact that there was no need for her to say more. So she would simply look at them in silence.

New Year preparations always start in Luzhen on the twentieth day of the twelfth month. That year my uncle's household had to take on a temporary manservant. And since there was more than he could do they asked Liu Ma to help by killing the chickens and geese; but being a devout vegetarian who would not kill living creatures, she would only wash the sacrificial vessels. Xiang Lin's Wife, with nothing to do but feed the fire, sat there at a loose end watching Liu Ma as she worked. A light snow began to fall.

'Ah, I was really too stupid,' sighed Xiang Lin's Wife as if to herself, looking at the sky.

'There you go again, Xiang Lin's Wife.' Liu Ma glanced in exasperation at her face. 'Tell me, wasn't that when you got that scar on your forehead?'

All the reply she received was a vague murmur.

'Tell me this: what made you willing after all?'

'Willing?'

'Yes. Seems to me you must have been willing. Otherwise. . . .'

'Oh, you don't know how strong he was.'

'I don't believe it. I don't believe he was so strong that you couldn't have kept him off. You must have ended up willing. That talk of his being so strong is just an excuse.'

'Why . . . just try for yourself and see.' She smiled.

Liu Ma's lined face broke into a smile too, wrinkling up like a walnut-shell. Her small beady eyes swept the other woman's forehead, then fastened on her eyes. At once Xiang Lin's Wife stopped smiling, as if embarrassed, and turned her eyes away to watch the snow.

'That was really a bad bargain you struck, Xiang Lin's Wife,' said Liu Ma mysteriously. 'If you'd held out longer or killed yourself outright, that would have been better. As it is, you're guilty of a great sin though you lived less than two years with your second husband. Just think: when you go down to the lower world, the ghosts of both men will start fighting over you. Which ought to have you? The King of Hell will have to saw you into two and divide you between them. It really is a shame. . . .'

Xiang Lin's Wife's face registered terror then. This was something no one had told her up in the mountains.

'Better guard against that in good time, I say. Go to the Temple of the Tutelary God and buy a threshold to be trampled on instead of you by thousands of people. If you atone for your sins in this life you'll escape torment after death.'

Xiang Lin's Wife said nothing at the time, but she must have taken this advice to heart for when she got up the next morning there were dark circles under her eyes. After breakfast she went to the Temple of the Tutelary God at the west end of the town and asked to buy a threshold. At first the priest refused, only giving a grudging consent after she was reduced to tears of desperation. The price charged was twelve thousand cash.

She had long since given up talking to people after their contemptuous reception of Amao's story; but as word of her conversation with Liu Ma spread, many of the townsfolk took a fresh interest in her and came once more to provoke her into talking. The topic, of course, had changed to the scar on her forehead.

'Tell me, Xiang Lin's Wife, what made you willing in the end?' one would ask.

'What a waste, to have bashed yourself like that for nothing.' another would chime in, looking at her scar.

She must have known from their smiles and tone of voice that they were mocking her, for she simply stared at them without a word and finally did not even turn her head. All day long she kept her lips tightly closed, bearing on her head the scar considered by everyone as a badge of shame, while she shopped, swept the floor, washed the vegetables and prepared the rice in silence. Nearly a year went by before she took her accumulated wages from my aunt, changed them for twelve silver dollars, and asked for leave to go to the west end of town. In less than half an hour she was back again, looking much comforted. With an unaccustomed light in her eyes, she told my aunt contentedly that she had now bought a threshold in the Temple of the Tutelary God.

When the time came for the ancestral sacrifice on midwinter's day she worked harder than ever, and as soon as my aunt took out the sacrificial vessels and helped Aniu to carry the table into the middle of the hall, she went confidently to fetch the winecups and chopsticks.

'Put those down, Xiang Lin's Wife!' my aunt called hastily.

She withdrew her hand as if scorched, her face turned grey, and instead of fetching the candlesticks she just stood there in a daze until my uncle came in to burn some incense and told her to go away. This time the change in her was phenomenal: the next day her eyes were sunken, her spirit seemed broken. She took fright very easily too, afraid not only of the dark and of shadows, but of meeting anyone. Even the sight of her own master or mistress set her trembling like a mouse that had strayed out of its hole in broad daylight. The rest of the time she would sit stupidly as if carved out of wood. In less than half a year her hair had turned grey, and her memory had deteriorated so much that she often forgot to go and wash the rice.

'What's come over Xiang Lin's Wife? We should never have taken her on again,' my aunt would sometimes say in front of her, as if to warn her.

But there was no change in her, no sign that she would ever recover her wits. So they decided to get rid of her and tell her to go back to Old Mrs. Wei. That was what they were saying, at least, while I was there; and, judging by subsequent developments, this is evidently what they must have done. But whether she started begging as soon as she left my uncle's house, or whether she went first to Old Mrs. Wei and later became a beggar, I do not know.

I was woken up by the noisy explosion of crackers close at hand and, from the faint glow shed by the yellow oil lamp and the bangs of fireworks as my uncle's household celebrated the sacrifice, I knew that it must be nearly dawn. Listening drowsily, it seemed to me that the whole town was enveloped by the dense cloud of noise in the sky from the ceaseless explosion of crackers in the distance, mingling with the whirling snowflakes. Enveloped in this medley of sound I relaxed; the doubt which had preyed on my mind from dawn till night was swept clean away by the festive atmosphere, and I felt only that the saints of heaven and earth had accepted the sacrifice and incense and were reeling with intoxication in the sky, preparing to give Luzhen's people boundless good fortune.

7 February 1924

Rou Shi 柔石
[Jou Shih]

Zhao Pingfu, who used the pen-name Rou Shi ('Soft Rock'), was born in 1901 to a small merchant family that had memories of a grander past. In 1917, while training to be a teacher in Hangchow, he joined the new literature movement. Most of his working life was spent in education until 1928, when the suppression of peasant risings in his native county of Ninghai, Chekiang, led to the dissolution of the county educational bureau that under his control was reforming the school system. He went to Shanghai, where he devoted his time to left-wing political and literary activities, editing a number of short-lived journals that introduced foreign writing and woodcuts, particularly from northern and eastern Europe. He was a close associate of Lu Xun. In 1930 he joined the League of Left-Wing Writers openly and the banned Communist Party in secret. As the representative of the former he attended the first National Congress of the Chinese Soviet Districts.

In January 1931 he was arrested by the police of the British-controlled International Settlement in Shanghai. After being handed over to the Kuomintang authorities he was secretly executed the following month.

His stories are typical of much of the writing at this time in that they express dissatisfaction with the state of society and sympathy for the common people without showing much understanding of them. The influence of nineteenth-century Europe is much more obvious in his stories than is that of traditional Chinese written or oral literary forms, with the result that they only had meaning for other members of the tiny group of left-leaning westernized intellectuals concentrated in Shanghai and a few other big cities.

'Slaves' Mother' is one of the many stories from the 1920s and 1930s portraying the wretched state of women in pre-liberation China. This was something that any Chinese writer could not fail to be aware of, particularly by contrast with what he had read of Europe. Even in the grandest feudal household women suffered abominably —as had been incomparably demonstrated in the great eighteenth-century novel *Dream of the Red Chamber*—and it was not necessary to look very far to find cases of terrible oppression in contemporary life.

The woman in this story goes through an experience that was far from exceptional, and her sufferings were limited by comparison with what some endured. She meets no violence, is fairly well treated, and is allowed to return to her own family at the end. If she does not struggle against her fate it is because she accepts it; others in her situation killed themselves or ran away.

Slaves' Mother

Her husband was a leather merchant. He bought wild-animal skins from the village hunters and oxhides to sell in the big city. Sometimes he did a little farming too, helping transplant rice seedlings in the spring. He could plant so straight a row that if five others were working in a paddy-field with him they put him at the end of the line as marker. But things were always against him; his debts piled up over the years. It was probably because everything had gone so badly that he had taken to opium, drink, and gambling, which had finally turned him into a cruel and loutish fellow, poorer than ever and no longer able even to raise a small loan to tide them over.

His destitution brought with it a disease that turned him a withered yellow-brown all over: his face went the colour of a little bronze drum, and even the whites of his eyes turned brown. People said that he had the yellow liver sickness, and the children called him Yellow Fatty.

One day he said to his wife, 'There's nothing for it. If we go on this way we'll even be selling our little cooking pots before long. Looks as though you'll have to provide the solution. No use your staying and starving with me.'

'Me?' his wife asked dully. She was sitting behind the stove holding her baby boy, now just three years old, as she fed him at her breast.

'Yes, you.' Her husband's voice was weak with sickness. 'I've pledged you.'

'What?' His wife almost fainted. There was a moment of silence in the room before he continued, gasping for breath, 'Wolf Wang came here three days ago and went on and on demanding that money back. When he went I followed him as

far as the Two Acre Pond. I wanted to do myself in. I sat
under the tree you can jump into the pond from and thought
and thought, but I hadn't got the strength to jump. Besides, an
owl was hooting in my ear, and it made me so scared I came
home. On the way back I met Mrs. Shen who asked me why I
was out so late. I told her everything and asked her to borrow
some money for me or some clothes or jewellery from a girl that
I could pawn to keep Wolf Wang's wolf-eyes from glaring
around the house every day.

'She said, "Why are you keeping your wife at home? Look
how sick you are yourself." I couldn't say anything, just
looked at the ground, but she went on, "You've only got one
son, and you couldn't spare him. But what about your wife?"
I thought she was going to tell me to sell you—"Even though
you are married there's no other option when you're hard up.
Why keep her at home?"

'Then she said straight out, "There's a gentleman of fifty
who has no son and wants to marry a second wife. His first wife
won't agree, and will only let him hire one for three or four
years. He's asked me to look out for a suitable woman. She must
be about thirty and have had two or three children. She should
be quiet, well-behaved, hard-working, and willing to obey the
first wife. The gentleman's wife told me that if these conditions
were met they'd pay eighty or a hundred dollars for her. I've
been looking for someone for several days but I can't find the
right woman."

'Then she said that meeting me made her think of you:
you're just what's wanted. She asked me what I thought about
it and forced me to agree though the tears were in my eyes.'

At this point he hung down his head and his feeble voice was
silent. His wife said nothing; she seemed quite stupefied. After
another silence he continued; 'Mrs. Shen went to the gentleman's house yesterday. She says he was delighted, and his wife
was pleased too. They'll give a hundred dollars. You'll be there
for three years, or five if you don't have a son in that time.
Mrs. Shen arranged the date as well—the eighteenth, five days
from now. She went to sign the contract today.'

His wife was trembling right down to her stomach as she
forced out the question, 'Why didn't you tell me before?'

'I walked round and round in front of you yesterday but I couldn't bring myself to do it. Think it over. We're done for if you won't give us this way out.'

'Is it settled?' the woman asked, her teeth chattering.

'As soon as the contract's signed.'

'Curse it. Is . . . is there no other way out, Chunbao's dad?' Chunbao was the name of the child she was hugging.

'Damn it, I've thought it over and over. But we're so poor we'll have to do it to stay alive. I don't even know whether I'll be able to transplant rice this year.'

'Have you thought about Chunbao? He's only three—he can't do without his mum.'

'I'll keep him—you've weaned him.'

He had gradually lost his temper. When he walked out through the door she began to sob.

She remembered what had happened just a year ago. She was lying on her bed like a corpse after giving birth to a daughter, though a corpse would have been in one piece. Instead she felt as though she had been torn limb from limb. The new-born girl lay on the floor in a pile of straw, crying loudly as she drew in her arms and legs.

The umbilical cord was wrapped round the infant and the afterbirth lay beside it. She longed to draw herself up to wash the child, but even when she lifted her head up her body was immobile on the bed. She watched her husband, her cruel husband, as with flushed cheeks he placed a bucket of boiling water beside the baby. 'Don't, don't,' she cried with the last of her strength, but without a moment's thought or a single word the man who had been so savage even before he was ill took the new-born baby in his brawny arms and thrust her into the boiling water like a butcher slaughtering a lamb. Apart from the bubbling of the water and the hiss as the flesh absorbed it there was no sound from the little girl. Why hadn't she herself cried aloud? Why had she accepted her unjust end so quietly? Thinking back she remembered that it was because she had passed out feeling as if her heart had been torn out. Memory seemed to dry up her tears. 'Fate's against me,' she sighed. Chunbao pulled out her nipple, looked at her, and said 'Mummy, mummy.'

c

The evening before she was due to leave she sat in the darkest corner of the house. The oil lamp was burning as dimly as a fire-fly in its niche. She was hugging Chunbao and resting her head on his. Her thoughts seemed to be far away; she herself did not know where. Slowly they came back to her son. 'Chunbao, Chunbao,' she said softly.

'Mummy.' The child smiled as he sucked her nipple.

'Mummy's going tomorrow.'

'Eh?' Not quite understanding, the child buried his head in his mother's bosom.

'Mummy won't be coming back. She can't come back for three years.'

As she wiped her eyes the child stopped sucking to ask, 'Where are you going, mummy? To the temple?'

'No, to a family called Li over ten miles away.'

'I'll come too.'

'You can't, love.'

The child angrily went back to drinking her milk, of which there was all too little.

'You'll stay at home with daddy, darling. He'll look after you. He'll let you climb into bed with him and play with you. Be a good boy and do as he tells you. Then in three years' time. . . .'

Before she could finish the child said miserably, 'Daddy'll hit me.'

'He won't hit you any more.' As she said this she stroked his forehead with her left hand. There was a scar, now healed, where his father had struck him with the handle of a spade three days after murdering his new-born sister.

She was going to say more to her son when her husband came in. He walked up to her, pulled something out of a pocket, and said, 'I've got seventy dollars here. I'll get the other thirty ten days after you go there.' After a pause he went on, 'They've agreed to send a carrying chair for you.' After another pause he added, 'The carriers will come after break-fast.' With that he left her and went out again. She and her husband ate no supper that evening.

There was a spring drizzle the next day, and the chair

carriers came early. She had not slept all night. First she had
mended some old clothes of Chunbao's. Although spring was
nearly over and summer would soon begin she had brought out
the tattered padded jacket the boy wore in winter to give to
his father, who was already asleep. After that she had sat
beside him wanting to say something, but the long night
dragged past without her saying anything. When she did pluck
up the courage to speak she made only incomprehensible noises
and the sound seemed to come from outside her, so she lay
down to sleep.

Just as she was forgetting her worries and drifting off to
sleep Chunbao woke up. He pushed her and told her to get up,
and as she dressed him she said, 'Be a good boy at home. If
you don't cry your dad won't hit you. Later on I'll buy some
sweets, darling, so you needn't cry.'

The child, too young to understand sorrow, opened his
mouth and began to sing. She kissed him on the lips and said,
'Don't sing or you'll wake up your dad.'

The carriers were sitting on a bench by the door, smoking
and talking about what interested them. Soon Mrs. Shen
arrived. She was the old matchmaker from the next village
and experienced in the ways of the world. As soon as she came
in she said, brushing the rain off her clothes:

'It's raining. That's a lucky sign. Your family is going to
prosper from now on.'

The old woman scurried round the room, hinting to the
child's father that she wanted her money: it was through her
efforts that the contract has been arranged so smoothly.

'Quite frankly, Chunbao's dad, for another fifty dollars the
old fellow could have bought himself a concubine,' she said.

Then she turned to the woman, who was still holding her
child to herself, to tell her that it was time to be moving.

'The carriers,' she said very loud, 'want to get there in time
for dinner, so you'd better hurry up and get ready to go.'

The woman looked at her as if to say that she did not want
to go and would sooner starve to death at home.

The words were on her tongue, and the matchmaker knew
it. She went up to the woman and said with a sickly smile,
'You silly girl, what can Yellow Fatty give you? That other

family has plenty of food and to spare, and with over thirty acres of land they're very well off. Their home is their own and they have hired hands and oxen. The first wife is very good-tempered and considerate: whenever she sees you she gives you something to eat. The old fellow—well, he isn't really old— has a very light complexion and hasn't grown his beard yet.[1] Because he's such a scholar his back is a bit hunched, which is very refined. The only thing is that you must watch your words. The moment you get out of the sedan chair you'll see it all. I'm a matchmaker who's never told a lie.'

Wiping her tears away the woman said very softly, 'But I can't bear to leave Chunbao behind.'

'Don't worry about him,' said the old woman, putting a hand on her shoulder, and bringing her face close to Chunbao and his mother. 'He's three now, and as the saying goes, a three-year-old can leave his mother, so he'll be all right without you. If you make the effort you can have one or two more there. Then everything will be fine.'

The carriers outside were impatient to be off, and grumbling, 'She's no blushing bride, so why all the weeping.'

The old woman took Chunbao from her and said, 'Let me take him.' The child began to cry and struggle, but the old woman eventually managed to drag him outside. When she was in the chair the woman said, 'Take him indoors, it's raining.'

Her husband sat there motionless, his head in his hands. He said nothing.

The two villages were about ten miles apart, but the carriers only put the chair down for a rest once in the journey. The spring drizzle blew in through the cloth sides of the chair, soaking her clothes. A woman of fifty-three or fifty-four with a fat face and calculating eyes came out to meet her. This must be the first wife, the woman thought. She stole an embarrassed glance at her and could say nothing. The older woman helped her up the steps in a very friendly way as a man with a long, thin face came out of the house. He took a good look at his new second wife and said, his face heaped with smiles, 'You've come very early. Your clothes are wet.'

---

[1] Only old men normally let their beards grow.

Ignoring his remark, the older woman asked her, 'Is there anything else in the chair?'

'No,' the new wife said.

Some women who lived nearby were peering in through the main gate. They went indoors.

She did not know where she was. All she was thinking about was her old home and how she could not bear to leave Chunbao. It was clearly true that she should be glad about the three years now beginning. Both the new family and the new husband she had been hired to were better than her old ones. The soft-spoken scholar was indeed a good and kind man, and even the senior wife was far better than she had expected her to be. She was so considerate and she told her all about her thirty years with her husband from their splendid wedding right down to the present. She had given birth to a baby fifteen or sixteen years previously who was, she said, such a pretty and clever little boy, but he had died of smallpox before he was ten months old. She had never had another child. She had thought her husband ought, well, to take a concubine, but she never made it clear whether he did not because he loved her, or because he had never found the right girl. This state of affairs had gone on right up to the present. Talking about it made her, straightforward as she was, jealous, sad, happy, then depressed. Finally the older woman spoke her hopes out straight although her face was red:

'You've had several children, so of course you must know more about *that* than I do.'

With these words she left her.

That evening the scholar told her all sorts of things about the family, though in fact it was nothing more than boasting and trying to win her favour. She was sitting beside a long table, a redwood one the like of which was not to be found in her old home. As she looked at it in a daze the scholar sat down on the other side of it and asked, 'What's your name?'

She stood up without answering or smiling and walked over to the bed. He followed her over and asked with a titter:

'Feeling shy? Missing your husband? I'm your husband now.' He laughed very quietly and tugged at her sleeve. 'Cheer up. You're missing your baby, aren't you? Still. . . .'

Instead of finishing what he was saying he tittered again and took off his long gown.

She could hear the senior wife scolding someone in a loud voice outside. She could not make out at first who was at the receiving end: was it the kitchen maid or was she scolding her? At any rate, it was for her benefit that the older woman was losing her temper. The scholar, now in bed, said:

'Come to bed. She's always going on like that. She used to be very fond of one of the labourers, but ever since he got too friendly with Mrs. Huang in the kitchen she's been going for her all the time.'

The days passed. Her old home gradually dimmed in her memory, as her present situation slowly became more real and familiar to her. All the same, Chunbao's howls still echoed in her ears and she occasionally saw him in her dreams, although he became increasingly indistinct as her present life grew more complicated every day. She now knew that the senior wife was suspicious, and that for all her show of generosity to her she was so jealous that she watched the scholar's every move as closely as a spy. If ever the scholar met the new wife first and talked to her, the senior wife would suspect that he was giving her something special and call him to her own room to give him a piece of her mind. 'Have you been bewitched by that fox-spirit?' 'You ought to have more sense of dignity.' These were the sort of remarks that the new wife heard her make more than once. From then on she would scurry away if ever she saw him coming in when the older woman was not with her. When the senior wife was there the new wife had to give way to her which was only natural, but if anyone else noticed the new wife giving way, the senior wife would lose her temper with her and say that she was deliberately making everyone think that she was cruel. Later on menial household tasks were heaped upon her as if she were a servant girl. She tried to be clever and wash the clothes that the older woman had changed out of, but the senior wife said:

'You needn't wash my clothes. You can tell Mrs. Huang to wash yours too. Dear sister,' she continued, 'would you mind having a look at the pigsty? Why are those two pigs squealing?

Perhaps they're hungry. Mrs. Huang never gives them enough to eat.'

Eight months had passed, and that winter her tastes began to change. She wanted to eat fresh noodles and sweet potatoes instead of rice, but after two meals she was tired of them. Then she wanted to eat ravioli soup, but too much of it made her feel sick. Next she wanted pumpkin and plums although they were summer things that could not be had then. The scholar realized what these changes foretold. He smiled all day, eagerly fetching any of the things she wanted that he could find. He went out himself to buy her some tangerines and sent someone else to buy oranges. He walked up and down the verandah reciting something to himself that nobody could make out, and when he saw her milling flour for the New Year holiday with Mrs. Huang he told her to rest although she had only done a few pounds: 'Take a rest. Let the hired hand do it—after all, everyone eats the New Year cakes.'

Sometimes when everyone else was talking in the evening he would take a lamp and start reading the *Book of Songs*:

> *Qua qua cries the osprey*
> *On the island in the river.*
> *The beautiful maiden*
> *Is a fine match for the gentleman.*

'Sir, you're not taking the official exams,' said the hired hand once, 'so why read that?'

He rubbed his beardless cheek and said happily, 'Do you know about the joys of life? About "the candlelit night in the bridal chamber, one's name on the list of successful candidates"? Do you know what those two lines mean? They are the two most happy things on earth. I've passed through that stage, and now I've got something to be even happier about.'

Everyone except his two wives burst out laughing.

All this made the older wife look extremely cross. She had been pleased when she first heard that the new wife was pregnant, but when she saw what a fuss the scholar was making of her she resented her own failure to have another child. In the third month of the new year the other woman stayed in bed for

three days because she was feeling ill and had a headache.
The scholar wanted her to rest, and when he kept asking her
what she wanted, the senior wife really lost her temper. She
said that the new wife was just pretending to be delicate and
nagged at her throughout the three days. She started by mocking her unkindly, saying that since coming to the scholar's
house she had grown high and mighty and was putting on a
concubine's airs with her backaches and headaches. She was
quite sure she had not been so spoilt in her own house and
probably had to go round begging for food like a pregnant
bitch, right up to the moment of birth. But now she was
putting on her fine and fancy manners because the old fool—
this was how the older woman referred to her husband—was
making such a fuss over her.

'Everyone has had sons,' she once said to Mrs. Huang in the
kitchen. 'I was pregnant myself for over nine months and I
just don't believe it can make you feel that ill. Besides, this
son isn't here yet. He's still on the king of Hell's register—how
can we be sure that it won't be a monster? She'd better wait until
the brat is born before being so high and mighty and putting
on those airs in front of me. She's showing off a bit too early.'

That evening the woman had gone to bed before supper, and
when she heard all this sarcasm and abuse she began to sob
quietly. The scholar, who was sitting fully dressed in bed, shook
and sweated with fury when he heard it. He wanted to button
his clothes up, get up, and go and hit her. He wanted to grab
her by the hair and lay into her until he had worked off his
fury. But for some reason he could not summon up the strength as
he was trembling down to his finger-tips and his arms felt limp.

'Oh dear,' he said with a low sigh, 'I've been too good to her.
I've never hit her once in thirty years of marriage. I've never
even flicked my finger-nail at her. That's why she's as difficult
as an empress today.'

He rolled over to the other side of the bed where the new
wife was and whispered in her ear:

'Don't cry, don't cry. Let her yap away. She's like a doctored
hen—she can't bear to see anyone else hatch an egg. If you can
produce a boy this time I'll give you two jewels—a green jade
ring and a white one.'

Before he could finish he was unable to bear any longer the jeering laughter of his senior wife that he heard through the door, so he undressed quickly, buried his head in the quilt, and moved towards her breasts.

'I've got a white jade one. . . .'

Her belly swelled day by day until it was the size of a bushel measure. The older wife finally hired a midwife and even started making baby clothes in brightly patterned cotton when other people were there to see her.

The sixth month of the old calendar,[1] when the heat of summer was at its greatest, passed in hope. Autumn began and cool breezes started to blow through the country town. One day, when everyone's hope was at its highest pitch, the atmosphere in the house was thrown into confusion. The scholar was extremely anxious. He paced up and down the yard with an almanac in his hands reading it out as if he wanted to learn it by heart. 'Wu-chen, jia-xu, the year ren-yin'[2] was what he kept repeating lightly to himself. Sometimes he cast an impatient glance at the room with closed windows from which came the low groans of a woman in labour; otherwise he looked up at the sun masked by cloud. He went to the door of the room and asked Mrs. Huang who was standing outside:

'What's happening now?'

Mrs. Huang nodded continuously and said nothing. Then she breathed out and replied:

'It'll be born any minute now, any minute now.'

He picked up his almanac and started walking up and down the verandah once more.

This went on until, as the evening mist began to gather and lamps were lit in the room like wild flowers in spring, a baby boy was born. While the baby bawled inside the room the scholar sat in a corner, almost weeping with happiness. Nobody in the house was interested in eating supper, and as they sat at the unappetizing meal the senior wife said to the servants:

'We won't let on that he's a boy yet so as to keep bad luck

[1] About July.
[2] The scholar was working out the time and date of the baby's birth in terms of the traditional calendar.

away from the little brat. If anyone asks, you are to say that it's a girl.'

They all smiled and nodded.

A month later the baby's soft, little white face was reflecting the autumn sunlight as the young wife suckled him, surrounded by the neighbouring women. Some were praising the baby's nose, some his mouth, and some his ears. Others praised his mother, saying that she looked fairer and stronger than before. The senior wife and the baby's grandmother were giving instructions, protecting it, and saying, 'That's enough for now. Don't make him cry.'

The scholar racked his brains for a suitable name for the child but could not think of one. The senior wife thought he should choose one from the words 'long life, wealth, and glory' or 'happiness, office, longevity, and blessings.' 'Longevity' or some other words with the same meaning would be best, like Qixi or Pengzu. The scholar thought them too common and did not agree: they were names that anyone might have. He leafed through the *Book of Changes* and the *Book of History* and searched high and low, but after a fortnight and then a month he still had not found a suitable one. In his view it had to be a name that would bring the child luck while also meaning that he had been given a son in his old age. One day he was holding his three-month-old son while looking through a book for a name for him. With his spectacles on his nose he carried the book over to the lamplight. The baby's mother was sitting silently on the other side of the room with her mind far away when suddenly she opened her mouth and said:

'I think we should call him Qiubao.'[1] All the eyes in the room turned towards her as everyone listened to what she had to say next. 'He was born in the autumn, wasn't he? So he's an autumn treasure. Let's call him Qiubao.'

'Yes,' the scholar said immediately, 'I've put a great deal of thought into it. I'm over fifty, in the autumn of my life, and the child was indeed born in the autumn. Autumn is the time when everything comes to maturity. Qiubao is an excellent name.

---

[1] Literally 'Autumn Treasure'.

And it's in the *Book of History*, isn't it? "And there will be an autumn." I'm having my autumn now.'

Then he praised the child's mother, saying that study was useless and intelligence was inborn. All this made the woman feel awkward, just sitting there. With her head bowed and a sad smile she said, holding back her tears, 'It was only because I was missing Chunbao.'

Qiubao grew every day into a child who was charmingly inseparable from his mother. He had extraordinarily large eyes that gazed tirelessly at strangers and could recognize his mother at a distance with a single glance. He clung to her all day, and although his father loved him even more than she did, the child did not like him. The scholar's wife pretended to love the child as if he were her own, but the boy's big eyes saw her as a stranger and looked at her with tireless curiosity, clinging more closely to his mother. But the day when his mother would be leaving this house was drawing nearer. The jaws of spring bit the tail of winter and the feet of summer were always close behind spring. This put a problem in the front of everyone's mind: the three years would soon be up for the child's mother.

Because he was so fond of his son the scholar suggested to his wife that they should pay out another hundred dollars and buy her for good. But his wife's reply was:

'If you're going to buy her you'd better poison me first.'

The scholar snorted angrily and said nothing for a long time. Finally he forced a smile and said, 'Just think of that poor child without his mother.'

'Don't I count as his mother?' asked the senior wife tartly, with a cold smile.

There were two conflicting feelings clashing in the mind of the child's mother. On the one hand the words 'three years' were always in her brain, and three years would pass easily even though she was now living like a servant in the scholar's house. Besides, the Chunbao of her imagination was as lively and adorable as the Qiubao in front of her, and although she could not bear to part with Qiubao it would be even worse to lose Chunbao. On the other hand she would like to stay in this house for good because, she thought, Chunbao's father was not fated to live long and his disease would carry him off to a very distant place in a few years. So she asked her second husband to bring Chunbao here, too, so that she could have him with her.

Once she was sitting exhausted on the verandah in the early summer sunlight that has such an amazing power to make you so drowsy that you start imagining things. Qiubao was asleep in her arms, her nipple in his mouth, and she somehow felt that Chunbao was standing beside her. She stretched out her hand to take hold of him, wanting to say something to the two brothers, but there was nothing beside her after all.

In the doorway further away from her stood the older wife, staring at her with her kind face but evil eyes. The woman realized with vague regret that she should escape as soon as she could; the older woman was watching her like a spy. Then the child in her arms cried, and she could only cope with the senior wife by inventing things to do even when she was not really busy.

Later the scholar changed his plan. He now wanted to send for Mrs. Shen to ask the former husband of Qiubao's mother if he would agree to continue the arrangement for another three years for another thirty dollars—or at most fifty dollars. 'When Qiubao is five,' he said to his senior wife, 'he'll be able to leave his mother.'

His wife, while telling her Buddhist beads and reciting 'I dedicate myself to Amitabha Buddha', replied:

'She has her elder son at home. You ought to let her go back to her original husband.'

'Just imagine poor Qiubao without his mother at two,' continued the scholar, his head lowered.

The older woman put down her beads and said, 'I can bring him up, I can look after him. Do you think I'd try to kill him?'

At this last remark the scholar started to walk away, but the older wife went on behind him:

'That child was born for my good as well. Qiubao is mine. If we have no descendants it will be your family that dies out, but remember that I depend on your family. You've really been taken with her. You've gone so senile you can't think straight any longer. You're so eager to have her with you—how

much longer do you think you're going to live? I'm certainly
not going to share a place with her in the ancestral temple.'

She apparently had more cruel and biting things to say, but
the scholar was by now out of earshot.

That summer a boil appeared on the child's head and he
ran a slight fever. The senior wife went everywhere to consult
goddesses and ask for Buddha-medicine to smear on the baby's
boil or pour down his throat. The child's mother did not think
it was a very serious illness and was not happy to see the young
creature cry himself into a terrible state, so she would tip the
medicine away discreetly when he had drunk only a few mouth-
fuls of it. This made the senior wife sigh aloud and say to the
scholar:

'Just look! She doesn't care in the least about his illness. She
even says he's not really losing weight. Only love that comes
from the heart is genuine; superficial affection is false.'

All the woman could do was wipe away her tears in secret.
The scholar said nothing.

At the time of Qiubao's first birthday the family laid on a
noisy banquet in his honour that lasted all day. Thirty or
forty guests came, bringing clothes, noodles, silver lions to
hang round his neck, or gilded figures of the god of longevity
to pin on his hat. All these presents arrived in the guests'
sleeves. They wished him great success and long life. The host's
face gleamed and shone as if the colour of the sunset were reflected on his cheeks.

But just when the feasting was about to begin, that evening, a
visitor came into their courtyard in the dim light of dusk.
Everyone looked closely at him. He was a destitute-looking
countryman with patched clothes and long hair, and under
his arm he carried a bundle wrapped in paper. The host
greeted him with some astonishment and asked who he was.
His mumbled reply confused the host at first before it came to
him in a flash that this was the leather merchant.

'Why, have you brought a present too?' the host asked
quietly. 'You really didn't have to.'

The visitor looked all around him before answering:

'I . . . I wanted to. I've come to wish the baby long life. . . .'

Leaving his remark apparently unfinished he started to open

the paper parcel that was under his arm. With trembling fingers he untied several layers of paper and took out the four characters for 'Longevity like Southern Mountains'. They were made of silver-plated copper and each was about one inch square.

The scholar's wife came over and examined him closely. She seemed rather angry, but the scholar invited him to join the feast. The other guests all whispered to each other.

Two hours of eating and drinking had put everyone in high spirits. They were playing guess-fingers, the drinking game, and competing in the downing of large bowls of rice wine. The house seemed to shake with the din. Only the leather merchant was sitting there quietly although he too had drunk a couple of cupfuls, and the other guests were ignoring him. When the general excitement had died down the guests hastily swallowed a bowl of rice, exchanged polite remarks and went away in the light of two or three lanterns at a time.

The leather merchant went on eating to the very end, only leaving the table when the servants came to clear up the soup bowls. He went to a dark corner of the verandah where he met his hired-out wife.

'Why did you come?' she asked in a very sad voice.

'It wasn't because I wanted to; I had no alternative.'

'But why did you have to come in this state?'

'How do you think I got the money to buy the presents? I had to rush around all morning pleading with people to lend it to me, then I had to go into town to buy them. That made me tired, hungry, and late.'

'How's Chunbao?' the woman asked.

Her husband paused before replying.

'It's about him that I've come.'

'About Chunbao?' She sounded alarmed.

'Ever since last summer,' her husband slowly replied, 'he's been getting terribly thin. He became ill during the autumn. I hadn't the money to pay a doctor or buy medicine for him, so now he's worse than ever. If we can't find some way of helping him he may die any hour.' After a moment's silence he continued, 'I've come to borrow some money from you.'

The woman felt as if several cats were clawing and biting her

inside and chewing up her heart. She longed to weep, but today
was the day on which everyone had come to wish Qiubao well,
so how could she follow their good wishes with sobs? She
gulped back her tears and said to her husband:

'I haven't any money either. They only give me twenty cents
a month for pocket-money, and I don't have the use of any of
that because I have to spend it all on the baby. What are we to
do?'

After a silence the woman asked, 'Who's looking after
Chunbao now?'

'I left him at a neighbour's. I must go back this evening, so
I'd better be off.'

As he spoke he wiped away his tears. The woman said,
sobbing, 'Wait a moment. I'll go and see if I can borrow some
money from him.' She went away.

One evening three days later the scholar asked her, 'What
happened to that green jade ring I gave you?'

'I gave it to my husband that night. He took it to pawn.'

'But I lent you five dollars,' said the scholar angrily.

'Five dollars wasn't enough.'

'You always prefer your first husband and son,' continued
the scholar with a sigh, 'no matter how good I am to you. I
was wanting to keep you for another couple of years, but now I
think you'd better go next spring.'

The woman sat there impassively, not even weeping.

A few days later he said to her, 'That ring was very valuable.
When I gave it to you I meant to pass it on to Qiubao. I'd
never have imagined you would pawn it. It's a good thing *she*
doesn't know about it—if she did the row would last three
months.'

The woman became thinner every day. There was a dullness
in her eyes, and her ears were filled with mocking and abusive
voices. Chunbao's illness was preying constantly on her mind
and she was always on the look-out for a friend from her own
village or a visitor who was going there to bring her the news
she longed to hear—'Chunbao is better.' But there was never
any news. She wanted to borrow two dollars to send him some
sweets by a visitor who was passing that way, but no such

visitor came. She used to stand holding Qiubao beside the main road that passed near the main gate looking at the way home. This made the scholar's senior wife feel most uncomfortable.

'She doesn't want to stay here,' she kept saying to him. 'She's longing to go flying back there as soon as she can.'

Some nights she would cry out as she lay sleeping with Qiubao in her arms, which frightened him and made him howl.

'Why did you do that? Why?' the scholar asked as if he were interrogating her.

She patted Qiubao, humming and not replying.

'Did you shout because you dreamt that your first son had died?' he continued. 'You woke me up.'

'No, no,' she hastily objected. 'I thought I saw a grave-mound in front of me.'

The scholar said nothing else, but gloomy images kept coming up before her eyes and she wanted to walk towards the grave.

At the end of the winter the birds that were about to leave were twittering in front of her window all the time. First she weaned the child and then she had a Taoist priest perform the appropriate ceremonial. The separation, the eternal separation, of mother and child had been decided on.

Earlier that day Mrs. Huang had whispered to the scholar's senior wife, 'Shall I arrange for a chair to take her back?'

The scholar's senior wife, who was telling her beads, said, 'Let her walk. The chair would have to be paid for at that end and she hasn't any money. They say her real husband can't even afford to eat, so she shouldn't be extravagant. It's not far. I've walked ten or a dozen miles in my time, and her feet are bigger than mine. She'll do it in a few hours.'

When the woman dressed Qiubao that morning tears streamed down her cheeks as the child called 'Aunty, aunty'— the senior wife would only let him call his real mother 'aunty' as she herself had to be called 'mummy'—and she answered him through sobs. She was longing to say something to him like: 'Good-bye, my darling son. Your mummy has always been good to you and you must be good to her in the future and forget about me.'

But she could not bring herself to say it. Besides, she knew that a child of one and a half would not understand.

The scholar came up quietly behind her, put his hand under her arm with ten twenty-cent pieces. 'Here, take it,' he whispered, 'it's two dollars.' When she had finished doing up the child's buttons she put the coins in her bosom.

The senior wife came in again, and when she had watched the scholar go out she said to her: 'Let me hold Qiubao so that he doesn't cry when you leave.'

The woman said nothing, but Qiubao, most unwilling to leave her, kept hitting the senior wife in the face until she said angrily:

'You'd better go and have breakfast with him. Give him to me afterwards.'

Mrs. Huang urged her as hard as she could to eat plenty. 'You've been like this for a fortnight,' she said. 'You're even thinner than when you came. Look in the mirror and you'll see. Do eat a bowl of rice. You've got ten miles to walk today.'

'You've been very good to me,' the woman replied in a detached way.

The sun had now risen high and it was a beautiful day. Qiubao still did not want to leave his mother. When the senior wife snatched him cruelly away he kicked her in the belly with his little feet and pulled her hair with his little fists, howling at the top of his voice.

'Let me go after dinner,' said the woman from behind.

The senior wife turned on her and said cruelly: 'Pack your bundle and go. It'll be the same whenever you do it.'

The child's howls grew fainter in her ears.

As she packed she could still hear him crying. Mrs. Huang stood beside her trying to console her while keeping an eye on what she put in the bundle. Finally she set off with her old bundle under her arm.

She could hear Qiubao crying as she went out through the main gate and could still hear him as she slowly walked the ten miles.

The road, under the warm sun, seemed as endless to her as the sky. As she walked beside a river she longed to rest her feeble feet and jump into the water. It was so clear she could see herself in it. But after sitting on the bank for a while she had to start moving her shadow in the same direction once more.

The sun was past its height when an old countryman told her in a village that she had five more miles to go.

'Uncle,' she said to him, 'please could you arrange a sedan chair for me. I can't walk any further.'

'Are you ill?' the old man asked.

'Yes.'

She was now sitting in a cool shelter at the edge of the village.

'Have you come from the village?'

After a moment's silence she replied, 'I'm going there. This morning I thought I could do it on foot.'

The old man was understanding enough to ask no more questions before going to find two chair porters and a chair. Because this was the rice transplanting time no hood could be spared for it.

At what seemed to be about three or four in the afternoon an uncovered chair was carried down a narrow, dirty village street. In the chair lay a middle-aged woman with a face as shrivelled as a dried-up cabbage leaf. Her eyes were half shut with exhaustion and her breathing was weak. The people in the street all gazed at her with astonishment and pity, and a crowd of children followed the chair shouting and yelling. It was as if something strange had arrived in the silent village.

Chunbao was one of the children following the chair. He was shouting as if he were driving a pig, but when the chair turned into the lane leading to his own home he stretched out his hands in amazement. Then it reached his front gate. He stood stock still, leaning on a pillar some way away from it. The other children stood timidly on either side of the chair. As the woman stepped out her eyes were too blurred to recognize as her own Chunbao the six-year-old boy in ragged clothes and with matted hair who was no taller than he had been three years ago. Then suddenly she started crying and called 'Chunbao'.

The children were startled. Chunbao was so frightened that he went indoors to hide in his father's room.

The woman sat in the murky room for a very long time. Neither she nor her husband spoke. As night fell his drooping head straightened up and he said: 'Cook us a meal.'

She had to get up. After walking round the room she said weakly to her husband:

'The rice jar is empty.'

Her husband laughed bitterly. 'You really have been living with the gentry. The rice is in that cigarette tin.'

That evening her husband said to her son:

'Go and sleep with your mother, Chunbao.'

But Chunbao started to cry in the alcove. His mother went up to him, calling him by his name, but when she tried to caress him he dodged away from her.

'I'll hit you for forgetting her as fast as that,' said her husband to him. She lay with her eyes wide open on a dirty and narrow plank bed with Chunbao lying beside her like a stranger. In her numbed brain a fat and lovable Qiubao was fidgeting beside her, but when she put out her hands to hug him he turned out to be Chunbao. Chunbao, now asleep, turned over. His mother hugged him tight, and as he snored lightly he lay his head on her chest, stroking her breasts with his hands.

The long night, as cold and lonely as death, dragged interminably on and on.

Guo Moruo　郭沫若

[Kuo Mo-jo]

Guo Moruo, born to a rich landlord family in Szechuan in the early 1890s, was educated in his own province, then in Shanghai and Japan, where he studied medicine. His writing was at first heavily romantic, and he was one of the founders of the Creation Society, a literary clique that advocated pure self-expression. He was one of the pioneers of western-style free verse in China, reacting against the restraint in theme and form of traditional poetry with wild outpourings full of western names and imagery that now read as a badly dated product of the intellectual excitement and confusion of the time. His work became more politically committed later.

From 1925 he was teaching literature at Zhongshan University in Canton, then a revolutionary centre, and in 1926 he took part in the Northern Expedition as deputy director of the Political Department of the headquarters of the revolutionary forces. It is from this period that the material for 'Double Performance' is drawn. The capture of Wuhan by the combined efforts of Kuomintang and Communist organizations came at the high point of their united front, which collapsed all too soon afterwards when the Kuomintang right wing massacred Communists, labour leaders, and many of their own left wing who did not change sides or, like Guo Moruo, flee.

Guo went back to Japan, where for the next ten years his attention was mainly devoted to the study of ancient China. He also wrote stories, plays, and some volumes of autobiography. With the outbreak of the Sino-Japanese war in 1937 he returned to his own country and was active in the patriotic literature movement in Hankow and Chungking. In 1943 he went to the Soviet Union, and soon after going back to China he had to flee again, this time to Hongkong. In 1949 he went to north China, and since then has been one of the older intellectuals most enthusiastic in support of the People's Government, holding a multitude of high positions including the presidency of the Chinese Academy of Sciences

As a short-story writer he was influenced by the melancholy and introspective mood of much Japanese fiction, and many of his stories were set in that country. This piece, undoubtedly autobio-

graphical, has an ebullience in keeping with the mood of a revolution when it seems to be going well.

Double Performance

This episode took place at the time of the October Tenth
Festival in 1926, when the armies of the Northern Expedition
had taken the walled city of Wuchang.

As the storming of Wuchang after a forty-day siege and the
capture of Liu Yuchan and Chen Jiamo coincided with the
October Tenth Festival, the enthusiasm of the Hankow masses
had risen to fever pitch.

Some days earlier the Hankow Y.M.C.A. had decided to
invite Deng Yanda, the head of the Political Department, to
give an address, and the organizers of the meeting had plastered
the streets with posters in gold on red urging people to come
along. But on the evening Deng Yanda was exhausted after his
efforts in the fighting and had, besides, other duties that he
could not get away from, so he asked me to stand in for him.

After nine that night, when the Y.M.C.A. people had come
several times to urge me to hurry up, I went along to give the
speech for Deng, dragging Li Heling, who was in charge of the
organization of the Propaganda Section, along with me.

As it was long after the intended time when we reached the
Y.M.C.A. we were taken straight into a big hall packed with a
huge audience.

No sooner had we sat down on a row of chairs at the back of
the platform than one of the people who had come to get us
(probably one of the organizers) went over to the big, rather
western-looking man who was chairing the meeting and had a
whispered conversation with him. The leader of the meeting
nodded to us in greeting and opened the meeting.

Not only did he look westernized; his very intonation was
western.

'The meeting, brothers, is now open. Let us all stand up and
sing a hymn.'

Everyone stood up. The hymn number must have been

chosen earlier. From the two rows of girl students who were sitting in front of the platform on the right-hand side an older woman went over, sat down at the organ placed at an angle across the right-hand corner of the hall, and began to play. The others started singing.

After the hymn the leader started to pray, and when the prayers were over he made the opening speech. It was solemn and rhetorical. Probably all Y.M.C.A. organizers are orators as their eloquent tongues are their sharpest weapons.

It was rather a long speech, lasting perhaps half an hour. Naturally I cannot remember the whole of it, but its main theme was that Sun Yatsen[1] had been a Christian.

'The Northern Expedition,' said the leader, 'has defeated the northern warlords. And whose disciples are the Northern Expedition's commanders? They are the disciples of Sun Yatsen. Whose disciple was he? He was the disciple of Our Lord Jesus. Thus it is that all who believe in Our Lord Jesus win final victory; the victory of the Northern Expedition is his victory.'

Then he went on to praise Deng Yanda in the highest possible terms, saying, 'This great revolutionary is like George Washington or Napoleon. He is a man without precedent in Chinese history.' But what came next was again the argument that he was a disciple of Sun Yatsen who was a disciple of Christ.

The leader continued by saying how very disappointed he was that exhaustion had prevented Deng Yanda from being present. 'We shall have another opportunity to invite this great revolutionary to expound his lofty revolutionary theories. This evening we must content ourselves with listening to the representatives that this great revolutionary has sent along to talk to us.'

He signalled to me to begin amid a storm of applause from the hall.

This way of doing things was the standard Protestant one, and the reason for it was no mystery. Deng Yanda was holding three jobs at the time: Head of the Political Department, Governor of Hupeh Province, and Commanding Officer of the

[1] Sun Yatsen (1866–1925) was for forty years the leader of the nationalist revolution in China.

Mobile Office of the General Headquarters. In fact as well as
in name he had the prestige of being a man 'with three heads
and six arms'. This top Y.M.C.A. organizer was quite right to
call him 'a great revolutionary without precedent in Chinese
history', to invite him to give a speech so as to make propaganda for Christianity, to be infinitely disappointed because he
could not come in person, and to despise an obscure underling
like myself. But this was the high tide of the 'National Revolution', and the guiding spirit was 'Down with cultural aggression'.
Before going to the meeting I had been sure that the Y.M.C.A.
had only asked Deng to give a speech because they were scared
of the power of the revolution, but even if they were intending
to make use of us they could have been a little more accommo-
dating and cut out all that formalistic ceremonial to spare the
speaker embarrassment. I had never imagined that they
would make the speech into so trying an occasion. With his
thoroughly Christian way of thinking he was taking me for a
lamb to be dragged to the altar and sacrificed in atonement for
sin. He said that as one was either the disciple of a disciple of
Jesus, or else a disciple's disciple's disciple, the victory of the
revolution was a victory for Jesus. He should have noticed the
fact that ours was the banner of 'Down with cultural aggression' even if we were nothing but mere underlings. It was of
course his responsibility to make propaganda for his religion,
but didn't one have the responsibility to propagate the revolution? He was so faithful to his own responsibility and so clever
at making his propaganda, but he treated one as a sacrificial
lamb waiting helplessly while he, the Pharisee, piled up the
faggots round one.

With the hymn, the prayers and the opening speech I was
now so worried that I did not know whether to laugh or cry,
and was feeling wretched because there seemed nothing I
could do about it. Li Heling was feeling the same way judging
by the furious expression he wore as he kept glancing at me as
if to ask whatever we were to do about it. Before I had thought
of some answer to indicate to him the opening address was over
and the leader was gesturing to me to speak.

The wild applause seemed to be driving me, the sacrificial
lamb, to the slaughter.

Just as I was saluting the audience and the leader, who was on the point of setting fire to the faggots, a providential rainstorm was sent from heaven to put them out. A brainwave of the sort that sometimes flashes out of the blue when you are writing came to me at that moment.

'Before making my proper speech,' I said, 'I must perform a little ceremony. The leader, as a Christian, has just performed Christian ceremonies. But we are soldiers of the revolution, and as such have to carry out a revolutionary ceremony. We choose a chairman, who declares the meeting open and reads the late President's testament. Then we have three minutes' silent mourning for him. Only then can I speak. I would like to make Comrade Li Heling chairman.'

This suggestion made the listeners go wild. Their applause was longer and louder than it had been before, and it showed no sign that it was going to stop. The hall was full of friendly faces. I knew that the listeners were mine. When Li Heling stood up and announced that the meeting was open everyone became serious.

Li Heling, a very quick-witted man, opened the meeting in just the right way as acting chairman, then signed to me to speak.

There was another burst of wild applause.

I must have spoken for about fifty minutes, and while I cannot of course remember every word of what I said, I still have a very good idea of the broad outline. This is because my ideas and the objective realities have not changed since then.

I said that I fully understood Jesus Christ and his followers. I had read the Bible and been very fond of reading it for a time, almost to the point of deciding to get baptized. Why had I not been baptized? Because I had realized that we Chinese were in no need of baptism. Ever since the Opium War we had all been Christians from birth, and we spent our whole lives following Christ's teachings. Christ said, for example, that you should love your neighbour and even your enemy. If somebody stripped you of your overcoat you should present him with your shirt. If somebody wanted to strike your right cheek you should let him strike your left cheek too. We Chinese could claim without the slightest hypocrisy to have practised his teaching of love. How could you prove it? Some people had stolen

Hongkong, so we insisted on letting them lease Kowloon.
Some others had snatched Vietnam, and we had insisted on
giving them the Vietnam-Yunnan railway. Others again had
occupied Korea, and we had offered them Manchuria and
Mongolia. We Chinese were really more Christian than any
Christians. Christ had said that if you wished to accumulate
wealth in heaven you should abandon your earthly wealth. It
was harder for a rich man to enter the kingdom of heaven than
for a camel to go through the eye of a needle. How did we
Chinese make out on this? We had got rid of all our earthly
wealth long ago. We had thrown away all our resources that
could produce wealth—banks, mines, railways, postal services,
inland river and sea shipping, factories, markets. . . . We
Chinese were now as thin as a thread, and even if the heavenly
gates were no bigger than the eye of a needle we were fully
qualified for entry.

I did all I could to put this indirect line of reasoning over. It
went down very well, and there was a continual rumble of
laughter and applause.

Finally I referred to the huge leader of the meeting as a
'great missionary' just as he had referred to Deng Yanda as a
'great revolutionary'. I said that as a Chinese and a believer in
Christianity he was a double Christian and possibly more
Christian than Christ himself. However I was sorry for him for
being stuck in Hankow like Jesus nailed to his cross, unable to
use his divine powers. He should really have gone to London,
Paris, New York, or Tokyo to make those camels shrink till
they were thin enough to go through the needle's eye.

Now that I had the whole hall laughing I brought the speech
to an end amid fervent applause.

The 'great missionary' really was a giant of a 'great missionary'. He used the end of my speech as an opportunity to
continue his talk to the audience.

This time he was extraordinarily flattering about me, saying
not once but twice that I was an 'unprecedented' orator. The
reason I was so fine an orator was because I was a follower of
Sun Yatsen, who was a follower of Christ. He wanted everyone
to believe in Christ so that they could also become great
orators.

This was too much for Li Heling, now beside himself with fury. He began to speak and, where my speech had been polite and indirect, his was deliberately down to earth and direct.

He said that Sun Yatsen's belief in religion had been a thing of his youth; all his life he had not taught people to believe in religion but had taught them to make revolution. He explained what sort of a thing religion was, how it had harmed China, and how it was incompatible with revolution; for proof of how some swindlers in the pay of Christianity talked utter nonsense and tried to manipulate everything there was no need to look further than the present occasion. The words rolled off his Paris-trained tongue for a full hour, making the 'great missionary' quite ill at ease.

Then Li Heling asked the audience to stand up and sing the 'Song of the National Revolution'.

Since the troops of the Northern Expedition had entered Wuhan this simple song had spread everywhere. As soon as Li Heling raised his head almost everyone in the hall joined in the singing, with even the mission society's organist accompanying.

Next came the shouting of slogans. Li Heling would shout one, then everyone else shouted it after him. When he shouted 'Down with the religious policies of cultural aggression' the girl students from the mission schools, in the two front rows on the right, seemed to echo him particularly loudly, as if this was their first chance to get their own back after being tricked for so long.

When the slogans had been shouted the crowd, full of excitement after all the cries of 'Long live . . .', poured out of the hall like a flood-tide through a collapsed dike.

The 'great man' was now desperate. 'Please don't go,' he shouted in a hurt voice, 'we haven't prayed and sung our hymn yet.'

Voices in the crowd could be heard saying, 'Who wants prayers? Who wants hymns? We won't be singing hymns now.'

Nobody with less strength than that of the people would have been able to hold back that tidal wave as it broke.

4 June 1936

Mao Dun 茅盾
[Mao Tun]

Shen Yanbing, who uses the pen-name Mao Dun, was born in Chekiang in 1896. After being educated in Nanking and Peking he was one of the founders of the Literary Research Society started in 1921. Like the other literary clubs of the time, its ideas were somewhat vague, but at least they were based on a commitment to realism. Apart from working as an editor for the Commercial Press for seven years, he was first secretary to the Propaganda Department of the Kuomintang and then editor of a Wuhan newspaper during the period of co-operation between the Communists and the Kuomintang that came to an end in 1927.

He was one of the founders of the League of Left-Wing Writers in 1930, and right through until Liberation he was active in literary politics, nearly always in areas not under Communist control. His best-known work is the novel *Midnight*, published in 1932, which analyses the corruption of Shanghai's ruling circles at the time with great insight.

Mao Dun tends to be at his most perceptive and readable as a fascinated observer of the life of members of the middle and upper classes before 1949, writing with understanding and a certain affection. His stories on rural themes seem by comparison to be fictionalized essays on agrarian economics. 'On the Boat' has something of the atmosphere of frustration in wartime Szechuan, the western stronghold of the Kuomintang government to which millions of 'downstreamers' fled up the Yangtse to avoid the Japanese invasion of the eastern provinces.

From 1949 to 1964 Mao Dun was Minister of Culture. His removal was one of the first signs that political control in art and literature by the intellectuals of the 1920s and 1930s was coming to an end. He has published little of note since 1949.

On the Boat

The third blast of the ship's siren died away. There were, as usual, five precious minutes that gave the slower people their last chance.

Both decks were crowded. Between the morning mist that shrouded the peaks on the other bank and the surface of the river, the steam from the boat's funnel swirled lazily over the turbulent and dirty waters. In the distance the river broadened, and the slanting sunlight turned a fast eddy to the left into thousands of golden stars.

There was no wind. The smell of sweat from the people on both decks added to the stuffiness. The upper deck should have been cooler, because it was higher than the lighters around and open on three sides; the canvas at the sides of the boat had also been rolled up. But the big funnel that came up through the saloon was as hot as a stove, despite the panelling that surrounded it. Another smaller funnel not three feet away from it, and two ventilation pipes from the engine room, were also too hot to get close to. In cold weather both the space inside this triangle and the area around it were much used; now they were left empty, which reduced the capacity of the upper deck and made it seem more crowded.

'There'll be some breeze when the boat sails,' was the thought in everybody's mind. Five minutes felt like a very long time.

From above their heads came more hooting as hot, thick steam came down through a crack in the saloon roof. At the same time a shrill, vibrating whistle, even more painful on the ear for being mingled with the echo, came from the lighters. After both noises had stopped a deep, even throbbing slowly grew stronger. The engines had started. The lighters seemed to be slipping backwards.

The last batch of passengers to come on board surrounded the big funnel and occupied the triangular space. They sent out a crowd of sentries as far as the way up to the bridge. On the companion-way from the lower deck a pair of heads kept appearing indecisively and then suddenly disappearing again. As the boat slowly turned they finally made up their minds to press on upwards. A middle-aged man led the way. He was wearing faded khaki drill trousers and a somewhat worn green woollen uniform jacket with a round identification badge on the left breast. His top button was undone, and the big bag he was clutching looked heavy. He looked into the darkness of the cabin, frowned, and turned back to shout down the companion-way, 'Come up, at least there's more air here than there is down there.'

A woman holding a baby appeared slowly at the top of the companion-way. Another child of seven or eight was holding on to the back of her dress.

She moved forward along the 'sentry line' by the rails on the port side, aiming for a tiny space by the way up to the bridge. But as they passed the entrance to a cabin the man looked in and saw to his surprise that it was not as crowded as he had imagined. They changed their plan.

According to the board nailed up over the entrance, this cabin was the 'Defence Post', but as this boat was only ever sent on journeys upstream of less than two hours, during which it remained in the area of 'Greater Chungking', defence was not needed, making this cabin a special area on the boat. According to the shipping company's tickets, there was only one class on board; yet, either from custom or from personal inclination, local people, particularly the porters from the countryside, all went below; while the downstreamers always rushed to the upper deck, which only differed from the lower one in that it was higher and the light was better. There was more air of course, but the coal-ash was unbearable if the canvas on both sides of the boat was rolled up. The upper deck was a hotchpotch: modern girls, businessmen in Western clothes, official personnel, locals, downstreamers, countrywomen carrying babies in pouches on their backs, skilled mechanics with Kiangsu and Chekiang accents, young messengers carrying the insignia of their departments. As for the small cabin, the downstreamers never went in, perhaps because they felt they were not up to it socially, or perhaps because it was too stuffy.

On both sides of the small cabin were doors with little windows in them, but the crowd of patrolling 'sentries' outside cut off the breeze and kept out most of the light. When the man and his wife first stepped inside everything was so black that they dared not move. As their eyes began to get used to the darkness the first thing they saw was a man whose propped-up arms embraced almost half the long table in front of him. Benches were fixed along all four sides of the cabin, and the two long tables in the middle would be used later by the crew when they ate. Now they were almost covered by the odds and ends of hand luggage carried by the passengers, but only as far as that pair of arms. Inside the defence line they formed was a brown army jacket, a pistol belt, and uniform cap, on top of which a magazine lay open. The huge man sitting there looked as though he were reading it.

There was an obvious space on the bench beside him big enough for an adult and a child. The woman carrying the baby glanced at her husband. 'You sit there,' he said, as he went on looking for a place for himself.

The woman with the baby made her way along the narrow gap between people's knees and the edge of the table, carefully walked round black leather jackboots that sternly complemented the outstretched arms propping up the head, and reached her destination, only to find that what had been an empty place was not in fact empty. There, quite unambiguously, as if standing to attention, was a pair of feet in black leather shoes with their heels on the bench and their toes in the air. They looked very solid. Her first 'Excuse me' met with no response. She said it again louder. The man whose feet were at attention realized what was happening and grunted. The woman with the child, losing her patience, turned and was just going to sit down when the feet grudgingly withdrew some six inches.

'Would you give me a little more room please,' the woman asked as she sat down.

'Oh, how annoying. Still, it's a lot more comfortable here than on a bus.' He cocked up his head, though goodness knows who he was talking to. 'I was once on a bus,' he said with a smile, 'when all the room I could find was a space like this one, the size of the palm of your hand. I had to sit on the edge of my backside for four miles.'

Nobody took any notice, not even the woman or her husband, who had found somewhere to sit down to the left of the entrance. The child of seven or eight preferred to squeeze his way outside, where he stood between the legs of adults, his little face over the rail.

The man who looked as though he were reading the magazine had gleaming black hair. Perhaps it was a little long, and, because he had used too much or too little cheap hair oil, a lock of it kept falling over his eyes. When it did he would suddenly jerk his head back and, instead of lowering it again straight away, he would look around till his stare fastened on something in front of him.

It was the side view of a woman whose long and delicate eyebrows slanted into the hair in front of her ears. Her hair had been permed, but not in an obvious way. As she was knitting her head was bent forward, so that her two short plaits had slipped forward past her little ears to hang down beside her sensuous face. Her plump body was covered by a pale blue dress, though, as she was sitting at an angle with one leg over the other, her white thigh was revealed. She interrupted her knitting to keep straightening the hem of her dress; every time she put a hand out to do so her delicate eyebrows frowned slightly as if they were confirming the number of eyes that were staring at that part of her. She began to feel too awkward to look up. The woman sitting next to her at an angle so as to be facing her, looked a few years younger, but this may have been because she was suckling a baby, which made her quite unselfconscious: she boldly bared her breast to feed the baby, and let her permed hair blow around freely.

'Now you've found him, what are you going to do? Have you decided yet?' asked the woman feeding the baby. Before she had opened her mouth you could have told from the look of her that she was a downstreamer; and now that she had spoken one could have guessed that she used to live in the north.

'I think I'd better talk to a lawyer about it first,' the other woman replied quietly. She did not change her position at all except that she stopped knitting.

'Quite right, talk to a lawyer first. I can introduce you to a reliable one. He used to practise in Shanghai. He's very successful.'

The woman in the light blue dress sighed gently. Then, probably because she had sensed that the steady gaze from the other side of the room was still fixed upon her and had no intention of moving, she suddenly frowned and pursed her lips as if to say, 'Disgusting. What a dirty expression.' She twisted her lips into a half-smile and cautiously raised her head. At that moment a black shadow suddenly blotted everything out. A strange figure had appeared. He was wearing a locally-made broad-brimmed straw hat and a cotton gown that was somewhere between blue and black. His feet were bare, and he may have had no trousers under his long gown. In his left hand he held an oil-paper folding fan, and in his right a round straw one. Round his waist was what looked like a very broad ammunition belt in which he carried all kinds of folded paper fans. He was obviously a fan-seller taking the paddle-steamer to sell his goods at the port.

This fellow stood in front of the two women. Openly taking it that the steady stare from the other side was meant for the treasures that weighed down his belt, he began to sing their praises.

The magazine-reading posture was resumed. Someone called out 'Fan-seller!' from the other side of the cabin, and the broad-brimmed straw hat went swaggering over. Nothing escaped the glance of the magazine-reader even though he was looking down. He realized that his field of vision was clear once more, and the lock of hair had fortunately fallen forward again. When he jerked his head back this time he looked first to his side. He noticed the little face suckling at its mother's breast as well as the tiny finger pointing at a small, red oblong object inside the defence line formed by his own big arms. On the red object were the golden line and three gold stars of an army captain. It was fastened to the collar of the khaki army jacket.

One of the arms that had been propping up his chin moved to cover the collar. Then his glance flashed forward for a moment before he buried his head once more in the magazine in front of him. He appeared to be reading with great interest.

The woman in the pale blue dress and her companion were whispering to each other now. The bamboo knitting needles were lightly gripping the skin beside one of her plaits, and the other hand was toying with the hem of her dress.

'Over ten dollars for an oil-paper fan!' The sentence came over clearly from the opposite entrance.

The two women looked up as if they had been startled by

this noise. When they realized what it was they laughed quietly. The woman suckling the baby stared suddenly into her companion's face and said in a low voice, 'Do you know how much he's still got stacked away? He's trying to fool you. A mere million or two? Everyone says he's over the ten million mark.'

Instead of answering her the other woman only smiled a disappointed smile.

As the morning mist had slowly dissipated, the clear golden sun made life intolerable for the people on the side of the boat on which it shone. Sweat poured from everyone and they were unbearably thirsty. Pedlars, smelling so bad that one wanted to retch, pushed their way through the crowds. Their bamboo baskets, long and curved with indented sides like old-fashioned silver ingots, were full of cigarettes, bread, fried buns, and the like, but contained nothing to quench one's thirst. Yet the thirstier people became, the more they talked, till the whole boat was one great hubbub. The harder their tongues worked, the faster the boat seemed to go.

The small cabin was marked by the overwhelming pre-dominance of southerners talking in northern dialect. Strangers started disjointed conversations with one another. The only points of common interest they found were, apparently, food, drink, and pleasure. The fan-seller was made into a general topic of discussion for a full ten minutes because the price of his fans led to talk about prices in general and brought out the inevitable 'Banknotes are worth nothing these days.' To this a fat old man retorted loudly, 'Everyone says that, but nobody ever finds one in the street. I haven't ever found even a ten-cent note.' He laughed aloud, delighted with his words of wisdom. But that was the end of the conversation on prices.

When they broke up into twos and threes who knew each other the conversation became more lively. Discussion on winnings and losses the previous night was particularly heated. Without it the hot, stuffy journey might have been quite in-supportable.

The 'infantry captain', his head still propped in his hands, never spoke a word. He continued to look as though he were reading his magazine, but he never turned the page. Perhaps

D

he was trying to learn some passage by heart. More likely, he was studying the two women facing each other with too much interest. He alone knew.

As the boat entered the mouth of the Jialing river the news flew round that an air-raid signal had been hoisted. This was a new stimulus when the possibilities of casual conversation had been almost exhausted. 'One or two?' someone asked at once. Nobody knew. A few people who were particularly interested pushed their way through to the rails to look, but they could see nothing.

At this moment the boat sounded its hooter again. They had reached the harbour, and the high, sloping river banks could be seen again.

The air-raid question was dropped as everyone struggled to squeeze their way down to the lower deck, ready for dis-embarkation the moment the boat came alongside a lighter. The lower deck had been packed before, but now that there were twice as many people on it they all accepted being crammed in together, their noses pressed against the backs of each other's necks. Nobody was bothered about the heat and the smell of sweat.

This uncomfortable period normally lasted only ten minutes at the most, but this time it was exceptionally long. The people who were jammed in the middle, and could see nothing but a black mass of heads, were growing impatient, when the people in front suddenly started pushing backwards, shouting things that could not be heard distinctly. Then some voices came from the companion-way to the upper deck calling, 'Come up, come up, the boat's turning round.' The densely packed crowd of people would take a long time to disperse through this single steep and slanting exit.

By the time they realized what had happened the boat was out of the mouth of the Jialing river and heading back on full power. The original shout about an air-raid signal had been true. Just when the boat had been drawing alongside the lighters the urgent alarm had followed, and the regulations laid it down that boats had to leave when there was an urgent alarm as it would have been dangerous to stay alongside the Chungking wharf.

Everyone on the boat was at last talking about the same thing, though there were conflicting views. Some people felt that, as the boat had arrived, the passengers should be allowed ashore to find their own way to the air-raid shelters, which would be much better than staying on board. Another view was that as the urgent alarm had already gone there would not be time to get into town even if they did manage to climb up from the river: it was safer to be on the boat than to be caught in the open. Finally the discussion centred on where the boat was going to shelter.

'We should choose any quiet place, wait there till the all clear, then go back to Chungking.' This was the comment of the man who had given the woman a foot or so in which to sit down and who was now pacing up and down the cabin. The fat old man who had regretted never having found a ten-cent note in the street shook his head and said, 'Impossible. It's bound to go back.'

'But won't the shipping company lose that way?'

'Lose what?' retorted the fat old man, opening his eyes wide.

'They've still got to take us to Chungking, and they'll also have lost the trade they would have had coming back from Chungking this time.'

The old man snorted a laugh. 'That's not the way the company will see it. They'll take you back to where you started from for free. If you want to go to Chungking again later you will have to buy another ticket.'

The conversation was cut short at this point by the noisy argument starting up again. 'There's no question of getting our money back on our tickets. These are losses we've had to suffer through enemy action. But the Japanese planes might not come now that the sky is so cloudy. The moment the alarm was given the sun disappeared.'

This remark drew everyone's attention. The weather had indeed changed. Goodness knows when or from where they had come, but clouds now filled the sky, making the closeness even more terrible. Everybody felt a weight on their chests which made breathing difficult.

The boat went downstream fast, and it was only a moment

before it had passed all the places where people knew it might have sheltered. There could no longer be any doubts about the fat old man's judgement. The man who had made the optimistic remark decided to find himself some other pleasant dream, but as his former territory had already been divided up by others he had to find a corner into which he could squeeze himself. He shut his eyes and went back to sleep.

The woman with the two short plaits, who was wearing a pale blue dress, said with a sigh, 'We've had to be on the boat for all this time only to be taken back to where we set out from.' Her face looked old and anxious, perhaps because her two plaits were sticking to it.

Lao She 老舍

Lao She, the name under which Shu Sheyu (Shu Qingchun), wrote, was born the son of a Manchu imperial guard at the end of the last century; his father was killed in the invasion by the eight foreign powers shortly afterwards. His childhood and youth were hard, which enabled him to learn much about the life and language of ordinary people. In 1924 he went to London to teach Chinese, not returning to China until 1930. Over the next twenty years he produced many stories, plays, and novels written in a natural and easy Peking dialect that few could rival. Much of his work was humorous, weakened at times by a possibly English-influenced mildness not suited to the harsh realities of twentieth-century China.

During the war against Japan his work had a new bite to it, scourging traitors and profiteers with due savagery and celebrating the self-sacrifice of the Chinese soldiers. In 1946 he accepted a State Department invitation to visit America, coming back to China at Liberation some three years later. From then until his reported suicide in 1966 he was too busy as an official and member of countless delegations and committees to write much. Perhaps he found it difficult to fit into the strict new China.

'A Brilliant Beginning' is one of the more incisive of his pre-war stories.

A Brilliant Beginning

Old Wang, Old Qiu, and myself put a bit of money together and started a small hospital. Wang's wife was matron: she had risen from nurse to doctor's wife. Qiu's father-in-law was administrator and treasurer. Wang and I had decided that if Qiu's father-in-law fiddled the accounts or ran off with the money we would regard Qiu as his father-in-law's guarantor and put the squeeze on him. Wang and myself were old cronies, and as Qiu had come in on the act late we always had to be on our guard against him. Whatever you do and however many people may be involved, you must always have your friends and keep

your wits about you. If you don't you'll soon be in a mess.
With us two and Mrs Wang we would have outnumbered
Qiu three to one if it had come to a fight. The father-in-law
would have helped Qiu, of course, but he was so old that Mrs.
Wang alone could have pulled out all the hairs of his head. To
be fair, Qiu was quite an able bloke. He specialized in removing
piles and did it beautifully, which was why we had invited him
in on the business. But if he'd asked for trouble we wouldn't
have been at all kind to him.

I looked after medicine, Wang dealt with syphilis, Qiu was
in charge of piles and other surgery, and Mrs. Wang was matron
and head of obstetrics: this made four departments in all. What
we knew about medicine, to be quite frank, was practically
nothing. You get what you pay for, and our medical charges
were very low. Where we ran the racket was on syphilis and
piles: Wang and Qiu were our great hopes. Mrs. Wang and I
just played supporting roles. She was no doctor, though she did
have some experience of child-birth as she had borne a couple
herself. As for her skill in delivery, I would never have en-
trusted a wife of mine to her ministrations. Still, we had to have
an obstetrics department as it was so profitable. After a smooth
delivery the mother would have to stay for ten days or a fortnight, and we would just have to give her a little gruel or rice
boiled soft to get money from her every day. If the birth was
awkward we could think up some solution on the spot. We
weren't going to be put off by the smell of dirty nappies.

So we started business. Our name 'Hospital for the Masses',
had been advertised in all the papers for a fortnight. It was a
good name: anything that's to make money mustn't forget
'the people' these days. If you don't make money out of them
where else can you make it? That's the truth, isn't it? Of course,
we didn't say this in the advertisment as the people don't like
the truth. What we wrote instead was that we were 'sacrificing
ourselves for the people, bringing happiness to our compatriots.
Entirely scientific, entirely for the people, we are thoroughly
versed in Chinese and Western medicine and utterly free of
class discrimination.' What we spent on these advertisements
made quite a dent in our capital. Having invited the masses in
we had to deal with them. Nobody could tell from the adver-

tisements how big our hospital was. In the picture it was a big three-storeyed building. We used a photo of a nearby transport company. In fact it was six rooms in a single-storeyed building.

Now we were in business. In the first week of surgery we had a lot of people come for consultations, and they really were 'the masses'. We gave the more respectable among them various kinds of soda water no matter what was wrong with them. A week later we could formally collect our fee. As for the real, genuine masses, we didn't even give them soda water. I told them to go home and give their faces a good wash—they were so filthy that medicine would have been wasted on them.

One evening after a long busy day we held an emergency conference. It was no good appealing just to the masses, we had to bring in other people too. We all wished we had not called it the Hospital for the Masses. We'd never make a packet out of the masses without the top people. A hospital isn't like a paraffin company. Had we realized it earlier we would have called it 'Hospital for the Aristocracy'. Goodness knows how often Old Qiu had dipped his scalpel into the disinfectant, but not a single pile had come along. Could the rich old men with piles be expected to come to a Hospital for the Masses?

Old Wang had an idea. The next day we would hire a car that worked and take it in turns to go out in it and fetch our grannies and aunts. As soon as they reached the gates the nurses were to help them inside. When we'd done this thirty or forty times the neighbours would be quite impressed. We were all full of admiration for Old Wang.

'Hire a few that don't work as well,' was his next suggestion.

'Why?' I asked.

'Negotiate with a garage to lend us a few that are being repaired and park them in front of the hospital gates for a day. They should hoot every now and again. When the patients hear hooting all the time they'll think lots of people are coming here in cars. And people outside will be most impressed at the sight of a great row of cars parked at the gates all day.'

We followed his plan. The next day we brought all our relations along, gave them a cup of tea then took them home again. The two nurses were so busy always helping them walk in and out that they didn't sit down all day. The broken-down cars

that could only hoot were brought there at dawn, and they took
it in turns to honk every five minutes. From sunrise on they were
surrounded by children. We took a photo of the cars and sent it
round to the evening papers for publication. Old Qiu's father-
in-law wrote a classical essay describing the magnificence of the
stream of cars. That night the hooting was so bad that we could
not eat, our heads were spinning so.

You had to give it to Old Wang. As soon as we opened the
next day an army officer drove up. Old Wang was in such a
hurry to go out and welcome him that he forgot how low the
doorway was and raised a huge bump on his head. It was
V.D. Old Wang did not notice the bump. His face was
wreathed in rosy smiles as if he would not have minded seven
or eight more.

In a few moments the officer was being given a shot of 606.
Our two nurses took off his jacket and supported his arm with
their four hands: Mrs. Wang lightly touched the tip of the
needle a couple of times with her fat little forefinger; and only
then did Old Wang give him the jab. Not realizing what was
happening, the officer looked at the nurses and said with
gusto, 'Wonderful, wonderful!' When I said something he
agreed to have another, which Old Qiu, ready to make the
best of a piece of luck, had already prepared: jasmine tea with a
little salt added. Old Wang told the nurses to take the officer's
arm, Mrs. Wang touched the needle again with her fat little
index finger, and in went another syringe of jasmine tea. The
officer expressed his delight once more, and Old Wang gave
him a third shot for free—of Dragon Well tea this time.

In our hospital we were very particular about tea, and always
used Dragon Well and jasmine. For two injections of tea and
one of 606 we relieved him of twenty-five dollars (it was ten
dollars a shot with a reduction of five dollars on three). We
told him that he would have to come back, and guaranteed to
cure him in ten visits. After all, we thought, we had plenty of
tea.

Having paid his fee the officer did not want to go. Lao Wang
and I started flattering him. I praised him for not concealing
his infection. As he had come to us for early treatment his V.D.
would definitely present no danger. Venereal disease was a

great man's affliction, it was glorious and splendid, and a few shots of 606 would cure it. What was alarming was when some shop assistant or secondary school student tried to cover it up and went off to see a quack, or furtively bought medicine to treat it himself. Those medicines must be awful—they were only advertised in public lavatories. The officer agreed absolutely and told us that though he had already been to hospitals for it over twenty times, he had never had such pleasant treatment for it before. I didn't take the matter any further.

Old Wang carried on from there: V.D. wasn't really an illness at all—all it needed was a few shots of 606. The officer thoroughly agreed, and he had evidence to prove it: he never waited till he was thoroughly cured before going whoring again. All he needed was a few more shots. Old Wang, agreeing absolutely, offered to treat the officer as a special client. If he were to come over a long period he could have the treatment at half price: five dollars a shot. Alternatively he could have a monthly arrangement with as many injections as he liked for a hundred dollars a month. The officer thought this a splendid idea provided it was always done the way it had been today. We smiled and nodded, not knowing what to say.

No sooner had the officer's car left than another one drew up and four maids helped a lady out. The moment they were out they asked if we had any special rooms. I pushed one of the maids aside and lightly took the lady's wrist. When we were in the inner courtyard I pointed to the large office-building of the transport company. 'The special rooms there are all full. But you came at just the right time as we have two first-class rooms here'—I pointed to our little rooms—'so perhaps you can make do in them for the time being. Actually they are even more comfortable than the ones upstairs; save all that rushing up and down, don't you think, madam?' The old lady's first words were music in my ears: 'Ah, you're talking like a real doctor. Why do patients come to hospital if it's not to be comfortable? Those doctors in the Dongsheng Hospital are absolutely inhuman.'

'Have you been to the Dongsheng then, madam?'

'I've just come from there. The monsters!'

While she cursed away at the Dongsheng (which to be honest

is the biggest and best hospital here) I helped her over to the little room knowing perfectly well that if I didn't get her to curse at the Dongsheng she would never agree to stay in so small a place. 'How long did you spend there?' I asked. 'Two days, and they were nearly the end of me.' The old lady sat down on the bed.

I put my leg against the edge of the bed. There was nothing wrong with our beds except that they were rather old and tended to collapse. 'Why did you go there?' I had to keep talking to prevent her from noticing my leg.

'I'd rather you didn't ask me, it makes me so angry to think of it. Just think, doctor, I have stomach trouble and they wouldn't let me eat anything.' The old lady was on the brink of tears.

'Nothing?' I opened my eyes wide in horror. 'Stomach trouble and nothing to eat? That doctor was a savage. At your age. Madam must be eighty.'[1]

The old lady swallowed some of her tears and smiled slightly. 'I'm still young. Only fifty-eight.'

'The same age as my mother. She sometimes suffers from stomach-ache too.' I wiped my eyes. 'You stay here, madam, and I guarantee we'll cure you. The treatment consists of looking after you well. Eat whatever you feel like, then you'll feel better and won't be so poorly. Isn't that so, madam?'

She was weeping again, this time with gratitude. 'Doctor, I do like a bit of solid food but they insist on making me eat thin gruel just to spite me.'

'Your teeth are good. You should certainly have solid food,' I pronounced solemnly.

'I keep getting hungry, but they would only let me eat at mealtimes.'

'Fools.'

'They put a little glass stick in my mouth in the middle of the night just when I was going to sleep. They were taking something or other.'

'Shameless behaviour.'

'When I asked for a bed pan the nurses said the doctor was

[1] Attributing great age to her was flattery, not an insult.

just coming so I would have to wait till he had examined me.'

'The wretches.'

'When I'd managed to sit up the nurse told me to lie down.'

'Very tiresome.'

We were getting on so well now that I think she would not have gone even if the room had been smaller still. I felt I no longer needed to prop the bed up with my leg. Even if it collapsed she would have made allowances.

'Do you have nurses here?' she asked.

'Yes, but it doesn't matter,' I replied with a smile. 'You can have the four maids you brought with you staying in the hospital. Your own people will look after you perfectly well. I won't let the nurses set foot in here if you prefer.'

'That will be wonderful. But do you have room for them?' She seemed beside herself with delight.

'Of course. Why don't you take this whole courtyard? Apart from the four maids you could bring your cook over to prepare the dishes you feel like eating. I'll only charge for you. The maids and the cook can stay free. It'll be fifty dollars a day.'

She sighed. 'We'll do it this way then; I don't mind what it costs. Chunxiang, go back and fetch cook, and tell him to bring a couple of ducks with him.'

I regretted only asking her for fifty dollars. I wanted to slap myself in the face. Luckily I had not said that the medicine was included, so we could make up for it on that. From the way she'd come she must have had a son who was divisional commander at the very least. Besides, if she was going to eat roast duck every day she wouldn't be leaving inside a week. We could take a long view.

The hospital was really something now. The four maids scurried to and fro, and the cook had built a cooking stove at the foot of the wall. It was just like a wedding. We didn't feel inhibited about sampling the old lady's fruit and we had quite a few pieces from her ducks. None of us thought of examining her as we were concentrating on looking at the goodies she had brought.

Although Old Wang and myself were now well set up Old Qiu was rather put out. His knife was always in his hand, so I

kept well out of his way in case he tried his hand on me. Old
Wang urged him to be patient but his pride would not let him
feel easy until he had earned the hospital a few dozen dollars.
I admired the spirit.

After lunch somebody actually came to have his piles removed, a very fat, big-bellied man in his forties. Mrs. Wang
thought that it must be for child-birth until she made out that
he was a man and reluctantly handed him over to Old Qiu.
Old Qiu's eyes went red with anticipation. After a few words
his knife went into action. The fat man screamed with pain and
begged him to use an anaesthetic.

Old Qiu had an answer for that: 'We didn't say anything
about anaesthetic. It will cost you another ten dollars. Do you
want it? Quick.'

The fat man did not even dare to nod. Old Qiu applied the
anaesthetic, cut again, and said, 'You've most certainly got a
fistula. We never said anything about cutting that out. Do you
want me to go any further? If I do it will cost you another
thirty dollars. Otherwise we've finished.'

I was most impressed with Old Qiu. To grab the man and
then to squeeze the money out of him was really smart work.

The fat man raised no objections, and we reckoned that he
could not possibly do so anyhow. Old Qiu's technique was
superb, and he announced crisply as he cut out the fistula, 'I
can assure you that this should really cost you a couple of
hundred, but we're not crooks. We just want you to tell people
about us when you're better. If you have time tomorrow come
in for a check-up. My colleagues won't find a single bacterium
with their forty-five thousand X microscope.'

Not a sound came from the fat man. Perhaps he was speech-
less with rage.

Old Qiu had made another fifty dollars. That evening we
bought some wine and asked the old lady's cook to do us a few
dishes. They consisted largely of the old lady's ingredients.
We discussed our enterprise over the meal, and decided to add
abortion and cures for opium addiction to our services. Old
Wang suggested putting the word round quietly that we carried
out medical examinations, and would give a clean bill of health
when filling out the forms for anyone trying to get into a school

or take out an insurance policy even if they had already got their shroud and coffin ready—provided, of course, that we had our fee of five dollars. This proposal was passed without any bother. Old Qiu's father-in-law finally proposed that we should all put a few dollars towards a signboard. Although the idea was as old-fashioned as you would expect from a man of his age, he put it forward with the best interests of our hospital at heart so we raised no objection. He had thought of the words to go on it as well: Mercy Through Merciful Arts. A bit corny, but just what was wanted. I suggested that he should buy an old signboard in the market the following morning. Mrs. Wang said that we should have it painted and ready to hang up some time when a wedding procession band was around to provide the music. Old Wang was particularly proud of this delicate touch of his wife's.

Ye Zi 叶紫

[Yeh Tzu]

The father of Ye Zi (real name Yu Helin) was a petty official until in 1926 the tide of peasant organization and militancy combined with pressure from his brother to persuade him to abandon his career and join the revolution. The next year, when he was fourteen, Ye Zi left middle school to enter the military academy which was run by the then revolutionary authorities in Wuhan.

When armed counter-revolution crushed the peasant movement in his native county of Yiyang, Hunan province, he rushed home to find that his father and one of his sisters, now members of the Communist Party, had been executed. He had to flee from home with sixty-four copper coins in his pocket and all his other belongings—mainly a few old-fashioned romances—in a small basket. At first he wandered around the country trying to become a heroic swordsman like the heroes in these stories and avenge his family; then he became a common soldier, but finding nothing but meaningless suffering in this life he deserted and made his way to Nanking, where he arrived in 1928 as a toughened sixteen-year-old still burning with hatred for the state of Chinese society. He started to read contemporary Chinese writers and European literature in translation. The next year he went to Shanghai, where he spent most of the rest of his short life. In 1933 he joined the Communist Party.

His own writing began at about this time. His stories have a power that is rare in the work of his contemporaries, and most of them deal with the central theme of modern Chinese history: the peasants' resistance, armed and otherwise, to oppression. This choice of subject marked him out as almost unique at a time when others concentrated on the sentimental miseries of impoverished students, or tended to portray peasants either as noble savages or as pathetic wretches. Ye Zi's peasants fight back. His early death from tuberculosis in 1939 was a great loss to Chinese literary development. Had he lived longer he might have done much to bridge the gap between the very different literary worlds of westernized Shanghai and the Communist capital, Yenan, a small town deep in China's rural hinterland. It is curious that the cultural authorities of the 1950s and

early 1960s should have allowed his writings to lapse into comparative obscurity when compared with the publicity that such men as
Ba Jin or Lao She received. His first volume of short stories was,
however, published in English translation by the Foreign Languages
Press, Peking, under the title *Harvest* in 1960.

Stealing Lotuses

I

One evening when the sun had just set the old red-nosed hired
hand and Qiufu, the boy who looked after the water buffalo,
came running into the young master's room.

'What about it, Master Han?' said the old hired hand in a
low voice, fingering his beard and grinning. 'What about
guarding the lake?'

Master Han put down the primer he was holding and said:
'I'll go. My father has agreed.'

'Really?' asked the boy Qiufu, coming between them.

'Yes.'

The old hired hand moved his hand away from his whiskers,
grinned again and said, 'Then we needn't go to the lake this
evening?'

'No, you can go and booze.'

Young Qiufu was beside himself with delight. He had arranged to go fire-raising in the rushes with Xiaogui from the
other end of the village tonight, so it suited him very well not
to have to go and guard the lake. As for the old labourer, a
smile spread right across his face at the thought of drinking.
Making a mocking, comical, and somewhat obscene gesture
he said 'Be careful' and went out.

'Come back,' said Master Han suddenly.

Qiufu and the old hired hand turned round.

'Tell the hands in the husking mill not to go to the lake on
any account tonight unless. . . .' He pointed to the gleaming
whistle hanging in front of his chest. 'Do you understand?'

'Yes,' replied the old hired hand.

2

The moon slipped out from a dark ring of clouds.

Cassia and Chrysanthemum, who had been sent ahead to

reconnoitre, ran back panting. They were covered with tiny beads of sweat. They reported to the all-wise Mrs. Yunsheng:

'Yes, tonight will be all right. Neither the red-nosed servant nor the young so-and-so are there, and all the hired hands have gone off drinking and gambling. . . .'

'Then who's guarding the lake?'

'Well,' said Cassia awkwardly, 'he's back from the foreign school in the provincial capital.'

Mrs. Yunsheng nodded and fixed her gaze on Cassia with a wicked and highly significant smile.

Cassia blushed, bowed her head, and opening wide her liquid and mischievous eyes she went for Mrs. Yunsheng with great fury:

'What are you grinning at, Mrs. Yunsheng? You, you. . . .'

'Not at you. I'm laughing at that monster back from the foreign school. Hurry up and tell Aunt Taisheng, Taoxiu, and Li Seven's daughter. The more the better. When the moon's full our boats will meet in the forked lake.'

'Yes, we'd better get them. . . .' Cassia, still angry, hurried back to the upper village leading Chrysanthemum by the hand.

3

The lotus pods would soon be too old. Sighing at their wretched fate, their bowed and withered faces were just managing to hold themselves up above the waters of the lake. Most of their leaves, now like broken fans, could barely keep three or four dried bones waving in the breeze. The cold late September dew covered the banks of the lake, and in the distance, among the boundless expanse of rushes, large and small fires started by naughty boys flared up from time to time.

Master Han crept to the side of the lake and sat in a big rowing-boat looking up to the high ground and the unattainable stars in the sky. He made no sound. His brain was filled with those mischievous and liquid cat-like eyes of hers and her sun-browned face tinged with a delicious girlish pink. He remembered the chance he had lost in June and the unforgettable smile he had glimpsed while strolling beside the lake during the day.

'Yes, they're bound to come' he said to himself. 'I won't

blow the whistle however many of them there are. I just want
to catch the one with the liquid eyes.'

None of the school beauties under their queen could compare
with her. They used hair-oil, powder, and exotic scents; they
wanted you to obey them and do everything for them. But the
natural girl here, perfumed with sweat and mud, had such rosy
cheeks and liquid eyes. . . .

He waited in happy anticipation. He did not care that the
dew was gradually soaking him, or that the lake breezes made
him shiver. He braced himself, summoning up the stamina he
had needed in the ten-thousand-metres race at school and kept
his eyes fixed on the mouth of the forked lake.

The moon had slowly climbed to its highest point.

4

'Go on ahead, Cassia.'

'Why do you want just me to go? You. . . .' An angry
Cassia turned her cradle-shaped lotus boat that was not ten
feet long across the mouth of the lake, shattering the moon in
the water with her little oar. Those nearest to her could see
that she was blushing to the roots of her ears.

'He won't be able to hurt you, you fool.' Mrs. Yunsheng
moved her boat forward so that the two boats floated beside
each other like a pair of ducks. 'Bring him over here and we'll
help you.'

Cassia was still refusing. She did not want to do it even though
she knew that the others would not let her come to grief. She
remembered what an animal the wretch from the foreign school
had been that time she had been enjoying the cool of the
evening back in June.

Mrs. Yunsheng and Li Seven's daughter tried to encourage
her and put her mind at rest. At last she silently lifted her oar.

Her head was bowed so low it almost touched the bottom
of the boat; her heart pounded fast with anxiety. As her lotus-
seed gathering boat slipped between the stalks and leaves of
the plants she heard a lightly whispered call. She turned round
and saw that Mrs. Yunsheng and the others, who were far
behind and dropping slowly back, were calling to give her
resolution and courage.

She pulled herself together and started to row for all she was worth. Her boat shot like an arrow towards the southern bank.

5

Master Han had been looking for her so hard that his eyes were almost worn out when he saw a lotus-boat racing towards him, recognized the familiar slim graceful figure, and was intoxicated at the skilful way she rowed. In his delight he started rowing his heavy boat after her for all he was worth.

Cassia, gritting her teeth, teased him into going round in circles after her. When she had almost reached the others she deliberately stopped, and headed straight for his boat.

Master Han stretched out his hand to grab her boat and she jumped across into his. As he embraced her the whistle round his neck fell into the water.

The two of them fought and grappled with each other.

A dozen lotus boats rushed forward like a flight of wild ducks and surrounded them. A dozen women jumped into the big rowing-boat.

Cassia was rescued and Master Han captured.

'Tie him up with his belt.'

Master Han tried to shout, but a large handful of raw cotton was stuffed into his mouth.

Cassia was crying. She had lost. She scratched twice at Master Han's face and scratched hard; Master Han's eyes opened wide in pain as blood poured down his cheeks.

'You little wasp,' said Mrs. Yunsheng, pointing at him and giving him a piece of her mind. 'You've never suffered in your whole life, you bastard. Looking for a bit of fun, were you?'

'Ha! We'll leave him to spend the night here on his own.'

An icy mocking laugh came from somewhere in the crowd.

6

The moon was slowly sinking in the west.

As a dozen lotus-seed boats went to and fro across the lake a dozen pairs of scissors snipped in unison.

Cassia was still feeling indignant, wiping the tears away as she cut off the lotus pods, gathering fewer than anyone else.

Mrs. Yunsheng tried to cheer her up:

'Never mind, dear. We all know what you went through. We'll all give you some of ours.'

As the breeze blew up over the lake irregular waves snatched at the stems and leaves of the lotuses, rocking the boats like cradles.

'Hurry up or the hired hands will catch us.'

Every boat was now full and each of the women was very happy. There was no old man yelling at them, no vicious hired hands rowing after them in pursuit.

When they came out of the mouth of the forked lake again they were still singing quietly:

> *Stealing lotus, stealing in the middle of the night,*
> *When everybody is fast asleep.*
> *The rich don't know how the poor folk suffer,*
> *But the poor know what the rich are really like.*
> *Row fast, punt for all you're worth,*
> *If the lake guards chase us we'll never get away.*

7

Rice wine had made the old hired hand's nose redder than ever. When he crawled lazily out of his dog's hole of mouldy rice straw the next morning the sunlight had already reached the bottom of the wall.

He rubbed his eyes with some old raw cotton and staggered into the young master's study.

'Master Han, Master Han.'

A gust of cold autumn morning air came out of the study. The old man was now full of suspicion. He said to himself:

'That's funny. He must have been bewitched by those she-devils.'

He ran back to this dog's hole and shouted at the boy Qiufu to get up. His hair had all been burnt off by the fires he had started the previous night.

'You little devil, damn you. Quick, go and find Master Han.'

The old man and the boy dragged Master Han's boat back across the lake only with great efforts.

Master Han's face was swollen like a judge's, and his bloody scars had dried purple. He gave the old hired hand a vicious slap round the ear and shouted roughly:

'Where were you all? Dead? Damn you!'

The hired hand did not know whether to laugh or to cry. He wiped his nose hard.

'But you didn't blow the whistle, master. Why?'

'Damn you,' muttered the young master in a voice that seemed to have disappeared after his previous raucous shout. 'Come on. Come with me while I tell my father. Their leader was Yunsheng's wife, damn her. She still owes us rent and money. I'll have her husband put away for three years. That'll show them what I'm made of.'

The boy Qiufu stood there stupidly, holding his singed head, gazing with his filthy eyes at the young master and trembling for fear that another blow would land on his head. What ever could have happened, he wondered, for the young master to be tied up all bloody night?

20 February 1935

Zhang Tianyi　　张天翼

[Chang T'ien-i]

The son of a high official family whose fortunes declined after the overthrow of the Qing dynasty in 1911, Zhang Tianyi was born in Nanking in 1906 or 1907 and moved around during his childhood, publishing his first article as a student in Peking in 1925. Between 1931 and 1937 he published four novels and six volumes of short stories while working as a school-teacher, journalist, or petty official. During the war against Japan he wrote some lively though rather romantic stories about the fighting. In recent years his published work has mainly been children's fiction; he was also on the editorial board of *People's Literature* for some time.

The rickshaw puller, one of the few members of the working class with whom intellectuals came into daily contact, figured in their stories quite often. It is a mark of Lu Xun's quality that the rickshaw puller in a story he wrote in 1920—'A Trivial Incident'—is shown not in a ridiculous and pathetic way as in this and many other pieces, but as a man of dignity and courage. Zhang Tianyi's attitude, however, is much more typical of middle-class writers.

Zhang Tianyi's short stories are generally satirical; he was particularly good at satirizing the middle class, and self-important officials. He is generally regarded as one of the ablest exponents of the art of the short story during the 1930s. His style and language have a freshness and economy none too prevalent at the time.

Generosity

The rickshaw had been going very slowly along the road for a couple of hundred yards. The puller, a man in his forties or fifties, was bracing his shoulders and pressing down on the shafts for all he was worth to stop them jacking upwards. At the end of his nose a round drop had collected that was swaying, about to fall.

'Where to, sir?'

No reply. The gentleman stared in front of him, his twisted lips pressed tight together. He looked like a giant newt.

Vegetable sellers were jostling each other and calling their wares in the street. Although they had already filled the pavements with their loads they apparently felt they needed still more room, so they had spread out into the middle of the road.

The rickshaw man zigzagged along the road. Whenever a wheel went into a rut and tipped the rickshaw to one side it hurt his wrists. The gentleman in the seat moved himself further back into it and tucked his hands into his sleeves to make himself more comfortable. But the vehicle threw him from side to side, obliging him to take them out again to steady himself. He was sure it was because they were going too slow.

'Hey, what's the matter? Are you exhausted or something?'

This question came just when the puller was concentrating on getting across a heap of broken pieces of ice. He was bent so far over that the curve of his back hid most of his head from view. Suddenly the shafts shot into the air, throwing the gentleman back and shaking him up inside. The gentleman let out an angry snort, roaring something between his few teeth.

But the rickshaw puller had started an argument with a youngster who was carrying vegetable baskets. Their faces were only six inches apart and from their mouths poured streams of curses that they seemed to know by heart.

The gentleman in the rickshaw felt he had the right to intervene in the affairs of these vulgar people. Stamping his feet he said, 'Stop arguing. Move.'

The rickshaw man turned to look at him. His forehead was steaming, and beads of sweat had formed in his two-inch-long beard.

'He trod on the footboard of my rickshaw and broke it. That's no joking matter, sir. Bloody fool. No sense at all. Why's he fussing because I bumped into him?'

'How dare you say that!' The gentleman leant forward, making the shafts drop.

'What do you mean? I wasn't talking about you.'

'Hmm. Well then, what were you talking about just now? What's wrong with the board? Tell me.'

The rickshaw puller freed one hand to wipe his face with a grey cloth. The shafts took the opportunity to shoot upwards. He immediately pushed down on them hard, groaning with pain. At the same time he was being very careful to avoid those slippery pieces of ice on the road. His legs in their worn blue cotton trousers moved very unsteadily, which suggested that they were ulcerated.

'Just look,' he was muttering in a voice kept low for fear he would be overheard, 'the board's broken and I'll have to pay to get it repaired. I'll get you, you cocky sod. And what about him too, only paying me forty coppers for taking him this far, and throwing his weight about too?—Where is it, sir?' he said in a louder voice. 'Aren't we there yet?'

He wrinkled his nose and the drop fell to the ground. There were red lines across his hand where the skin was cracked, and the salt in his sweat was making it hurt.

It was now a little after eleven, the gentleman thought, though he was fairly sure it was not yet twelve. After lunch he'd have to go back to the city to report on the job. Damn the puller for charging forty coppers.

The gentleman, however, said nothing aloud as he sat there with an air of the greatest confidence. If the puller was talking too much for him he would shout with a falsetto screech, 'Shut up. Go faster.'

This was the way he always dealt with the lower orders. He was going to have to pay forty coppers just for sitting in the rickshaw for an hour, and that rogue was actually complaining it was too little. He moved his behind further back into the seat and thrust his arms firmly into his sleeves, but he was still uncomfortable. He did not usually take rickshaws. If Chen had not been on the point of leaving he would not have been in such a hurry to recover those five dollars from him. Otherwise he would not have been such a sucker as to spend forty coppers. His mouth was clamped tight as if he were afraid of something being thrust into it.

'Are we there yet, sir?' asked the puller with a sigh. There was no answer.

The gentleman had in fact seen the front gates of Chen's house. He did not say so because he hoped that if he made the journey a bit longer the puller might be too exhausted to take another step, in which case he would not have to pay. Otherwise the fare would be a bad loss.

Someone suddenly yelled from a car behind them. To avoid it the puller had to take the rickshaw into the side of the road although there was a deep puddle there. The car went hooting by.

'Excuse me, excuse me,' panted the rickshaw puller. The left wheel went into a rut, throwing the gentleman to one side. The puller put all his strength into his arms as he bent his back to pull on the shafts. He did not notice as he made this tremendous effort that his right foot was bent right back in the air. When it landed on the ground he slipped.

As it crashed the rickshaw gave out a loud crack. The puller fell to the ground, his body slumped over between the shafts. The gentleman was flung forward. He landed on the puller and rolled down beside him.

Everyone in the street crowded round, the wet vegetable baskets rubbing against them. Some youngsters were shouting something and a number of older people pushed forward to look at the rickshaw and mutter.

A lady stamped, rubbing her shoulder with her right hand and making indignant noises.

The gentleman scrambled to his feet and glanced at the puller lying on the ground. Then he looked at his hands and saw that they were now dirty. He had not suffered a scratch, though the lapel of his fur-lined gown was rather dusty.

The rickshaw man, he thought, had asked for this trouble. He'd complained about a job that was bringing him forty coppers and grumbled all the way. Now he was going to teach the rogue a lesson. He rubbed his knees and wrists, frowning. The spectators watched eagerly, clearly hoping that he was going to roll up his sleeves and invite them to inspect his wounds.

But it did not happen. The gentleman shot them a quick glance as if to say how extremely tiresome this whole business was, and started to clean the dirt very carefully from his case. 'Damn him,' he kept saying, 'damn him.'

The crowd was growing all the time, and everyone was trying to squeeze in towards the centre. The only person to succeed was a man in a Western suit wearing a triangular badge. He casually pushed aside those in front of him as he squeezed his way through. It seemed that he alone had the right to do so.

When the businessman had brushed the dirt from his clothes he threw out his chest and got ready to deal with the rickshaw man who had caused the trouble.

The rickshaw man was struggling to rise but could not manage it at first. There was a gash between his fingers and his badly grazed thumb. His knees, after being scraped along the frozen ground, were hurting ferociously. The top of his foot had been dragged along the road too, and was twisted so badly it was numb.

'It's his own fault for not looking where he was going,' said an old man.

The rickshaw man raised himself from the ground on his hands. His arms shook. He looked up and met the gentleman's eyes. He was standing above him with his arms on his hips and the corners of his mouth turned grimly down. 'What are you going to do about it? Tell me.'

A schoolboy of medium height jumped up to look over from the edge of the crowd. 'Take him to the police station,' he shouted, 'take him to the police station.' He pulled a face and ran away laughing.

Although he was now rather unsteadily on his feet, the rickshaw man could not straighten his legs. The furrows in his face seemed to be frozen there. A hole in his trousers showed his grimy knee from which blood was spurting.

He ignored all that. He was giving the rickshaw a very thorough check to see whether it had been damaged. He cursed beneath his breath, sniffing.

The man in Western clothes with a triangular badge looked at everyone, took up the pose of an orator, and started to lay down the law. 'Don't put the blame on anyone else. If someone takes a ride in your rickshaw you are responsible for their safety. . . .'

'That's right,' the gentleman added at once. He coughed and went on: 'Damn the man. He'd been muttering insolently for a long time before, too. Who do you think you are? You were happy enough to take me as a passenger. But now you're trying to push me around. Very well then.'

The puller was propping himself against a telegraph pole with one hand and looking closely at the spokes of the rickshaw's wheels. His head was bent as he waited to find out what the gentleman was going to do.

Several mouths started to give the gentleman advice. Of course it had been careless of the rickshaw man, but he had been injured, so that ought to count as punishment enough. He should drop the matter. Going to the police station would not be very pleasant.

There was a deep silence as everyone looked at the gentleman's newt-like mouth. He pursed his lips, wrinkling his chin. Suddenly they opened and he said quietly, 'All right. I'll let him off lightly.' As he turned to go his fur-lined gown swung apart for long enough to give a glimpse of a grey lambskin lining that had once been white.

Sighs came from many a nostril, and a number of people clucked approvingly. What a kind gentleman he was. The Western-clad man made another speech on the theme with much shaking of his head.

The rickshaw man gnashed his teeth and screwed up his nose. His eyes began to water. 'I've got to go back to the west city. Damn your eyes for making me come all this way. The bloody rickshaw company is going to give me trouble about this too.'

'Forget about it,' said a man in his forties with a sigh. 'You're lucky to have met such a generous man. If it had been somebody else just think what they might have done.'

'He's really generous,' repeated another pedlar.

Everybody watched the gentleman walk away and in through the front gates of a house.

As he reached out to knock on the gate the gentleman cast a glance back. Then he put his hand in his pocket and found that his packet of copper coins was still there. The hint of a smile flitted across his face. He wished that could happen every time he took a rickshaw.

Ai Wu   艾芜

Ai Wu made a name as a short-story writer with the publication of *Nan xing ji* (*Southern Travels*), a collection of stories based on his journeys in some of the remoter parts of Yunnan province and in south-east Asia. In these wanderings he met opium smugglers, inn-keepers, overseas Chinese workers and businessmen, members of minority nationalities, peasants, and many other kinds of people he would not have met as a student. The collection could be regarded as a local equivalent to *Down and Out in London and Paris*.

During the war against Japan he wrote patriotic stories and novels, and he continued to write after 1949. He has held a number of posts in the literary establishment.

On the Island

As the cold concrete had woken me at first light I had got up and started putting on my clothes. The pale blue sea with brown sails on it spread peaceful and fresh in front of my eyes like a vast picture on a wall. This was because the walls of the room only came up as far as my stomach, and above them there was nothing but a pillar every few yards; so that there was no need to go out on to the verandah to look at the view.

To my right the mainland was bathed in the dawn light, which picked out in bright, clear colours the coastline studded with coco-nut trees as it wound far into the distance where sea and sky met. The black peaks that towered above the island to the left looked very imposing and solemn. Where the foot of the mountain touched the sea threads of black and yellowish smoke rose from a modern city with red-roofed houses. I found myself forgetting about the irritation of spending a night in detention and thinking happily that, say what one might, this was a good place.

But the old chap of about fifty next to me who had been grumbling ever since we had been brought to the island suddenly sighed. I thought he was going to start moaning again, but instead he stood staring fixedly at the mainland with his mouth shut tight and his hands pressed against the wall. I followed his look and saw that there was something in the forest on the distant coast that was hurrying towards us puffing black smoke. The smoke danced and disappeared above the trees along its route. Then came the shriek of a whistle as the train stopped, letting its smoke climb straight up into the sky as it gradually thinned out. Now I realized why the old man had been sighing. He had told me the previous day that he was going to take a train to some faraway place after the boat had brought him here.

Last night he had tossed his emaciated body to and fro on the concrete, muttering from time to time things like:

'What sort of regulations are these, making the steerage passengers suffer like this?'

As this was April in the tropics the ports we had embarked from—like Madras, Calcutta, and Rangoon—had all been proclaimed Indian Ocean typhoid ports, so that the government here had told the epidemic control station to disinfect us unclean third-class passengers for a week before we could be allowed ashore. On being brought here under escort the night before we had seen all our luggage taken off to a disinfecting room, which meant that we had to sleep on the concrete floor that night with nothing to cover us. The first part of the night had been pleasantly cool, but later on the damp sea breezes blew in, making us cold. It had been even harder on this old man. Before dawn I had heard him having a fit of sneezing followed by coughing. His withered fingers were now pressed against the wall, his thin, slightly opened lips still slightly shivering as if the morning wind blowing in from the sea were too much for him. He was now gazing at the sea, on which two brown steamers were crossing, one going from the mainland to the island and one the other way. They were both packed with passengers on upper and lower decks. White foam surged up at the front and the back of the boats, making two lines of ripples on the mirror-smooth surface of the sea. The startled sea-gulls who had been floating there flashed and wheeled around the dawn sky on their silver wings.

'I should have paid the extra to travel second class,' mumbled the old man in an excited, dreamy voice. I tried to soothe him by saying that if he could resign himself to waiting the few days would be gone in no time. To my surprise he shot me a startled glance and hastily changed his tone, as if he regretted talking so incautiously just now. 'I wish I'd brought more money with me. . . . It would have been a lot better.'

It sounded forced, and an unnatural blush reddened his wrinkled cheeks. After a pause he went on, apparently feeling he should reply to my remark, 'You think I should resign myself to it, do you? Well, I can't. I've got urgent business.' He shook his head and examined the building with an uneasy and rather frightened expression on his face.

The building was about sixty yards long by twelve or so wide and empty of furniture. At one end were seven or eight short, black Indians from Madras who were now sitting cross-legged in a circle on the concrete drinking coffee, which they had brewed themselves, from brass cups. At this end there was another Chinese sleeping on the floor as well as the old man and myself. He was fast asleep, snoring deeply, and was wearing only a pair of black cotton trousers. The shirt he had draped over the top half of his body in the night had slipped to the floor, revealing his tanned and sturdy chest and arms. The morning sea breeze and the coldness of the concrete seemed not to affect him at all. It was as if everything here was just right for him.

I had got to know him during our three days on the Indian Ocean. As he had been travelling without a ticket the captain had savagely humiliated him on finding him out, throwing him into the stern in irons. He had thought nothing of it, staring back with a mocking smile at everyone who came to look at him and boldly singing. Someone asked him curiously, 'I was wondering how you got on board.'

'I was wondering what would stop me getting on board.'

He would always give a proud answer in the same terms as the question put to him. To go from India and Burma to the Malayan Peninsula and the Straits Settlements you needed a passport, without which you could not buy a boat ticket. Next came a very strict customs inspection. This time even the seamen had been made to come ashore with their bedding to register and be disinfected. Thus this stowaway drew the liveliest interest.

As this was my first sea voyage I had stayed in the stern day and night to have a better view of the sea, which meant that he became my closest neighbour. I found his songs on my lips. Once when I heard him singing a sea-chanty I had asked him if he had ever been a sailor.

'Why not? After all, I'm helmsman now.'

With a clever wink he had lifted his manacled hands and moved them from side to side. Suddenly he burst out laughing. 'He's a rum one,' I'd thought. 'You'd never get the truth out of him.' I stopped asking him what he really was. But the old man had greeted him when we were herded on board the anti-typhoid office's boat, and had very politely placed an opened tin of beef curry in front of him when we were eating on the island the previous night. This came back to me now, so I asked the old man, 'Do you know him? What is he?'

The old man weighed me up and did not reply. He looked towards the sea and said, 'This would be a wonderful day for a walk.'

Then he went to the empty ground between our building and the one opposite. This was bigger than the building. At our end was clean sand with umbrella-like trees, under which two Indian women with gold rings in their noses had made a stand for a frying pan with some bricks and were cooking pancakes with butter. The other end was concreted over and had taps. Some Indian men, dressed in white, were silently praying to the west. Like the two women at our end they were from Bombay and were staying in the other building. This then was a camp: two buildings and a piece of waste ground surrounded by iron railings with a little gate on the right-hand side that was kept locked. Behind us and to the left were many more such camps.

A white man and two Malay doctors came in and ordered us men from the two buildings to line up on the sand and strip to the waist. First of all the Englishman inspected us, rapping the slow undressers with his stick. Then the Malay doctors took each of us by the wrist and gave us a smallpox vaccination. The old man, who was standing next to me, made a pathetic face when the Englishman came to him, bowing and saying, 'I salute you, sir,' in Malay. He went on to plead with him in the same language to be allowed to hurry home to see his sick son. He assured the officer that he himself was free from disease and that he could be allowed to go that very day without the least worry. As he spoke his nose was running, the bones were sticking out of his skinny chest, and he was coming out in goose-flesh. The Englishman paid no attention to him, turned his head away, after bending it to listen to him, and walked on.

The strapping youngster who had been asleep indoors was now standing next to us. As the Englishman walked away he looked at the railings and said, as if to tease the old man, 'There'd be no problem about going. You'd just have to jump over.'

'Then why don't you?' I asked with a smile. He stretched his arms out and solemnly replied, 'Why should I? I couldn't find a better place than this, even if I paid to stay there.'

Towards noon the Indian orderlies who kept the place swept opened the gate in the railings and told us to come out of the camp to fetch our food, which was issued on the beach not far away. The place where we had been the night before looked like a shop. Two or three short Indian Muslims, with skins that were neither black nor dark brown, weighed out our rations and also sold tins and other kinds of food. We three were given our food together. The young man handed the potatoes and dried fish to me, took the rice and the little packets of tea himself, and then made a lordly expression at the old man, saying, 'I'm sorry, but would you mind taking that bundle of firewood?'

Seeing the effort it was for him to carry the firewood I asked him to swap loads with me. The young man shot me a glance that clearly meant I was to mind my own business. As we walked back he chaffed the old man: 'I don't suppose you've done this sort of work these ten years or more, Proprietor Li.'

The old man made no reply. His pale cheeks reddened again.

When it came to cooking, the young man was the boss again. He made me sit under the tree and peel the potatoes, while he squatted beside the fireplace that he had improvised from three bricks and watched the pot of rice. He made the old man do all the tiresome jobs like cutting up the firewood and cleaning the vegetables. Every now and again he would mock him or tell him off: 'Hey, you old fool, that's not the way to chop wood.'

While the old man was away washing the vegetables I asked him to stop this cruel game which I found repulsive.

'Do you think this is cruel, my friend? Do you know how he used to treat us? Don't imagine that he used to stop at swearing at us. He kicked us with the toecaps of his leather shoes.'

The youngster swung his leg at the stove to show me. Then he brought his temper back under control, or so it seemed, and said, 'But now I'll satisfy myself with teasing him. But if I wanted to settle old scores. . . .' He glanced with contempt at the old man and was silent. Trying to get to the bottom of it, I asked another question:

'What did you do when you worked for him?'

'Ask him. He'll remember.' The young man turned his attention to building up the fire, his jaw clenched.

We took the food over to eat in the cool of the verandah. The young man sat in the middle like the head of the household, quietly finding fault with the old man as we ate. The old man, well aware that he was deliberately trying to make things difficult for him, kept replying with angry glares.

'You expect your rice to be here without your having to shed a drop of sweat for it. You're like a weasel wanting to eat swan's eggs. There's nothing so terrible about having to cut a bit of firewood or clean the vegetables. Nobody's making you break rocks on a mountainside. We're not like some people in those bloody places'—he pointed at the mainland and the city on the island with his chopsticks—'who are as lazy as pigs and boot you up the backside. Phew! This dried fish has gone right off. Damn the bastards.' He went on to complain that the vegetables here were not good enough.

The old man was very restless that afternoon, pacing up and down the verandah, only stopping for a while to shade his eyes and look into the distance whenever the wind carried over the sound of a whistle.

When the Englishman and the Malay doctors came to inspect us again the next day, his pleas were even more pathetic than before. Never mind if they would not let him go, he said, but please would they transfer him to another camp. This time the Englishman opened his mouth, but it was only to say

'No'. The youngster said nothing as he looked at the old man
and twisted his mouth into a grin.

As the old man was thoroughly ill at ease and had eaten so
little, he stopped walking up and down or looking at the sea.
He was sitting out of the way quietly coughing.

The youngster, on the other hand, seemed to be in very high
spirits. He climbed up on the wall and sat facing the sea with
his back to one of the pillars and singing 'Like a bird in a cage,
I have wings but I cannot fly away' at the top of his voice
over and over again.

That evening we were given back our luggage. The old man
carefully put his things close to mine, and when the young man
was asleep he took me outside to sit on the verandah and said
to me, with a toadying expression on his face, 'You'd better
keep a good eye on your things. . . . He's rotten to the core, he'd
stop at nothing. Look at him—what he's got with him wouldn't
cover the palm of your hand.' He coughed. 'It's not that I'm
afraid of him, but I don't want to be tainted by him. In
Rangoon he never paid his boarding-house bills. Everyone
knew. You saw him yourself under arrest on the boat. It's not
the first time either. I've seen more of him. For him to be
giving me lectures!' He coughed again. 'Do you think that
after fifty years I don't know that if you expect to eat you have
to sweat for it? It's nonsense coming from him. Just look at
him—all he needs is a beggar's staff and bowl. I had a high
opinion of him when he was a kid; he was keen and hard-
working. When he grew up he went to the bad, starting with
stealing. Now he's rotten to the core. I don't understand why
the red-haired devils have these regulations, treating decent
people and criminals together. It wouldn't be so bad if you were
ill, but what can be the reason for keeping healthy people
locked up in here? That son of mine was practically on his
deathbed, and now I don't know how he is.'

A sigh led to another fit of racking coughing. He hurried off
to spit on the sand. The sea was now black, with only the red
lights of a few fishing boats bobbing up and down. You would
have forgotten that the mainland had been to the right of you
in the day-time if it had not been for the occasional light
shining through the trees that concealed the railway station.

E

The island to the left was a blaze of colour, with lights shining
from every house; the city looked even more beautiful and
lively than it did by day. The old man looked at it for a while,
sighed and said, 'So near, but so different. . . . You must have
distinctions between high and low in the world. . . . It's bound
to be hard on decent people like you or me in a lousy place
like this.'

As the brightly-lit ferry crossed the water you could see the
passengers above and below decks more clearly than by day.
'In fact,' I replied, pointing at them, 'some of them are having
a hard time too. Those who are travelling third by boat or
train aren't as well off as we are at this moment. If we look a
little further, could you be sure that nobody is diving into the
sea from that dock in the hope of earning a meal?'

'Of course they are, of course they are,' the old man was
quick to reply. 'Mind you, they deserve no better. Some
people are bone idle, some are crooked, some go in for whoring
and gambling, some. . . .'

I interrupted him with an angry question: 'Do you mean to
tell me that there isn't a decent man among them? I've known
many myself.'

He hastily changed his tack. 'Of course, of course, there must
be. But'—he coughed—'let me tell you that what I was saying
is very important. It's all a matter of the fate a man is born
with. And luck is vital too.' As the old man talked on I saw
how obstinately he clung to his class prejudices about life, and
since there was nothing that could be done about them I
stopped arguing with him, yawned, and said, 'It's late. Let's
go to bed.'

The first thing he did when he went inside was to check
whether the locks on his cases had been tampered with. Next
he looked at the string round his baskets to see if it had been untied. Finally he rearranged the cases and baskets so that the
knots and locks were all next to him. He sat on his bedding on
the floor and, instead of going to sleep, he felt the brass fittings
on them one by one as they were spread out near his feet,
counting, sighing, and occasionally coughing.

The light that stayed on all night made it hard enough for us
to go to sleep, and with the old man's tiresome coughing as

well it was even more difficult. Still, the light gave me a much clearer view of what he was like during the night. The odd thing was that although obviously sound asleep and snoring he would sit up and look all around with his eyes wide open like a sleep-walker whenever he heard anybody get up to go out and relieve himself.

The next night I slept well as I kept further away from him, but he was kept awake by coughing as his illness grew worse. When the Englishman came to inspect us during our fourth morning on the island the old man dragged himself to his feet but was so dizzy that he collapsed again.

'Serve him right,' was the young man's delighted first reaction, 'serve him right. It's much better to be a poor man like myself and sleep soundly till dawn. I'm not scared of anyone stealing my stuff—I haven't got any.'

Later, as the old man's incessant sad and mournful groans were cutting us to the heart, the youngster frowned and said to me angrily, 'I wish I could kick him away. I can't stand any more of it, I really can't.'

I suggested that a doctor should be sent for and asked the guards to move him to the infirmary.

When this request was passed on the answer was that a doctor was just on his way. Afternoon and evening passed without any sign of one. All that happened was that the sick man's groans grew louder. The youngster's muttered imprecations turned into crude abuse as he reckoned that all the red-haired devils and Malays deserved to die too.

After we had reported again that night how urgent the situation was the Englishman and the Malay doctors came along, reeking of liquor. Their diagnosis was acute pneumonia. If the sick man had the money he could be ferried over to the big hospital on the other island the next morning, but if he hadn't there was nothing that could be done for him and he might quite well die here before long.

I bent over the old man to tell him that he would have to pay to go into hospital and asked if he really had brought plenty of money with him so that he could go there the next day. Gazing at me with his bloodshot eyes opened wide in a crazy stare he listened as I repeated this several times over. At

last he raised his trembling hand to point at a brown leather
case next to him. Then he dropped his hand and shut his eyes.
He said not a word. His mouth was still wide open as he gasped
for breath.

I straightened up and looked at the youngster, who was
standing beside me scratching his hair. He was rather worked
up. Then he hurried out of the room looking very anxious
about something.

I went out on to the verandah for a breath of fresh air after
the doctors had gone. No lights were rocking on the pitch black
sea. Only the rare and occasional light showed that the city
on the other island was still there, and with the mountains the
same colour as the sky they shone like stars. Far away, where the
sea joined the sky, a lighthouse winked at the lonely ocean.
When I had been standing there for quite a time I noticed the
young man sitting silently under the verandah with his head
in his hands.

'What are you doing?' I asked him. 'Why don't you turn in
for the night?'

Several moments passed before he threw his arms apart and
answered me: 'It's funny, but something I've thought of is
depressing me.'

'What?' I asked, going over and sitting down beside him.

'I once worked as a rubber tapper in Sumatra. The bloody
shack we lived in was a ruin, full of rats. They even came out
in the day. We used to kill them with sticks in our free time.
They're real crafty, rats, and when they jump around or
dive into their holes it's almost impossible to hit them. When
you're lucky enough to get one you feel happy. Well, the
depressing thing I was talking about happened like this. Once
I went into the room by myself and saw one in the middle of
the floor. I grabbed a stick as quickly as I could, shut the door
quietly, and stopped up the rat-holes. We'll see if you can get
away this time, I thought. I was really excited. As I was only
looking at the rat I didn't watch where I put my feet and I
kicked over an empty wash bowl. Damn, I thought. To my
amazement the rat didn't move. It might have been stone
deaf. I poked it with the end of my stick and it fell over. It was
so weak that it took it a long time to stand up. It tried to run

away but it couldn't. It must have been ill. I lifted my stick to kill it, but for some reason that I couldn't understand I hadn't the strength to do it. My excitement had all gone. But I wasn't really sorry for it. It wouldn't have mattered at all if I'd killed it. All I wanted was to feel happier.'

He rose to his feet and paced up and down with a heavy tread.

When I went to bed I could not get to sleep for a long time, so I lay there with my eyes shut and rested. At first I could hear sad songs of separation from the distant camps where the southern Indians were kept, but gradually they died away. Some night birds flapped their wings among the trees in the yard. The sound of the waves beating against the shore was now soft and now loud.

At about midnight I saw the young man get up, walk round the room and cough a few times. When he was sure nobody had moved, he went to the sick man, bent down, and apparently felt him all over.

How low can you get, I thought, as I lay there motionless in the hope of seeing it through to the end.

As I watched he quickly found a string of little objects that he put into the lock of the brown leather suitcase. By the time I had realized that they were keys the case was open. He took out a wallet so fast that he must have known where it was beforehand. I was appalled by the thought that if he took all the old man's money it would be the death of him. But instead of taking money out of the wallet he put a roll of something into it from his own pocket. He returned the wallet to the case, which he shut and locked, put the keys back into the sick man's pocket, crept over to his own place and went back to sleep. I was mystified. Whatever was he up to? I deliberately rolled over to let him know that I was not asleep. He lifted his head to look at me, then lay down again.

The next morning the English sent a Chinese along to ask the old man how much money he had with him. He wrote all the details down in his notebook, then just to be on the safe side he asked the old man to count the money in his wallet to make sure that it was as much as he had said. I noticed the trace of a grin on the face of the young man beside me. All his smiles that I had seen in the time we had spent together had shown traces of cunning or mockery apart from this one, which was full of satisfaction.

As the old man raised his sick head he could not help saying with a sigh, 'They're messing us about. Call this epidemic control! Look what a state they've got me into. On top of that, they won't let us land if we're healthy and they let us ashore if we're sick. They're just making fools of us.'

'It goes without saying,' the young man said bitterly to himself, 'that the red-haired devils are dirt. And as for that old fool, if he hadn't been ill I'd have shown you—and I wouldn't have cared how high and mighty his ancestors were.' He closed his mouth round a cigarette and said no more.

I suddenly realized that last night he had been returning the money he had stolen the night before. I nodded knowingly to him and said, 'Last night. I saw.'

In between puffs he at last told me frankly a great deal about his past. It was not at all like the joking way in which he had answered questions about himself before. He admitted that this was his trade, and reckoned that it was good fun.

'Just think,' he went on, tapping the ash from his cigarette, 'how conceited some people are. I mean, it's not as if they had an eye or a nose more than the rest of us. What's so marvellous about them? It's just that they dress well and have a bit more money in their wallets. I can't stand people like that. When I first learnt this trade it was just for fun, not to use seriously. But later, when I kept meeting people like that—on trams, in crowded places, everywhere—I thought, What are you so stuck up about? I'll take you down a peg. It was terrific, a real laugh. I couldn't stop myself doing it. I was hooked on it like opium. Sometimes I took wrist-watches and fountain-pens. I know it was wrong, but I couldn't help it.'

'What have your takings been like this time?' I asked with a smile.

'I'm flat broke.'

'What will you do when we land?' I couldn't help feeling anxious on his behalf.

'I'll start up straight away.' He raised his eyebrows and reverted to his usual mocking smile. Then he took a deep drag on his cigarette, threw it to the ground, and walked away. 'They may even invite me to stay with them for a few days,' he joked. 'It would be too unfriendly of them to make me go to the effort of working as soon as I go ashore.'

On the day we left the little island we all lined up on the beach for our final inspection. As we were given permission to land we were happy despite the scorching sun. Before we boarded the ferry the police came over from the other island and took the young man away in a motor-boat. As it drew away he stuck his grinning head out of the cabin door and waved to us very gaily. It was as if we and the Indians were all standing on the shore specially to see him off.

There was no breeze, and the pale green waters of the sea around him looked scalding hot as they reflected the sun's powerful glare.

24 September 1936, Shanghai

Zhao Shuli   赵树理

[Chao Shu-li]

Zhao Shuli, born in Shansi in 1903 or 1905, had at the time when this story was written spent nearly all his life in his native province, studying intermittently in his own village, the local town of Changzhi, and the provincial capital Taiyuan, learning the techniques of the popular folk-music and ballad styles, and working as an entertainer, a schoolteacher, and a journalist. In 1939 he started to do cultural work for the Eighth Route Army in the Taihang Mountains, a stronghold of the anti-Japanese struggle in south-east Shansi, where his main job was running local papers.

His first big success was 'The Marriage of Xiao Erhei', a story about free choice in marriage in the villages. It sold over thirty thousand copies in the backward Taihang mountain region alone, a circulation that few writers could then rival on the national scale. 'Meng Xiangying Stands Up' is not one of his best-known pieces, but it deals with the eternal problem of village women taking part in politics in a lively and realistic way. In this story, describing a real woman, the language is much closer to that of the traditional story-teller than to that used by the Westernized novelist of the city or to the semi-classical style of most newspapers of the day. It was a story that could be read aloud to and enjoyed by peasants, or understood without too much difficulty by the newly literate revolutionary cadres in the anti-Japanese base areas where the Communists were encouraging the people to start organizing themselves to fight and produce in order to defeat famine and the invader.

For many years Zhao Shuli's work was held up by the powerful literary official Zhou Yang as the embodiment of the principles Chairman Mao laid down for literature in the Yenan talks. More recently Zhao came under attack for failing to have enough sympathy for the development of socialist agriculture. Whatever truth there may be in these accusations—and they do not appear unfounded—his contribution to the sinification of the Western-style short story and novel has been an important one, and his earlier work describes some aspects of rural Shansi during the war against Japan in a way found in no earlier writing about the Chinese countryside. There have been reports of his death since 1966.

Meng Xiangying Stands Up
A true story

1 *The old rules and new reasons*

By the Qingzhang river in the south-east corner of Shexian county lies the village of Xiyaokou. Niu is the most common surname. A mile to the west, in the village of Dingyan, the predominant name is Meng. The Nius and the Mengs are both large clans, and they have intermarried for generations. In the old days, when you could not call women by their personal names, you can imagine how difficult it was to find a particular woman who had one of these surnames because there were so many women known as 'Mrs. Niu from the Meng family' or 'Mrs. Meng from the Niu family'. Meng Xiangying, who came from Dingyan and had married into Xiyaokou, was herself a 'Mrs. Niu from the Meng family'.

Do not imagine that just because the two clans have inter-married for generations every couple is very happy. Indeed, many are the reverse. This is wild hill-country: as they used to say in the old days, 'the mountains are high and the emperor is far away', which could be brought up to date as 'the mountains are high and the government is far away'—it is some fifteen miles to the district government office. For this reason the customs here have not changed much since the last years of the Qing dynasty. For women the old rule still holds good that as a daughter-in-law you have to put up with beating and abuse, but that once you become a mother-in-law yourself you can beat and curse your daughter-in-law. If you don't you're failing to put up a good show of being a mother-in-law. The old rule for men in handling their wives is, 'a wife you've married is like a horse you've bought—you can ride them or flog them as you like.' Any man who does not beat his wife is only proving that he is afraid of her.

Apart from following all the usual rules, Meng Xiangying's mother-in-law has a distinction of her own—a sharp tongue.

When she was young she used to have a lot of friends outside the home, and though her husband did not approve he was scared of quarrelling with her because she could beat him whether it was an argument or a slanging match. If her own husband was intimidated by her, what chance could her daughter-in-law have?

The old village rules and her mother-in-law's sharp tongue ought to have been enough to put paid to Meng Xiangying, and on top of this there were things in Meng Xiangying's own background to make her position even worse. In the first place, she had nobody in her own family to protect her. Her parents had died when she was eight, leaving her with only a twelve-year-old sister and a baby brother. Later on her sister had also married into Xiyaokou, but because her sister's in-laws and her own were on bad terms her sister could not even come to her wedding, with the result that she had to see herself off in the bridal sedan chair. With a family like this behind her, there was nobody to speak up for her when she was beaten. Secondly, her own family was destitute. Thirdly, because she had lost her mother so young she had not learnt to sew well. Fourthly, she had natural feet. In this area women with natural feet are thought as odd as women with bound feet where natural ones are usual. And lastly, since she had been running the home from when she was a child she was not prepared to let her mother-in-law put upon her as she pleased. To the mother-in-law these were all reasons why she deserved to be beaten and cursed.

2 *She could not even cry*

Someone who has been cruelly wronged but has no way of protesting cannot usually help weeping, but Meng Xiangying did not have much chance of doing even that. Had her parents still been alive, she could have gone to cry in their house, but with only a ten-year-old brother there it was not merely difficult for her to go and cry on his shoulder, she had to go on looking after him when she did cry. Had she got on well with her husband she could have turned to him for a weep at night when her mother-in-law mistreated her; but as he was the one who generally gave her the beatings she suffered on his mother's orders, it would only have been asking for a second dose if she had gone crying to him.

Meng Xiangying did have one or two people to whom she could take her troubles. Her sister was a close neighbour, and she could cry whenever they met. There was also Changzhen, a young wife in the family next door who had to put up with the same sort of beating and abuse from her mother-in-law as Meng Xiangying did from hers; the two of them could weep on each other's shoulders. Apart from this she could cry by herself when she hung home-made paper out to dry on the wall. It was by the paper-drying wall that she cried the most, and the lapels of her cotton tunic would become soaked right through as she wiped the tears away with it.

Finding another chance to cry once caused some trouble. She had harnessed the donkey to the roller to grind some millet, and she burst into tears as she scooped the grain into place. An uncle of her husband's happened to meet her and ask her why. Unfortunately her mother-in-law turned up just as he was making some critical remarks about her. Realizing that he had been overheard, he took advantage of his position as her husband's brother to criticize the mother-in-law to her face. For fear that he would expose the faults of her own youth, she did not try to rebut him directly. All she could do was to change the subject.

The mother-in-law had long been against Meng Xiangying talking with outsiders, particularly with other young married women. In her own experience, when young wives got together it was always to compare the faults of their mothers-in-law; so whenever she found out that Meng Xiangying had been talking to the women in the neighbouring houses she would discover some wrongdoing for which to beat and curse her. Although it was to a man that Meng Xiangying had been talking this time, her mother-in-law had heard herself being criticized with her own ears. 'The so-and-so,' she thought, 'she must be spreading the dirt about me outside every day. I'll have to teach her a lesson.' According to the old custom, when a mother-in-law wanted to find fault with her daughter-in-law she was as thorough as a donkey going round and round the rolling mill-stone: she did not miss a step. As it happened Meng Xiangying had carelessly smashed a brush-handle with the roller that day, so her mother-in-law used this as a pretext for abusing Meng Xiangying's parents. It became so unpleasant that Meng Xiangying could hold herself back no longer.

'Stop that, mother. I'll bind it up for you.'

'Bind up your mother's ———,' replied her mother-in-law.

'My sister will lend me a new one to replace it.'

'Replace your mother's ———.'

Mending it would not do, replacing it would not do, and on top of that she had to hear all this abuse of her mother. Meng Xiangying was now so furious that she had the courage to say, 'My own mother has been dead for many years. You're my mother now. You're swearing at yourself, mother.'

'——— your mother.'

'Mother!'

'——— your mother.'

'Mother! Mother! Mother!'

Mother-in-law stopped swearing. As she had met her match in her daughter-in-law, swearing gave her no pleasure. 'The so-and-so's got an even sharper tongue than I have,' she thought. 'I'll have to think of some other way to deal with her.' Later on she did indeed change her methods.

3 *She could not die*

One day Meng Xiangying asked her mother-in-law for some cloth with which to patch her husband's clothes, and the mother-in-law told her to ask the father-in-law for it. According to the old rules she should not have had to ask him for patching cloth, and when Meng Xiangying argued the point with her mother-in-law, leaving her without a leg to stand on, the mother-in-law started abusing her again. The mother-in-law, realizing that she could not possibly win against Meng Xiangying who was in the right and prepared to argue, hurried to the fields to call her son.

'Meini' (this was Meng Xiangying's husband's name), 'come back at once. I can't do anything with that young madam of yours. She wants to eat me alive.'

As she could not control the young madam, Meini had to come back and flaunt his authority as young master. The moment he arrived he grabbed a stick and went for Meng Xiangying—according to the old rules there was no need for him to bother to ask why. But Meini did not have much authority himself, being a lad of only sixteen, and a year younger than his wife, and Meng Xiangying snatched the stick back from him.

This caused real trouble. By the old rules, when a man beat his wife she was expected to take a few blows and then run away, after which somebody else would take the stick from him and that would be the end of the matter. But Meng Xiangying had not simply refused to be beaten and to run away, she had actually disarmed him, making him feel thoroughly humiliated. In his rage he picked up a sickle and hacked a bloody wound on Meng Xiangying's forehead, from which the blood kept gushing out even after they had been pulled apart.

The people who broke up the fight seemed to think that Meini had done wrong. Nearly everyone said that if he had to hit her, he should have done so anywhere but on the head. They were only saying that he had hit her in the wrong place. Nobody asked why he had hit her. By the old rules there was no need to ask why a man had hit his wife.

After the fight everyone dispersed as though it were no business of theirs. The only person not to take so casual an attitude was Meng Xiangying herself. If her head had been cut open when she was completely in the right, and nobody was going to say a fair word for her, then it seemed that there was nothing to stop her husband from hitting her whenever he wanted to. Was this to go on for ever? The more she thought about it the more hopeless it seemed. Finally she decided on suicide and swallowed some opium.

As she did not swallow enough she did not die but started retching violently. When her relations discovered this they poured some dirty water, in which combs had been cleaned, down her throat, which made her bring it all up.

'If you like swallowing opium that's fine,' her mother-in-law said. 'I've got a whole jar of it. I hope you can swallow the lot.' Meng Xiangying would have been glad to, but her mother-in-law did not produce it.

Another time, when Meng Xiangying came back after dark from working in the fields, her mother-in-law would not let her eat and her husband refused to allow her indoors. The yard gate was shut, as were the doors of her mother-in-law's and husband's rooms. She was left standing by herself in the yard. Changzhen, the young married woman who lived nearby, came to see her, as did her sister. They whispered a few words to her from the other side of the yard gates, which she dared not open. Changzhen and her sister were crying quietly on one side of the gates, while Meng Xiangying cried quietly on the other. Later she sat under the eaves and cried herself to sleep. When she woke up her mother-in-law and husband were both still sound asleep, the yard was quiet, the sky was bright with stars, and her clothes were soaking wet.

She had nothing to eat the next morning or at noon either, so, reckoning that she could not go on living, she went back to her room while her husband was taking his siesta in his mother's room and hanged herself.

Her neighbour Changzhen came to see her again, and when she heard that Meng Xiangying's in-laws and husband were fast asleep she thought this would be a good chance to talk. Changzhen got such a fright when she went into the room and found her hanging from the rafters that she screamed and ran out. The shouting that ensued brought a lot of people to the rescue, including Xiangying's sister, who held the body in her arms and sobbed.

After a lot of effort had been made to revive her, Xiangying opened her eyes. She saw that she was in the arms of her sister, who by now seemed to be made of tears.

Both her attempts to kill herself had failed. She had to go on suffering.

4 *How she became a village cadre*

In 1942 a worker came from the Fifth Sub-region to Xiyaokou. When he asked them to choose a leader for the Women's National Salvation Association the villagers suggested Meng Xiangying. 'She can talk,' they said, 'and that means she can keep a firm grip on what is right.' But nobody had the courage to discuss the proposal with her mother-in-law. 'I'll go myself,' said the worker, but he met with some opposition. 'She won't do,' said Meng Xiangying's mother-in-law. 'She's a

failed suicide. She couldn't cope.' No matter what arguments
he used, they were met with 'she couldn't cope'. Why did
Meng Xiangying's mother-in-law refuse so obstinately to let
her become leader? This was something to do with Notquite
Niu. (He is a former enemy agent who has come over to our
side, and they call him Notquite because he has not yet reformed properly.)

When the troops of Zhu Huaibing[1], that expert trouble-
maker, were stationed in this area, Notquite Niu was a big
man in the village. Later, after Zhu Huaibing fell and the local
security chief went over to the enemy, Notquite Niu made
contact with him a couple of times in enemy territory. Then,
when the Fortieth Army[2] was stationed in Linxian county,
Notquite Niu got on good terms with them too. He certainly
knew how to run with the hare and hunt with the hounds. He
was very close to Meng Xiangying's in-laws. When Meng Xiangying's father-in-law Niu Mingshi ran into debt over his paper-
making and had to make his land over to someone else as
security, leaving himself none, Notquite rented him an acre.
Notquite's wife had been as sociable as Meng Xiangying's
mother-in-law when younger, and through introducing friends
to each other the two women had themselves been friends for a
long time. As Notquite Niu was an important man and Niu
Mingshi's landlord, and as the two wives were such old friends
as well, the two families were on very close terms. Although
Niu Mingshi kept only three-tenths of the grain he harvested
and had to give the remaining seven-tenths to Notquite, he and
his wife still felt honoured at being on good terms with such an
important man.

After the fall of Zhu Huaibing this area came, in name at
least, under the control of our Shansi-Hopei-Shantung-Honan
Border Region; but in fact, because 'the mountains are high
and the government far away', most of the local people could
be swayed by what Notquite Niu and his friends said. Every
few days Notquite would announce that the Japanese or the
Fortieth Army were coming at any moment; and whichever it
was, he always said the Eighth Route Army was no good. Meng
Xiangying's father-in-law was only half convinced by this;

[1] A Kuomintang commander.   [2] Kuomintang.

after all, there had been no sale for his home-made paper after
the beginning of the Anti-Japanese War until the Eighth
Route Army came. They encouraged the revival of paper-
making, and arranged for the paper to be bought by the
government, which had started everyone making it again. Niu
Mingshi had himself made a lot of money by making paper,
and had taken less than two years to redeem the land he had
made over to someone else as security for a loan. He could see
that the people who had been coming to buy paper for the past
two years were all from the Eighth Route Army, so he knew
that they were really far from being 'no good'. But when he
heard Notquite's stories he would start to change his mind
again: so important a man, after all, must know what he was
talking about. While Meng Xiangying's father-in-law was half-
convinced by Notquite, but at the same time doubtful too, her
mother-in-law became the faithful disciple of Notquite's wife.
It made no difference to the mother-in-law who bought their
paper, or how the land had been redeemed—she followed one
leader: Notquite's wife. When Notquite's wife said the Fortieth
Army would be coming soon, she expected it the next day or the
day after. When Notquite's wife said the Fortieth Army would
shoot all the present village cadres, she thought the right thing
to do was to tell all the cadres' families to get the coffins ready.
As you can imagine, such a mother-in-law could not possibly
approve of Meng Xiangying becoming the leader of the
Women's Association.

The worker, a young man, lost his patience when all his
arguments were met with 'she couldn't cope' by Meng
Xiangying's mother-in-law. 'If she can't,' he shouted, 'then
you'll have to.' To his surprise this did the trick. Meng Xiangying's mother-in-law had always thought that being a village
cadre was dangerous because sooner or later you were bound
to get shot by the Fortieth Army. The reason why she did not
want Meng Xiangying to be one was not so much out of love for
her as that she was afraid of being in trouble herself as a cadre's
relation. This was why, after all her refusals, the worker's
suggestion that she should do it herself threw her into a panic.
She would get into less trouble by having her daughter-in-law
as a cadre than by being one herself. So she became much more

amenable: 'It's none of my business, none at all. If she can cope, let her.'

The worker had won. From then on Meng Xiangying headed the Women's Association.

5 *Uncontrollable*

As a village cadre she had to go to meetings. Meng Xiangying would say to her mother-in-law, 'Mother, I'm going to a meeting,' and off she would go. Mother-in-law was astonished at the idea of a young woman going to a meeting, but she could not stop Meng Xiangying for fear that the worker would make her take the job on herself. Although she felt that the Eighth Route Army was 'no good', she reckoned that her own capacity was even smaller; if she resisted openly, then unless the Fortieth Army came to her rescue early the next morning there was nothing to stop the worker taking her to the district government office at noon.

Meng Xiangying's mother-in-law had mixed feelings about women taking part in meetings. She would have liked to go along and have a look, but decided she had better not; if she did, the Fortieth Army would say when they came that she had gone to meetings organized by the 'Eighth Route faction'. The next day her curiosity made her go along to find out what a lot of young women together talked about at a meeting. Her investigations shocked her. The women wanted emancipation; they were against being beaten and sworn at by their mothers-in-law and husbands; they were for ending foot-binding; they wanted to gather firewood, fetch water, and till the fields; they wanted to do the same work and eat the same food as the men; they wanted to go to winter school. In her view this was rebellion. If mothers-in-law and husbands could not beat young wives, who would? Surely someone had to beat them. Her second daughter-in-law, Meng Xiangying (her older son and his wife were farmers in Xiangyuan), had feet that she would not allow her mother-in-law to bind small enough no matter how she was beaten and cursed; surely she did not have the nerve to demand that they be allowed to grow bigger still. Would women who gathered firewood and fetched water still be women? She was uncontrollable enough while illiterate, but if she learned to read and write she'd be even more high and mighty. What was the world coming to?

Meng Xiangying was not particularly bothered by her mother-in-law's worries. With the worker's help her job ran smoothly. She went to a lot of meetings and frequently attended winter school. When a young wife was beaten by her mother-in-law or bullied by her husband she told Meng Xiangying, who told the worker. Then there would be meetings, criticism, and struggle.

The harder Meng Xiangying worked at her job, the more information on her the mother-in-law gathered. 'I can't control the so-and-so,' she said to Meini, now that she could neither beat nor swear at her. 'She tells everything to that worker. What are we to do about her?' Meini had no solution. He sucked in his breath, and his mother sucked in hers.

When Meng Xiangying came back from gathering firewood her mother-in-law pulled a face and muttered, 'Disgraceful'. When Meng Xiangying carried some water in, her mother-in-law pulled a face and muttered, 'Disgraceful'.

To promote the unbinding of feet, the worker told Meng Xiangying to be the first to unbind, and she was. Mother-in-law pursed her lips, and her glare followed Meng Xiangying's feet around.

The young women in the village were not like Meng Xiangying's mother-in-law. When they saw Meng Xiangying gather firewood, some of them went along to gather it with her. When they saw her fetch water, some went to fetch water with her. When they saw that she had unbound her feet, some unbound theirs. Not all the husbands were like Meini. Many of them were progressive. One said, 'A woman with natural feet can work as well as a man.' Another was of the opinion that if women fetched firewood and water men had to waste less time on these odd jobs. A third view was, 'Notquite Niu is always saying that the Eighth Route Army is no good, but I think the things they stand for are all fine.'

No matter what everyone else thought, Meng Xiangying's mother-in-law was developing a stronger and stronger dislike for her. Now that she could not beat or swear at her there was no way of working off her resentment, so she decided to have a conference with Notquite Niu's wife. One day, on her way to the fields, she saw Notquite's wife ahead of her. 'Wait for me,' she shouted, but instead of waiting Notquite's wife went faster. The mother-in-law ran after Notquite's wife to catch her up, only to be told:

'Our two families are going to be seeing less of each other. Don't think your second daughter-in-law is very fashionable with her unbound feet. When the Fortieth Army comes they're sure to say she's an Eighth Route Army wife. If your family has connections with the Eighth Route Army, we're not going to get into trouble on your account.'

These few words turned Meng Xiangying's mother-in-law numb with horror from her head to the soles of her feet. Resentment had been building up inside her for days, but she had never imagined that the situation could be so terribly dangerous that even this conversation was impossible. She went straight to Meini to see if he had any ideas, but he had not. The two of them sat there sucking in their breath as before.

6 *She can't even be sold*

Once, when the villagers were going to Taicang Hamlet for a struggle meeting against the enemy agent Ren Erhai, Notquite Niu and his friends said to them, 'Off you go then. The Fortieth Army thinks the world of Ren Erhai, so if you're in the struggle against him watch out for your head. The Fortieth Army will settle the score with you the moment they come.' Remarks like these terrified Meng Xiangying's parents-in-law and husband. Although none of them dared to try and dissuade her directly, they all turned pale. 'This time we're in for real trouble,' whispered the mother to her son. 'Real trouble,' he whispered back.

The strange expressions they wore worried even Meng Xiangying. When she spoke to the other young women about it some of them said it might be best to stay away. Unable to make up her mind, she asked the worker if it would be all right not to go. 'It's not compulsory,' he said, 'but if the masses are going, the cadres should too.' Meng Xiangying had no answer to that, so she decided to go. She wondered if she could avoid having to say anything.

In Taicang Hamlet she saw a crowd, even bigger than one

for the opera, filling the square. Far more people wanted to speak than could get a word in, and Ren Erhai hung his head, not daring to look anyone in the face. Her attitude changed at once. She did not believe that so many people could all be unconcerned about being shot: obviously there would be no trouble. Before long she was leading the Xiyaokou villagers in shouting slogans against Ren Erhai.

After this struggle meeting she became bolder, no longer believing the enemy agent's rumours about a change of regime, and working with more enthusiasm than ever. Her mother-in-law was just the opposite. No sooner was Meng Xiangying back from the meeting than Notquite and his friends were saying, 'Sooner or later she's for it.' In cold fear her mother-in-law racked her brains until she found what seemed to be the ideal way of dealing with Meng Xiangying.

One day the mother-in-law said to Meini's aunt, 'After two bad harvests there's no food in the house. Meini had better take his wife to his brother's in Xiangyuan.' It was true that there was nothing to eat in the house, and Meng Xiangying would have been delighted to be separated from her mother-in-law, but now that she had started work in the village she had to carry on with it. That evening her mother-in-law had another talk with Meini's aunt while Meng Xiangying was at the literacy class for women. As the oil for the class's lamps was kept at her home Meng Xiangying came back to fetch it, and she overheard a snippet of their conversation.

'She should be taken to Xiangyuan and sold,' her mother-in-law was saying. 'Our Meini's young. There'll be no trouble getting him another wife.'

'Aren't you afraid she'll report it to the Eighth Route Army there?' asked the aunt.

'No. Xiangyuan is occupied by the Japanese.'

This was enough to tell Meng Xiangying what her mother-in-law's brilliant scheme was, and she lost no time in telling the worker. 'As she hasn't told you directly,' he said, 'don't question her about it. Just say that you are too busy here and can't go.'

As she would not go there was nothing her mother-in-law could do about it. Her plan had come to nothing.

7 *The heroine emerges*

That summer Pang Bingxun and Sun Dianying went over to the Japanese with the Fortieth and New Fifth Armies, after which the Eighth Route Army smashed them in Linxian. When all the Notquite Nius heard that several thousand men of the Fortieth and New Fifth Armies had crossed the Zhang river and were heading north, they were just getting ready to spread the news when they learnt of their capture by the Eighth Route Army in a Japanese strongpoint. Instead they kept quiet. But the fact was plain to see, and they could not suppress news of the victory. As soon as the village cadres heard the news they were delighted, and they gave it a great deal of publicity. From then on there was a general change of view. Even the people who had previously believed Notquite's talk about a change of regime now realized that it was his regime which had collapsed. In these much happier circumstances Meng Xiangying's work naturally went more smoothly than ever.

Unfortunately that autumn brought the worst of a string of disastrous harvests. No rain fell throughout the summer, and the crops were so dry you could almost have lit them like matches. The ears of millet that autumn were like gong-mallets with things like wax tapers a mere inch long on them. The maize did not even reach the height of a man's thigh, and half an acre yielded scarcely enough to fill a small basket. Then there were weeks on end of rain and dull days in the autumn, so that not a grain of millet was harvested. The weeds grew taller than the crops.

The government urged everyone to gather wild plants to eat during the famine. When the village cadres discussed this, Meng Xiangying was put in charge of organizing the women. Everyone in the village was depressed by the bad harvest, and some were even saying, 'We can't possibly survive after all these years of getting no crops in, so why should we bother gathering a few handfuls of leaves?' Meng Xiangying went to every house to encourage the women. 'We won't die, but we'll have to eat if we're not to,' was the sort of argument she used. Another was, 'It won't be any good trying to gather wild plants once autumn's over.' A third was, 'A mixture of wild plants and grain husks is better than husks alone.'

Besides talking, she took some of the keener women to make a start at the work. It now appeared that when some of the families without any food had said they would rather be left to die in peace they were only giving vent to bad tempers, because when they saw the courtyards of Meng Xiangying and her helpers filled with wild plants they went out gathering too. Meng Xiangying organized the women into four teams that went separately into the mountains every day. Within a week all the edible leaves had been stripped from the trees on the mountains nearby and were drying in the women's courtyards. When the area round their village was exhausted, they went to other villages; and when there was nothing left west of the river, they went east of the river. They went on until the autumn winds blew all the leaves from the trees. By then the twenty or so women had gathered some forty tons of leaves.

When they had finished gathering leaves they heard that a local herb could be sold for a dollar a pound, so Meng Xiangying now organized the women to collect it. Organizing this was easier because the huge piles of wild food that every family had meant that nobody was thinking now in terms of dying of starvation. Everyone was reminded of Meng Xiangying whenever they saw the leaves, so that no sooner did she mention organizing the women to gather the herb than everyone in the women's families said, 'Go with her. That girl knows what she's doing.' They gathered over ten tons of the herb, which brought in more than 20,000 dollars.

8 *Dividing the household*

It has been said that because Meng Xiangying could work to beat the famine, her mother-in-law and husband turned over a new leaf. On careful inquiry this turns out to be quite wrong.

Mother-in-law had no objection to eating the wild leaves Meng Xiangying brought back, but she disapproved of her going out to gather them. 'She's luring a gang of young women to go out.' 'Going out' originally had two meanings. There used to be a vicious kind of coal-mine boss who would buy workmen 'to the death' (which meant that if the man did anything wrong he could be beaten to death) and keep them locked up at the bottom of the pit, only letting them out to see the sunlight once every five or ten days. This was called 'going out'. The other kind of going out was when a prisoner was let out from his cell into the prison yard. Being locked up again in his cell was called 'being put away'. Meng Xiangying's mother-in-law was not totally against her going out, as was proved by the way Meng Xiangying used to go to the fields for harvesting and thinning seedlings when she was first married. The mother-in-law's idea was that she should be the one to decide when Meng Xiangying went out and when she was put away. According to the old rules, if a young wife went out of the house on her mother-in-law's orders she had to be back within the time set. If she asked to be allowed out, it was up to the mother-in-law to give or refuse permission; and even if permission was given, the daughter-in-law still had to have a careful look at her mother-in-law's expression before she went. She could be beaten, scolded, or given no food if she was late back. By the old rules it was unthinkable that Meng Xiangying should organize all the women in the village. This was why her mother-in-law felt that she could not possibly be allowed to go out like this.

Several other mothers-in-law shared such ideas. Notquite Niu's wife used this chance to spread a rumour that eating wild plants was no remedy, with the result that some of the older women would not let their daughters-in-law go. Meng Xiangying had to call the women to a special meeting to look into the matter before the rumour could be quashed.

After the tree leaves and the herbs had been gathered Meng Xiangying summed up her achievements and her mother-in-law did the same. Instead of adding up how many wild plants and herbs Meng Xiangying had gathered, the mother-in-law's summary was that she was less and less like what a daughter-in-law should be. In her view, a daughter-in-law should be like this: her hair should be combed as straight as a broom handle and her feet should be as small as lotus-leaf cakes; she should make tea, cook, husk millet, mill flour, offer soup and hot water, sweep the floor, and wipe the table clean. From the moment when she started the day by emptying the chamber-pots till she set the bedding out at night she should be at her mother-in-law's beck and call, without wandering off for a single moment. She should hide whenever she saw a stranger, so that outsiders would never know you had a daughter-in-law unless you told them yourself. This was how she felt daughters-in-law should be, even though she had not always lived up to it in her own youth. She felt that Meng Xiangying was getting further and further from being a model daughter-in-law: she wore her hair in a bun; her feet were getting bigger every day; she climbed mountains all the time; and, as if it were not enough for her to go rushing around her own village, she went off three or more miles away at times. Instead of discussing things with her mother-in-law and keeping some of them from the worker, she told him everything. As the mother-in-law made this summary she thought gloomily, 'What am I to do? I can't beat her, I can't swear at her, I can't control her, and I can't sell her. She won't regard herself as a member of the family much longer. Anyone would think the worker her own father.' After many sleepless nights she finally thought of a solution: to divide the household.

She asked Notquite Niu to be the witness to the division. It was a fair one—if it had not been, Meng Xiangying would probably not have agreed to it. Meng Xiangying and her husband took two-thirds of an acre of level land and the same amount of sloping land, but they did not get any grain. 'It's all been eaten,' her mother-in-law said, 'because we harvested so little.' After the division the husband went back to his mother's house to eat and sleep, which left Meng Xiangying free to go her own way by herself.

9 *Meng Xiangying's influence spreads beyond the village*

After the division, in which all the food she got was less than three pounds of turnips, she had nothing to eat but the wild plants. As she had no grain at the New Year, she borrowed nearly three pounds of millet, seven of wheat, and one of salt.

As the district government office is some fifteen miles away they could not oversee work there, and, besides, local cadres were very hard to find. The district Women's Association found it most unreasonable that someone as good as Meng Xiangying was both at working herself and at organizing others to beat famine should be driven from home and left to go hungry. Besides, it hindered work throughout the district. They asked higher authority for permission to issue her with some grain to help her out, and kept her there to organize some of the Women's Association work at the district level.

Meng Xiangying has been a most successful district cadre this year.

In the first month of the lunar calendar she was chosen as a labour heroine, and she came to the Fifth Sub-region's Labour Heroes' conference. As she was passing through Taicang Hamlet on her way back, the head of the Women's Association there asked her what lessons she had learnt about how to organize women. 'When there's trouble, explain the rights and wrongs,' said Meng Xiangying. 'Lead by doing the work yourself, and set a good example.' She went on to talk at length about organizing the women to unbind their feet, gather firewood, carry water, collect leaves, and pick herbs. Following her example the head of the Taicang Women's Association led the women of her village in digging a canal over a mile long and clearing two and a half acres of waste land.

On the fifteenth of the second month Meng Xiangying did some campaigning at the temple fair in Baishan Village (some thirteen miles from Xiyaokou). The women from many villages all thought her methods were good. This year the women in the seventh district of Shexian county have worked very hard at food production, and of the very many labour heroines many became heroines as a result of her influence.

Her own achievements have been even more remarkable. In the spring she organized the women to hoe 93 acres of wheat and dig two acres of level land as well as seven and a half of hillside. In the struggle against locusts that summer they cut over ten tons of grass for burning to smoke them out. There is no need for me to go into her other achievements—harvesting wheat, loosening the soil, raking with branches, stripping the twigs of the paper-mulberry tree, and gathering wild plants to eat—because it has all been reported in the press.

10 *Some questions*

Why are Meng Xiangying's mother-in-law and husband still on such bad terms with her? Is it because she walks too steadily now that her feet are a natural size? Is it because she does so much work that there is not enough left for them to do? Is it because she has loosened the soil too far? Is it because she has taken all the edible leaves from the trees?

Her mother-in-law has never made any such announcement.

I have not written about Notquite Niu or Meng Xiangying's mother-in-law and husband very respectfully. Am I giving them no chance to change in future?

Meng Xiangying is only twenty-two this year. Another chapter can be written at the Labour Heroes' conference every year, so we'll see who has changed for the better and who for the worse.

Gao Langting 高朗亭
[Kao Lang-t'ing]

Reminiscences and stories about the revolutionary struggles of the past are a popular form of writing in China today.

The author of this story was one of the founders of the Communist guerrilla movement in Shensi province in 1930 which, after learning the lessons of a number of defeats, was strong enough by 1935 to hold a firm base area in the north of the province where the various Red Armies from central and southern China could re-establish themselves and prepare for the war against Japanese aggression.

Huaiyiwan

A story of the North Shensi Guerrillas

In 1932 the landlord militia of Huaiyiwan under its commander Qiu Shukai was stationed in the goddess's temple that stood on an isolated hill. It would have been hard to capture their arms by direct assault.

That February we had just been defeated in an ambush in the Heng Mountains. We had no weapons left at all and only one dollar between us. Of us revolutionaries only Gao Wenqing, Liu Shanzhong, and myself were left. We sat on a sandy wall and wondered what we were going to do.

'I used to be a soldier in Yenan,' said Gao Wenqing, breaking the silence. 'There's a place there where I've got friends. We could go and join the army there. They won't know about what's happened here. We can work up a mutiny, take a few rifles away with us, and start up again.'

I agreed before he had finished speaking. Liu Shanzhong's reply was, 'Let's think it over.' After a discussion we said we would do it.

When Liu Shanzhong brought up the question of travelling expenses I fished out our last surviving dollar. 'That won't be enough,' he said. 'We'll have to think of something else.'

'As it's February third by the old calendar it'll be warmer by the time we get down there. I won't need this coat any more. If we can sell it for three or four dollars we'll be able to manage.' As he spoke Gao Wenqing grinned, bent down, and picked up his coat, then looked straight at us as he waited for our answer.

After two or three minutes' silence I looked up and said, 'Very well then. We'll cope when we get there. I don't think we'll die of starvation.' Liu Shanzhong laughed too and got up.

On the afternoon of the seventh we reached Huaiyiwan, found an inn in the main street that served food, and put up there. After a simple meal we sat and talked.

'Do you want any more, gentlemen?' asked the landlord, a tall man of about forty who came in and greeted us. Although this was an ordinary thing for an innkeeper to ask he said it as if he really meant it. Comrade Liu Shanzhong stood up and invited him to take a seat. The innkeeper offered his pipe round with both hands for each of us to smoke.

'Is business good?' I asked, to start the ball rolling.

'It's lousy. I only earned enough last year to keep myself fed. I couldn't afford any clothes.' He stroked his black moustache in a rather odd way with his right hand and sighed.

'Is business difficult now, then?'

'There's plenty of trade, but there are too many extra taxes. Of the forty dollars profit I made last year they took over twenty-eight.'

'What about this year?'

'They haven't sent the demands out yet. The commander and the local gentry have been discussing them for several days at Paijiawan, so I expect they'll soon be sending them.'

'Perhaps they won't be so bad this year.'

'Of course they will. They've been worse each year for ages now. Why should they be any better this year?'

'How big is your family? How much land do you work?'

'I've only got an acre or so of my own. That's not enough. But the rent for a landlord's land is too high: a year's crops aren't enough to cover it. There'd be nothing left for me to eat when I'd paid it. Apart from the terrible levies on this inn I have to pay out yet more tax on my land. They say it'll be fifty dollars for each tax-unit this year. I haven't got a hope.'

He struck a light and took several fierce pulls at his pipe. 'Things have been getting hopeless recently. The big landlords are demanding enormous rates of interest on loans. Last year my donkey died and I had to buy a new one. I hadn't enough money, so I had to borrow ten dollars from a landlord at eight per cent a month. In the six months since last March the interest alone has mounted to four or five dollars, and in a year interest and capital will come to a full twenty.'

'That's a terrible rate of interest,' I put in with a sigh.

'Never mind that,' the innkeeper said, not waiting for me to finish. 'Last May I had a demand for fifteen dollars security levy. They hounded the life out of me. Commander Qiu's men came to dun me for it, and, when I was a bit slow at letting them tie me up, one of them hit me. The two of them with guns forced me to go with them to the landlord's to borrow twenty dollars, and not a cent of it touched my hands. They took it all away with them. When I signed the contract with this other landlord he insisted on eight per cent for every ten days. When I complained that it was too much he demanded the money back at once. What could I do? They'd already taken it.' As he spoke his eyes began to redden.

'Cheer up, grandad,' said Liu Shanzhong and I, trying to console him. 'We poor people are going to stand on our own feet.' Slowly he looked up at us.

'What do you mean, stand on our own feet? With Boss Tuo of the Jiang family, and Commander Qiu, and all the landlords round here, nobody can stand on their own feet. If you can't pay the high interest all you can do is. . . .'

The door burst open and in ran the boy who had urged us to eat there in the first place.

'Come home, dad. The landlord's men have come to ask for the money you borrowed to pay for the mountain sacrifice last March.' The innkeeper sighed, frowned, and slowly got up. Then he took leave of us and led the child out with a heavy step.

As evening drew in the innkeeper's son came in with a linseed oil lamp that he put on the edge of the *kang*[1]. As soon as he had left there was a knocking at the door of the shop next door.

---

[1] A brick bed-platform that can be heated from underneath in winter.

'Have you any oil? Can you let me have some?' shouted the voice at the door.

'Yes, wait a moment.' After this reply came the sound of the door being opened. 'Why are you wanting oil at this time of day?'

'We're smoking opium at White Cabbage's place.'

'Who else is there?'

'Commander Qiu's officers. I wouldn't be fetching oil for anyone else.'

'Is the commander himself back yet?'

'Not yet. Got a packet of Hadamen cigarettes?'

'Yes. It'll cost you five hundred cash.'

'Let me have it quick. I don't care what it costs.'

The shutting of the door was followed by hurried footsteps echoing away.

'If the commander isn't at home the rats will be coming here whoring,' Liu Shanzhong muttered to himself.

'Let's take a chance and deal with him,' I said, looking at Kao Wenqing.

'What?' he asked quietly, with alarm in his voice.

'Qiu's younger brother was at the Normal School with me. We got on well, and I know something about their background. We can disguise ourselves as travellers, go to the barracks while the commander's away, and find some chance to capture the militia's rifles. What do you think about it?'

'Wouldn't it be safer to go to White Cabbage's place first and capture the officers' guns?' suggested Liu Shanzhong, turning to me.

'No,' I replied. 'If he's gone whoring he won't necessarily have one with him. And if he has got one he'll certainly be on his guard in a place like that where there could easily be trouble. I doubt whether we'd find it at all easy to get it.' The other two nodded in agreement. We all sat there in silence, our heads in our hands. When I'd thought it out a little further I went on with my proposal. 'We should go there in the daytime pretending to be the commander's friends. They'll have no reason to be suspicious of us. At some time when they're not expecting it we'll give each other the wink and seize our chance.'

'What'll we do if the commander comes back?' As he

thought things over Gao Wenqing asked this and other similar questions.

'We won't wait till then,' put in Liu Shanzhong, not waiting for me to speak. 'If we go we can't be longer than three or four hours. If we see an opening we'll act; otherwise we'll have to leave. As long as the commander's away we'll have the initiative. We'll only strike if we're certain of success, and if we're not we'll leave. What do you think, Langting?'

'Very well then.' I turned to Wenqing and asked him what he thought.

'We've got to do it,' he said, 'there's no doubt of that. The problem is how.'

'We'd better think our method out carefully. The cleverer it is the better.'

The discussion came to an end. We packed our simple luggage, thinking about the coming day.

The morning of the eighth was extremely fine. We had our breakfast, bought two packets of Hadamen cigarettes, and set out from the inn. We crossed the river and climbed the hill, heading for the goddess's temple.

'I wonder whether we'll be walking back or whether we'll be carried back,' joked Gao Wenqing, rubbing his eyes.

I gave that remark a serious answer. 'Walking, of course. Before we attack them they won't dare to try anything on us.'

'But we must be careful,' put in Liu Shanzhong. 'None of us must show even a hint of nerves.' We looked at each other and nodded, then sat down near the defence works to get our breath back.

There were no sentries at the barracks gates, which were shut.

'Open up,' I shouted, stepping forward and knocking on them.

'Who's there?' came the answer as a door opened inside the compound.

'Me,' I replied in a friendly voice.

'Who do you want to see?'

'The commander.'

'He's out.' The voice from inside was gradually coming closer to the gates.

'When will he be back?'

'This evening, or tomorrow at the latest.'

'Please open up, then. We'll wait for him. We have important business to discuss with him.'

'How many of you are there?'

'Three of us.'

'Wait a moment while I tell the lieutenant.' As he spoke his footsteps faded away. Two minutes later we heard more footsteps returning. The men gave the barracks gates a heavy shove, undid the chains, and opened them. Two oddly-uniformed men came rushing out, each with a rifle on his shoulder.

'Have you come to see the commander, sir,' asked one who was wearing a brown scarf round his waist.

'Yes,' I nodded.

'How do you gentlemen know our commander?' asked the other one. He was wearing black clothes with white puttees and a sash.

'When we were serving under General Su together.' As I spoke a third man came out. Over his unbuttoned black clothes that revealed his chest he had thrown a black-patterned satin jacket. An old-fashioned sharkskin spectacle case, from which fluttered a piece of green silk, was sticking out of his pocket. We examined this new arrival.

'Please come in and sit down. I must apologize for not coming out to escort you here.' Before we had even reached the gates he was greeting us in this way, his faced wreathed in smiles.

'May I ask your name, colonel?' said Liu Shanzhong, flashing his white teeth in a grin.

'The name's Qiu.'

'He's our lieutenant,' explained the soldier in the brown scarf, not waiting for him to finish.

'Forgive us. It's a great honour,' we said almost in unison, going on to chat politely about the weather.

'As you gentlemen are all strangers to me I beg you to enlighten me about yourselves.' At this suggestion from Lieutenant Qiu we each introduced ourselves. He very courteously allowed us to go inside first.

Lieutenant Qiu took us to their office, which was also their bedroom. The first things we saw when we went in were two rifles hanging on the wall with their ammunition belts. It

looked as though there were five or six clips in the two of them.
There was a padlocked brown box on the floor, and woollen
rugs from Yulin were spread on the *kang*. The middle-aged man
in a long gown, who was sitting cross-legged on it, rose to his
feet to greet us when he saw us coming in, and then sat down
again on the *kang*.

'This is the commander's cousin, our instructor Mr. Zhang,'
said Lieutenant Qiu, introducing us to each other, after which
we all sat on the *kang*. Two soldiers with guns stood on the
floor beside us, lighting our cigarettes and pouring our tea.

As we drank our tea we talked about our 'deep friendship'
with Commander Qiu. As we went on they became more and
more convinced and treated us with ever greater respect. The
two armed men took off their rifles and ammunition pouches,
hung them on the wall, and left the room one after the other.
The lieutenant and the instructor became very informal with
us, treating us as if we were members of the family.

While we were gossiping with them we exchanged glances
with each other, and, under cover of going to the lavatory,
we agreed to get them into one of the living caves during the
midday meal and then strike. We had spied out where the
guns were: apart from the four in the office there were another
two hanging on the wall above the *kang* in the mess.

We had been talking for over three hours.

'Food's ready, sir; where will you have it?' asked a cook.

'Bring it in here,' was the lieutenant's laconic reply.

'No need,' we interrupted, 'we'll eat in the mess. It's warmer
there and it'll save our friends the trouble of rushing about.'
The cook hesitated, waiting for a decision, and after trying to
resist our suggestion several times the lieutenant finally agreed.

'Very well then, set the table on the *kang* in the mess.' This
order given, the cook went out. We lit our cigarettes and continued the conversation. Before long one of the privates
appeared to ask us to come along for the meal.

When we got to the mess the food was already on the table.
The lieutenant pressed us to eat first, but we insisted that everyone should eat together. After more polite refusals we all finally
sat down round the table. Several militiamen stood around the
room to wait on us.

F

As we ate the three of us exchanged glances. Before we had eaten our fill we put down our bowls.

'Please carry on. We're going inside to rest.' I stood up, took my leave of the lieutenant, and stepped off the *kang* with the other two.

'Yes, that's all right, you go in and . . . smoke. We'll be along in a moment.' The lieutenant had his bowl in his hand and his mouth was full of food that he had not had time to swallow, which was why his reply came out a few words at a time.

We went back to the office in the barracks. The four rifles were still hanging quietly on the wall, and there was nobody else in this cave. Our eyes opened wide and we grinned as we exchanged glances. Gao Wenqing was the first to jump on the *kang* and take down a German rifle. He tried the bolt action lightly a few times and then pressed in a clip of ammunition. He jumped off the *kang* and ran back to the mess.

'Don't move. Hand your guns over and no harm will come to you,' he shouted, kicking open the doors to the cave in which was the mess, pointing his rifle at the members of the militia as they ate. I was close behind him, and while he was shouting and keeping them covered I rushed in sideways with my head ducked down, jumped on the *kang*, and grabbed the two rifles and ammunition pouches from the wall.

'Sir . . . sirs, are you going to . . . hurt us?' asked the lieutenant, the instructor, and the privates as they raised their hands, their faces pale with terror.

'We won't kill you if you hand your weapons over without making any trouble,' I replied, taking the guns from the wall. I slung one of them over my shoulder, kept the other in my hands, and put the two ammunition belts round my waist. Then I turned to them and asked which of them kept the key to the box in the office.

None of them said a word. They looked at each other.

'If you don't tell us we'll shoot you one by one right here.' I added in a harsh voice.

'I . . . I've got it,' said the instructor Zhang, pulling a key on a chain from his wallet and handing it to me with a trembling hand. I leapt off the *kang* and rushed back to the office. As I ran in Liu Shanzhong had just gathered up all the guns and ammunition from the office and was clattering out with them slung all over him. We ran straight into each other. I went past him into the room, opened the box, and found that, apart from account books and other pieces of paper, it contained a roll of silver dollars over a foot long and twenty-nine bank-notes. I took them all and ran back to the mess.

'Whose money was it in the box?' I asked the militiamen.

'Three of the notes are the cooks' . . . and about a dozen of the silver dollars . . . were for provisions. The rest . . . were, were the taxes collected the day before yesterday.' Instructor Zhang was in a great hurry to get his answer out.

'How much of it in fact was for provisions?' For a long time this further question produced no answer. When we were growing impatient I changed my tack: 'Would fifteen dollars cover it?'

'Well . . . yes . . . no. . . .' Zhang would not come out with the exact amount. I counted out three notes and fourteen silver dollars, put them on the edge of the *kang*, and said, 'We don't want the cooks' money and the food money. Here it is.' Not one of the cooks said a word as they looked at us with their pale faces.

'Here's another forty dollars—five dollars' demob gratuity for each of you,' I continued, counting another forty out and putting them on the edge of the *kang* too.

'You're very generous, sirs.'

'The guns are public property and anyone is entitled to use them. We don't want your money.'

'Please take it with you for travelling expenses.' At last they all began to talk.

'Listen carefully,' I said with vigour. 'We, my friends, belong to the Red Army that is led by the Communist Party. We work for the poor and only kill crooked officials, evil gentry, and local bosses. We don't touch even a needle or a thread of the poor. You too are hungry, unemployed, and oppressed, so we have no intention at all of harming you. If you want to come and join the Red Army with us you can do so later, and if you don't want to do that you can go back home and farm. Whatever else you do, you must stop working for the bad gentry and the landlords and oppressing ordinary folk like yourselves.'

'Yes, yes,' they all agreed.

'Goodbye, friends, we're off now.' I stepped outside and locked the door of the cave. The three of us danced happily towards the barracks gates with the muffled voices of the militiamen in the cave still audible:

'Goodbye, Red Army sirs.'

'Thank you, Red Army sirs.'

We fired off three rounds on the little hill where the goddess's temple stood to celebrate our victory. Then we three lads left Huaiyiwan heading southwards with our six guns.

Under the Party's leadership these three men and their six rifles developed through several phases and despite a number of setbacks to become the Twenty-seventh Red Army at the end of 1934. It is now a guard regiment in the Border Region.

Sun Li   孙犁

One of the finest Chinese writers to emerge in the 1940s, Sun Li came to literary maturity during the Anti-Japanese War as a cultural worker and journalist in central Hopei, where he began to publish poems, essays, sketches, and stories. The necessities of war forced him to be concise, a habit that, unlike some other writers, he did not lose in the easier conditions after Liberation. Having spent so much of his life until then in the countryside in and around his native county of Anping he knew the peasants well, writing about their struggles with insight and sympathy; unlike some writers he does not condescend in his treatment of them. His admiration for the spirit of peasant women and girls who shouldered so many of the burdens of the war and fought another campaign— for their own freedom—at the same time is reflected in many of his stories.

Yet despite his own rural background and his work in the villages as a school-teacher before the Japanese war and a cadre from then until the 1950s, Sun Li describes the peasants as an observer rather than as one himself, like the cadre from outside in 'The Blacksmith and the Carpenter'. This piece, an example of what the Chinese would classify as a 'middle-length story', was the result of six months the author spent in a village in Anguo county in 1952. As he said in an interview in *Chinese Literature*, 'I drew the plot from life, and Old Li, Old Fu, Six, Nine, and Man-erh (Manr) were all based on real people. . . . Some episodes, though, were taken from my own childhood.' By strict political standards he would be criticized for concentrating on middle (that is, neither good nor bad) and backward characters, presenting them as rather more glamorous than the activities on whose efforts the future of the village depends. Class struggle is shown indirectly through the clash and development of personality. But the story has a charm and an honesty that is hard to resist, and it has value as a study of what is more formally labelled the spontaneous tendency to capitalism in the countryside in competition with the growth of the collective spirit after land reform. Other writers have dealt with this problem in its more dramatic aspects; Sun Li shows us the forces at work in an ordinary, unspectacular way as a few individuals choose between the easy, selfish life and the hard work needed to build a new society.

The second part of the story, if it has been written, has yet to come out. In it the author planned to carry the account on to the high tide of agricultural co-operation in the middle 1950s. Until 1963 at least ill health prevented him from doing so.

Another translation of this story, by Sidney Shapiro, has been published in *Chinese Literature*.

The Blacksmith and the Carpenter
First Part

I

What leaves the deepest impression from childhood? If you were brought up in the countryside in the old days conditions were hard and there was not much cultural life. You would only see an opera once in several years and might not hear the gongs and drums of ballad singers in your village from one year's end to the next. So there wasn't much for children to amuse themselves with apart from the fields, the grave-mounds, the ruined kilns, and the willow copses outside the village.

The banging of axe and chisel in someone's yard would bring crowds of children running in. A carpenter, hired to build a new cart or put up a door, would place the piece of timber he wanted to plane against a wooden wedge, then he would bend over it and send the shavings flying up from his ever-moving plane like strips of silk before they fell beside the bench. The moment the children ran over to pick them up the master of the house, who was supervising the job, would shout,

'Clear off and play, children.'

But the hissing of the plane was bewitching and the carpenter's skill fascinated us. Besides, there were the flames rising above the wall from the wood fire where he used to boil his fish-glue and straighten timber. We couldn't tear ourselves away from this crackling fire, which was more attractive than ever if the carpenter was working at the beginning of winter as he usually was.

In the end we had to drag ourselves sadly away. The marvellous sound of axe and chisel would echo outside the courtyard, and the fierce flames would go on burning before our eyes. When I was a child I often wondered ridiculously when our family would be able to hire a carpenter. If I mentioned this ambition when we children were eating our supper back at home my father would reply angrily.

'Hire a carpenter? We couldn't afford it in a hundred years. If you're lucky it might happen in your time. Otherwise I can send you as an apprentice to Old Li, then you'd be able to spend all your time with axes and chisels.'

Old Li Dong was the only carpenter in the village. He was a tall fellow with a brown beard and a pock-marked face. It seemed most unlikely that I could be apprenticed to him as we children knew he was not taking anyone on. None of his six sons were carpenters; like all the other children they spent their days with baskets on their backs collecting beanstalks in the fields.

Yet hope never dies, and there were, besides, many other ways of enjoying ourselves. In late spring or early summer there would be more clanging, and a roaring stove would be set up in the village street. This clanging sounded even more heroic and the fire was even more splendid. They could be heard and seen from far away. The blacksmith Old Fu and his stove were back in the village.

They came at the same time every year, like the swallows who nested on the roof-beams. Just before the wheat harvest and the busy period in the autumn, he tempered sickles, hoes, and spades and also made everyday objects for the peasants. As soon as he came everyone brought out the things that needed repairing and the scrap-iron and steel with which to do the job.

Old Fu Gang was known as 'the handyman'. He was about fifty. His thin, dried-up face looked like the tongs he held in his left hand and the hammer he held in his right; it was the colour of the anvil he used to put on a big tree-stump. His short beard looked like rust. He stripped to his waist, round which he tied an oilcloth apron that sparks had honeycombed with holes over the years. Tattered pieces of cloth protected his feet from the sparks that flew when he hammered hot iron.

Old Fu had two apprentices. The elder one swung the

hammer, put water on the whetstone, and sharpened knives, while the younger pulled the box bellows and cooked the meals. Even when his face was streaming with black sweat, the younger apprentice would still pull away at the puffing bellows with his head held high and one foot planted firmly in front of him. The children clustered round him would show their heartfelt admiration for his noble attitude to his work.

'Watch out!' When the smith brought a piece of red-hot iron out of the furnace he would quietly warn the children. They scattered, followed by the sparks that flew in all directions to the clanging of the hammer.

The children would have stayed there watching for ever if their parents hadn't come to collect them. They didn't even know what it was they liked seeing: was it better to watch a door-hinge or a chain being made? Childhood! What worlds do you remember when you look back on it reflectively?

The blacksmiths worked in the village for over a month each year. They got up early and went to bed late. In the morning, when everyone else was still wrapped in a quilt, you could hear their hammers in the street, and their furnace would still be burning long after dark. At night they slept beside their stove without any kind of shelter or tent over them. Only when it was raining steadily did they tidy up their wheeled stove and go to somebody's house.

They usually went to Old Li the carpenter's place. Old Li was very poor and his wife had died leaving him six children. A few years earlier he had hardened his heart and sent the eldest to learn a trade in Tientsin, entrusting several of the others to the care of relations and friends. Then he had put his tool-box on his back and gone off to the North-east. In those distant parts he learnt and suffered a lot, but he came back empty-handed. After that he took some of his children to live in the spare courtyard of someone's house, and life was harder than ever.

Old Li was a sociable fellow and he knew from his own experience about the hardships of being away from home. As his friendship with Old Fu was a very deep one he called him not 'handyman' or 'Old Gang' as some of the other older people did but 'relation'.

On rainy days the blacksmith's forge was moved to his court-yard, where they worked in an old husking shed. To thank his 'relation' Old Fu would always find the time to mend Old Li's carpentry tools, tempering or sharpening those that needed it. Old Li repaid this help on his slack days by changing the handles of Old Fu's hammers and repairing the box bellows.

Although they always called each other 'relation' you could not say what exactly it implied. Was it because one of Old Li's sons had taken Old Fu as his godfather or because two of their children were betrothed?

People would sometimes ask them, 'Are you relations by marriage or adoption?'

'By adoption,' the loquacious and cheerful carpenter would say. 'Any of my six sons you choose can call you godfather.'

'By marriage would be fine too,' replied the blacksmith, a man who didn't talk or laugh lightly. 'I've a daughter at home.'

But whenever he mentioned his daughter his face would immediately darken like red-hot iron being put into a bucket of water. His wife had left him this young daughter when she died.

'Bring the girl here next year,' said Old Li one evening when the two of them were sitting in the shed and smoking. As Old Fu had said nothing Old Li brought the subject up, knowing it was the only key that would unlock his old friend's tightly sealed lips and allow the sorrows hidden in his heart to come flowing out.

'It'd be another mouth to feed,' said Old Fu, his head bowed. 'Daughters are such a nuisance.'

'What about me? I've got six children,' said Old Li, unable to hold back his tears.

Although they understood each other so well when they talked like this it was hard to go on. Although each wanted to help his friend in his troubles they realized that there was in fact nothing they could do, and merely to console each other seemed pointless.

At this moment Old Li's youngest son, Six, asked his father to come to bed. Old Fu looked up at Old Li and said, 'I think Six has the most spirit of all your sons, and he's the brightest too.'

'I'd like you to take him as your apprentice one day.' Old Li hugged the boy. 'Is your girl as old as he is?'

'How old is Six this year?' Old Fu asked.

'Eight,' Six replied.

'That girl of mine is eight too,' said Old Fu. 'As she's a head shorter than you she should call you "elder brother".'

2

The next year, when the wheat was ripe, Old Fu did indeed bring his daughter with him. He made a seat for her on the side of his handcart. The seat was, of course, very small, and she clung to the cart with her right hand as she sat cross-legged on an old cushion. They had been travelling for five or six days, staying in small inns and getting covered with dust. But she was very excited because she was going to spend a long time with her father, her only relation. This made her very happy.

As soon as they reached the village they went to Old Li's house. Old Li was delighted. He invited all the little girls who lived nearby to come and play with his young guest.

'What's your name?' the girls asked.

'Nine,' she replied.

'Have you got eight big sisters?' they asked.

'No, there's only me,' she answered.

'Then why are you called Nine?' The girls were puzzled. 'Here you're called after your place in the family, like Six who's the sixth son.'

'I was given my name when my mother was alive,' the young guest said with some embarrassment. 'I was born on the ninth of the ninth month.'

'Oh.' The other girls now understood. 'Are you allowed to wear a plait where you live?'

'Mm.' She was rather shy. A dazzling red thread bound her heavy plait.

After playing with these girls for a few days she made friends with Six. She realized that Six and she were as close in friendship as were their two fathers. As it was difficult for Old Fu to have his daughter with him when he was busy he made Six and Nine a little shovel each one night for gathering firewood. Old Li fitted handles to them, and then sent them off into the countryside every day. Six would stride ahead with a big basket of red thorn on his back and his shovel in his hand. Nine would follow close behind carrying a slightly smaller basket, and they went deep into the wilds.

Six disliked gathering firewood from village to village; he was like an explorer always wanting to go where others rarely went. Though he covered such great distances he didn't work properly as he wasted so much time walking. If he startled a nesting bird it skimmed across the ground and came down again as if it were leading him on, and Six followed it for flight after flight. Sometimes he chased a half-grown rabbit, thinking that he could catch this one, but he always failed.

'We'd better hurry up and get some firewood,' Nine urged him.

'What's the hurry?' said Six. 'We can fill a basket before we go back tonight.'

'Shouldn't we fill two baskets each?' asked Nine.

'Even if we filled three every day we wouldn't become rich,' Six scolded her severely.

He walked slowly through the grass looking carefully at the ground, made a mark, and watched it. Later he threw his basket down and called to Nine, 'Watch this hole and don't let it get out this way.' He went back to the place he had marked, bent down, and started to dig fast with his shovel.

To their delight they caught a short-tailed field mouse, which they put in a little wooden box when they returned home that evening. Carpenters' houses are always full of wooden boxes.

As the next day was very windy they played at Six's home instead of going out. When his father had gone off to his job Six took the mouse out and said to Nine:

'He must be fed up after being in the box all night. We ought to let him run around on the floor.'

'What'll we do if we can't catch him again?'

'It'll be all right as long as we block the drain.' Six put the mouse on the floor. At first it crouched at his feet without moving. When Six hissed and pushed it with his foot it ran round the room, then suddenly disappeared down a hole.

'See if there's any water in the vat,' Six ordered Nine anxiously.

It was dry. He seized the scoop, rushed to the salt vegetable jar, scooped out some brine, and poured it down the mouse-hole. When it had no effect he went to fetch some more.

'Uncle will tell you off when he comes back,' said Nine. 'Salt is very expensive.'

Six flung the scoop to the ground and smashed it.

The two of them had not enjoyed themselves at all. Six was very sad at the loss of his mouse, and Nine, brought up in a poor home where she never spoilt a needle or a thread, was worried about the scoopful of brine.

The wind blew fiercer and fiercer. They took shelter in the tumbledown husking shed, in the middle of which lay a large stone husker that was rarely used. Nine sat on the dust-covered base of the husker and Six climbed into the empty rotary winnower, curling up like a shrimp with his head upwards and going to sleep.

'You come in too,' he said to Nine, 'there's room for you.'

'No,' she said, being sensible. The wind was blowing so hard outside that the sky was blackened and the cobwebs in the roof were shaking. A huge spider was blown down then scurried back. Nine had no mother, and her father was working outside in the gale. Her new friend was asleep in the winnower. The memories of childhood stick in the mind, and even if you find yourself one day in a tall skyscraper surely the picture of that afternoon in the poky husking shed will appear before your eyes.

3

The Anti-Japanese War began that year. It swept across the plain as the first great storm to rock the foundations of the old way of life. From that year onwards the trials of war taught the new ideas of class struggle, and the suffering masses, including the sons and daughters whom they had previously regarded as a burden and impossible to bring up properly, began to smash the visible and invisible chains that had been passed down for generations. Two of Old Li's older sons joined the army.

In the chaos of war Old Fu the blacksmith could not go home at the usual time, and as his daughter was fortunately with him he was most unwilling to run the risk involved in the long journey at this time. Apart from helping on the land, the blacksmith and the carpenter had to do their bit for the war. It was not long before Old Fu's two apprentices joined an Eighth Route Army arsenal. That winter Old Fu and his daughter shoed the horses for the growing numbers of cavalry who were always passing by. Nine worked with a will. Once, when she was watching some soldiers leave, an ill-tempered horse kicked her on the forehead. It left a tiny scar. A medical orderly had bandaged it for her there and then; she never even cried. Everyone agreed that, far from spoiling her looks the scar made her more attractive.

In storms, gunfire, hunger, and cold, and in the excitement of struggle and victory Six and Nine ended their precious years of childhood. Old Fu was on good terms with the people of the village and everyone in the neighbouring hamlets knew him too. When he had to flee for safety the women would offer to look after the girl. Whichever village he went to people would care for the blacksmith's daughter, feed her, and give her somewhere to sleep. In the last two years of the war, with better harvests and more experience of guerrilla fighting, Nine always liked to travel with Six. Six, brave and careful, took good care of her. When they were together Nine, now just beginning to grow up, felt not only happiness at having a companion to give her courage but also another emotion quite close to it. As she never ran into any great dangers when she was with Six she sometimes believed his boasts.

'Don't go with anyone but me,' he often said to her, 'because the Japs keep clear of me.'

'Nonsense,' said Nine, following close behind.

'Stay with me and you won't go hungry or thirsty,' said Six with confidence. 'I'll get you food like a sparrow.'

Six seemed to Nine to be very clever. If it rained he always found her somewhere to shelter; even in the wilds she did not get wet. When she was hungry he would go a long way to find her something to eat. Many people were hiding in the wilds at the time and they all helped children. More importantly, her gratitude and happiness could overcome temporary hunger or cold.

After the Japanese surrender the blacksmith was eager to take his daughter to visit the home they had been away from for so many years.

The evening before they went Old Li fetched a jug of liquor to give Old Fu a send-off. Normally Old Fu was taciturn even when he was drinking, while the words would pour out of Old Li's mouth the moment alcohol touched his lips, like the Yellow River bursting its dikes. But this evening Old Li could only produce a few everyday remarks as the two old friends sat with a vegetable-oil lamp and the jug of liquor between them. In the end he bowed his head and said nothing.

This was very strange, so Old Fu asked, 'Is something worrying you?'

'Yes.' Old Li cheered up; he had been waiting for this question. 'There is something I want to ask of you. I've got six sons, and poor as I am I can't hope to do anything for them. But I think Six may have some promise.'

'You've spoilt him a bit,' interrupted Old Fu. 'Children should be brought up strictly.'

'You're right.' Old Li was in a hurry to say his piece. 'To put it frankly, I'm quite sure that Six and Nine could get on very well together. But how could a man as hard up as I am keep a daughter-in-law?'

He finished the bottle with one gulp and bowed his head again.

'I see what you're driving at,' said Old Fu, 'but if you're hard up I'm no better off.'

'But if you bring up a daughter you want to make a good marriage for her,' said Old Li, his head still bowed.

'The children are still young. Let's arrange it when we come back from our visit home.' With these cold words Old Fu ended what should have been a heart-warming talk. His old friend was chilled to the heart.

That evening Nine said good-bye to her aunts and grannies who lived nearby. The girls all stayed with her, and after visiting one house they all went in a group to the next. Six tagged along behind.

'Why are you following us?' the girls asked. 'You're a boy, and the guerrilla days are over.'

'He's saying good-bye to Nine,' some girls said.

'Go back to bed this minute, Six,' scolded some of the old ladies.

'I will come with her,' thought Six, 'and I won't go to bed. It's none of your business.'

Nine talked and joked with the others all the time.

The next morning Six and his father got up early to help Nine and her father pack their cart. In the dark shadows Nine whispered to him,

'We'll come back.'

4

There was no news of Old Fu and Nine after they went. It was said that their village was in an area occupied by Chiang Kai-shek's bandit troops. The next year the Liberation War was fought over the plains and many great things happened. In the land reform Old Li won as his share quite a lot of good land as he was both a poor peasant and a soldier's dependant. When his second son was killed in the Liberation War he was given some grain as compensation, and after the liberation of Tientsin[1] his eldest son who had been in business there brought him some money. His standard of living improved. When he heard of his second son's death he was sad for a time, remembering how everything had been difficult for the boy from childhood; he had even had to take his four brothers begging after their mother's death.

Old Li was now nearly sixty, and of his sons only Four and Six were living with him. For some reason that escaped him he was not very fond of Four. Six was his favourite. The old man thought that as he himself had led a hard and unsuccessful life, and as his older sons had never known good times when they were little, he should let Six enjoy himself now that they were better off.

Six was being more spoilt than ever. Although he was now grown up he did not want to go and work in the fields like Four, and he refused to have anything at all to do with such jobs as mucking out the pigsty. As he didn't enjoy pure idleness

[1] In January 1949.

he became a small trader. After the autumn harvest he would hull and roast peanuts to sell in the street, and in winter he cooked bean-curd and beat clappers at the cross roads. What he couldn't sell he ate himself. When his father was in bed at night he used to fill a bowl with bean-curd, add some shallots and ginger, and place it by the old man's head.

'Have some, Dad, it's hot.'

As the old man sat up and swallowed it he thought how understanding and good to him his son was.

Sometimes Six made a bowl for Four who fed the animals at night, but Four, frugal from childhood, never accepted any. 'Every bowl you sell,' he would say, 'means so much more earned. I don't need a bowl when I'm just going to bed.'

This made Six think that his brother was unkind. Whether he was selling peanuts or bean-curd Six never made any money. He had far too many friends in the street who would take a handful of the one or a bowl of the other, and even if they put it on account Six could never bring himself to put on a stern face and ask them to settle up. It was always Four who had to collect the debts at the end of the year. The girls were particularly bad. When they saw Six they took some peanuts and asked:

'Are they crisp? Do they taste good?'

'Try some,' said a grinning Six, hurrying to open his sack. Tasting was free and there were so many girls to dip in and take a big handful. On top of this Six would put them into their hands and stuff them into pockets that may have had small entrances but were very deep inside.

As Six was good-looking with a light complexion and a pleasant temper all the girls in the street liked him. Aware of it himself, he did all he could to strengthen and extend this good impression. When the war ended he was the first to let his hair grow with a parting. Instead of having it cut by the itinerant head-shaver he went to the hairdressers by the southern gate of the country town every market-day. At night his was the only electric torch in the village, and when he flashed it down the street giggling girls would surround him and say,

'Hey, Six, you're dazzling me.'

'Here, Six, let me have a go.'

When it rained he would put his Double Coin brand rubber shoes on specially to go visiting in, making a point of visiting the houses where the girls were pretty and the pools of rainwater in the yard were deep. When a girl saw through the window that he was coming she would scramble off the brick bed and say,

'Six, you've come at just the right moment. Take them off and let me wear them to go to the lavatory.'

'They'll suit you,' Six would say, taking the shoes off to give her. 'You should buy yourself a pair.'

'Where would I find the money?' the girl would say with a grin. 'Next time you go to town bring me back a pair of socks.'

'What colour?' Six would ask.

'You decide. You're always buying things and you have a good eye,' the girl would say, trustingly feeling in her trousers. 'Here's the money.'

'Don't bother,' Six would say, 'give it to me when I bring them.'

When he brought them back the girls would praise him for getting the colour and the size right but they never mentioned the money.

5

Old Li was too busy worrying over his newly revived business to take Six in hand. Recently he had replaced his old grey donkey with a chestnut horse. Although it was rather long in the tooth it was in very good condition, but when harnessed to the broken-down cart that had been allocated to him at land reform it didn't look right. He hunted everywhere and bought some elm and locust-tree trunks with which to make himself a cart. His carts were well known far and wide, and now, after a lifetime of building countless carts for others, he was very happy indeed to be building one for his own children. When he was travelling around buying wood he even bought a sapling of sandalwood, the carpenter's favourite tree, which he planted under his window and tended with great care. It marked the beginning of his new life. His yard was full of chickens, and he bought two more piglets for the sty.

He made Four help him strip the branches from the tree, and afterwards they propped them up in the yard like anti-aircraft guns. With the old man up above and facing downwards and Four sitting on the ground and looking upwards they took it in turns to pull the big saw down the inked line. Old Li was always getting at Four: if it wasn't for going askew it was for pushing the saw back wrongly. When Four suggested that Six should do some sawing the old man refused, which made Four say that he was unfair and started off a quarrel between himself and his father. The old man sometimes even chased Four round the yard with an adze.

Four hated being called stupid. Ever since the Anti-Japanese War he had been studying hard, reading books and papers, and going to evening classes every night. He was active in village youth work, and regarded himself as far better informed and more progressive than his father or Six.

The old man could not bear silence after a quarrel.

'When I was your age,' he said, 'I had already finished my apprenticeship. Nobody could match my skill in Harbin in the North-east where there were Japanese and Russian carpenters, let alone in this country. That was what the Russians, the rich Soviet people used to tell me.'

'They weren't Soviet then,' said Four, 'they were White Russians.'

'I made the screen in the guest room of the Accumulated Wealth Bank by the south gate of the county town wall. The big medicine merchants from Yunnan and Kwangsi praised those flowers in particular as being really well carved.' The old man became more and more excited as he spoke. 'That was the name the Bu family traded under. I was on very good terms with the boss.'

'But wasn't the Bu family overthrown by the poor peasants' league?' said Four. 'You can only say things like that at home. If you say them outside people will accuse you of having connections with landlords.'

'I made the sedan chair for the Cuis who live in Back West Street by the southern gate,' continued the old man. 'It was only used when the old lady went out.'

'They were big landlords too,' said Four. 'That sedan

chair was allocated to a poor peasant who uses it for moving dung.'

The old man pushed the saw down so hard that he nearly knocked Four backwards.

As the building of the cart drew near to completion, Old Li thought more and more of his friend Fu as there was some ironwork to be done before the cart could be finished. There were of course other blacksmiths nearby, but they were not good enough for Old Li. In the old days he and Old Fu had often made carts together. Their carts, it was said, made such a thunking noise on the road that you could tell from a distance that Old Li had cut the axles and made the joints and Old Fu had fitted the iron rims to the wheels. Old Li very much hoped that his old friend could come and help him make this cart perfect, as a worthy specimen of their many years of co-operation and a symbol of their deep and unchanging friendship. As there was plenty to eat and drink in the house these days he decided to send Old Fu a message asking him to come and bring his daughter with him. The children were the right age, and the way things looked now he was in a strong position to suggest a marriage again.

But he heard that they were still fighting over there, so he couldn't send a message.

When he thought of the wedding his mind turned to the question of where they were to live. The tumbledown compound he was staying in now would not be nearly big enough for the children to live in together even if it was true that the village had decided to give it to him permanently. He felt ashamed if, at his age, he still couldn't find a few rooms for his children to live in. This year the summer and autumn harvests had both been good, so he decided to put all his grain together and buy a house with it. He had previously wanted to use it to buy more land but he had heard that land wasn't very secure these days, whereas a house was always your own under any social system. That was why he decided to buy a house.

Four suggested that they should discuss the matter with his elder brother in the army, but Old Li said, 'No. He's a revolutionary cadre and disapproves of our making a good living.'

He commissioned a middleman in the village to assess some houses for him. Soon afterwards the middleman said that the widow in the back street wanted to sell hers. It had three northern rooms, whitewashed earth bricks, strong wooden doors, windows, and structure, and a big yard round which other rooms could be built. There was only one door at the moment. It was cheap at ten bushels of wheat. Besides, it was so close to where Old Li was living now that it would be easy to get there.

When Old Li thought it over he found the house very satis-factory and was going to pay a deposit. The widow made a condition that the new owner was not to move in until she died. Old Li was hesitant on this point as the widow looked very healthy and nobody could know how long she might live. Before long the middleman came back with the news that a nephew of the widow's was also after the house and had offered twelve bushels. This alarmed Old Li who paid the deposit and had some trouble with the nephew until, as the dependant of an army martyr, he was enabled by village arbitration to buy it.

Now that he had bought a house Old Li had much to worry about. Every few days he would go to look at it. If someone else's chickens were in the yard he drove them out. If children had broken the wall by climbing on it he built it up again. If the plaster on the walls fell off he mixed together some more and put it on. He cared about every little detail of the house, while the old widow didn't seem to take any interest at all as she wheezed and coughed on the brick bed in the eastern room.

That winter Old Li wanted Four to move into the western-most of the northern rooms there and take the animals with him, putting the horse trough outside. When he discussed it with the widow she would not agree to it, saying that the horse might drop its dung into her cooking pots. Their quarrel made her so angry that she packed up and moved to her daughter's. She put the word around that Old Li had forced her out, which made a very bad impression in the village. Even his son in the army heard about it somehow and wrote to his father criticizing him.

Old Li regretted this for many days and felt that he had brought trouble on himself. But as he had bought the house he

might as well move in, and on an auspicious day he, Six, and
Four moved into their new home. People wanted him to give a
feast and he had to comply.

Six always came back late at night, and Old Li would wait
up for him.

'Why did I buy this damned place,' said Old Li, 'if it wasn't
for you?'

'Mm.' Six buried his head in the quilt. 'Why is the new house
so cold?'

'You ought to behave properly,' Old Li warned him. 'You
shouldn't run around like that all day.'

Six was already sound asleep. His snores were even and
comfortable, a sound that the old man loved to hear. Old
people always feel happy to have a young son sleeping sweetly
beside them.

6

That same winter Six got together with a family of layabouts
in the village to sell beef dumplings. Every evening he wandered
up and down the main street with a wooden case on his back.

'Beef dumplings. Hot beef dumplings.' He carried on till
late at night.

The dumpling shop was in Idiot Li's house at the western
end of the village. Idiot Li's wife was the eldest daughter of a
disreputable family that lived off prostitution and gambling
near the eastern gate of the county town. She was born ugly.
Her left foot was crooked, her face was dark and pock-marked,
she had been blind in her left eye since childhood, and she had
a protruding growth on it. She was cunning by nature and not
even the new society could reform her. She was also very greedy,
and to satisfy her appetite would think up all kinds of strange
and original schemes.

Idiot Li was completely under his wife's thumb. From the
Anti-Japanese War onwards they had squandered everything
they had been allocated in all the political struggles. They
exchanged the land and the coarse grain that fell to their share
for wheat to sell as noodles, with the result that capital and
interest alike disappeared into their stomachs.

Selling dumplings this year with Six, Idiot Li's wife did not want to take on such light jobs as kneading the dough and making the casings. Before long she brought a younger sister over from their mother's home, and although she said it was to help with the work anybody could guess what her real objective was.

This girl looked quite different from her elder sister. People said that in the old days she had been adopted from another family and was not born to the same mother.

She was eighteen that year, and her name was Manr. She was married already though her husband had been away for some years. Manr grew prettier every year and she moved like a branch of blossom. Everyone in the county town knew her, and it was generally agreed that she was the most stunning girl in the region.

When she first came to her sister's house Manr behaved very quietly. She rarely went out. Every day, when her sister went visiting, she sat cross-legged on the *kang* chopping up the stuffing and making the dumplings; she rarely even raised her head. Idiot Li went to and fro in the room filling the cooking trays and looking after the stove. Six had nothing to do, so he used to sit on a bench at the foot of the brick bed and gaze at Manr with a cigarette between his lips. When her sister came back at night and Manr asked her what she would like to eat she always said at once, 'Why ask? Boil up some soup and we'll have dumplings.'

'You'll eat here, won't you, Six? You don't need to go home,' said Manr.

'Why bother to ask him,' said her sister with a smile. 'He's our partner so of course we must look after him well.'

Six was now here day and night, getting up to no good.

Manr gradually became restless as she sat on the *kang*. Every day she would find time to stand in the doorway. When she moved to her sister's house someone had put the news about, with the result that the pedlars who sold cosmetics and scented soap all followed her to the village. Three or more of them would put their loads at her sister's door, and if she did not appear they shook their pedlars' rattle-drums to a subtle and bewitching rhythm until they lured her out.

Later on she would go along the street on the pretext of

husking grain. Whenever she went out husking the tiny village was thrown into confusion. If it wasn't yet her turn to use the roller she left a brush beside it to show she was next and went straight back home. Young men gathered round the roller in increasing numbers, making the person who was pushing it round at the time feel most awkward.

When the roller was vacant the young men would go and tell her. A moment later Manr came out of the alley where her sister's house was, drawing all their eyes towards her. Their expressions were of every kind: some were bold and some were timid but they were all lit by passion and wild desires. They burned like an endless string of fire-crackers.

On her head Manr carried a big tray that she supported with one hand while she walked towards the roller as if nobody else were there. Her modish new flowered jacket showed its red lining when the wind blew up the front flap; the bell bottoms of her padded trousers brushed rhythmically against each other. Her embroidered shoes moved across the ground so smoothly and lightly that they seemed to leave no footprints.

Her empty hand moved to and fro as if she were dancing; it was as soft as if it had been made of dough. Her face was slightly flushed, and so as not to appear to be panting she kept her glistening lips tightly shut. She had undone the buttons at the neck of her jacket.

She went down the long street like a victorious general passing along the ranks of the troops he had to inspect. Some of the young men took a few steps backwards and others climbed to the top of the slope on which the wall stood to look down on her beauty from above.

When she reached the mill roller she turned round to put the tray on the ground. Then she stroked the shiny black hair that reached down to her shoulders and cast a glance over the young men.

She had come to husk millet, so she spread the grains out on the base of the mill and waited for her sister. When her sister did not come, as she had been delayed by something, she started to push the mill roller round herself.

She knew perfectly well that she would not have to do it

alone. But today although the boys all watched, postured, and even pushed each other none of them had the courage to come forward.

Whenever her turns of the mill roller brought her round facing the street she looked towards the western end of the village to see whether Six was coming. She very much hoped that he would. He had more sense than all these ninnies and was bound to come and help.

But Six seemed to have forgotten their arrangements: there was no sign of him. She could push the thing no longer, but not wanting to seem weak in front of the young men she pretended to have finished, stopped, went back to sweep up the grain, and turned round to pick up her tray.

'I don't think you've done it well enough,' said a young fellow called Dazhuang who was standing right at the front.

This youngster, Dazhuang ('Strong'), who was in fact extremely timid, could bear the sight no longer. He took pity on her, summoned up his courage and grabbed the empty pole for pushing the mill roller. This most uncharacteristic action so astonished all the other youngsters that they forgot to tease him as they usually did. Suddenly there came from the eastern end of the street a shriek like the strident and terrifying scream of a solitary woman woken from her dreams one winter night by a weasel among her chickens.

This was Dazhuang's wife. He had married very early and she was eight years older than himself. She had been obliged to put up with him for a very long time, and as he gradually grew up she had loved him the more and looked after him more strictly. He was usually very frightened of her, as scared as he was of his own elder sister or even his mother. He carried in his memory the years she had not only taken care of his food, drink, and so on but had even taught him how to speak and behave. But Dazhuang had never imagined that if he had happened to be with some other woman it would make his own wife so furiously angry. He gazed at her uncomprehendingly as he leaned on the pole.

'You shameless beast,' she said as she hurried up to him. 'It's nearly time to make the supper. What are you doing here? Why aren't you fetching water?'

'Uuh?' Dazhuang did not know what to say in front of all these people when his wife was so furiously angry.

'Are you deaf or are you dumb?' His wife's voice was shriller than ever. 'What have you come running over here for? You're nearly seventeen but you still haven't learnt how to behave.'

'He's still a kid. Let him off this time,' said the young men, laughing.

'Still a kid?' Dazhuang's wife hated people to say that her husband was young. 'Then when'll he grow up? Are you kids? A shit-eating baby wouldn't do anything as shameless as that. You're like a pack of dogs who all come out when a bitch goes down the street with her tail between her legs. You stretch your necks out till they're stiff and your eyes are popping out of your heads. I've been watching you for long enough, you filthy lot. If you don't know what you're like draw a bucket of water from the well and take a look at yourselves in it.'

This undiscriminating and confused scolding made the young men very annoyed, though none of them wanted to clash with her at this moment. They glanced and coughed at Dazhuang in the hope that he would pull out the pole, but he put up not a trace of resistance and even started to walk back home.

The boys gazed at Manr as she sifted the grain from the husks, her face the colour of red cloth. In this encounter the girl who had won the reputation in front of so many men of being dangerous when roused hung her head and said nothing.

But a struggle was about to begin none the less. Her sister had appeared at the western end of the street and was rushing this way as if towards a fire or a flood. As she was fat, as one of her feet was mis-shapen, and particularly because she could not see where she was going, she moved like a footballer dribbling into the attack: one moment she would be leaning forward with her arms bent and the next she would trip over herself and go rolling on the ground.

'Who are you calling a bitch?' She issued her challenge to battle when she was still some ten yards from Dazhuang's wife.

'If the cap fits, wear it,' said Dazhuang's wife, thrusting her chest out.

'My sister is a pure young girl,' said Idiot Li's wife. 'Her backside is cleaner than your face. You may be able to push your baby husband around but you can't bully a relation of mine.' She rushed over to the mill roller and pulled the pole out of it. Manr held her back.

'Why've you become such a goody-goody?' she shouted at Manr. 'You're disgracing me.'

She raised the pole and charged at Dazhuang's wife, who being much fresher than her adversary was able to grab it and pull it towards herself, sending Idiot Li's wife sprawling to the ground.

7

At this moment Old Fu and his daughter came back to the village after their long absence.

He was pushing his furnace as usual, and Nine was pulling the cart. Old Fu seemed older and more wizened than ever. His cart was now dilapidated—even its creak was no longer what it had been. Nine was taller and dressed in tattered old clothes. Her face was thin, her hair was full of dust and her shoes were split. Only the pure and warm light in her eyes showed how eager and happy she was to be back.

When they had pushed the cart to the cross roads Old Fu put down the carrying strap and greeted the people around. Nine pulled the kerchief from her neck to wipe the sweat from her face.

'We're back,' said Old Fu. 'But what are you quarrelling about?'

'It's nothing,' said the young men. 'Two women comrades with nothing better to do are practising a few holds on each other.'

'They shouldn't do that,' said Old Fu gravely. 'You've been living in our base areas all along, and that really is like living in paradise. You should have seen our place: life was terribly hard during the Kuomintang occupation. When Nine and I went back it was like falling into a trap. Still, we managed to stay alive.'

'What have the harvests been like in your place?' the young men asked.

'They were picking up again but we had another disastrous crop this year,' said Old Fu. 'You've been having an easy time, so if you don't do things properly you're letting down the Communist Party and Chairman Mao. I've been thinking of you all these years and I'm sure that as this is an old liberated area you must have made a lot of progress. Where's Six? Why isn't Six here?'

Old Fu looked at all the faces then turned round to his daughter. She seemed to have found something to interest her as she stood there gazing at the beautiful girl with the mobile eyebrows who was turning the roller. As she did not know her, Nine thought she must be a new bride.

'I saw Six chasing a pigeon at the north of the village a bit ago, but he's probably gone home now,' said a youngster. 'You should go and see your old relation: Old Li has been doing really well for the past couple of years.'

Old Fu took his leave of them and lifted up the shaft of the cart. As Nine pulled the rope she kept looking back at Manr.

Old Li was delighted to see his old friend again. He took him to the new house to see the cart he was building.

'I've been waiting for you, as you can see,' said Old Li excitedly. 'We can fix your furnace up in the yard here to-morrow. Just imagine how comfortable it is to work in a spacious yard like this.'

'It's very good,' said Old Fu. 'You could have a woodwork factory here without feeling cramped.'

'When this cart's finished I'm retiring,' said Old Li with great satisfaction. 'Transport is where the money is these days. Once the wheels of your cart start rolling you've got a fat wad of bank-notes. My eldest boy has been making a pile since the liberation of Tientsin. Although winter has only just started he bought this coat for me. But I can hardly work when I'm wearing it.'

Old Fu realized that he was rather cold as he looked at his friend's long coat of lambskin covered with fine black cotton cloth. The thought of letting his guest go inside to rest after his long journey did not cross Old Li's mind as he explained in detail his plan for rebuilding the house and took his friend to see the pigsty. Only when he opened the door of the northern rooms to show Old Fu the horse did he let him come inside and sit down.

The two old men had gone inside and Nine was just about to follow them in when she looked up and saw Six standing on the roof and waving to her. He pointed to the ladder that led up to it. Nine climbed lightly up to find Six lying behind some dry branches playing with a flock of pigeons. At the sight of the stranger the pigeons beat their wings and took off. The sun was setting and the red glow from the western sky was reflected on the smooth, whitewashed roof as the brown pigeons and white pigeons flew round above their heads, chasing each other, dipping and soaring.

'I saw you'd arrived some time ago,' said Six, 'but I didn't dare call to you with my father there.'

'What are you keeping all these pigeons for?' asked Nine.

'For fun,' Six replied. 'Yang Maor has just got a pair of pure white foreign ones from Peking, and they're terrific. I wanted to buy them but he won't part with them for love or money.'

'Doesn't the Youth League criticize you?' Nine asked.

'I'm not a member.' Six waved his hands, playing with the pigeons and making them swoop down and fly up again. 'Are you?'

'I've just joined,' said Nine, then she was silent.

'They're very interesting when you get to know about them,' said Six. He stood up and called, 'Pigeons, pigeons.' They landed in order along the eaves as they had been trained to do.

'Who's that girl, Six?' Nine had noticed the girl who had been husking standing on a roof a few houses away and wearing a bewitching smile that she could not understand.

'It's Manr, Idiot Li's sister-in-law,' said Six. 'The dumplings are cooked and I've got to go and fill the box. Let's go down.'

Six did not come home after supper. When Four found out that Nine was a Youth League member he said with great excitement, 'Have you brought your credentials with you? You can come to our study meeting this evening.'

'I brought them with me,' said Nine with a smile. 'I'd love to come to your study meeting. Do you have a job in the Youth League branch?'

'I'm responsible for propaganda,' said Four. 'As it's so sandy round here and we never have enough spring rain, the League has called on us to bore wells and plant trees so as to change dry fields to irrigated ones. It's a marvellous idea, but there are still a lot of people in the village who don't understand.'

'Only bloody you do,' said Old Li. 'I wish you didn't give me such a bad name in the village.'

'Why hasn't Six joined the League?' asked Nine.

'Search me. He says his brains aren't good enough and meetings give him a headache. But does he look like someone without brains?'

'You must help him,' said Nine. 'It looks to me as though his mind is on other things.'

'It might do more good if you talked to him,' said Four with a sigh. 'He's got no time for me. I'm nobody at home.'

'Stop talking nonsense.' Old Li was scolding him again. 'Where does that great prestige of yours outside here come from?'

'It's good for youngsters to be progressive,' said Old Fu, trying to soothe him. 'If people weren't like that you couldn't possibly be living as well as you are.'

'You're right,' said Old Li. 'The times are always moving ahead. But we should live the old way.'

8

As Nine was so concerned about Six, Four suggested that they should go and talk to him together. Four fed the animals, asked the two old men to look after the house, put together the documents he was to study, and went out with Nine carrying a small oil lamp.

'Why are you taking an oil lamp?' asked Nine.

'It's the Youth League study lamp. We don't keep it in the hall so that no oil gets wasted there.'

The word 'oil' brought Old Li shouting to the windows:

'Four! Have you filled it with our oil? Is your Youth League a paupers' league? Who ever heard of providing the lamp oil yourself for work? If you're nobody at home it's thanks to that oil.'

Four did not reply, but when he had taken Nine out he

stopped in the street and said, 'I don't know whether Six has come out to sell his dumplings yet.'

Six was not selling them that evening. Instead of his clear voice came Idiot Li's ear-splitting shout—'Beef dumplings! Hot beef dumplings!'

When Four asked him where Six had gone he answered rather offhandedly, 'Goodness knows. I'm not his boss.'

At the western end of the road they heard Six's voice coming from a big threshing ground outside the village. As the gates were ajar they could vaguely make out many trees growing inside and several piles of firewood. Under a tall willow by the wall Six and a girl were standing close to each other.

Nine stopped at the gates, but Four impulsively pushed them open and went in shouting, 'Six!'

The girl shot sideways as if something had run into her.

'What are you shouting for?' asked Six in a quiet and angry voice.

'What's up?' Four did not keep his voice down. 'What's so secret?'

'Stop yelling!' Six was even more furious.

Four shut up. He struck a match with a sudden scraping noise, lit the oil lamp he was carrying, and held it above his head, throwing its light all around.

'Heavens!' Six rushed forward, blew it out, and said, 'Why ever must you light your paupers' lamp all over the place?'

'So you're up to something you want to keep in the dark.' As he spoke Four walked round the tree. He collided with Manr who was hiding behind it and the two of them started to quarrel.

'You've done it.' Six stamped and there was a cooing sound in the tree. 'The pigeons have got away.'

'Only one's gone,' said Manr who had stopped quarrelling to look up into the tree. 'Shut up, all of you.'

The pigeon that had flown away, of whichever sex it was, missed its mate and circled in the night sky before landing in the tree again. Six now told his brother in a quiet voice that Yang Maor's foreign pigeons had escaped and they were trying to catch them.

By night the willow tree seemed to touch the stars, and its

bark was as smooth as a woman's skin. Six had taken off his shoes and socks and was spitting on his hands before climbing it.

'Don't risk your life: it's very dark,' said Four. 'I'm going home to fetch dad.'

'Stop laying on the big brother stuff,' said Manr. 'If it's worth three hundred thousand dollars[1] to catch one you can work out what two are worth, you great scholar.'

Nine could not bear it. 'You shouldn't take risks like that, Six.'

'Marvellous,' said Manr, smacking her lips. 'The girl who loves you has spoken.'

'Who are you?' said Nine. 'I don't know you, so why pick a quarrel with me?'

'Don't bicker,' pleaded Six. 'Don't startle my pigeons again. Pigeon, pigeon!' He was soon up in the fork of the tree.

'Let's go,' said Four to Nine. 'There's nothing we can do. If he falls and kills himself it'll be because he was fated to, and it'll serve him right.'

Nine went off with Four. She was very angry and worried.

'They seem to be a pair.' Manr dragged her words out.

'What's that?' asked Six from the tree.

'I was talking about the pigeons. They're on the southern branch.'

Four and Nine could hear Manr saying all kinds of frivolous things as she stood under the tree, urging Six on to dangerous deeds.

9

Nine met the village Youth League members in a landlord's house that had been confiscated during the land revolution. Many of them who had known her before asked with great interest about what had happened to her. Four lit his lamp and called them into the western room. This had originally been three rooms but they had now been made into one that was used by the Youth League and the village opera group. It was very cold. The windows had been smashed, the patterned paper on the roof beams hung down in cobweb-covered tatters, and

[1] Roughly £5

one of the doors was missing. On the north wall hung a small blackboard in front of which was a broken-down and oil-stained table. The floor was covered with long heaps of local bricks and dried mud which might have been meant for tables and might have been meant for chairs. If you sat on them it was cold, particularly for the girls, whose clothes were very thin, but they sat quietly on them all the same.

Four and a youngster called Guozao were the instructors. They looked after the lamps and explained to the Youth League members how to publicize well-boring and afforestation among the ordinary peasants. After an introductory talk there was a discussion.

It was now late at night, and even colder inside the room than outside, but the earnest discussions continued.

'Comrades, we must make our village rich and prosperous,' said Four. 'When that time comes we can build a really good hall so we won't have to hold our meeting in a cold room like this.'

'You're getting off the point,' Guozao warned him. 'What we're considering now is how to deal with the difficulties we've met in our publicity work.'

'In my opinion there are two big obstacles blocking the way forward for our village,' said Four, getting back to the point. 'One is Li Seven's rubber-tyred cart: the quick money you can make in transport tempts people to look no further than the end of their noses and encourages selfish capitalism. The other is Idiot Li's dumpling shop where all that loose behaviour makes people less keen on work. If our publicity is to be successful we must stop Li Seven from carting and put an end to Idiot Li's dumpling trade. Otherwise we'll be wasting our breath. They'll make solid profits and we'll achieve nothing.'

'I agree,' said Guozao. 'In the first place Six is your own brother, so you should tell him to get away from that bad company; and in the second place your father is building a cart to make his fortune. These two obstacles are in your own home, so you'd better tell us how you're going to deal with them.'

'The trouble is,' said Four sincerely, 'that my father won't take any notice of what I say. When I ask him if he's against the Party's call he says he's all for it. But when I suggest boring a well this winter he says we're too busy. That's my problem. Of course, I'm not giving in.'

'Let me help you,' said Nine. 'I don't agree that old people can't be talked round. When we were at home my father liked me to tell him about the new ideas. As for Six, we must help him make progress.'

'Yes!' The girls sitting behind her had said not a word for ages, but now they all shouted together as if they were being conducted in a choir.

'Helping Six is another problem,' said Guozao with a grin. 'That girl Manr has a much stronger pull on him than the Youth League.'

The girls objected to this view.

'If you don't believe me, just try dragging Six away from her.' Guozao stepped down from the platform.

After the meeting they all went home singing, and Nine was taken away by the other girls to spend the night with them. Guozao came from a big family that lived in a small house, so in the winter he often spent the night with Four. This way they could study and argue together. They went back to Four's place, fed the animals, shared some cold sweet potatoes left on the stove from breakfast, and wriggled into their quilts.

'My quilt's freezing,' said Guozao with a grin. 'It's tough for us with no firewood to burn to heat the *kang* bed and no wife to warm us up.'

'Overcome the cold,' said Four, breathing in the cold air. 'If we want to be bachelors we must overcome difficulties.'

'Do you think we really have to be single?' asked Guozao. 'I don't think we should rush into a decision on that.'

The chestnut horse was eating hay in the next room. Although its teeth were old they rang like iron as it chewed. The two youngsters were soon asleep, bathed in the clear moonlight that came in through the window.

10

Six and Manr were still in the empty threshing ground. Six had caught the pigeons long ago, and when he slid down from the tree Manr dragged him to a pile of barley straw. They

G

buried themselves in the soft, warm stalks. She pulled out some red string, tied the wings of the foreign pigeons, and fondled them happily, making them kiss and cuddle up together.

'When I sell them I'll buy a padded jacket,' Six said to her, 'as part of the present I should have given you when we first met. Besides, you've helped me a lot.'

'Our friendship isn't based on food and clothing,' said Manr earnestly. 'Buy one for that girl Nine.'

'Why?' asked Six.

'Because her face is so black,' said Manr with a laugh. 'She really is a blacksmith's daughter.'

'She works hard,' said Six, 'and she's a Youth League member.'

'What if she is!' said Manr. 'I belonged to the Youth League when I was at home. They criticized me, so I came straight to my sister's place. And there's nothing special about hard work in a girl.'

'What is special in a girl then?' Six asked.

Manr threw her head back with laughter. Six looked at her face, more beautiful and seductive than ever in the moonlight, and soon found the answer.

As a heavy mist rose before dawn, shrouding the trees and flowers covered with frost and snow, Six and Manr finally decided to go home. They stood up, brushed the straw dust out of their hair and clothes, and discovered that one of the precious foreign doves had been crushed to death under Manr's body. It was a crested cock pigeon, and Six was heartbroken as he held it in his hands. At that moment he would have given anything to bring it back to life but its heart had stopped beating and it was cold under its wings.

When they returned to Idiot Li's home the front gates and the door of the house were on the latch. Manr's sister was not shocked at their coming back so late, and Idiot Li did not even seem to hear them, so soundly was he snoring in his quilt.

Manr told her sister how they had spent the night catching pigeons and how miserable Six was because one of them had been crushed.

'That's nothing to be miserable over,' said her sister laughing in her quilt. 'Scald it, pluck it and chop it up and we'll have saved four ounces of beef. On a cold night like this I thought you two must have slipped out for something more serious than catching pigeons. Well, you had better get on the *kang* and slip into my quilt to warm up.'

She slipped out of her warm bedding to crawl naked into Idiot Li's quilt.

When Six left their house at dawn he met the owner of the pigeons, Yang Maor, at the gate.

Yang Maor was a short lad who dressed stylishly. On his tiny, pointed head he wore a felt hat that looked top-heavy. His head was continually moving and his little round eyes darted about very quickly.

'You're up early, Six.'

'So are you,' said Six, hanging his head sadly. 'What do you want?'

'I've come to see you.' Yang Maor thrust his hands into the pockets of the carrying pouch slung over the shoulders of his short padded jacket. 'We're good friends, so give me back my pigeons. When they hatch their first brood this year I'll give you one, and I mean what I say.'

Six did not reply.

'Alternatively,' Yang Maor moved a step closer, 'I've just trained a falcon to catch rabbits. It's flying off hunting at this very moment. I could give you that.'

Still Six said nothing.

'If you want money—though as mates we shouldn't let that come between us—' Yang Maor's lips were trembling and his head was cocked on one side, 'I can manage that. Give me the pigeons back and we can make some arrangement.'

'Some other time,' said Six, about to leave. 'I'm going to get some breakfast.'

'Well!' Yang Maor's eyes were flashing with anger. 'You've always been a good friend up till now. You can't treat me like this! Give me back the pigeons this moment or else you'll be stealing them.'

'What do you mean, stealing?' Six stopped and turned round to ask.

'Stealing my pigeons and stealing a married girl too.'

'Have you seen me doing it?' asked Six.

'Other people have, and even if they hadn't I'd expose you,' shouted Maor.

'Go ahead. Who cares?' Idiot Li's door opened and there was Manr. She had obviously only just dressed and tidied herself up; and her make-up was not properly on yet. She was leaning on the door-post with her hands behind her back looking at Yang Maor. 'I'd like to see you show us up. What proof have you got? Have you caught either of the parties in the act? Tell me! Don't come round here with your filthy talk this bloody early in the morning if you don't want a clip round the ear.'

Yang Maor, who had never seen so beautiful a woman as Manr in all his days, was stupefied by her pink and white face. He hopped forward like a sparrow in the snow, moving his feet but not his body and craning his head forward. His appearance was now the very opposite of his name Maor ('Mortise'). He was just like a sharp wedge being driven into a piece of wood by the carpenter's hammer. He looked Manr up and down from top to toe over and over again, drinking in her scolding like a guilty religious believer receiving divine reproof.

But then her voice that was like music in his ears stopped. She slammed the door and went back inside.

II

Yang Maor used to be a pedlar in needles and thread. In the old days he went to Baoding every winter to buy some of the things women need at the New Year and other festivals, which he took by train to sell in the hill country. There were some amusing stories about his dealings in the Western Mountains and they all had a very strong romantic flavour. But in all those years he had not made a fortune; he had nothing left from those days but a little blue-glazed earthenware pot.

A few days earlier a cadre from the provincial government had arrived in the village with an introduction from the county authorities. Whatever you thought he might be, he certainly seemed to be a senior cadre. When the question of where he was to stay was being settled he made the village cadres feel that there was something odd and unnatural about him. The usual thing would have been for such a cadre to ask to stay with a village cadre or an activist, which would have made both contacts between them and security easier. What gave the local cadres some misgivings was that this cadre wanted to stay with an ordinary family, and said that he wanted to see the backward as well as the advanced aspects of the village. They thought that he must be making secret investigations as part of a special mission. The deputy village head, used to eccentricity, did as he requested and took him to Yang Maor's house.

Yang Maor was a single man, and at first he gave his guest a warm welcome, clearing him a space, albeit a cold one, on the *kang*. As the cadre was not strong a small coal stove was lit in the room.

'Comrade Yang, couldn't we borrow a kettle and boil up some water instead of letting the stove burn for nothing?'

'No need to borrow it—I've got one.' Yang Maor produced the water-pot from the wooden cross-piece under the table, filled it from the vat, and placed it on the stove.

'Can you boil water in that porcelain pot?' the cadre asked.

'That's what's so good about it,' said Yang Maor. 'It's a porcelain glaze over an earthenware paste. It boils water fast and doesn't leak like an earthenware pot.'

But the top of the stove was already soaked and hissing vigorously. At first the cadre thought that there must still be water on it from the vat, but when he picked the pot up later and looked at it he saw a number of cracks in the bottom that had been widened by the heat. Apart from losing water it was in danger of being ruined by the fire. The cadre said,

'It's no good, Comrade Yang. It really leaks. It's useless.'

'It doesn't leak.' Yang Maor glared at him. 'If I say it doesn't leak it doesn't.'

'But it's obviously leaking,' the cadre said.

'It won't do for you to stay here. You must move somewhere else.' The cadre was mystified at being given his marching orders so abruptly.

He showed Yang Maor the big drops of water leaking from the pot and falling into the stove with a hiss.

Yang Maor did not even turn round to look.

The cadre could only roll up his bedding and find the deputy village head who had taken him there to tell him what had happened.

'Comrade,' said the deputy head with a smile, 'you wanted to see the backward part of the village, and Yang Maor can probably be regarded as a good example. I can give you some details on his background and life-story because I used to go trading with him when I was young. As you can imagine, it was extraordinarily difficult to be the partner of a chap like that. He was stubborn and quarrelsome; he fiddled the accounts, and would suddenly lose his temper and treat you as his enemy. But as he knew the Western Mountains and the way there very well, I put up with it and went along with him. Every year he came back only when he was flat broke. The reason why he went broke was not because he was greedy, lazy, or crooked but because he put so much into his grand passions. When he went into the mountains he was like a hunter going into the forest: his only interest was looking for a sweetheart.

'Whether a woman was pretty or ugly depended entirely on whether she suited him. With him everything that's his is good and can't be criticized. Even a dead chicken is a phoenix if he likes it. Every year he had to have one sweetheart. When he found his woman he would go nowhere else but to her village. Even in wind and rain he'd sit selling his wares at her gate. You can imagine how little he could sell in one small hamlet. He sat there until his capital was all gone.

'One winter he discovered another heart-throb. She lived high on the side of a mountain, and from the glimpse I once had of her from the back she wasn't at all bad-looking. She was wearing blue clothes and she had a flower in her hair which she'd combed till it shone. Yang Maor was so bewitched by her that when I wanted to come back in about the last week of the year he was still going to that village every morning and sitting at her door all day. When he was hungry he ate some dry provisions washed down with cold water from that pot. He shook that rattle-drum of his so hard that the skins at both ends wore through but still the woman wouldn't come out. One day he lost his patience. He went in and shook it in her yard just when her husband was coming back from the mountain. The husband drove him out with a carrying-pole and kicked his box of goods and water-pot down the mountainside. Yang Maor rolled down the slope with blood pouring from his head and passed out. I hurried there to rescue him and to pick up his things. When I looked at them I saw that they weren't much damaged except that the water-pot was cracked. "Your pot's broken, Yang Maor," I said. "It isn't," he said angrily. "At worst there's a hairline crack on it." "Yes," I said, "just like the crack on your head."

'That's what Yang Maor is like, comrade. He thinks of that woman to this very day. He says she fancied him and it was only her husband who was in their way. Please don't take it badly: we'll find you somewhere else to live. We've got another backward place in the village.'

12

Old Li now began working in earnest on the ironwork of the cart, and the smith's furnace was set up in the yard of the new house. It was a fine early morning and Six's pigeons were circling above.

Old Li was putting the finishing touches to the cart's body-work. As soon as the ironwork was finished, he thought, he could start painting it. As Old Fu lit the stove thick smoke curled up to the sky then came down into the yard again and dispersed. Nine pulled the box-bellows, while Four had been told to learn how to swing a sledge-hammer.

Old Li carried to the stove the scrap-iron he had been collecting for years, as well as some iron he had bought recently.

Nine was very lightly dressed in a lined blue jacket. To tie round her forehead and bind her hair, she had twisted up a towel which looked like the legendary Monkey's shrinking headband in an embroidered picture she had seen. Her face was brighter than ever and full of devotion to her work while she pulled the bellows lightly but steadily.

As Old Fu took the first lump of heated iron in his tongs and put it on the anvil Four hurried over to wield the sledge-hammer. Old Fu showed him what to do by tapping beside the anvil. As Four was not yet able to hit just the right place with just the right force his blows sometimes landed on the anvil itself and sometimes on Old Fu's little hammer. Nine let go of the box-bellows handle to strike some demonstration blows for him. With her example and help Four began to master the art.

While doing his carpentry Old Li had all his attention on them. He kept scolding Four, going on at great length about how stupid and hopeless he was. When they were taking a break Old Fu went over to Old Li and said:

'Your temper has got terrible, my friend. You shouldn't treat youngsters like that: you'll make his work worse, not better. If you tell him off for all you're worth all the time he's working he won't know what he's doing.'

'What a thing to hear from you,' replied Old Li. 'You're always saying that children should be brought up strictly. This cart means a lot to me, and the sooner it's finished the sooner I can use it to make money. We two must put everything we've got into building it.'

Building a friendship is as hard as growing a flowering tree. It can wither and die because of a moment's carelessness. As Old Li and Old Fu worked together on this job they both came to realize that things were no longer what they had been. When they had worked together for others in the past they had been like brothers, as close to each other as hand is to foot. This time Old Fu had a stronger and stronger feeling that Old Li was not working with him but was supervising him. Old Li was driving him so hard that he even showed disapproval if Old Fu stopped to smoke a pipe. What depressed Old Fu even more was that, although he had made so long a journey to be here, Old Li was acting as if the engagement between Six and Nine had never been mentioned.

In the last few days Old Li had just stood in the yard in a fur jacket inspecting his work and telling him what to do. Six would occasionally wander around the yard dressed in his best clothes and then disappear again. Old Fu, who had not been very well, carried on working conscientiously, wearing a tattered jacket. Some of the people who came to look every day were old friends of the blacksmith's who would at one time have come to admire his and Old Li's skill; today the spectators distinguished between Old Fu's skill and Old Li's business, paying no more attention to Old Li's carpentry. All they were interested in was his prosperous future.

The two old friends were now clearly in different positions, as Old Li was fully aware, and Old Fu soon realized too. This was the beginning of the tragedy. For many years he and Old Li had both hated and mocked the way 'the owner' behaved, but it was now his old friend who was openly acting as the owner, and towards himself at that. This was the fault of the bad old ways, not of the new society.

One mealtime, when the ironwork was nearly finished, Old Li said with a smile, 'Life is getting better for me, my friend. Don't laugh at me, but I've got to save up to buy Six and the others a house. I don't suppose you have to bother about that sort of thing.' Expecting him to mention Nine's marriage with Six, Old Fu raised his head to listen. It came as a shock to hear Old Li continue: 'I've got the impression that you're having a hungry year in your village.'

This last remark made Old Fu furiously angry. He pushed his bowl away, stood up, and said, 'I didn't come here as a famine refugee.'

He told his daughter to put the furnace out by throwing a bucket of water on it. Then he packed his handcart and wheeled it out into the street. Although many people tried to dissuade him, nothing would make the old man go back.

Nobody in the village knew the real reason why the two friends had split up. Four and Nine, inexperienced in the ways of the world, had never known anything so sad. Old Fu, thoroughly miserable, took Four to one side and said, 'Tell me, lad, whose fault is it?'

'It's fine this way,' said Four. 'You've solved a tricky problem for us.'

'What problem?' asked Old Fu. 'Don't you want to see us old fellows happy again?'

'We youngsters want to organize a well-sinking team,' said Four. 'This winter we're going to sink and pipe up the wells we need in this village. We've borrowed a drill already, but a lot of our gear needs repairing. We'd have asked you if we'd thought my dad would have let you. Now you've had a row with him you can help us.'

'Have you got any iron and steel?' asked Old Fu.

'There'll be enough,' said Four, 'we've all given some. Let's take your handcart to the Youth League office's courtyard.'

'We certainly need you, uncle,' the youngsters said when

they got there. 'Don't go back to your home village in Shantung. We've talked it all over with our village cadres; we'll
clear out the east room here for you and re-paper the windows.[1]
We'll bring firewood in every evening to heat your *kang*. You
can make your home here.'

<h1 style="text-align:center">13</h1>

Old Li was sitting by himself on a log in the yard. When Old
Fu had pushed his handcart out through the gates so decisively
he had thought that it would be just as well if such a friendship
came to an end. It wouldn't matter to him: he could find someone else to help him finish the job. Old Fu wasn't the only blacksmith in the world. Old Li took his axe and angrily drove the
nails into the cart's tail-board. But as he calmed down and
heard his axe echoing in the empty yard without a friendly
accompaniment of iron and steel he could not bear to go on
working, so he put the axe aside and sat down. His friendship
with Old Fu, he thought, had taken longer than a year or two
to build, and it had stood many hard tests. He rubbed his left
foot. One year when he and Old Fu were working for the same
family he had accidentally cut his foot with his adze because
he was feeling low. He had been far from home with no friends
near and very little money in his pockets. Throughout the
months while he recovered it had been Old Fu who had arranged for the doctor, bought the medicine, carried him around
on his back, and brought him food and water. He had, of course,
repaid this debt. In the scorching summer that followed Old
Fu had injured himself with some molten iron and he had looked
after him.

The question that troubled him was why Old Fu had broken
off their friendship. Was it because he was jealous of his success?
As he thought it over he realized that Old Fu had never been
that sort of man. Was it because he himself had become money-
grubbing and had treated his old friend shabbily? As he reflected on all he had said and done over the last few days his
sorrow was deepened by his shame.

[1] Traditionally Chinese windows were covered with paper instead of
with glass.

Six came in. Li looked at his son and all he could see was a grey air of uselessness about him. It was all for him that he had wanted so badly to build a cart and a house and had offended his friend. And the boy, who only cared about his own pleasures, had never given a thought for his father's feelings.

'Is the meal cooked, dad?' drawled Six lazily, standing in the sun under the window.

'It's cooked. I'm just waiting for you.' The old man sprang to his feet and went for Six with the axe in his hand.

The sharp-eyed Six turned and ran. He had been quarrelling again with Yang Maor, and Yang Maor who had just found out about the death of the cock pigeon was coming to argue with Old Li about it. Six ran into him in the gateway, hailed him and said:

'Never mind about our business, brother Maor. Please go and calm my father down before he kills me.'

Yang Maor had always been susceptible to flattery or a few polite words. He hastily accepted this commission, hurried inside, and raised his arms to stop Old Li in the gateway.

'Out of consideration for me,' said Yang Maor, 'go back inside and tell me quietly what's wrong.'

He pushed Old Li into the yard, found him something to sit on, and offered him a cigarette. Then he squatted down beside him and said soothingly, 'Hurry up and finish building your cart; don't waste this winter. This is the time to make big money. Look at Li Seven. He makes hundreds of thousands from every trip to Dingzhou. He made enough in three journeys to build a brick house, apart from the cost of feeding himself and the horse. Uncle, there's a brick house for sale in West Village at a fair price. Are you interested?'

'No,' said Old Li. 'I just don't care any longer.'

'All parents are the same,' said Yang Maor. 'They hate it when their children don't try. You were a friend of my dad when he was alive. You know how strictly he brought me up and how much effort he put into it. Even though I can't pretend to have brought him any glory it's only fair to say that I never disgraced him. I'm a straightforward bloke. I've fought injustice wherever I've found it, I'm prepared to have a knife stuck between my ribs for the sake of a friend, and I've never

been tight-fisted with my money. The fact that I've never
achieved anything at all in my time has not been because of
incompetence but because I'm fated to have a hard life. I
think Six is a good intelligent lad. He may be a bit wild, but
that's natural in a youngster. You hurry up and finish the
cart and give it to him. As soon as he has something serious to
do he'll stop running around, won't he?'

Old Li had gradually calmed down, and Yang Maor was
now bringing him back to his old train of thought. At this
moment Four came in and without saying a word he went indoors and sieved two lots of fodder for the animal. He slipped
out again holding something under his padded gown.

'What are you carrying?' asked Old Li.

'A broken spade.' Four had to stop and show him the object.

'Where did you find it? I've been looking for scrap-iron
everywhere in the past few days. Why didn't you tell me about
it?' Old Li flared up again.

'I picked it up the other year when we pulled down the
Japanese fort but threw it down somewhere because it was no
use to me. I'm going to mend it now that the high-ups have
called on us to sink wells.'

'Bloody rebellion everywhere.' Old Li stood up as he spoke.
'Put it back wherever you found it. The high-ups may be
calling on you to sink wells, but I'm calling on you to make a
cart. Old Fu won't work for me, so make yourself a meal then
come and help me with the nails.'

Yang Maor hurried over to calm him down again. Four went
off to fetch some firewood, slowly thinking out another way to
smuggle the spade away.

14

To draw Six into study and work, as Nine hoped to do, was no
easy matter. He would never go near such meetings and activities if he could help it. When cadres went to fetch him he would
say that production was the first priority at the moment, and
would act out the part by slipping off into the fields with a
firewood basket on his back. The cadres had also wondered
whether to start by reforming Manr. She was most approach-
able, but the young men were either too timid to go to see her

or else unwilling to invite suspicion. When women went to see her she always gave them a warm welcome, and if they were holding a child she gave it something good to eat, and hugged it and kissed it all the time. Any baby, no matter how shy or how naughty, was happy in Manr's arms, and the child's face would set off the youthful bloom of Manr's face and make her prettier than ever. Besides, she knew how to talk—when she started to talk and laugh it was as if her lips were oiled—and such encounters made the women comrades rather fond of her, so that their criticisms of her were always much milder than they would otherwise have been.

'Manr! A bright, clever girl like you ought to study. I'll come and call for you this evening. We can go to the night school together.' The women comrades tried hard to persuade her.

'That will be lovely,' said Manr with a smile, 'I've been longing to go and study. There's no need for you to come and call for me, dear: it's a rough road and your lantern isn't very bright. It would never do if you fell over something, carrying the baby. I'll take myself there. I know all the roads and houses in the village.'

'You really must come.' The woman comrade urged her once more.

'I really will.' Manr saw her to the gate and waved to the baby. When the woman comrade had turned the corner Manr's face became serious. When she'd thought it over she went inside and changed, then went into town to her mother's house. Whenever there was some movement in the village and meetings were going on all the time, she would not show her face for days on end. Sometimes she put in an appearance at the night school. She always sat in a dark corner. At the beginning of the lesson, when people had not yet settled down, she pretended to be listening very quietly; but when the others gradually became absorbed she slipped quietly out.

Whether she was living in her mother's or her sister's house she used to roam around outside the village by herself. The night was to her what it was to the birds and animals who are active after dark. On hot summer nights she drifted around like a firefly, unable to control the dreams and impulses that kept surging up in her. She dragged her intoxicated body round the village wall or walked to and fro in a clump of trees on a sandbank far from the village. The night made her very bold. Foxes looking for food on the sandbank often ran past and insects flew into her face or crawled over her, but she still sat there happily, caressed by the cool breeze and soothed by the warm sand beneath her. In winter the raging winds stirred up her wild emotions, and the snow-flakes that fell on her face might have fallen on a piece of red-hot iron.

Every night she stayed out until very late and only came home when nobody else was stirring. With a light and familiar step she came round the village wall and over the fence, then she pushed the door open silently and went to her *kang* without disturbing anyone in the house. She would be up early at dawn, fetching firewood and cooking the breakfast with spirit. Her work never suffered as her youthful vigour was limitless. But she was wasting the precious years of her prime and hovering on the brink of disaster.

Yet her talents were so many. Everyone believed that if only they had been planted in the right soil they could yield a rich crop. No matter how complicated a pattern of cloth or how unusual a type of shoe she could master it on sight and make it quickly and well. Her intelligence was like thin ice in spring or thin paper pasted across a window—penetrated at a touch. When the mood was on her she worked in the vegetable garden watering the plants, and she could rival the strongest boy in the speed with which she emptied the well in a single morning. She could carry nearly a hundredweight of beans in their pods over three miles to market.

At such times some of the older people in the village expressed their admiration for her and hoped that there would be some force strong enough to lead her back on to the right path. When the new Marriage Law was being explained in the village that year she had suddenly become active, going to meetings on her own initiative and asking people to read the papers to her while she thought them over quickly and seriously. The documents explained that women were equal with men, that they had already done a great deal of work, and would be doing even more for the country in future. But when she heard later on that some people wanted to turn the question under discussion into an investigation of sex relationships in the village she withdrew and went back to her dissolute way of living. This was why the deputy head of the village suggested to the youngsters that the senior cadre should be taken to Idiot Li's house.

Manr's mother came to see her that day. She was a woman in her fifties who still devoted great enthusiasm to the way she dressed. From her manner, when she came to see her daughter it looked as though she had been thinking deeply. When she saw Manr she said, 'Manr, your husband will soon be back. Your mother-in-law came to see us. It will soon be New Year, so you ought to go and spend some time at their house.'

'I won't,' said Manr. 'The marriage was arranged by you and my sister, so if you want to finish what you've started, and if my husband's coming back, you two had better pack up your things, get on the cart, and go see him.'

'What the hell do you mean by that?' said her mother. 'People are gossiping about the way you rush shamelessly around the village.'

'I don't care about their gossip,' said Manr, straightening out her shoes and socks as she sat on the *kang* with her head bent low over them. 'Let them chatter if they've nothing better to do.'

'You're getting a bad reputation, my little hussy.' Her mother clapped her hands together.

'I'm not the first in the family to have one.' Manr had jumped down from the *kang* and was gazing into the mirror, combing her hair. 'I'm following your fine example.'

This clash with her mother annoyed her sister, who said, 'Don't talk nonsense, Manr. Whose example are you following? You're not good enough to be my pupil. You had that affair with your Six all winter and didn't even get a new pair of padded trousers out of it. How dare you give us that sauce?'

'Then go and earn me a pair yourself.' Now that she was ready Manr lifted the door-curtain and went out.

She went to her sister's vegetable patch. It was next to the big sandy bank west of the village, and as Idiot Li's family was so lazy it had not been worked for years. The sandbank had by now overrun half of it and the little peach sapling in it had been bent right over by the drifting sand. Manr scooped the sand away with her hands, straightened the sapling, and wrapped its trunk in dry grass. She sat down in a part of the bank sheltered from the wind. A cock was crowing on the bank, and dried poplar leaves fell into her lap. A feeling of misery swept over her; she covered her face and started to cry. In this moment she understood herself, pitied herself, and hated herself. She realized where she stood: she was friendless and had to make her own way in the world. Had she gone wrong up till now? She started to reflect on the criticism and advice that had been offered her.

15

When she saw her sister and her mother leave the village she went back home by a roundabout way. On seeing Idiot Li helping a cadre to tidy up a room she was astonished. She knew that cadres had never stayed with her sister before as she was backward and dirty and had a bad reputation. The room they were tidying up, the inner one of the eastern part of the house, was deep in rubbish; a young donkey was kept in the outer one.

When she saw how awe-struck and uneasy her brother-in-law was in the cadre's presence it was obvious that he did not understand why the village cadres should have brought a high-up to stay in his place. He kept asking the cadre for instructions and moving his things around because he did not know what to do. The cadre's clothes and behaviour did not seem to Manr to fit the room he was going to stay in. From what he was wearing he must have come from at least as far as Baoding. He was particularly demanding about hygiene, and bent his own back to sweep out this place that had not been touched for centuries. For some reason that she did not understand Manr wanted to help him, bringing water in her own flower-patterned wash-bowl and sprinkling it on the dust that was swirling up from the floor.

'Where do you fit into this household?' asked the cadre, straightening his back.

'She's my young sister-in-law,' said Idiot Li with a mixture of pleasure and fear as he stood to one side.

'Oh, you must be Comrade Qi Manhua,' said the cadre,

looking closely at her. 'The village cadres have told me about you.'

'What have they told you about me?' Manr asked, bending low as she swept.

'Not much, not enough to explain someone,' said the cadre. 'While I stay here we will be one big family and gradually get to understand each other.'

When he had laid out his bedding on the *kang* Manr carried in some kindling, swept the stove, cleaned the pot, filled it with water, and said, 'Nobody's lived here for a long time. It's very cold. I'll light a fire under the *kang* for you.'

'I'll do it,' said Idiot Li as he stood beside her.

Ignoring him, Manr boiled the water, poured some into the wash-bowl, then went to the northern room to fetch her own soap and bring it to him.

'Have a wash. Did you bring a towel with you?'

That evening the cadre went to a meeting; it was the middle of the night when he came back. As he came in he saw a full thermos flask and a paraffin lamp with the glass wiped clean and the wick turned down standing on the very clean *kang* table. The *kang* was warm to the touch.

He heard the door of the northern room being opened as Idiot Li's wife came in, covering her breasts.

'Comrade,' she said, 'you must come back from meetings earlier in future. We always keep our door locked, and I can't sleep happily with it left on the latch.' With that she went out again and slammed the door.

The cadre wrote something in a notebook at the table by the light of the lamp and was just getting ready for bed when Manr came in without a sound. A new towel was wrapped around her head so that a large printed peony covered her forehead. Her face looked pale in the lamplight and she seemed exhausted as she sat down on the edge of the *kang*, and leant against the wall.

'Pour me a bowl of water, comrade,' she said with a smile.

'Still up as late as this?' The cadre handed her the bowl of water he had poured out.

'Yes,' she said, still smiling. 'I want to ask you what sort of job you're doing. Are you in charge of production?'

'I'm here to get to understand people,' said the cadre.

'That's new,' she smiled. 'Production cadres keep coming here all the year round like the little men on a revolving lantern. They want to see the millet and wheat yields. What do you want to see?'

The cadre smiled, said nothing and looked at the young woman. They were a man and a woman alone together in the middle of the night, something that would make ordinary people most suspicious, but her expression was pure, her eyes innocent and he could see nothing wicked about her at all. It was difficult to understand anybody, he thought, and at any rate he was unable to guess what was in the girl's mind at this moment.

'Drink your water and go to bed,' he said. 'Your sister's waiting for you.'

'They blew their lamp out and went to sleep a long time ago,' she said. 'I'm very tired and it's warm on this *kang* of yours, so I want to sit here a bit longer.'

The cadre brought out a newspaper and read it in the lamplight. He did not know whether this girl, if she was as loose and shameless as they said she was in the village, was trying to win his favour and avoid criticism by these manoeuvres, or whether she was acting out of youthful curiosity and an unselfish desire to be helpful.

'If you're here to understand people,' said Manr, holding her bowl of water in her hands, 'why come to this rowdy place instead of going to the activists' and model workers' homes?'

'What's so rowdy about it?' the cadre asked.

'While you're staying here, it is as if there were a trap beside a mound of grain or a pile of straw—the birds all fly away and won't eat here,' said Manr. 'It's not usually very quiet here. Normally my sister's room is packed tight every evening.'

'In that case I must be hindering you from earning your living,' said the cadre. 'I'll move out tomorrow.'

'As you please,' said Manr. 'I'm not Yang Maor. I'm not forcing you out. What I'm saying is that getting to know people isn't like looking at a picture—you can't do it just by sitting here. You can't do it quickly either. Some people put on an act and say all kinds of fine things to your face. Some people won't talk to you about anything and just wait for you to make a subjective judgement.' At first her voice trembled and she held back her tears, but she ended up sobbing. The tears streamed down her jacket. The cadre put down his paper in alarm, but Manr said nothing else. She tugged at her head-towel to wipe the tears dry, gravely put down her bowl, and went out.

Idiot Li did not come once during the night to feed the young donkey, which brayed, kicked the wall, and gnawed at its trough. Either because the room was warm or because a new guest was staying in it the rats were active, squealing as they wandered over the boxes, the table, the edge of the *kang*, and the window-sill.

The cadre lay awake for a long time. When he woke up early the next morning he saw Manr hurry in. She looked as though she was in the middle of washing as she was only wearing a red cardigan, with the sleeves rolled up and the collar open; her face and neck were covered with drops of water. She leant over the cadre, and as her breasts brushed against his face a warm fragrance came from them. Finally she picked up her soap box and hurried out.

16

The blacksmith's forge was put up on its new site.

'This time I'm going to be in charge of it,' said Nine to the other youngsters. 'After all, we're a Youth Well-Sinking Team.'

'We're behind you,' they said. 'We'll take turns with the sledge-hammer and the bellows. All we'll ask uncle to do is to watch and advise us.'

The iron and steel that the young people had brought along were odd scraps that had been buried in corners or in mud for years. Now they were to be tempered and made into a steel drill that could bore down underground and bring out the spring water. To the young people it was like tempering their own high enthusiasm into a force that would build up the country.

Nine's face shone in the light of the forge as the hammer in her hand struck the anvil with a familiar ring. It was not her first encounter with this heavy work. In her childhood she had helped her father to forge shoes and bits for more cavalry horses than she could possibly count. The clear ringing of the hammer in her ears made her remember the thundering of great bodies of cavalry on the roads across the plain during the war, a sound that had spoken of a young girl's first gift to her country—her rock-hard loyalty.

She may too have been reminded of an earlier time. Perhaps she was working today in memory of her mother who had died in her middle years after a life of poverty. When her mother bore her she had been put on a little *kang* beside the forge, and she had heard these sounds of labour night and day while her mother hummed lullabies to her from beside the bellows. Indeed, her mother had done this heavy work while still carrying her.

Although it was a bitterly cold morning her thin clothes were soaked in sweat. This was the first time she had worked with her friends to a plan that they had settled together. Her young companions were eager, co-operative, and considerate, which Nine found exciting and new. Her father looked excited too; in his long and hard life he had never even dreamt of anything like the scene that was now before his eyes.

The first snow fell while the young people were working in the fields. The snow gleamed as it slowly melted in the midday sun on the sandy bank nearby. A layer of damp earth covered the fields that had all been ploughed during the autumn. But the weather had already turned very cold and the land was frozen hard in the morning and the evening.

The tall pulley towers of the young people's well-sinking team rose in twos and threes across the plain. They were a marvellous new sight on the dreary plain, a sight that made one imagine flags flying in the breeze, windmills in foreign novels, water towers in railway stations, the head-gear at a coal-mine, or the scaffolding for a big city building. As the young people worked with all their might to tap the water their songs whirled around in the air like the wheels of their pulleys.

Four, Guozao, and Nine were one team. At midday they cut some bushes from a cemetery, gathered some twigs, and lit a fire to cook the dry provisions and millet that they had brought with them.

'As you know,' said Four to Nine, 'although we live on a plain the village is surrounded on three sides by sandbanks.

The one to the west of the village has come down from the hills, and its drifting sand is worse than a flood. When we have those sandstorms that blot out the sky every spring, the sand comes over walls and fences into our fields and vegetable patches. It smothers the garlic and shallot shoots, fills the furrows where the wheat's planted, and buries saplings. When the spring winds are over we have to go into the fields and sweep it away or even lie on the ground and blow it away to let the shoots that have been bent and whitened by the sand see the sun again. If you walk along the streets when the sand has poured into them it's like wading through a river. The sand comes in through the door and breaks the paper on the windows. The women have to sweep up several basketfuls of it every day. That's what our environment is like. The high-ups are dead right telling us to sink wells and plant trees. It's just what we need in this part of the world.'

'In the mountains where we live,' said Nine, 'we have drought every year. Ever since I can remember hot dry sandstorms have blown in from the valley to the north-west and given our little house a terrible battering. The stream in front of the house rushes along under the ice in winter but in spring it dries right up. We have to eat husks and the leaves of trees to get through the spring.'

They talked about how happy they would be if from this generation onwards the natural environment was changed, and the hardships of centuries were brought to an end. They would build up a village in which the harvests were good, there were plenty of trees, springs came gushing out, and canals criss-crossed the countryside. Just then something appeared on the southern sandbank that was right out of keeping with their conversation. Six came first on to the bank with a falcon on his right arm, followed by Idiot Li and his wife, each of whom was holding a dead rabbit. They stood on either side of Six like bodyguards, gazing and pointing into the distance. Behind the bank appeared Manr's pretty face like a half-hidden branch of peach blossom.

'Four,' said Guozao, 'your brother's getting cleverer than ever. He's taken up falconry now.'

'I can't understand that lot,' said Four. 'Six had a terrible quarrel with Yang Maor about the pigeons, but since Idiot Li took the three of them into town for a meal they've become good friends again and Yang Maor has lent Six his falcon.'

'What do you mean, the three of them?' asked Guozao.

'Manr went too,' said Four. 'She's their backbone, the heart of their organization, their guide to action. They'd be lost without her. I've heard that Yang Maor is now the best customer at Idiot Li's dumpling shop and he has a good feed off them every evening. Idiot Li's wife said to him, "Maor, you eat and dress well now but you're still not completely on your feet. I want to introduce you to a girl, but you'll have to take me out for a meal." And he did too.'

'Can you get Six to come over and help us?' said Guozao trying to provoke him.

As Four was wondering whether to do so or not the group turned round and disappeared in the direction from which they had come.

Others can treat something they casually hear or see as a joke and pay no attention to it, but it can weigh very heavily on people directly concerned. Nine sat gazing abstractedly at the deserted sandbank. She was still thinking about the village of her childhood. After the death of her mother she often used to sit by herself in front of the little window. Outside the window was a jujube tree on whose branches birds gathered to perch in the sun, sheltered from the wind. The birds seemed very friendly as they played together. The ones who perched and chirped close together seemed the friendliest, but before long one of them would hop off to another twig. A gust of wind would scatter them. There was also a tiny rush-pond in front of their gate. When the water was low the little fish crowded together and swam around a single water-weed, but when the stream rose in summer nobody knew what happened to any of them.

One soon tires of such uncomfortable memories. Nine stood up and said, 'We've had enough to eat and drink. Let's get back to work. I'll tread the pulley first.'

'Mind you don't fall down the well,' said Guozao with a grin. 'Do you know what? I reckon Six's dumplings will be inedible —they'll be made of rabbit.'

Nine trod the pulley vigorously, working like an insect in the dawn or the twilight. As the wheel went round she seemed to Four at the bottom of the well to be a striking and moving image of a young girl.

The more she worked the more relaxed and experienced at it she became and the sun moved slowly from in front of her down towards the west. She could see very far, as far as the two tall flagpoles in front of the Medicine God's Temple by the southern gate of the county town. She could see the people all over the countryside muck-spreading, collecting firewood, looking after sheep and oxen, and putting their vegetable patches in order. She saw Six and Manr hunting through the fields and heard the shouts of Idiot Li and his wife.

Guozao and Four, working below her, were talking about this very subject.

'Four, you know a lot of political theory so explain this one to me: we're doing a cold and tiring job here while your brother is fooling around with a girl. Is our way of life right or is theirs?'

'You've raised a very important question, the question of the philosophy of life,' said Four from the bottom of the well. 'Would you like to live like them?'

'Sometimes they annoy me but sometimes I'm a bit jealous,' said Guozao.

'I'm sure they think they're right,' said Four, 'but even they must sometimes be a little ashamed of the way they live. If they weren't they wouldn't scuttle off whenever they see us.'

'But there's still the old question—why can't he ever be reformed?' asked Guozao.

'I've been thinking that over for the past couple of days,' said Four. 'We're not likely to get results if we try to reform them through our efforts alone. When it comes to making someone politically aware, study and individual experience are important, but most important of all are social influences. Six is a good example—he's like the drought-ridden land we are trying to improve. If we work well we can tap springs of water, make the land bear harvests and even become high-yielding. But the sandstorms and drifting sands all around can still bury it and turn it back into a desert where not a blade of

grass will ever grow again. We must strengthen the positive
influences in society, just as we must extend the irrigated area,
reduce the drought-ridden area, and tap more sources of water
until the winds and the sand are defeated.'

'Yes, that may well be so,' thought Nine as she trod the
pulley-wheel bringing up load after load of sand and mud from
the bottom of the well. As she looked down it she saw new,
clear water appearing there. But what about love? It grew,
she thought seriously, in quite a different way from the friendship of childhood. Only a love formed with shared revolutionary
objectives and in the course of long and tough work could stand
up to the trial of life's many difficulties and be truly strong and
eternal. Of course, love could develop in the smiles of childhood
as well as in arduous work, just as some flowers bloom on calm,
windless ponds and others bloom on mountain crags, forcing
their roots deep into the soil, lasting out through drought, and
holding their own against storms.

17

The cadre had not come to the village just to find out about
living standards. He wanted to help someone with all the
enthusiasm that he had accumulated over years of work. He
hoped that with his help Manr would be able to change, and
knew that this would only be possible through work and study.
This was, of course, going to be very difficult as he was only
too well aware that he did not really understand her yet.

When Manr came back in triumph from her hunting expedition that evening the cadre was standing in the courtyard.
Idiot Li's house was in a large dilapidated compound. By the
north-west corner of the ruined wall was a pit for storing dried
cabbage beside which grew an old, moribund and hideous elm
with a dead top and a twisted, split trunk. One great branch
that should long ago have been broken off for firewood drooped
down into a neighbour's yard where it had become a chicken
roost. Several hens had flown up on to it to spend the night
there.

Manr showed no signs of her exhausting and happy day
rushing around the fields. She came back after her sister and
brother-in-law, who had returned dog-tired, covered in mud,

and carrying a rabbit each. She got herself ready with her clothes neat and clean and her hair combed before coming in. She walked past the cadre as lightly and casually as ever.

'Comrade Qi Manhua,' the cadre called to her, 'are you busy after supper?'

'No, I'm a lady of leisure,' said Manr with a smile. 'What do you want to do?'

'The Youth Leaguers are studying this evening. You should go along and listen.'

'They haven't asked me,' said Manr with a wily grin. 'I'm too backward.'

'Of course you can go. Cook the meal now; we'll go along together afterwards,' said the cadre.

Manr nodded and said nothing. The cadre could see from the expression on her face as she turned away from him that she was very angry. She carried some firewood over to the stove to cook the meal, and as she sat in front of it making up the fire she kept glancing out of the corner of her eye at the cadre who was standing in the doorway.

'Aren't you going out to eat, comrade?' Manr asked.

'Put a bit more millet on,' he said with a smile. 'I'll eat here.'

'Our food's no good,' said Manr, 'you won't be able to eat it.'

'Even if it's terrible I'll still give you grain tickets for it,' said the cadre. He stood in the yard until Manr had cooked the food.

By taking her time over it Manr spent twice as long as necessary cooking the meal. She thought of running out several times, but she was intelligent enough to know that the cadre was watching her just to prevent her from doing such a thing. She also realized that he meant well. She forced herself to be calm as they ate the meal together.

Her brother-in-law squatted in the outer room to eat, and her sister, not understanding what the trouble between them was, said nothing. It was as if she were keeping off some forbidden subject.

After they had finished eating it was dark. Seizing the initiative Manr put down her bowl first and said, 'Let's go, comrade.'

When they had gone through the front gate Manr ran
ahead. She was carrying a little torch.

'It's a good thing you've got that,' said the cadre.

'I'll lead the way,' said Manr. 'It's quicker to go round outside the village.'

She turned north from the alley and went out of the village.
As she walked so fast and her flickering torch gave too little
light the cadre could see nothing as he followed her. He kept
stumbling.

Manr leapt lightly over a low sandbank and headed east
along the inside of the village wall where the ground was very
soft and many trenches had been dug for trees. The cadre
staggered along, his feet often sinking into the sand. He had to
walk slowly in order not to get too close to her and be confused by her torch.

'Hurry up,' said Manr. 'They've probably started. I don't
want to be late.'

'What kind of way is it you're taking me?' asked the cadre,
only half joking. 'This isn't the main road.'

'What do you mean, the main road?' said Manr. 'The
quickest way is best. There's a well here. Mind you don't fall
down it.'

The cadre worked his way round the well by feeling the
windlass. Finally came a steep slope down which Manr jumped.
The cadre virtually slid down it.

'Careful, there's a fence.' Manr slipped sideways between
the thorns, which caught the cadre's clothes.

'Take this.' Manr turned round and handed him the torch.
She went along a path covered with piles of broken bricks and
old tiles and in through the back gate of a big temple that the
cadre had visited before. As they went through the main hall
he shone the torch on the statues of limbless or eyeless Buddhist
immortals who stood at all angles along the walls. Manr
walked past them without taking any notice, slowed down,
and said:

'Comrade, have you ever been to the temple fair here on the
eighth day of the fourth month? It's fantastic. The wheat
comes up to your waist then, and while the old ladies worship
Buddha here the village lads take the girls they've brought

with them into the wheat fields outside the village. If you go into the fields at midnight the couples rush out of the furrows and fly away just like birds. It's terrific fun.'

'What's fun about that?' asked the cadre.

'It's only what I've been told,' said Manr. 'I've never been here when it's been as lively as that. During the Anti-Japanese War the guerrillas in this village were terribly brave. They used to mount guard on the top of the three-storey hall in this temple or even on the heads of the statues and shoot at the enemy when they were making search-and-destroy sweeps here. The nuns carried their ammunition for them. They've all gone back to ordinary life now. One of the youngest and prettiest of them is the daughter-in-law of the deputy village head.'

'These stories about the Anti-Japanese War are much better,' said the cadre.

'Then let's not go to the meeting,' said Manr, stopping and turning round. 'Let's go back home and I'll tell you stories all evening.'

The cadre shook his head.

'Are you sure I won't be struggled against?' Manr asked in a hushed voice as they came out of the hall.

'Absolutely,' said the cadre. 'Now why don't we go to the meeting?'

'A nun once hanged herself here,' she said, pointing to a big tree in front of the hall, 'because there was no freedom to love then. I saw her when she was alive. She could play the pipes and she was very pretty.'

The cadre said nothing. A gust of wind swept across the tips of the trees and the top of the roof.

'I'm scared.' Manr suddenly turned round and nearly flung herself into the cadre's arms. Her voice was shaking and he could hear her teeth chattering. He held her up and he flashed the torch in her face. It was pale, and she had rolled up her eyes so that only the whites were showing. She was talking incoherently and weeping.

'What's the matter?' asked the cadre in alarm.

'I saw her, I saw her,' she shouted.

Hysteria, thought the cadre. It surprised him that she should suffer from that complaint.

The first person to run into the temple from the street on hearing her shout was Six, who was going past on his way home after giving Yang Maor a rabbit. It was only when Six rushed up that the cadre realized the position he was in was open to suspicion: being with a woman in this state on so dark a night and in so lonely a place. He explained to Six how he came to be here with Manr.

'Help me, carry me home,' moaned Manr when she heard Six's voice.

'Very well,' said the cadre. 'Help by carrying her. Do you know the way to her home?'

'Yes.' Six squatted down as he spoke and put her arms over his shoulder. Manr went on weeping, her tears dropping on Six's neck. In the street she calmed down, pursed her lips, and blew lightly on the back of his neck. At first he was a little afraid, but when she put her lips to his cheek and gave him a hot kiss Six knew at last that there was nothing wrong with her.

18

Old Li regarded Six's coming expedition with the cart as an event of the greatest importance. After it was built he put all the skill of a lifetime into finishing the paintwork during the winter which was earlier than he had planned. One evening he invited Li Seven to a good meal and said:

'Seven, I'm entrusting Six and this new cart to you. Please look after him well and teach him all you've learnt in half a lifetime of carting. Make him drive straight and don't let him turn the cart over.'

Li Seven agreed at once, and added:

'Don't worry, I won't stand by and watch him suffer. We plan to go to Shimen this time. What do you think we should bring back?'

'Bring back whatever we can make a big profit on,' said Old Li. 'You decide. But as it's a new cart don't bring coal on its first journey.'

'In winter,' smiled Li Seven, 'coal's the most profitable thing to carry. Still, when we get there we'll decide. Otherwise we can carry a mixed load.'

When he was half-drunk Old Li had this to say to Li Seven:

'During land reform there was something of a split between us. But I never regarded you as a rich peasant; I always classified you as an upper middle peasant. Of course, your grandfather and father were rich peasants, but after you and your brothers divided up the inheritance you were mainly a carter and didn't hire much labour. I didn't think it was enough to make you a rich peasant, though it would have been pushing it a bit hard to say you were a middle peasant, which was what the argument was about then.'

'That's all over now,' said Li Seven. 'At the time I really hated losing that mule, though later on I sold some stuff and bought it back. Because of my bad class origin I don't like to have anything to do with people in the village. I get a decent living from my carting. Frankly speaking, a man with ability and brains can eat and drink well without having to work in the fields. I don't have to stint myself when it comes to having the best. When I'm at home I eat whatever Idiot Li has to sell. If I'm away I have steamed cakes or fried noodles in inns, and when I get back on the cart there's a full bottle of good liquor in my coat. Whenever I feel like it I bend down and take a swig.'

'I really admire you,' said Old Li. 'You are the only member of all the families that were overthrown who has recovered fast.'

After Li Seven had gone Old Li went to feed the animal several times. At the first cock-crow he woke Six and loaded the fodder for him. While Six got the cart ready Old Li arranged the shafts and the harness, fastened the girth, and oiled the wheels. Six ate his breakfast and drove the cart out into the street before dawn. The early risers who were out were all full of praise for it. Old Li was walking along backwards in front of it, levelling the ruts in the road and giving his son a stream of instructions.

When they left the village Li Seven took the lead in his large cart drawn by two animals. Yang Maor, who wanted to buy some goods in Shimen to sell over the New Year holiday, was riding on it. Once through the village wall Li Seven cracked his whip to get the cart rolling at a good speed, ran after it for a few yards, then jumped aboard. He turned round to see Six get on his likewise. Old Li only went back into the village after he had watched Six's cart disappear round the sand dune.

At the cross roads the village head stopped him and said that he hoped he would join the co-op. To counteract Old Li's fears he told him with great enthusiasm how co-ops were run in other villages and how compensation was paid for carts and draught animals. None of this seemed to make any impression on Old Li. As he walked home people noticed that his normally springy and confident stride had become hesitant and uncertain.

As the carts passed the sand dunes they suddenly stopped. Manr, who was waiting under an old poplar tree holding a small bundle, stood up and clambered on Six's cart.

Li Seven roared with laughter and flicked his whip. Behind the two carts rose a cloud of dust.

19

Every day Old Fu had the supper ready when Nine came home. Knowing that his daughter was doing heavy work he boiled millet for her just as he had always done when he was working at the anvil. Every day father and daughter sat on the inside *kang* and ate their supper by the light of a small oil lamp.

Old Fu had noticed that his daughter had been very silent for the past couple of days. Thinking that she must be overtired he said:

'Several of the mutual-aid teams brought me my money today for the odd repairs I've done for them during the past few days. I didn't want it, but they made me keep it. They said that, as we were away from home and had no crops of our own, we had to support ourselves by our work. As it's nearly New Year you ought to buy yourself some new clothes.'

'I don't need any,' said the girl, her head bowed. 'My old clothes will do for New Year as long as I wash and fold them properly. You need a new padded jacket, father, your old one's worn out.'

'I'm too old for fine clothes,' said her father. 'The village head told me that the mutual-aid teams are going to join together in a co-op next year. He wants us to join because the co-op will need smiths. I said I'd wait till you came back to talk it over. You must help me decide whether to join or not.'

'I'm all for joining,' said Nine with a smile, 'It's the best thing we could possibly do.'

'I agree,' said her father with excitement. 'Of course, we could go home and join the one there. But the work is further ahead here and, besides, we've got a lot of friends in this village. So let's join here. The village head said he hoped Six's family would come in too because work would be much easier with carpenters as well as blacksmiths in the co-op. But Old Li is crazy about carting and doesn't want to come in. I haven't seen Six for days. Have you?'

The girl said nothing.

'Are you feeling ill?' he asked, watching her closely. 'Why aren't you eating?'

'No,' she said, 'I'm just a little tired.' She went to the outer room to clear up the bowls and pots.

'My quarrel with Old Li,' said her father from the inner room, 'is just a family quarrel, something between us two old men. It doesn't matter at all. Don't let it bother you.'

'It doesn't,' said Nine. 'I don't think you've been too well this winter, dad. I wish you'd take it easier.'

'Don't worry about me,' said the old man with a smile. 'I'll get better when spring comes. As there's no meeting tonight you can clear up and have an early night.'

Nine arranged her father's bedding on the *kang*, shut the door behind her, and went to join the other girls.

It was a fine night with a very full, bright moon. Nine stopped in the courtyard and listened. Her father was not coughing as he usually did after blowing out the lamp and lying down. She felt much clearer and calmer, a state of mind that went with the clear winter night and the moon shining above her head. She looked hard and thought she saw for the very first time the little rabbit in the moon.

20

The whole of childhood is like a small boat sailing down a river in spate during spring. As you remember it everyone was happy and lively, but in fact its full white sail bore the scars of winds and storms. Did the boat surge bravely forward, never held up by counter-currents or shallows? Memory, like its cargo, is sometimes light but sometimes it weighs heavy.

But the fire of youth is unquenchable, and as you learn to

handle the tiller you confidently sail for thousands of miles with a huge cargo. What you hope for is not a calm journey with following winds but the strength to crash through terrifying waves and to hold your course in the face of any difficulties.

Spring 1956

He Guyan   和谷岩
[Ho Ku-yen]

The Korean War, in which the Chinese helped the North Koreans to throw the American forces back from the Chinese border to the area of the 38th Parallel, was of enormous psychological importance to the Chinese as in it they showed themselves that they could resist successfully United States military power provided they were prepared to pay the price. Although the same basic principles of warfare developed in China by Mao Tse-tung and others during the previous decades still held good, new techniques had to be evolved to meet the challenge of an enemy far better equipped than almost any of Chiang Kai-shek's units had been.

One of the biggest problems was supplying a large army along a road system under constant attack from U.S. aircraft. The terrain left the drivers with few alternative routes, and Chinese air cover could only protect them for part of the way. Thus much depended on the courage and ingenuity of the drivers combined with the tireless efforts by the Korean peasants to keep the roads repaired, an aspect of the situation on which this story is silent.

Another translation of this story has been published in *Chinese Literature*.

Maple Leaves

One autumn evening, as the sun was reddening the western sky, Hu Wenfa walked briskly out of the gully in which he was billeted. He was a driver in the Second Transport Company. He stuffed his last steamed bread roll into his mouth and brushed the dirt and crumbs off his uniform with his greasy hands as he walked to the shelters where the trucks were kept.

The shelters were in a wood to his right. Of the dozen or so that had been dug along the foot of a hill all were now empty except the one in which Hu Wenfa's new GAZ truck squatted like a great dark green beast with its shoulders hunched. Outside the shelter Hu Wenfa's assistant Wang Zhixiu was stretched out snoring happily on his greatcoat, which was by now dirt-brown right through to the fleece lining.

Hu Wenfa smiled at the sight, kicked him gently on the leg, and said, 'Wake up, we're going.'

Wang Zhixiu scrambled to his feet, looking blearily at Hu Wenfa. Then without a word he took the bucket that was beside him and went down to the river to fetch some water. Hu Wenfa opened the bonnet, inspected the engine closely, and oiled it. It was only when they were both sitting in the cab that Wang Zhixiu asked, as if he had only just been woken up, 'What's it this time?'

'Taking ammo from divisional stores to the strongpoint on Height Four One Two.'

'But haven't three trucks gone already?'

'Yes. Three went, but planes got two of them on the way. I don't know how the hell it happened. How could two grown men let their trucks be hit by a ruddy plane? They're still waiting for the ammunition on Height Four One Two. We've got a tough one today, young Wang. We've got to cross some air-strafed interdiction zones and another that's under artillery fire. If a plane gets us tonight our record of thirty-five thousand kilometres of safe driving will be snatched from under our noses.'

'We won't let it happen.'

'I hope not. Let's get one thing clear from the word go—no sleep for you this evening.'

Young Wang yawned as if to suggest that Hu Wenfa was wasting his breath saying anything so obvious and replied, 'Start her up.'

The motor roared into life. Long after the truck had bumped its way up to the military road Hu Wenfa kept looking round to see if Wang Zhixiu had gone to sleep.

Wang Zhixiu was an odd sort of bloke. Although he was only just twenty there were already two deep furrows in his brown forehead. He was quiet, unflappable, and always seemed to have the hint of a smile on his face. His eyesight was good and he worked with a will. The only thing wrong with him was that he was such a glutton for sleep. It made no difference where he was: whenever he had a moment to spare he would spread his greatcoat out on the ground and lie down on it. Within two minutes he would be right out, and neither wind nor rain could wake him.

There were two things that could shake him out of this habit. One was when something had gone wrong with the truck. This would fill him with so much energy that even the company commander or the political instructor would be wasting their breath telling him to go to sleep. His soft, warm greatcoat might have turned into a bed of nails as he climbed over the truck or lay underneath to repair it. If it was a minor fault he might take a nap when he had put it right; but if there was something seriously wrong he would work at it all day through till the truck had to be moving again at night. He could not be bothered to eat properly on the job. He would ask someone to fetch him a couple of steamed rolls, and if there were none of those to be had, he would wash a biscuit down with a mug of hot water. He never let Hu Wenfa have anything to do with day-time repairs because he felt that the driver needed sleep more than his mate did. He only asked Hu Wenfa's advice when the problem was one he could not cope with himself.

The other thing that could stop him from sleeping was an urgent assignment like today's. Hu Wenfa need not have worried on that score. When they came across enemy aircraft at night they drove without lights under a blanket of darkness. Wang Zhixiu would rock to and fro breathing lightly as he sat beside Hu Wenfa as if he were asleep, but at any moment he might suddenly shout, 'Stop! Bomb crater!' then jump down from the truck to see how deep it was and whether it was possible to go round it. If it was not possible he would take his shovel from the truck without a word. Within ten minutes the hole would have been skilfully filled.

Hu Wenfa's character was the opposite of Wang Zhixiu's. He was an alert and active man of inexhaustible energy who wanted to get on with any job he was doing as quickly as possible, and was never happy when driving at less than sixty kilometres an hour. This often made Wang argue with him. Once when they had been crossing a zone under artillery fire Hu had wanted to go flat out, but Wang had been dead set against it. Instead of going into all the details he just said slowly, 'However fast you drive you aren't going to be able to race the shells.'

'What do you suggest then?' Hu had asked him.

'I'm all in favour of going fast along decent roads, but the ground in front of us here is honeycombed with craters. If you drive like a madman a crash will be enough to write off the lorry even if we dodge the shells.'

On Wang's advice Hu had taken it quietly. All that happened to them was that shrapnel tore some holes in the truck's canopy.

Another time they had to cross a river in winter when the water, covered in a thin sheet of ice, was higher than the surface of the bridge.[1] The wooden bridge itself, about a kilometre long, was invisible; all that could be seen of it were a few wooden posts. Hu Wenfa's idea was to go straight along the line of the posts, reckoning that as the rivers were never flooded in winter the bridge was bound to be there under the ice. Wang Zhixiu would have nothing of it. After an argument he jumped down from the truck. 'A truck costs a fortune,' he said, 'and we can't fool about with it. I'm going to make sure.' He took off his cotton-padded trousers, socks, and boots, then leapt into the river. Although lumps of ice kept bumping noisily into him he said nothing as he felt his way across along the posts and confirmed that the bridge really could be crossed. His teeth were still chattering audibly when he came back and climbed into the cab. When Hu Wenfa advised him to put his greatcoat back on at once he replied in a matter-of-fact way, 'It's nothing to what our mates have to put up with at the front.'

Wang Zhixiu was a meticulous but slow worker. Hu Wenfa was always pulling his leg about the way he took his time, to which Wang would coolly reply that by taking their time the Chinese People's Volunteers would wear the Americans out.

The difference between the driver and his mate was like that between a straight and hard *Cunninghamia* tree and a tough, flexible mountain creeper. Hu Wenfa had not liked working with Wang Zhixiu at all to begin with; but by now he felt he would never find a better Number Two.

Wang's life was very simple, and seemed to consist of nothing

---

[1] Bridges were often built below the surface of rivers during the Korean war to hide them from U.S. aircraft.

other than driving, going to classes, eating, and sleeping. He
was not interested in singing, dancing, or playing cards, and as
far as Hu Wenfa could see there were only two things of which
he was really fond. One was a coloured picture of Chairman
Mao he had bought at a stationer's when he went back to
Andong (on the Chinese side of the Korean frontier) three
months earlier. As Hu liked it too he let him paste it up in the
right-hand corner of the cab. The other thing Wang liked was
the maple leaf of the Korean autumn. Before every journey
he would break off a spray of the red leaves to put in the cab
by the picture of Chairman Mao, and when they withered he
would replace them with fresh ones. Hu Wenfa, with the veteran
truck-driver's passion for tidiness, liked to keep his cab as neat
as a bridal chamber. Once he removed the leaves and threw
them out when Wang was not around, but a new spray was
there when they set out the next day. 'What do you want those
mucky leaves in the truck for?' he asked. 'They get in the way.'
'No they don't,' replied Wang. 'I didn't put them in your
steering wheel.'

'You're going cissy with all your leaves and flowers.'

'Don't you like them then?' asked Wang with a grin.

'No.'

'You will soon enough.'

'Never. They smell bad and they look worse.'

Putting the leaves to his nose Wang replied, 'I suppose
you've never been to my province, Jehol?'

'No.'

'Our maple forests cover mountains and plains. You should
see them in autumn. Whole mountains turn red—from light
red to purple and crimson. The most beautiful flowers in the
world aren't a patch on them. When I joined the army the
head of our engineering team took me to the top of a hill and
showed me where the construction site had been measured out
below. "When you come back from Korea after victory," he
said to me, "a big factory will have been built there. By then
you won't be able to recognize your own front door." I heard
that they'd started work on it soon after I joined up. It's a great
thing to have a factory built, but I wish I'd remembered to
tell him not to cut the maples down.'

'We're industrializing now,' interrupted Hu Wenfa, 'so of course trees must be cut down when necessary.'

'The fewer the better. If they're really in the way they can be moved and replanted. It would be very good to have a line of maples round the outside of the factory.'

When the first star began to shimmer in the sky a lorry loaded with ammunition was roaring south. It was too dark for its number-plate to be readable, but a spray of red maple leaves danced like a flame behind the ammunition lorry's windscreen when another truck coming towards it flashed its headlights.

Wang was feeling sleepy again. 'We haven't had a single plane so far,' he said with a gigantic yawn. 'I hope it's all going to be as peaceful as the last few miles.'

'Not a chance. The Yanks won't be that obliging. Where are we coming to now?'

'We're almost at Jiuhuali.'

'We'll have to be careful. This is where it begins.'

'Stop and let me climb on top. I can see a lot farther from up there.'

At just the moment when the truck stopped one, two, and then a dozen flares lit up in an S-shaped pattern in front of them, turning the sky a lurid white. The truck's shadow was picked out clearly in the road. 'Damn,' said Hu furiously. 'Talk of the devil. You're too bloody clever.'

'Let's go then.'

'O.K.'

Hu slammed the cab door shut and shouted, 'Hold tight, Wang.' The truck shot forward like a hurricane. Knowing that the enemy aircraft was circling above him Hu could not leave his lights on all the time. But there was the danger of driving into a bomb crater. He used all his skill as he shot forward, flashing his lights on obstacles for about as long as it takes to blink. They were out again before the pilot had time to mark his position. Hu Wenfa had played blind-man's-buff with enemy aircraft more often than he could remember, and he had always won.

Young Wang was clinging to the top of the truck and probing into the night with his eyes as if they were searchlights. One or two kilometres later, when they were almost through the area lit by flares, he suddenly heard a grating roar. He turned and saw the black form of an aircraft diving towards them under the flares. Instinctively he banged the top of the cab three times and shouted, 'Stop!' As the brakes slammed on, a stream of blue tracer shells exploded and sent sparks dancing on the road two or three yards in front of the truck. The aircraft could not come back straight away, so after this strafing run the lorry raced forward even faster than before. Wang felt his stomach being all but shaken right out of him as he clung to the sides of the truck, his eyes fixed on the sky. The aircraft was soon diving on them again, coming in lower and faster this time. Wang thumped the cab three times again to tell Hu to stop. Instead Hu turned his lights on and drove flat out for several dozen yards. Then the lights went out again as the truck made a fast right-hand turn off the road and into a wood. Wang heard three explosions behind him and saw that thick smoke was blotting out the stars. Blue streaks were bouncing off the road.

Hu Wenfa stopped the truck under a tall tree, jumped down from the cab, blew his nose hard, and said, 'Blast! It's like a toad jumping on your foot—it gives you a scare even though it doesn't bite you.'

'Is the truck O.K.?' asked Wang, scrambling down from the top.

'Yes.'

'When you did that crash turn I thought it was because you couldn't stop.'

'If you try the same trick twice you give the game away. The sod would have got me if I'd done it again.'

Wang was full of admiration for Hu Wenfa as he remembered where the three rockets had just exploded. 'That's another tip I've picked up from you,' he said. 'You know your stuff all right.'

As the aircraft had now lost its target it dropped more flares. The tree just covered the truck. Wang looked at the sky that was a pale yellow in their glare and said, 'The bloody plane's still hanging about.' Hu pulled his greatcoat over his head, lit a cigarette, took a deep drag, exhaled and replied,

'He's welcome to fly round in circles up there. The more of their fuel they burn the better.'

Ten minutes or so later the sound of its engine faded away in the sky. The last flare slowly burned itself out and dropped as a glowing red spark. They climbed back into the cab and drove back to the road. Some half a dozen kilometres later a large mountain loomed up in front of them, and on the other side of it were flashes like sheet lightning. Hu stopped the engine and leaned out of the truck to listen. There was an unbroken roar of exploding shells. 'We'll have to be careful on the way up that: it's the King of Hell's Nose. The road's narrow, the mountain's high, and it's under permanent shelling. You can't use your headlights or drive fast. Being hit by a shell isn't worth worrying about, but if we go into a ravine that'll be our lot.'

'Start the engine. They won't be able to get us.' Wang opened the side window of the cab and put his head and arms outside to watch the narrow, winding road that the truck was climbing. Wang's clipped shouts could be heard clearly over the shells and the engine: 'Left . . . further left . . . that's it . . . straight ahead . . . slower . . . slower, shell hole . . . right. . . .'

The truck kept stopping for Wang to jump out, grab his shovel, and walk ahead to find which way they could go. After countless stops and bends they were almost at the top. Just when they were going to follow the hairpin bends down the southern side there was a great flash and what sounded like a roll of thunder as a huge volley of shells exploded on the slope. Stones and branches showered on the truck. They were choked by the shell smoke that swept into the cab. Hu Wenfa cursed furiously and stopped the engine. Wang hesitated for a moment, quietly jumped out, and strode southwards through the smoke. It was two or three minutes before he came back. 'What's it like?' Hu Wenfa asked.

'The road surface has been blown to bits. I think we can get across if we take it a bit faster. Whatever you do, don't stop. Let's go.'

Wang leant out and shouted as he had before: 'Left . . . left . . . that's it . . . careful . . . right . . . straight ahead.'

The lorry rocked from side to side in the shellfire like a small boat in a stormy sea. At times the cab was tilted at such an angle that they fell out of their seats, and Hu only righted the truck with a tremendous effort. As Hu clung to the steering-wheel his hands ran with sweat, and he clenched his teeth till they hurt. On either side were cliffs and deep ravines, and at any moment a whole cluster of shells might explode beside him. Not that he was worrying about this; the one thought in his mind was to follow Wang's instructions and press on without stopping.

'Left . . . left. . . ,' Wang was shouting hoarsely. 'Mind the crater . . . slower . . . slower . . . right. . . .'

As soon as the last word was out of his mouth flames leapt up all around the truck with powerful shock-waves that almost lifted it clear off the road. Wang was thrown back into his seat. Hu grabbed his arm with one hand and asked, 'Are you all right, Wang?'

'Don't stop. Never mind about me. Keep going.' Wang dragged himself up and seized hold of the window. 'Faster,' he shouted, louder than ever. 'Left . . . left . . . that's it . . . carry on . . . right, shell hole. . . .'

The lorry went down the southern slope of the mountain round the hairpin bends. There was a continual explosion of shells on the road and the mountainside that showered the truck with a hail of stones and shrapnel. All Hu could hear was Wang's voice shouting, 'Left . . . turn right . . . carry on . . .' until they drove into a deep gully. Hu breathed a sigh of relief. 'We're through,' he said. Then he turned to Wang and added, 'But for your sharp eyes we'd have ended up in a ravine tonight.'

They drove along the gully for nearly a mile until somebody appeared from behind a boulder, stopped the lorry and asked, 'Are you the ammunition truck?'

Hu Wenfa jumped down from the cab and said, 'Yes. Are you the Second Detachment of the Zhenjiang unit?'

Before the other man had time to reply a group of men came out of another gully saying softly to each other, 'Hurry, the ammo's here.' They were all round the lorry in a moment.

'Have you come to help unload the truck?' Hu asked one of them who was wearing a greatcoat.

'No. We've come to collect the ammunition.'

'Blimey,' interrupted another soldier, 'you really had us
worried. If you'd been any longer we'd have run right out.
Got any grenades?'

'Plenty.'

'Do we need them! We've been hard at it ever since sunset.
Let's get the stuff unloaded.'

Hu Wenfa could hear a continuous rumble of hand-grenades
going off almost as fast as machine-guns on the other side of a
nearby mountain. 'Wang,' he shouted in his excitement, 'come
and help unload.'

The others were bustling on and around the lorry. With so
many men on the job the load was soon off. Because he had been
sweating heavily Hu was very thirsty, so he went into a dug-out
with the ammunition detail for a drink of water. Thinking
that Wang must be thirsty too after shouting so many instructions on the journey he filled a water-bottle for him. When he
was almost back at the truck he called Wang a couple of times
but nothing moved. He looked into the cab and saw Wang still
slumped against the window with one arm dangling and the
other cradling his head. Hu shook him by the shoulder. 'Hey,
wake up. Time to turn round and go back.'

Wang still did not move.

Hu Wenfa put his hand out to feel his head and was horrified.
He jumped into the cab, groped for the torch, and saw in its
light that Wang's face was the colour of earth. There was no
light in his half-closed eyes. One of Wang's hands was clutching
the clothes on his chest. Blood was dripping from his wrist
down to his trousers and the seat.

Hu Wenfa lifted him up and poured a little warm water into
his mouth. He shouted loudly at him a couple of times. It was a
very long time before he heard the familiar voice murmuring,
'Hu. . . . We got through. . . . I won't be going back with
you. . . . Be very careful . . . in the interdiction zones. . . .
Watch the road. . . . Whatever you do . . . don't stop in the
interdiction zones. . . .'

Wang was growing heavier and heavier. Hu lifted up his
head and looked through the windscreen at the lightning-like
flashes from the other side of the black mountain in the distance
and the red fireballs climbing into the sky. 'Open your eyes

again and look, Wang,' he was thinking. 'Our boys are going
to wipe them out.' As he brushed against Wang's icy cold hand
his heart contracted and something warm welled up in his
throat. He buried his head in Wang's chest and wept.

After Wang's death Hu Wenfa became rather quiet. He
rarely rocked his head and whistled as he had before, and he
was often seen lost in thought in front of the lorry. The political
instructor and his comrades all felt sympathy and concern for
him. They too were all saddened by Wang's sacrifice. Some of
them even said anxiously when Hu Wenfa was not in earshot
that they doubted whether he would finish his 35,000 kilometres of safe driving now that he had lost so good a mate.

In the tense days of that autumn Hu Wenfa's truck drove as
usual along roads knee-deep in mud. He beat 42,000 kilometres
before 7 November. The whole company held a meeting to
celebrate and they expected that this would certainly cheer him
up. He was as gloomy as ever. Even he could not have explained
what was on his mind. As the truck drove through the Korean
mountains pock-marked with craters, maple woods would
flash past the windows. Every time he saw the rows of maples
on some mountain pass he would think of his dead friend.
Wang had been like a single maple tree on the plains of China.
Compared to the vast forests it was next to nothing, but it was
just such trees that made up the forests. Although maples did
not have the scent of flowers they were more beautiful than any
flower on earth, particularly when the cold winds of autumn
bit through to the bone after the heavy frosts had begun.

His new mate had not been in the company long before he
discovered that his teacher, Hu Wenfa, had the strange habit of
putting a spray of maple leaves beside the picture of Chairman
Mao in the corner of the cab. Once the truck started, the pink,
crimson, and purple leaves would rustle and dance. In the light
of an oncoming headlight they were like flames.

February 1955, Peking

Fang Shumin 房树民

Unlike the writers of the older generations, the younger authors in China tend to be known only through their work. We may suppose that Fang Shumin is a young writer from Hopei province, since that is where the stories in his 1964 collection *Lanterns in the Snow* (from which 'The Moon on a Frosty Morning' is taken) are set.

'The Moon on a Frosty Morning' reflects the acute struggles in the villages brought about by the bad harvest years of the early 1960s, when collective agriculture came under great strain but was finally saved by the determination of such peasants as Cassia in this story. It is also a sign of the times that a woman is shown as one of the village leaders, a sharp contrast with the passivity of the heroine in 'Slaves' Mother'.

The Moon on a Frosty Morning

Cassia had just fed her one-year-old baby and was covering her head with a towel to go to the fields, when her four-year-old son Shigour said to his granny, 'Why are you making shoes for my father? He's away.'

'I'm not making them for that spineless father of yours.' She rubbed the awl against her hair and thrust it hard and angrily through the sole of the shoe. 'I'm making them for your mother.'

'But her feet are too small for those shoes,' Shigour protested solemnly.

'Out of the way, brat.' With Shigour driven away the old lady handed her daughter-in-law the black canvas shoes for which she had just finished making the sole.

'Oh well,' she said, smiling till her eyes creased right up, 'you can't blame the boy. You've been so busy these last few months rushing all over the place through mud and water. No wonder these great boots aren't proper women's shoes. Try them on.'

Cassia tried on the new shoes and found that they fitted perfectly. Even she could not help laughing. Then she tucked a sickle in her belt and hurried off to the threshing-ground.

The threshing-ground lay to the north of Bean Hamlet, as the village was called. It was bigger than last year, and heaped within new fencing in the middle of it were two huge mounds of bright red sorghum that had yet to be milled; the corn-cobs stacked in frames built of sorghum stalks gleamed in the autumn sun like a golden palace, and the piles of late millet were pushing at the fence round the threshing-floor, making it lean like an overhanging cliff.

The rich fragrance of grain drifted across the threshing-floor. Although it was now late autumn and the light north-west wind blowing across the fields was reminding everyone that the cold season had begun, Cassia felt only warmth at the sight of the fine harvest on the floor as she cut off the sorghum tops with her sickle.

Eyes sparkled as people returning to other counties from market passed the threshing-floor. They sighed with admiration and said, 'What a good harvest they've had in this team.'

'Indeed,' somebody agreed awkwardly. 'Looks even better than the Cherry Orchard Team we passed earlier.'

'A fat lot you know. They left the famous Cherry Orchard Team behind months ago.'

'Which team is this then?' asked the ill-informed man with another sigh.

'Bean Hamlet.'

'At last. So this is the famous "poor Bean Hamlet",' a voice said with a hoarse chuckle. 'The paupers have managed a decent harvest this year—like a blind man catching an eel.'

This last remark stung Cassia as she worked. There was an explosion in her head as she flung a bundle of sorghum tops to the ground, flicked her short, untidy hair back and shot a furious glare at the hoarse, middle-aged man. He blushed in fear and embarrassment. She softened her expression, suddenly realizing that she had no reason to lose her temper like an eighteen-year-old. A woman of thirty-two should be more tolerant; besides, she was deputy work-team leader. She waved to the men in the road and smiled at them. 'Are you thirsty, friends? Take a rest on the threshing-floor.'

'No thanks,' one of them replied. 'Looks like a good harvest you've had this year.'

'It certainly is,' she shouted happily, stepping back with her strong legs. An old man in a little felt hat jumped off his grey donkey and croaked, 'Hey, comrade, Come here, comrade.'

A cheeky youth beside him who was grinning all over his face grabbed him and whispered: 'You're asking for trouble, you shameless old devil. You're not on comrade terms with her.'

When Cassia heard this she ran to the fence and said to the old man, 'Never mind that nonsense, uncle. You go ahead and call me "comrade" as bold as you please. What do you want to say?'

The old man shifted the pouch-sack on his shoulder before relaxing and letting himself reply. 'I came through here on the way to market during the floods in July, and the oceans of water covering the fields made me think that you'd been washed out again. After two bad years running I was sure you'd be going hungry again this year. I'd never have dreamed you could get this good a harvest.'

Cassia waved her sickle and laughed, her eyebrows raised. 'You can't have been to market since then. You may have seen the floods, but you didn't see how we fought against them.'

The old man now apparently understood everything. He took off his hat, nodded, jumped back on his donkey, and rode away. Cassia smiled as she watched them go off towards the Grand Canal ferry. The full evening sun cast a golden light over her tanned face. The boundless plain beyond the village and the fields of green wheat shoots that covered it gave her a feeling of expanse and excitement. At the same time she was a little depressed. She had wanted badly to tell those strangers who did not know the story how their village had fought against the flood. But she must put all such ideas out of her head. Anyone would think that Bean Hamlet was not tough enough. As she gazed into the distance deep in thought she saw a trail of yellow dust rising from the road behind the brick-kiln. She knew it came from a rider and trembled as she realized that it must be Big Wu galloping at that speed. Just then she heard some women on the threshing-floor crying out, 'It's Big Wu,' 'It's him, it's Big Wu.' Unable to think of anything else she dropped her sickle and ran after the other women and the children towards the road. Shielding her eyes with her right hand she made out a chestnut horse pounding through the dust, and the bare-chested man astride it was indeed Big Wu, the team leader.

'Big Wu.' She was waving and shouting.

The chestnut horse carried its rider to the fence. The tall rider, a man in his forties, dismounted with a leap into a cloud of dust and put his hand on the horse's back.

'Have you been impatient waiting for me to come back? Come and take a look at our horse.'

Cassia was the first to reach it. 'It's a fine sturdy beast,' she said.

'It's kicking,' shouted Big Wu, deliberately frightening the women and children so that they scattered like chickens. Cassia alone stepped forward and grabbed it by the mane. When it shook its head violently, she pinched its nostrils shut and forced its mouth open.

'Be quiet, you devil.' It whinnied, pawed the ground, and then calmed down. 'What did you want to make it do that for?' she said to Big Wu, adding, 'Tell me quickly, how old is it?'

'Six. It's a strong one all right.'

As she kneaded the horse's back she could not hold back her praises. 'And such a glossy coat. What breed is it?' 'It's Mongolian—from beyond the Great Wall.' 'Good.' Then she anxiously asked, 'Have we bought her yet?' 'I paid on the nail and I've got the papers to prove it.' 'Good.' Cassia tugged at the reins as she said, 'Yesterday Tiedan and I built the stable, and last night Grandpa Baishun was chosen as stock-keeper. He's so pleased he's spent the morning cooking and rolling feed. I'll take him along to be watered and fed. I've got the cart with iron-rimmed wheels ready at the granary door to take the state grain, so you'd better go there and check the grain. Now that we've got our horse we must load the cart tomorrow morning, and I'm going to drive it. After two years on relief grain from the government our team must be first to deliver.'

'Fine, fine,' Big Wu cut in. 'You take him over to Grandpa Baishun for a feed, and I'll be with you when I've checked the grain.' Just as they were about to move Big Wu suddenly remembered something. 'Cassia,' he shouted. 'Wait a moment. I've got good news for you.'

'I didn't hear a magpie this morning,'[1] she said, turning her head, 'so I don't see how there can be any good news for me.'

'Shigour's dad, your husband Waizi, is coming back from Cherry Orchard tonight.'

Cassia was shattered. This sudden news was like being hit on the head with a brick. Try as she did to control the anger that surged up inside her she could not help her face turning pale and her voice shaking as she replied, 'Don't you dare mention his name. Our family is getting along very well without him.'

'Keep your temper, Cassia,' said Big Wu. 'If he's seen he was in the wrong and is willing to come back you should be ready to help him. The return of the prodigal is something to be pleased about.'

'So am I expected to send a bridal chair with eight porters to fetch him?' Cassia asked indignantly. 'If he had the nerve to leave he can have the nerve to sleep out in the village's reed beds.'

'Hmm,' said Big Wu. 'Waizi wasn't in that sort of mood at all. When we met at the market he grabbed hold of me and wouldn't let me go. And when he asked me about his mother, yourself, and the two kids, his eyes were red although he is a grown man.'

'It's none of his business,' Cassia cut in, sounding as if she were gnashing her teeth. 'We haven't starved to death.'

'Listen,' said Big Wu. ' "Waizi," I said to him, "your wife has changed. These last months she's really been doing things. She's a candidate Party member and has been elected deputy team leader." '

'You seem to have enjoyed gossiping with him, you old gasbag,' she interrupted again.

'The best part of the story is still to come,' grinned Big Wu. 'He hung on to my hand until I said, "Let me go, I've got to buy a horse for the team." Tears were pouring down his cheeks,

---

[1] A magpie is thought to bring luck in China.

so I asked him if he wasn't all right staying with his in-laws.
"Don't ask me about that," he said. "I've heard all the news
from Bean Hamlet. If they'll have me back again I'll. . . ."
"What'll you do?" I asked him, and he started howling. "Never
mind, Waizi," I said. "If you know you've gone wrong you
should come back and admit it; from now on you must forge
ahead with all the rest of us. I'll back you up this time. When
will you be coming home?" His answer came back like a shot:
"Tonight".'

Cassia was so angry that she stamped her foot and flung out
her arm. 'I never signed any undertaking to have him. Even if
he does come I won't have him back.'

'Oh well,' said Big Wu, still trying to win her round, 'you
should at least let him stay tonight. He's coming back this
evening, whether you let him stay on can be decided later.
After all, we can't ignore him now he's turning over a new leaf.
Look! The horse is eating Old Deng's fence. Take him away
this moment!'

It was night by now. The north-west wind that had been
blowing across the plain had dropped, and the frozen stars
shivered in the late autumn cold. Cassia let the horse relieve
itself, then watered it beside the well. Grandpa Baishun tethered
it in its newly-built stable and fed it as carefully as if he were
fingering a jewel. A moment later Big Wu was there, standing
under the swinging hurricane lamp and saying happily, 'Mmm.
That feed smells good.' With a nod to Grandpa Baishun
he said to Cassia, 'I've checked the state grain. The stuff in
the sacks is all up to standard—first-rate stuff—so it can be
taken in first thing tomorrow. When I've had a drink of water
I must be off to the river bend to hear how the labourers from
our village are getting on with the canal. Which of the men
should take the cart?'

She stretched out her arm. 'I told you I was going to drive,
didn't I?' He shot a sidelong glance at her and, seeing the
determined way her eyebrows were raised, could only smile.
It would have been a waste of time to say anything more.

She was a long time settling in the new horse with Grandpa
Baishun before going home. As it was the end of the lunar

month there was not even a sliver of moon above the trees. She
felt her way into the courtyard and grimly remembered to
wedge the gates shut by sticking a pole hard against them. In
the house she heard her mother-in-law ask sleepily from the
darkness, 'Is that you back? Shall I light the lamp?'

'No,' Cassia replied quickly. 'Are the children asleep? Why
are you still awake?'

'I rocked them to sleep. Why did you have to make such a
noise shutting the gates? We haven't used the date-wood pole
for months, so why shut the gates with it tonight?'

'I thought the wind would blow them open.'

'Fool,' the old woman went on, 'idiot. Didn't you notice that
the wind had dropped ages ago?'

Cassia did not want to tell her mother-in-law that Waizi
was coming back that night in case the news gave her a seizure
and killed her. She climbed on to the *kang*, but no matter
which way she lay she could not get to sleep. She gritted her
teeth and hardened her heart, longing to hear him trying to
force the gates while she lay there on the *kang* and would not
get up to open them. He could freeze—he had asked for it.
As she lay there her heart would start to pound at the slightest
sound from the yard, but as she waited she heard no loud noise
to follow.

An evening in July flashed before her eyes. That night when,
with one cloud-burst following another, she had waded home
from a team meeting through the floods, her feet heavy with
mud, supporting herself with difficulty on the vegetable-garden
fence. Just as she and her mother-in-law had been looking for
a big spade in the shed they had heard squelching footsteps
in the yard. She had opened the door and said, 'Oh, you're
back.'

The stocky Waizi had come in and was wiping the mud off
his feet while she lit the lamp and asked him, 'Where've you
been? We shouted ourselves hoarse trying to get you to the
team meeting.'

'I went to Cherry Orchard,' he had said.

'What a thing to do,' she had replied, flaring up. 'You just
don't care about the team's crops. Big Wu's been elected team
leader and he'll be a good one. He's taken men and women from

our village down to the river bend as fast as they can go to drain the water out. But you had time to go and visit the children's granny. What do you mean by it at a time like this?'

'You want to know what I was doing?' said Waizi with a laugh. 'I was negotiating. It's all settled. Tomorrow the whole family moves to Cherry Orchard.'

Cassia had been stunned. 'What? What did you say?'

'What's the point of thinking about nothing but work all the time? Can't you see that this poverty-ridden hollow has been a frog pond for two years running? Even the team's donkey has starved to death. Now this year's rains have drowned us again. There's nothing to stay for. The sooner we find some dry land the better.'

Cassia had realized at once what he was thinking. 'Frightened of starving?' she had said. 'Want to sneak off, don't you?'

Waizi had tilted his head to one side and replied, 'Say what you like as long as you understand that tomorrow we're shutting the place up and going, bedding and all.'

'Who's going?' she had asked.

'All of us,' he had said.

At this she had flared up and shouted furiously, 'You can clear off by yourself. You may have it all nicely worked out, but nobody's going with you.'

The stocky Waizi had rushed forward and grabbed her. 'Stay where you are. Where are you going with that spade?'

'Get away from me,' Cassia had said, breaking away from him. 'I'm going to drain off the water and guard the dike with Big Wu. This is a crisis. I've got no time to waste talking to you.' Waizi had raised his hand, but Cassia had moved her spade instantly to parry it, screaming 'Don't touch me. If you lay a finger on me you'll get a dose of this.' With their quarrel the room had felt as hot as a kiln; gongs were being beaten outside to tell everyone to go to the dike at once, the boy was crying, and the adults were shouting at each other. It had been too much for the old woman, who released a torrent of abuse on him: 'Worthless wretch, evil son, get the hell out of here and eat and drink as well as you can.'

When Cassia had come back the next day from her work at the river she had tried to win him round, but he was so set in his twisted ideas that when she had finished he just replied, 'The flood waters are here to stay. This dump won't ever get rich. Are you coming with me or aren't you?'

'No,' Cassia had said, steeling herself, 'I won't go.'

'If you're not coming that's your lookout. Mother and Shigour are coming with me.'

The old lady had jabbed her finger at his nose and said, 'You're not going to take even a hair of any of us, not one hair.'

Red-faced and hoarse, Waizi had issued his last warning: 'Very well then; don't come if you don't want to. But don't expect me to be nice to you when you come begging from me in the autumn.'

This had made the old lady angrier than ever: 'If that's how you're going to talk to us you'd better clear out at once. Go off and hatch your plans, my fine lad. There may not be much flesh on us but our bones are hard, really hard.'

Waizi had wrapped up his bedding and gone, his pipe between his teeth.

His last superior glance at them was deeply etched on Cassia's mind. The thought of it still made her almost burst with indignation; she gave an involuntary and contemptuous snort. This woke her mother-in-law, who rolled over and asked:

'Are you cold?'

'No, mother, I'm boiling hot.'

She tried as hard as she could to calm herself down as she lay there in the dark, her eyes wide open, struggling to drive away the image that flickered in front of them. But it hovered there more clearly than ever. She imagined him coming back and apologizing to her. She would tell him straight out that what he'd done had been completely wrong, and it had all been because he had not had confidence in the group and the people's commune. . . . She fell into a doze. When she woke again a little later there was still no sound from the courtyard. 'He hasn't come back,' she thought. The crescent moon setting in the south-west was filtering its light through the window, and she could hear the first cock-crow of the morning. She could stay in bed no longer. The old lady leant over to her and said:

'Why are you tossing and turning so?'

'Keep your voice down, mother.' Cassia sat up smartly and felt for her clothes. 'I've got to get up early to take the tax grain in.'

'You'll be frozen right through this early in the morning,' the old lady said, 'so mind you wear a jacket over your green tunic. I finished the soles of your new shoes last night and put them by your pillow. Have you found them?'

'I've put them on,' Cassia replied.

'It'll be a long, cold journey, so wait till I've boiled you some noodles and egg.'

'No thanks.' Cassia got down from the *kang*. 'I must be on my way before the third cock-crow. I can get something to eat on my way through Zimu township.'

She groped lightly for her child's head, kissed his lips, and went out. She felt the cold in the courtyard at once, pulling her warm hands straight away from the frozen window-sill and sucking in her breath. There had been a frost that night, the first since last winter, and the young crows perched in the locust tree in the yard were cheeping miserably. Some dead leaves, covered in white, were drifting to the ground. She looked up again at the golden crescent of the moon in the south-western sky and at the stars shimmering in the cold air, overcome with a warm feeling of pity. It had been the height of summer when Waizi left wearing only a thin shirt and trousers. He would choose the cold season to come back, the pig-headed fool. Well, if he wanted to come back he'd have to change his way of thinking.

She regretted her anger of the previous night. He hadn't come back, so she need not have blocked the gates so securely. She went over and worked the heavy date-wood pole loose. As she stepped through the gates all her courage could not stop her from gasping with fright: there was somebody squatting in the shadows outside.

'Who's that?' she called.

The man did not look up. He stayed there with his arms clasping his shoulders and his head buried in them.

There was no need to ask any questions. The faint moonlight was bright enough for her to see that it was Waizi.

29 October 1962

Wang Xingyuan 王杏元
[Wang Hsing-yüan]

Wang Xingyuan is a young writer from Kwangtung province who published in 1965 the first part of a long novel set in a village in eastern Kwangtung. In 1967 he was a member of a group of writers who visited Vietnam.

This story, first published in 1963, illustrates the clash between the loyalties of clan and class that has been so often a feature of the Chinese countryside in transition. There is nothing unusual about a youngster with only a few years' schooling taking such testing jobs in the teams and brigades of the people's communes, as the only members of the older generation with the necessary experience tend to come from the richer sections of society and thus not have the same sympathy for collectivism. It is easy to imagine the importance that proper accounting has for the commune members' morale—if some are credited for work not done, and the efforts of others go unrewarded, enthusiasm is bound to suffer. The number of work-points each member of the commune earns during the year decides the size of his share of the harvest. There are a number of methods by which work-points can be allocated, varying from daily assessment by a work-point recorder as in this story to a monthly meeting at which all the members of a production team decide together what the work of each is worth.

The Iron Inspector

Everyone for miles around is full of praise for the way Apricot Village has gone from poverty to prosperity by increasing production over the past year or two. All the villagers think that this year will be better than ever, and anyone who goes there can see the truth of it. The soil has been improved in sixty or seventy per cent of the village's two hundred or so *mu*[1] of paddy fields, and each *mu* has already been given sixty to seventy carrying-pole loads of fertilizer of some sort or another.

[1] A *mu* is a fifteenth of a hectare, or about one-sixth of an acre.

Hoeing and the care of the rice-shoots are all up to date. The mountain streams have been cleared, the paths between the fields have been weeded, the dikes round the paddy-fields have been trimmed neatly into shape, and the way the fruit trees have been pruned and heaped around with earth has made the mountainside orchards look like gardens. Since the beginning of spring the peasants have been working hard, competing with each other in skill and ability. As soon as the team leader gives the order they set to work like a platoon of soldiers. This whole atmosphere should be enough to convince anyone that this year will be even better than ever.

How was it that Apricot Village, which used to be called Three Kinds Village, improved so quickly? Ask any of the villagers and they will tell you, 'We've got the Communist Party to show us the way, there are good cadres in charge, and we've trained able men like our "iron inspector" who can cope with anything.' But not so fast. You've never heard of this 'iron inspector'. If you are curious enough to inquire further I can guarantee that anyone who asks more about him will be full of admiration for his unselfish sense of justice.

The reader does not know who this 'iron inspector' is, does he? He is no bigwig, only a humble work-point recorder called Li Zhenping, a seventeen-year-old with parted hair, a boyish face, clever eyes, and a very strong character. His mother will tell you that he is a poor orphan who lost his father as soon as he came into the world. He was reared on thin rice porridge and salt vegetables, and he grew up wandering through mountains and fields as he clung to his mother's skirt. He only started primary school in 1956 at the age of eleven. Although he had hoped to go on to secondary school, it happened that when he finished his primary education the team's work-point recorder had just walked out on them. As the villagers wanted Zhenping, the Party secretary said to him, 'Come back and take over. You can't let the accounts get into a mess by refusing to help us.' The secretary persuaded him in this one conversation to go home and enter 'The University of Work'.

He made a start worthy of a tiger or a dragon, and the villagers were pleased with him from the moment he left his studies. He was extremely conscientious about setting quotas, assigning work to people, posting work-points on the wall, and everything else. He did it all very carefully. He was friendly too, and used to read the paper aloud to the villagers after he'd entered all the points. He put a picture of Chairman Mao on the wall of the work-team's office to liven it up, and covered the walls of the little village hall with New-Year pictures, scrolls of birds and flowers, and newspaper cuttings, making the place look grand and cheerful.

No needle is sharp at both ends: Li Zhenping could not use an abacus to calculate work-points. He had to add them up every night with pen and paper. Seeing what a lot of trouble this was for him the members of the team urged him to learn how to use an abacus. He made up his mind to do so. But when he brought the subject up somebody coughed drily in the corner and said, 'Hmm. It's finding a teacher that will be difficult. The only problem about learning to use the abacus is when the teacher is worried that the pupil will learn so fast that he'll soon be better than he is himself. But if you found a teacher you'd have no trouble learning.' The speaker was Li Zhenping's uncle Li Wanben, and his remarks drew many mocking glances from everyone else. 'That's right,' somebody said, 'it's only natural for an uncle to teach his own nephew.' 'He didn't get any business when he advertised for pupils,' snorted somebody else. At this comment Li Wanben slipped off without another word.

This Li Wanben was well known in the village as a calculating monster. He was famous for being grasping and selfish like an old silkworm that gobbles up big leaves: he could work out ways of getting bones from eggs. In the old days he had been quite a rich trader with a good 'reputation'. When the commune was set up he refused to use its lavatories. He used his family's excrement to feed three big dogs he was raising at home. One morning the dogs started fighting for his shit when he went to feed them, and in the mêlée one of them bit his backside. He lay idle on his stomach in bed and sent his wife to tell the team leader that he had a bad cold and to ask for the money to get it treated. When the money was refused he wept and made a great fuss. Then someone told the team leader what had really happened and revealed his dirty secret. His prestige was completely destroyed. The people in the village who gave out nicknames changed his name from Wanben to Wangben ('Origin-forgetter').

'Wangben it shall be then.' When he accepted the nickname the villagers thought he had seen the error of his ways, but it would have been harder to change his nature than to draw blood from a turnip by peeling it. They often saw him coming back in the evening from working in the communal fields with an agonized expression on his face, walking on tiptoe, and bent double with a hand pressed to his belly. At first they thought it must be belly ache, but on repeated observation they realized that the old rogue was holding back his urine to water the vegetables in his private plot by the village.

Li Zhenping wanted nothing to do with a man who had so bad a name. He could learn from the brigade accountant. But when Li Zhenping was eating lunch the next day Li Wanben came in with an abacus under his arm to teach his nephew. 'We shouldn't let our sewage be wasted by flowing into someone else's stream,' said Li Wanben. 'You must get with it and learn all the tricks.' The boy's uncle seemed so sincere that Zhenping's mother insisted that he should take lessons from him. Now that Wanben had come round to their house Zhenping had to agree, unable as he was to refuse. Thus it was that Zhenping mastered addition, subtraction, multiplication, division, and the 'under nine technique'—everything except pounds and ounces—in eight midday rest periods and nine evenings.

Skill strengthens the will, as the saying goes. Now that he knew how to use the abacus Zhenping rattled away at it to his heart's content as he calculated work-points; and Wanben, feeling that he now had a well-placed supporter, started to get up to his tricks again. The way he divided the labour in his family was that his eldest son went up to cut firewood on the hillside to sell for ready cash, while his daughter-in-law had to toil away at their private plot. Thus when the commune members set out for work in the morning his son and daughter-in-law were the support troops who only reported in long after the others had started. Apart from being the last in, they were the first out when it was time to stop work. Li Wanben

himself did not start late or finish early, but he carried a little
bamboo basket at his waist and dropped his mattock to chase
any frogs or edible locusts he saw. If they dived into one of
the low dikes round a field he insisted on breaking it down.
When exhausted by the pursuit he would sit down at the edge of
the field for a smoke. This enabled him to feed his huge
numbers of hens, geese, and ducks; and without this 'joint
state-private enterprise' he reckoned that he could not have
managed to survive.

While Wanben was up to no good every day Zhenping went
daily to the fields, keeping his eyes skinned to see how hard
each commune member was working and whether those who
were not on the system of contracting to carry out a particular
job were up to the minimum standard; he also inspected the
quality of contracted work. Seeing how disgracefully his uncle
Wanben was behaving he went up to him and said, 'You must
fill your quota, uncle.' 'Quota my foot! I've eaten more salt in
my life than you've eaten rice.' Wanben gave his nephew an
evil glare and started resentfully to work.

One day Li Wanben had been extremely lucky: he had
caught two basketfuls of frogs in one go. This was going to be
the day on which the commune members put Zhenping's
integrity to the test. The job Wanben had undertaken to carry
out for the work team was to plough and harrow a piece of
land in the date orchard somewhat bigger than a *mu*. He had put
too much weight on the plough, leaving the ground looking as
though it were covered in mountain ranges, and even after he
had harrowed it the soil was still uneven and not properly
broken down. Among the villagers some were worried that
Zhenping might not be clever enough to avoid being taken in
by Wanben. Some were making all sorts of critical remarks
and others were warning him. Aniu, the work team leader,
slapped him on the shoulder and said, 'Now we'll see whether
you're a pillar of strength or not.'

Zhenping wondered how, feeling more on his guard than
ever. That evening he was still pacing up and down in the date
orchard examining the land his uncle had ploughed and harrowed. He really had done a very shoddy job. When calculating
the work-points that evening Zhenping felt awkward with the

abacus and used pen and paper instead. He was bursting with
anger and determined to humiliate his uncle that night. He
worked out everyone else's work-points first, deliberately leaving his uncle's to the last. Li Wanben was as pleased as punch
that day. He squatted in a chair by the accounts desk with a
grin so broad that his eyes were half closed while he waited
for his points to be worked out. As he saw his nephew passing
over him again and again to work out the others' points first
his face darkened. Was his own nephew, the student he himself
had taught, daring to turn on him like this? He coughed
occasionally as a hint to Zhenping.

When the points of everyone in the team except Wanben
had been worked out Zhenping thought for a while before
saying to the commune members, 'I hope you will all report
anyone doing shoddy work.' After a long silence the deputy
team leader lost patience. 'Write down the truth,' he said
decisively. 'I'll back you up if there's any trouble.'

'Hmm. How can I know how shoddy it was? Everyone must
report on him.'

Zhenping had been intending to say straight out who it was
who had worked badly, but he decided to give his uncle a
chance to show a little political awareness. The owlish gaze
his uncle fixed on him showed that there was no hope, so he
said to Wanben, 'You're the one who's worked badly, uncle. I
think you ought to re-do the piece of land in the date orchard.'

'What?' said Wanben with an evil glare, adding through
clenched teeth, 'Very well. Write it down then. I've finished
with you.' He slapped the desk and stalked out.

Zhenping sat there quietly as Wanben's clogs could be heard
stamping out through the door. The commune members burst
out laughing. 'Zhenping,' someone said, 'you're like the barber's
apprentice whose first customer was a hairy old man. We're
going to see what you're like with the razor now.' 'It's a steel
one,' said Zhenping with determination. 'Unless he does it
over again I'll only give him three-fifths of the points. If he
doesn't like it he can lodge a complaint against me.' With that
he wrote down the points. To pay off the favour Wanben had
done him, and to leave himself under no obligation to anyone
as work-point recorder, Zhenping transferred five of his own

points to Wanben as a very fat fee for teaching him the abacus. Although the team members said the points should be given to Wanben from the general pool, Zhenping refused, generously wrote down the transfer, and went. The people who had been waiting to see Zhenping face this test had to clap and laugh. 'Good. Apricot Village really has got an iron inspector.'

When an unhappy Li Zhenping went home and opened the door he saw that his uncle and his mother were chatting about something. 'No need to ask,' he thought, 'he's complaining to mother. I don't care. He can complain as much as he likes.' He went straight into the inner room, climbed into bed, burrowed under the bed-clothes, wrapped them around himself, and waited for the complaints to begin.

'You're getting much too big for your boots,' said his mother. She was very embarrassed by Wanben's complaint and at the sight of her son she lost her temper. Without going into the rights and wrongs of the question she grabbed the bamboo pinchers she used for driving her hens and started to belabour Zhenping as he lay there on the bed. 'Nothing will stop you. How could you show so little feeling, and you an educated boy?' Giving one whack with every phrase she made the dust fly out of Zhenping's bedding. He neither moved nor cried. His mother went on beating him till Wanben snatched the pinchers from her and said, 'That's enough. Don't be like a puppy chewing a stone that somebody has thrown for him. It doesn't really matter if I've been hard done by. It must be because my ancestor Shunxing didn't leave a legacy of good deeds. That's why his descendants are all like worms in the ground that get chopped up by other people's spades. You'll have to eat your way through many more sheaves of rice yet before you're in a position to lay down the law, my lad.' Zhenping's mother turned to Wanben and apologized to him profusely. When at last she saw him out she said, 'The boy is still very inexperienced. He'll need a lot more of your advice in future, uncle.'

That night she went on and on at the boy as if she were reciting scriptures, scolding him for 'trying to block out the sun with a chopstick.' At first he ignored her, but when he could bear her nagging no longer his temper flared up. He leapt out of bed and shouted at his mother, 'The more you go on with

your capitalist and lousy feudal ideas the more they stink.'
After this outburst he went back into his quilt and shut his
ears to all his mother's abuse. He felt that what he had done
was honourable and right and did not care who attacked him
for it. At the same time he was aware of how sharp and complicated the struggle in the villages was and how difficult it
was to do the right thing.

When the commune members went to the fields to harvest
the winter wheat and pick peas the next morning Zhenping
went with them as usual. Li Wanben's family started work
particularly early. Everyone noticed that he had no basket at
his belt and was working very conscientiously. When he had
to watch the frogs that he could not catch leaping around in
the fields, it was as if lumps of his own flesh were jumping about.
The other commune members were quietly delighted. Seeing
how well Wanben was now behaving the team leader Aniu
said to Zhenping, 'As long as you bake it in ashes the prickly
eel can't do you any harm.' Then he turned to Wanben and
said provocatively, 'How terrible. Such a pity to see all those
frogs hopping about with nobody to catch them.' Grinding his
teeth so hard that he almost broke them, Wanben angrily
raised his sickle and cut a frog in half.

As several days went by Wanben had to watch his ducks
laying smaller and smaller eggs or even stop laying altogether.
But it was not worth catching frogs for them if he lost work-
points for it. Neither could he bear to feed them on rice. For
Wanben, a man who calculated his every move, to be reduced
to such a state made him hate Zhenping to the very marrow
of his bones. After four days of solid hatred he managed to
think up an evil plan. When nobody was looking he threw a
packetful of broken glass that he had collected into the team
office through the crack between the doors. 'That'll cut his
feet to shreds,' he thought. 'Now we'll see if he can come into the
fields to spy on me.' You cannot be on your guard against a
danger you do not know about; and as Zhenping, his bare legs
covered in mud, was the first to unlock and go in at midday
several jagged pieces of glass cut right into the soles of his feet.
He collapsed, blood gushing out. The commune members
helped him, as soon as they heard about it, by removing the

glass and bandaging his wounds. Wanben too pretended to sigh when he heard the news, but really he was chuckling to himself, 'Try boiling the head of an ox and a chicken in the same pot and you'll see which has more flavour.'

This sneak attack on Zhenping meant that he was unable to go to work. He had to stay at home and recover. The cadres, the team leader, and he decided that this must have been a trap set by some evil person. The cadres urged him to carry on and not to weaken. He was also greatly consoled and encouraged by the concern the commune members showed for him. Now that he could not go out with the others the bamboo basket reappeared at Wanben's waist and disaster struck the frogs in the fields once more. When one horse stops the others rest. Those who shared Wanben's stinking outlook began to slacken as well. Zhenping could no longer go on sitting around when he learnt of this. He could not let anyone make trouble and hold up production now that it was well into spring and the rice shoots would soon have to be transplanted. Even though he could not work with the others he could sit beside the fields and help the team leader to keep an eye on things. He would sort them out.

Three days later he limped out to the fields on crutches. When his mother and the other commune members tried to hold him back and make him rest, he threw the crutches away and said, 'They don't hurt at all.' When he reached the field he sat beside it and watched. Thus Li Wanben's plan to get rich was foiled by the iron inspector once again.

After the spring harvest the rice shoots were transplanted. Apart from what was sold to the state or kept for the seed nearly all the wheat, peas, and sweet potatoes were shared among the villagers on the basis of work-points. It worked out that each point was worth a little over four pounds of wheat and three of peas, as well as some sweet potatoes. They had worked hard and now they were being amply rewarded. They were all delighted to receive the fruits of their labour apart from Li Wanben. He went round with an evil face, making snide remarks and saying that he had been robbed and bullied by the cadres. He and his sympathizers made a lot of bother. They threatened not to work and demanded transfers to other teams.

These troubles were the work of Wanben too. The team leader Aniu was an imperturbable man who knew how to cope no matter how Wanben twisted and turned. As for Li Zhenping, his feet were now toughened up again and he was determined to carry this battle through to the end. Several days after the share-out his cousin came from the county town to visit them, and Zhenping's mother talked about the rights and wrongs of what he had been doing. Wanben came along too to make his complaint. When he had heard both sides of the story the cousin, who was a government worker, took Zhenping to one side and said, 'It was right of you to put the common good above your personal feelings; but all the same, we cadres have to weigh up the character of every commune member and be patient in educating and reforming them. . . .' This explanation made Zhenping realize that he had not done nearly enough to change his uncle's way of thinking. Then he thought that trying to change his thinking at this stage would be a waste of time, like a hen pecking at a closed clam. At last an answer came to him. At noon the next day, when his mother was not there to know, he slipped over to his uncle's with a scoopful of his own family's wheat in the hope that this would mellow Wanben so that he could then tackle his uncle's attitude of mind. But when he reached his uncle's front door and called out to him, Wanben came out and spat at him and gave him a vicious glare like that of a ghost seeing a fire. 'Damn you! My evil star.' With that he slammed the door.

As Zhenping stood under the eaves wiping the spit from his face, he glared back at the door feeling humiliated and angry. 'If you won't reform that's your look-out,' he said at last, marching off in a great fury.

One day about a fortnight later Zhenping went to the marketing and supply co-operative to arrange for the sale of some home-made baskets, brooms, and such things. Instead of going straight back that afternoon as he had intended, he went to the clinic to buy some basic medicines for the village's first-aid worker. While he was there Li Yongfu happened to ring up the clinic asking for a doctor to visit his sick son. The doctors were all out. Rather than let one take the mountain path by himself, Zhenping felt he'd better wait till one came back and go with him. The pediatrician did not return till evening. Zhenping took him back to Apricot Village that night, and it was nearly ten by the time they reached Li Yongfu's place. Zhenping hurried back to the office without stopping at Li Yongfu's.

He unlocked the door, went in, and turned on the light. A tray had been turned over. When he switched on his torch for a closer look he found to his horror that a basket of wheat and another one of beans were missing. A desperate search failed to reveal any sign of them. Who had stolen them? Another hunt round the room revealed a cigarette end that he recognized as his uncle's. Wondering how it had got there he hurried over to the team leader Aniu's house.

It was a pitch-black night with not a star to be seen, and as he rushed along in his impatience his torch danced around like a firefly. When he was past the second lane he heard scurrying footsteps in the third, and he looked up just in time to see a dark figure flit across it. His eyes probed the night like searchlights now that he was thoroughly alerted. He ran after the figure to the beginning of the third lane and shouted, 'Who's there?' Then he heard a sound and saw the dark figure drop something. Running up and shining his torch on it he saw that it was the wheat seed stolen from the team office: 'Third Team' was painted on the basket in big red letters. He started off in pursuit again, shouting, 'Stop thief, stop thief!' All the dogs in the village started to bark as his shouts woke the sleeping commune members. With Zhenping after him the dark figure stumbled and ran in terror past the third lane and back into the first lane, not realizing that it was a cul-de-sac walled off at the end. 'Stop thief. He's stolen the team's seed,' shouted Zhenping when he reached the entrance to the lane. Zhenping's mother was the first person to open her door, and she came to the threshold brandishing a carrying-pole. 'Where is he?' she asked Zhenping. 'Where is the damn thief?' 'At the end of the alley. Catch him, mother. He's stolen the team's wheat seed.' 'Right then.' After a quick search she saw a piglet jump squealing out of the sty of the house opposite. Without a moment's hesitation she charged at it, waving her carrying-pole. Just as she was about to bring it swinging down she heard a hoarse, imploring voice saying, 'It's . . . it's me.' 'Oh . . . it's you.' She recognized it immediately as Wanben's. As she stood rooted to the ground with shock, not knowing what to do, she saw Wanben shoot out of the pigsty and into her house. She shut the door and shouted, 'He's got away. Stop thief!'

'Where did he go?' asked Zhenping, shining his torch around in his own house. By now everyone in the lane had opened their doors and joined the hunt, and in answer to all their questions Zhenping's mother waved and said, 'The thief went over the wall.' They all came rushing down the lane. When Zhenping reached the wall at the end of it he saw that as there was no ladder the thief could not have got over it. This made him curious. He searched the woodpile and pigsties nearby. No sign of him. The way his mother was shaking all over as she shut the door aroused his suspicions. 'Afraid of the thief?' he asked. His mother made a tutting noise and said, 'Forget about it. He's miles away by now. Go to bed.' 'All right. But I'll cook a bowl of rice first—I'm hungry.' He pushed his mother aside and went into the kitchen. As she could not stop him she went in with him, shutting the door of the room behind her. He shone his torch under her bed, on the stove, and in the corners. He was just going to climb up into the loft, which she knew would be disastrous, when she grabbed hold of him and whispered, 'Son, this is terribly important, terribly important.' 'I'm seeing this through to the bitter end,' he replied, shoving her aside and storming up the ladder. In the beam of his torch he saw Wanben crouching like a dog under a cupboard and gazing pathetically at him.

Wanben, who had been dissatisfied with the share-out after the spring harvest, had been watching for a chance to destroy Zhenping. That evening he had taken advantage of his absence to go along to the team's office with skeleton keys and steal some wheat. Now he was caught—like a junior devil who had run into the great wizard's net. Zhenping hesitated for a moment at the sight of him, stunned at meeting his enemy so unexpectedly. He glared malevolently at his uncle. Now that the cat was out of the bag Zhenping's mother pointed at the tip of her son's nose and began to scold him under her breath: 'You'll be the death of me. Even an ox's horn bends inwards,

I

so you ought to show some consideration for your own family. The gods themselves sometimes make mistakes. If your uncle has gone wrong the right thing to do is to criticize him on the quiet. What else can you be thinking of?' 'That would be like wrapping dogs muck up in clean white paper,' said Zhenping, flaring up. 'You'll see what I'm going to do.' He turned to go downstairs.

'I'm not dead yet,' she said, hanging on to him with both hands and not letting him take a step. 'Even if you have no consideration for him please show me some.' 'I'll show none for anybody.' Seeing the hard expression on Zhenping's face Wanben pretended to be tough and said, 'Let him go. It must be the fault of our ancestors that we're in this state now.' Zhenping ignored him and insisted on going downstairs, dragging his mother to the top of the ladder with him as she would not let go. 'How can you be so heartless,' she pleaded. 'You've no more chance of stopping me than of pouring all the water out of the reservoir in the mountains.' At this his mother lost her temper. 'I'll do it, I'll do it,' she said, slapping him in the face and making him so angry that his hair stood on end. As he thrust her forcefully aside he heard the team leader Aniu shouting, 'Where's the thief, Zhenping?' 'Here,' Zhenping shouted back, his voice shaking the whole village and making all Wanben's cronies tremble.

The cocks crowed. The 'iron inspector', the public-spirited recorder of work-points, realized that this was his moment of victory at last.

TWO MODERN
STORYTELLERS' STORIES

The storyteller's art has received much attention in the 1960s as it is one of the most effective ways of bringing political and other messages to ordinary people, particularly in the villages, who are not usually in the habit of reading for pleasure. The older storytellers have been urged to drop the traditional subject matter, often drawn from the novels of the Middle Ages, in favour of new, revolutionary themes; and youngsters are being encouraged to learn the art. The mixture of prose and verse in the first of these two pieces is an interesting reminder of the continuing vigour of old forms used by professional storytellers some thousand years ago.

The first of the two pieces, both of which date from the early 1960s, is based on a real co-op founded in Xisishilipu village, Zunhua county, Hopei province in 1952 by Wang Guofan (Wang Guxing in the story) and Du Kui (Du Hong). The plot of the story sticks very close to the account of this co-op in *The High Tide of Socialism in the Chinese Countryside,* a collection of articles on the co-op movement in China that appeared in 1955. In an editorial note to this article Mao Tse-tung held up the frugality with which this co-op had built itself up through its own efforts as a model to the whole country. Since then the co-op has become part of the Jianming Commune, and a much fuller history of it has been published. The second story is one of many on the improvement of farming methods.

Tang Gengliang 唐耿良

[T'ang Keng-liang]

The Paupers' Co-op

In a certain county of Hopei stands a mountain called Changyu, and in the valley below lies Changyu Village, a village always known for its poverty: poor hills, poor water, poor soil, and poor people, too. Poor hills? A mass of rocks and sand bare of trees. Poor water? Light rain used to seep so fast through the stones and sand that after a few days of sun the fields were burnt dry; but heavy rain made the mountain torrents flood, flattening the crops or sweeping them away. Poor soil? The district was hilly, with sandy soil, so of course its yields were low. Poor people? The village had 154 households, but three out of four consisted of poor peasants or hired hands, of whom several dozen had to beg for a living.

Soon after Liberation came land reform, when the poor and lower-middle peasants were given some land of their own. But lack of tools, draught animals, fertilizer, and funds made it impossible to grow good crops or to cope with drought and flood. Some of the former poor peasants and hired hands found themselves having to sell their newly-won land.

The few Party members in the village cudgelled their brains day and night to think of some way out. One of these, Wang Guxing, was a big, burly man and a good farmer. He foresaw that the 1952 crop failure would make it hard for the villagers to last through the winter; and it would be a disgrace if they had to apply to the state again for relief. Our brave Volunteers are fighting the enemy over in Korea, he thought one evening, but instead of doing our bit for the country we ask for thirty tons of grain and large relief loans every year, besides more than a hundred suits of padded clothes each winter. We can't let this go on. But how are we to change these poor hills? Will we paupers ever be able to stand on our own feet?

His thoughts were cut short by a knock on the door. When he opened it in came Du Hong, a younger Party member, bluff and outspoken. 'Have you heard, Old Wang?' he boomed. 'Li Ying's selling his land to Guo Rui.'

'What?' cried Wang. Of course, Li Ying had so many mouths to feed that although his eldest son was a hard worker they could never make ends meet. But land is a peasant's life— what would they live on if they sold it? 'Go and tell him not to sell, Du Hong,' said Wang. 'We'll all chip in to help if he's broke.'

'It's no use. I've already tried. He just said, "You're in the same boat, so how can you help? Even if I scrape by now, I can't last out till next year's harvest. I'm going to sell and have done with it!" What he told me next really upset me. Guo Rui had sneered at him, "To have land you must be born lucky. You paupers aren't fated to own land. Your shares of land won't put any meat on your bones." '

That made Wang Guxing see red.

Who was this Guo Rui? A landlord's stooge who'd got off lightly during land reform and was now growing brash again.

'Tell Li Ying not to sell,' said Wang. 'We'll help him out. I'll go and consult the district Party secretary. We don't want a new lot of poor peasants and hired hands, much less a new landlord class, or we'll have to have land reform all over again.'

'Right,' said Du. 'I'll go straight away.'

Wang Guxing went that same night to see District Party Secretary Cao. He was back the next morning and told Du Hong, 'Good news!'

'What good news?'

'The district cadres are examining some directives on agricultural co-operation. They want to have another try at setting up a few co-ops. Secretary Cao said, "So long as we poor stand together and follow Chairman Mao's line on agricultural co-operation, we can join forces in co-ops. If we pull together we can make the earth produce gold. Step by step we'll shake off our poverty." '

'Very good,' cried Du. 'I've been wishing we could have a co-op ever since I heard that other districts were trying them. We must make a go of it.'

Wang called together all the Party members to pass on

Secretary Cao's advice. Then they went off to try to persuade the villagers to form a co-operative.

This wasn't easy. Why not? Because co-ops were something new. No one had any idea what they were like or what their advantages were. So most of the peasants had doubts.

Some said, 'If so many people are thrown together there are bound to be quarrels and fights, even families breaking up.'

'Several dozen households farming together? They'll never agree. Everything will be messed up.'

'Too many cooks spoil the broth. Too many sons means none support their father. We're better off without co-ops.'

But the Party members didn't lose heart. They went on canvassing. And finally twenty-three households agreed to take the co-operative road proposed by the Party.

'Good,' said Wang. 'We'll start with twenty-three households. If we make a go of it, others will want to join.'

A meeting was held to set up the co-op. The twenty-three families who went saw at once that they were all poor peasants, the poorest in the whole village. This really was a Paupers' Co-op. They elected Wang Guxing as chairman and Du Hong as vice-chairman. When they reckoned up their assets, the co-op owned nearly forty acres of land, but no draught animals at all except for three legs of a donkey. Three legs of a donkey? Well, this donkey was the joint property of five households. Four of them had joined the co-op, but not the fifth; so one leg of the donkey didn't belong to the co-op. That meant they had a three-quarters share in this donkey. And not having a single ox or cart, how were they to till the land? The fields here are normally manured in winter. But with only three legs of a donkey it would take them till after midsummer to manure nearly forty acres! What was to be done? They couldn't invest any money, because most of them didn't even know how they were to manage till the New Year.

'Rope in a couple of rich peasants,' one suggested. 'They've got oxen and carts for us to fall back on.'

'That wouldn't work,' said Du Hong. 'We'd only get snubbed. Someone asked Guo Rui to join, and he promised to think it over, but he's been sneering behind our backs that we paupers are toads who want to feed on craneflesh. "They're starting a co-op without capital," he is saying, "and want me to join because I have draught animals. They must be dreaming! If these paupers can run a co-op, a worm can fly to heaven and become a dragon." Doesn't that make you mad? We paupers will have to grit our teeth and get this co-op on its feet by ourselves.'

Old Li Ying said, 'Du Hong's right. But if we can't buy oxen, carts, and fertilizer, it won't be easy to farm. Why don't we ask the government for a loan like the one they made to us when we had mutual-aid teams? They should give us more help now that we're starting a co-op.'

A good many people nodded in approval. But Wang stood up and said, 'I don't agree.' Why not? 'Our co-op's only just starting,' he explained. 'How can we beg from the government before we've anything to show for ourselves?'

'But our co-op has problems,' argued Li Ying.

'Maybe. But so has the government. Our Volunteers are fighting in Korea and need the whole country's support. We can't increase the government's burden. How could we suggest such a thing? Besides, we'd have to pay back the loan. It's no good saddling ourselves with a debt before we start producing. We must find our own way out of our difficulties.'

'All very fine,' replied Li. 'But we're broke. You can't squeeze oil out of a stone. What's to be done?'

'We each have a pair of hands. If we all set to, we can cope.'

'Of course, we've got hands,' said Li. 'But where's the money for animals and carts to come from?'

Wang pointed out of the window. 'There! Animals, carts, tools—we'll get the lot up there!'

All eyes turned to the mountains ten miles away. They couldn't for the life of them see how they were to provide animals and carts.

'The mountain's covered with brushwood, isn't it?' Wang continued. 'Cut some and sell it, and we'll be able to buy all we need.'

Du Hong jumped to his feet crying, 'Fine! I'll take all our able-bodied men up there tomorrow, Old Wang, while you stay here and get ready for the spring ploughing.'

'Let me go while you stay in the co-op,' countered Wang.

'No, no. You're commander-in-chief and I'm the vanguard. You've got a good head on your shoulders. Our co-op's only just set up, and if the landlords and rich peasants slander us or make trouble you can deal with them here much better than I can. But I'll make a better job of it up in the hills.'

'All right then,' Wang agreed.

So it was arranged that Du Hong should take eighteen able-bodied men with him the next morning. They would get oxen, carts, and tools from the mountains with their own hands.

It was after noon before everything was settled. Wang walked home, feeling hungry, and found his wife busy mending a padded jacket. He went over to the stove. The pan was empty.

'Why haven't you cooked the dinner yet?' he asked his wife.

'We've no rice or flour in the house,' she said. 'There's nothing to cook.'

'Never mind,' he told her. 'I'll go and borrow some food from a relative.'

He picked up a sack and went out.

The relative from whom he borrowed some grain invited him to share their meal; but, saying that he had eaten, Wang started for home. He was really cold and hungry now, his face blue with cold in the north wind. But his spirits were high as he thought about the work to be done after the nineteen men had gone. Someone called him. It was Li Ying's eldest son, Li Yi.

'What's up?' Wang asked.

'Dad sent me to tell you he can't go to the mountains to-morrow.'

'Why not?'

'We've nothing to eat at home. He doesn't like leaving us. . . .'

This was a real problem. Then Wang's eyes brightened as they fell on his sack. Plumping it on the ground, he said, 'That's simple. Take this sack of grain, and your dad can leave with an easy mind.'

The lad didn't want to take the grain. But when Wang insisted that he had enough at home and had borrowed this for the others, the boy shouldered the sack and hurried cheerfully home.

Meanwhile Wang was thinking that as it was cold and the ground was frozen they should see that the men cutting brushwood were warmly clad and well fed. Li Ying wouldn't be the only one with difficulties. Every one of the twenty-three households was poor. Some were probably short of grain, warm clothes, or shoes. They'd have to call on them all to find out about their problems and help solve them.

Forgetting his own cold and hunger, he went to see Du Hong instead of going home. He found him having supper.

'What's up?' asked Du.

'I'm wondering if our co-op members going to the mountains tomorrow will cause any problems for their families.'

'Why should they? They all agreed to go.'

Wang explained how Li Ying had run out of grain. 'This trip to the mountains is our co-op's first venture,' he said. 'We've got to make sure it's a success. You and I must do our job very thoroughly.'

'Yes, you're right, Old Wang. You think of everything.'

With that the two of them made the rounds of all the co-op members.

It turned out that each household had its difficulties. But when asked, the poor peasants straightened their backs and said, 'They're not worth talking about. We can cope without troubling you about every little thing.'

Some offered to lend a measure of grain or a pair of old shoes to those worse off than themselves. So all the snags were smoothed out, and the co-op members were very much touched by their leaders' thoughtfulness.

'Don't worry!' they told them. 'We'll put our backs into cutting enough brushwood to buy the tools and animals we need to make our co-op a going concern.'

Du Hong clapped Wang on the back. 'With this spirit we could move mountains!' he cried.

Deeply stirred himself, Wang answered, 'The harder times are, the better we must look after everybody. The work will go much more smoothly if our co-op members feel really close to us.'

It was dark by the time they finished their last call and Wang and Du separated. By now Wang's belly was rumbling. He remembered the grain he'd borrowed and sent to Li Ying. How was he going to square things with his wife? Nearing home, he saw her sitting in their doorway, and at the sight of his empty hands she asked, 'Where's the grain?'

He told her just what had happened. She said not a word, but tears ran down her cheeks. My man's right, of course, she was thinking. But what about us?

The two of them carried in some vegetables that had been put out to dry in the yard, carefully picking up each leaf from the ground and all the fragments on their clothes. After putting these precious last supplies on the vegetable pile, she told her husband with a sigh, 'These and a few handfuls of beans are all we have left.'

Wang wanted to comfort her but didn't know how. He was convinced, however, that the twenty-three households could take the greatest difficulties in their stride if they were really in step.

The next day he led the women to the fields to prepare for the ploughing, while Du Hong and his eighteen men marched off briskly to the mountains.

> Were they hard pressed? Not they!
> They coped the poor men's way.
>
>   Just see these men!
>
> Nineteen paupers of one heart and mind
> Plaited straw ropes and whetted their old sickles;
> Dry rations and bedding-rolls on their backs,
> They left their village and went into the hills.
> Among the treacherous rocks, the towering peaks,
> By day they cut brushwood, and they slept in an old
>   temple at night.
> The wind cut like a knife, snow whirled like feathers,
> But the poor have grit and courage higher than heaven.
> Despite their troubles they wrested treasures from the
>   mountains,
> And after a hard fight came home laden with spoils.

In twenty days they cut more than twenty tons of brushwood,

which they sold in town for 430 yuan. Was everyone pleased!
These paupers had never handled so much money.

They called a meeting of the whole co-op to discuss how to
use it. To start with, nobody spoke. Why not? Everyone was
wondering how to manage till the New Year.

At last Li Ying said, 'Chairman, the New Year will soon be
here, and none of us has a cent. In the past we'd have borrowed
from the rich, but this year they refuse to lend. They say,
"Your co-op's got all that cash; you paupers are flush now;
you don't need a loan," I think we should share out part of
this 430 yuan, so that every home has dumplings for New
Year.'

This proposal met with considerable support.

This is awkward, thought Wang Guxing. They have sweated
their guts out in the mountains for this cash, and it seems only
fair to let them enjoy the New Year; but we'll all suffer if we
share out this money. So he said, 'It's only natural to want a
good New Year; but if we share out this money we can't buy
oxen and carts or grow good crops. We'll be in the same fix
next year. "Don't burn in one day wood it took three years to
carry home." We must look ahead. If we tighten our belts now
for the sake of a good harvest next year, and make a go of the
co-op, we'll be sure of a happy New Year and we shan't have
to worry the rest of the time either. Let's work out the best use
for this money.'

That made sense to the rest. They had to cut their coat according to their cloth. A bad harvest later would be a high
price for dumplings now. They decided to tighten their belts.
Instead of sharing out the money, they went to town and bought
an ox, a mule, a cart, and nineteen sheep. The whole co-op
exulted over these purchases.

But these new assets themselves created new problems. They
had no pen for the sheep, no harness for the cart, no fodder
for the ox. What were they to do? Ask the members to help.
Being poor they could only make poor contributions. Each
family gave two planks of wood, two nails and two trusses of
straw. Then they built a pen for the sheep and a byre for the
ox with these and with stones from the river bed. That still

left the problem of fodder and harness unsolved. Wang pointed through the window with both hands: 'Get them from the mountains!'

Not all the men could be spared during the spring ploughing, so only nine were sent this time. After roughing it in the hills for twenty days, they carried back more than two hundred loads of brushwood, which fetched 210 yuan. Apart from harness, they bought another mule, eleven more sheep, and a bean-mill to start a side-line in bean-curd. So now the paupers' co-op owned, in all, one ox, two mules, thirty sheep, a cart, and three legs of a donkey. Its members were full of enthusiasm.

But willing as the paupers were to work, they were still hard up, and long before harvest time they ran out of grain. Some cooked a whole basket of greens with a handful of rice; others had nothing at all to put in the pan. When Dai Ming collapsed in the fields from hunger, Wang took him home and made him a broth of the last few beans in their house. He and his wife now had to make do with wild plants.

Hunger affected the co-op members' work and their morale too.

Li Ying started grousing in the fields, 'If I hadn't joined the co-op,' he said, 'I could have sent my son out as a hired hand. That way I'd have had one less mouth to feed and some cash at the end of the year. Now we haven't so much as a grain of rice, yet he expects us to feed him.'

Li Ying's boundary stones were in the way of the plough, and one co-op member started to move them away. But Li growled, 'Don't waste your time shifting those. After the autumn harvest I'm leaving the co-op. I'd only have to lug them back again.'

Later someone urged Wang Guxing, 'Let's pick some of our unripe crop, Old Wang, just enough to keep us from starving!'

'And spoil our harvest? No!' said Wang. 'We must tighten our belts now to reap more grain later on. We'll find some other way out.'

The Party members talked it over and solved the problem again the poor man's way. They would cut brambles, strip the leaves off for compost, and sell the stems to buy grain.

Guo Rui was doing his best to put a spoke in their wheel and wreck the co-op. 'Those paupers are desperate,' he gibed behind their backs, 'and no one will buy their brambles. Their bellies are rumbling with hunger. The sooner they break up the co-op, the better for them.'

Du Hong leapt with rage when this came to his ears.

'It's no use flaring up,' said Wang. 'We don't have to sell to him.'

He got the co-op members to make baskets and crates out of the brambles, and they sold these in other villages. But the small sum of money raised did not buy enough grain to go round. Wang let others have his share. When they realized this and protested, he said, 'Never mind. We've still some grain at home.'

He was growing paler and thinner every day. Some neighbours who checked up on the quiet, found that his family was living on husks and weeds.

The Party had taken an interest in this new co-op from the start. When the district Party secretary learned of its predicament, he hurried to Changyu Village with a loan.

'Don't worry about us, we're all right,' said Wang Guxing. 'I guarantee no one will die of hunger!'

'All right, are you?' retorted Cao. 'You're as pale as a ghost, man!'

Wang covered his face with his hands and laughed. 'That's my natural colour. I'm not hungry.'

'Not hungry? You haven't eaten a grain of rice for days.'

'I don't mind missing a few meals if the co-op can grow strong enough so that none of our members need ever go hungry again. Besides, the Party and the government have much bigger problems to cope with. We don't want to add to their burden.'

With Party members like these, who always put others first and work so whole-heartedly for the common good, thought Secretary Cao, they're bound to make a success of the co-op. 'Comrade,' he said, 'if people have problems, it's up to the state to help. Buy some grain with this fifty yuan, and go on finding ways to tide yourselves over. If you succeed, co-operation will take root in this poor mountain valley. And that will be wonderful.'

They bought grain for the co-op with the loan. Deeply touched, one member fingered the grain and declared, 'They say that nobody is as dear as a mother. But the Party cares for us better than a mother. Just in the nick of time the Party's sent us this loan to see us through.'

That made them work harder than ever. They put plenty of manure on the fields and kept them well weeded, so that the crops grew well. When the peasants working on their own saw this, they realized that co-operation was better. Some of them secretly made up their minds to join the co-op after the harvest.

Now only one person was worried. Who? The landlord's stooge Guo Rui. I must find some way to wreck the co-op before these paupers set it on its feet, he told himself. I shall compete with the co-op and outdo it! My family has a donkey, three oxen, thirty sheep, four pigs, and over five acres of good land. With all my livestock and capital, I'm sure I can show these paupers where they get off.

Part of his land lay next to some of the co-op's fields. He decided to sow the same crop and do whatever the co-op members did. Like them, he sowed an acre to maize. At first both crops did pretty much the same. In summer, when the co-op manured its plot with sheep droppings, Guo Rui used pig-dung instead. But whereas the co-op's twenty-three families had plenty of hands to carry manure and spread it, only three of Guo Rui's family worked on the land. It was a long way, uphill and down, from his home to the field; and he and his sons were so busy carting manure that they had no time to spread it. That afternoon Guo Rui noticed that the co-op had just about finished, while he still had a good deal of dung to carry. He gritted his teeth and filled basket after basket to the brim. His two sons sweated under their loads till they felt that their backs would break; the donkey's legs nearly buckled under the weight; and Guo Rui himself panted as he staggered along. Though they worked with all their strength, they got only half their dung to the field by the time the co-op was spreading its last lot. Guo Rui dumped his load and went back for more without even stopping for breath. But before he reached the village the co-op members had knocked off and started for home, singing and chatting. Fuming inwardly, he decided to make one last trip. But his back was aching, his two sons were worn out, and however hard they beat the donkey it would not budge. They had to take lighter loads and stop every few steps to rest. At the end of this trip it was dark, so they left the dung piled by the field to spread the next day.

When they reached home and sat down to supper, it started to thunder. Then for over an hour there was a downpour of rain. Guo Rui cursed and swore and could not sleep all night. First thing the next morning he and his sons dashed to the field. Their whole pile of pig-dung had been washed away—into the co-op's land, too, which was lower than theirs. The maize there was green and sturdy after its soaking, thanks to all the dung, while Guo's by comparison was lank and droopy. In his rage, he sold two sheep and bought some chemical fertilizer in the town.

When Du Hong saw this he asked, 'Why don't we buy some fertilizer too?'

'We must stick to our poor men's way,' said Wang Guxing. 'Let him fertilize his fields; we'll hoe ours well. Loosening the soil is as good as a dressing of dung. Take my word for it, a few extra hoeings will do more for the crop than his fertilizer.'

Guo Rui wasn't worried when he saw them hoeing. All you paupers can do is work your heads off, he thought. Just wait till you see what this fertilizer does to my maize! Little did he know that he had applied too much. As the sun blazed down, the leaves of his maize started wilting. Father and sons made haste to water and weed the field, but it was too late. And when Guo tried to hire a labourer there were none to be found. Why not? Because all the paupers had joined the co-op, and the peasants working on their own had no time to spare.

The co-op's maize grew tall and strong. By harvest time each cob was about a foot long, as plump as a pestle, and covered with symmetrical golden kernels the size of horses' teeth. Guo Rui's cobs were no longer than a fountain-pen, no thicker than a man's thumb, and only had a few scattered kernels.

Now the harvest was shared out. Li Ying's family of seven owned two acres of land and three of its members worked. The previous year in the mutual-aid team they had harvested six

piculs of grain; this year in the co-op they got forty-one. Li Ying
jumped for joy and caught Wang Guxing by the arm. 'Let's
move those boundary stones away, chairman,' he cried. 'They
use up a furrow or two of land, and get in our way as well.'

'Don't let's fag ourselves out shifting those,' chuckled Wang.
'We'll only have to help you lug them back in a few days.'

'Come off it, chairman! My mind's made up. I'm in the co-op
for life. You couldn't get me to leave even if you kicked me out.'

It had been a tough year, but already the paupers' co-op
had shown the advantages of co-operation. After the harvest
sixty new families joined, bringing the total up to eighty-three
households. Hard work and thrifty management enabled the
co-op to forge ahead every year, so that by 1956, three years
later, Changyu Village had changed out of all recognition.
Every household entitled to had joined the co-op, and now they
combined with three neighbouring villages to form a co-
operative of the more advanced type. By now their poor
mountain valley had grown rich, the barren hills were smiling;
flinty tracks had been transformed into smooth highways,
thatched huts into tiled stone houses; and every single family
had surplus grain and money in the bank. Strange to say, more
people were getting married, too. What's strange about that,
you ask? Well, for Changyu Village it was a big thing. The
place had been so poor before that the Changyu girls refused
to marry local boys, and girls from outside wouldn't come to
Changyu either. In fact, they had had a saying:

> The hills are strewn with stones galore;
> The village has bachelors by the score.

And now? Not only did the local girls marry village boys, but
girls from other villages gladly came here as brides. In 1956
alone, twenty-four young couples married.

Marriage is a good thing, of course, but its effect on production was rather bad. How's that? The young fellows had
been working for all they were worth, assembling cheerfully
before the bell sounded and charging off like tigers to the fields
as soon as the team leader assigned them jobs. And now?
Now that they were married, they went to work later. Some-

times not until the work bell had stopped ringing did the newly-
weds saunter out; and in the fields each kept looking right and
left to see where the other was. Before sunset they were thinking
of knocking off and through cupped hands would hail each
other: 'Hey! Time to pack up!' A few hours apart seemed to
them such a long separation that they had to walk home side
by side. With all this starting late and stopping early, a job
that should have taken one day took two, and as time went by
the work suffered. Sometimes a young fellow would simply fail
to show up. If taken to task by the team leader, he would retort,
'What does it matter? Deduct it from my work-points! I've
grain in my bin, and money in the bank, I don't care.'

Wang Guxing raised this problem with the Party committee.

'In our parents' day,' said Du Hong, 'newly-weds were too
bashful to greet each other if they met in the lane. But these
young couples nowadays cling together like sticky rice—
there's no parting them! We must come down hard on the
slackers.'

'That wouldn't get us anywhere,' said Wang. 'Let's call the
young people to a meeting this evening and talk it over with
them.'

After supper, the twenty-four pairs of newly-weds and the
village's unmarried girls and lads assembled in high spirits.

'I've a tricky question to put to you,' announced Wang.

'Fire ahead, chairman. We'll answer it, don't worry.'

'All right then. Tell me, how is life today?'

'That's easy,' said one lad. 'Life today is fine.'

'And how did we come by this fine life?'

'By hard work.'

At this point Du Hong sprang to his feet. 'Hard work?' he
boomed. 'Tell me this, then. Your grandad and your dad
sweated their guts out, but one starved to death, the other
hanged himself. And your family couldn't even afford coffins
for them. Just wrapped some matting round them, didn't
they?'

This silenced the young people, until one of them hit on the
answer. 'We owe our good life today to the leadership of the
Party.'

'Right!' said Wang. 'The Party saved us. Got us to organize

co-ops, to make our poor mountain valley yield good crops, so that now we paupers live like human beings. Without Party leadership, we would have sweated our guts out and got nowhere. Don't you feel you're letting the Party down? A young husband and wife should be loving, but not so loving that they slack at work. Compare today with the past. The better our life is, the harder we should work. Besides, the good times are just beginning for us—we've only taken the first step up the mountain. We're still a long, long way from communism. This is no time for slacking.'

The young people's faces were red. They all saw the matter now in the right perspective. The next morning as soon as the work bell rang, the young men once more charged like tigers to the fields.

Things got better year by year in Changyu Village. In 1958, several co-ops merged in the Guangming People's Commune, with Wang Guxing as its chairman. Now it is 1962, just ten years after the co-op was set up. What earth-shaking changes these brief ten years have seen! In 1952 they started a co-op with a three-quarters' share in a donkey. Today they've gone a long way towards mechanizing agriculture. They have tractors to plough the fields, electric pumps, motors to hull rice, trucks to transport their produce. Yes!

> Three legs of a donkey then, and men drew the plough;
> They've mules and horses, trucks and tractors now!

Ten years ago there was more sand than soil on the stony hills, so that the crops were spoiled by flood or drought. In these ten years they've built reservoirs and canals, changing the sandy hillsides into irrigated fields; they can water the crops in time of drought, and pump out excess water in time of flood. In place of six hundredweight an acre, they now raise one and a half tons or so, and the once barren hills are covered with fruit trees. So Changyu Village today has rich mountains, rich water, rich soil, and rich people, too.

Six families out of ten have built new houses. Take Li Ying's younger brother Li Shen, who used to live in a tumbledown thatched stone cottage which let in the wind and the rain.

Now he has a spacious five-roomed house with a granite foundation, walls of brick with black mortar between, glass window-panes flooding the rooms with sun, a flat cement roof, and bright electric lights. If you stand on a hill in the evening and look down, the electric lights are like pearls gleaming in the dark, and Changyu Village is a beautiful sight! There was not a single bicycle here in the old days, but now there are 137. Even old Li Ying has bought one, and he can ride it no hands!

Truly:

> This village took the fine collective road,
> Made lakes high in the hills, canals below;
> Its co-op started with a three-legged donkey,
> Now trucks and tractors rumble to and fro.
> The paupers have transformed once barren hills,
> And there's a lesson here for all of us:
> By self-reliance, hard work, and sheer grit
> We'll make our country still more prosperous!

Xu Daosheng 徐道生
[Hsü Tao-sheng]

and

Chen Wencai 陈文彩
[Ch'en Wen-ts'ai]

Two Ears of Rice

In our new society, all the hundred and one professions produce their own experts.

The Zhang Family Production Team of a commune near Shanghai had a member called Zhang Yougu, known as a local expert in seed cultivation. He had a square ruddy face, shaggy grizzled beard, and bushy eyebrows, while the thumbs of his horny hands were as thick as yams. When he didn't go barefoot he wore straw or rush sandals. You could tell at a glance that he was a seasoned farmer.

Whenever Zhang Yougu had time to spare, he roamed the countryside taking a good look round. Other people going to market or to a commune meeting would take the road, but he insisted on taking a path through the fields. So seldom was he at home that his wife used to complain, 'Look at you, dropping in for meals as if this were a canteen or just coming back to sleep as if your home were an inn. When you do show up, you're like a bus pulling up at a stop for a minute before roaring off again.' But although she nagged she was secretly pleased, because she knew that her old man was working for the common good. So she never tried to hold him back.

Why did Zhang spend so much time rambling through the fields? He had his reason. Good bamboos, he used to think, produce good bamboo shoots; good seeds yield a good harvest. To raise our output of rice we must have good seeds. The same amount of manure and the same field management produce different yields depending on the quality of the seeds. So

Zhang Yougu was always on the look-out for high-yield rice seeds for his production team.

One autumn day, when the fields were a mass of gold and the late rice was nearly ripe enough for harvesting, Zhang rambled out again after finishing work. He kept his eyes skinned as he strolled this way and that. When he reached the ninth patch of paddy he caught sight of two ears of rice swaying in the wind some way off. They were quite enormous, over-topping the rest by a good three or four inches. The sight warmed his heart. Truly:

> You can wear out iron shoes searching in vain;
> Then all at once your wish you gain!

He rolled up his trouser legs and raced to the spot. Parting the paddy on either side, he examined these two plants from tip to root, then from root to tip again. Ha! The heavy ears nodded in the breeze on their thick stems. He counted. One ear had 284 grains, the other 316, making exactly six hundred, no more and no less! Feasting his eyes on them, Zhang pinched, stroked and fingered the ears, longing to pick them at once and take them home. But that wouldn't do. They weren't quite ripe. Yet if he left them there, they might be damaged by the strong north-west wind. He was in a quandary until he spotted a clump of reeds by the stream. The very thing! He hurried over and pulled up a few, with which he built an enclosure for the two plants. Now they were as safe as houses. He inspected them first from one side, then the other, with rising jubilation. The next thing he knew, the moon was up and the frogs were croaking. Aiya! he thought, I haven't had supper yet.

Zhang trudged home, grinning from ear to ear. As soon as he crossed the threshold his wife called out: 'Look at you, old man! Not coming home till so late. Where have you been? What kept you all this time?'

'Today the bus ran late,' he chuckled.

'It's no use talking to you,' she complained. 'You've always got some excuse.'

The days sped by until a week had soon passed. The late rice was being harvested field by field. After knocking off work, Zhang went back to pluck those two ears. In the week since he first saw them, they had grown more golden and the grains had filled out. He stepped up to them, picked them very carefully, and went home joyfully with the ears in his pocket.

As soon as his wife set eyes on him she cried, 'Well, wonders will never cease! What brings you home so early for a change?'

'A wonder indeed,' he replied. 'They ran an extra bus this evening.'

'Oh, that's nothing special,' she said airily. 'We can all have supper earlier this evening.'

As they ate their supper, Zhang Yougu could not take his mind off the six hundred seeds in his pocket. His wife, meanwhile, was thinking: I must find time tomorrow to sow those bean seeds of ours. 'Tell me, old man,' she exclaimed, 'where did you put those beans we kept last year for seeds?'

'Seeds, did you say? Six hundred! Think of it.'

'Is that all? We had more than that, surely.'

'That's a lot. Two hundred and eighty-four plus three hundred and sixteen. Figure it out for yourself. That's exactly six hundred seeds, no more and no less.'

His wife couldn't make head or tail of this. When she asked for an explanation, she realized that her old man had misunderstood. Zhang chuckled inwardly too at the thought of it, as after supper he found the beans for his wife. He then fetched a piece of cellophane, dusted it, wrapped up the two ears of rice and put this small package away.

When the sun was as high as a bamboo pole the next morning, Zhang unwrapped the two ears and put them on the roof to sun, hurrying home before sunset to put them away again. He did this for several days until they were dry. Now, he thought, they can be stored away until sowing time next year. Where's the best place for them? Hung up? No, the seeds might drop out. In a drawer? No, the rats would eat them. Ah, that's it! He cleaned out a short length of hollow bamboo, slipped the ears inside, sealed up both ends and tucked this container away in one corner of the living room, where no hens could get at his seeds, no rats drag them off. They were as safe as houses.

Time flew by, and soon it was the twenty-fourth day of the

lunar twelfth month, when the custom in the villages is for each household to do a thorough clean-out. Zhang Yougu had a meeting in the commune that day, so his wife would be all on her own. A model housewife, she got up bright and early to set about her cleaning. First she swept the kitchen, then the living room and bedroom, and finally the courtyard. After that she had a good look round to see if any dirt had escaped her attention. Everything seemed spick and span until she noticed a black object in one corner of the living room. What was it? Why, she'd nearly missed it. She hurried over and picked up the bamboo container, thick with dust. Whatever was inside it? She shook it and heard a faint rustling. Aha, she thought, my old man must have caught some crickets during his rambles and put them in this. She removed one stopper, and out fell two ears of rice. Is that all? Why should he leave these here? she wondered. Her first impulse was to throw the ears away, but grain was too precious, 'I know what,' she told herself. 'I'll add them to the team's rice which is still sunning outside.' No sooner said than done. She stepped to the door and threw the ears on to the pile. Then she took the bamboo container to the kitchen and tossed it on to the wood stack before sitting down to make rice dumplings for their supper. Little did she know the trouble this was to cause.

What meeting was Zhang attending in the commune? A meeting on seeds. The commune Party secretary announced that to raise the yield of rice good seeds must be chosen. When Zhang told them about the two fine ears he had picked the previous autumn, the Party secretary urged him to go ahead and grow more. Zhang started back in high spirits, his thoughts running on his six hundred seeds. When he reached home, he saw at a glance that the place was spotless.

'Good for you, old girl!' he cried. 'You're a model house-keeper, all right. The whole place is as clean as a new pin.'

His wife, busy making dumplings, was surprised to see her old man back so early and complimenting her too as soon as he crossed the threshold. Beaming with smiles, fairly walking on air, she said, 'Well, didn't you tell me that cleanliness makes for good health?'

She was cut short by a sudden yell from her husband. 'Aiya! That bamboo container—did you see it?'

'What a fright you gave me, shouting like that! I thought something serious was up. If it's that bamboo you want, it's by the stove.'

Zhang dashed into the kitchen and grabbed the bamboo. But when he picked it up he found it empty.

Another yell set his wife wondering, 'What now?'

'Didn't you see two rice ears in this?' he demanded.

The husband was burning with anxiety, but his wife, cool as a cucumber, hadn't even turned a hair.

'Those two rice ears?' she said. 'I picked off the grains and threw them on to that pile outside.'

'What's that?' he bellowed. 'You're crazy!'

Why is he calling me names? she wondered. Not one squabble have we had in all the years we've been married. Has attending a meeting in the commune gone to his head? Or did he get a dressing-down? Is he trying to take it out on me? Well, I'm not putting up with that.

'Who are you calling names?' she protested. 'What's so special about going to a meeting? Two ears of rice aren't pearls or agates. Pearls and agates are worth money; but what's so special about two ears of rice?'

By now her old man was fairly burning with rage. 'So pearls and agates cost money! Those two paddy ears of mine were priceless!'

The rage Zhang was in made his back start aching again from an old injury. Turning away from his wife, he stumped angrily towards the door. He nearly tripped over the bamboo, the sight of which added fuel to his fire. A vicious kick sent it rolling to the threshold, and as it rebounded out fell two golden grains. With eyes for nothing else, Zhang lost no time in retrieving the container, from which he emptied out another four grains. Two plus four made six! Six left out of six hundred —at least that was better than nothing. He gathered the seeds together, determined to keep them safely this time, and slipped them one by one into a glass jar. Where could he store it? After careful consideration, he put this jar away with his voting card.

And there the seeds stayed until after the next year's Grain Rains,[1] when it was time to sun them. He had just taken out the jar one afternoon when the team leader called from the yard, 'Yougu! Come here a minute, will you?' Leaving the jar on the table, Zhang went out.

Zhang Yougu had an eight-year-old granddaughter, Xiaohong, whose dearest pet was a hen. Xiaohong had fed this hen since the day it was hatched; it was she who let it out of its coop, and she who shut it up at night. The hen, a fair size now, was devoted to her. Each morning when Xiaohong set off to school with her satchel, the hen would escort her to the gate; and there it would meet her when she came home again. But today when Xiaohong came skipping home, to her surprise there was no sign of her hen. She ran to the coop and found that it was laying. Xiaohong walked quietly into the house, put her satchel on the table and took out her arithmetic book to do some sums. But before she had opened the book the egg was laid and the hen ran in, clucking, to announce to its young mistress the good news that it had laid an egg. A reward of grain was given for each egg laid, and this clucking was a reminder. Xiaohong went at once to the kitchen, but found the door locked.

'I'll give you something in a moment,' she promised. 'Just wait.'

She sat down again to her homework, but the hen continued clucking indignantly. It hopped on to a stool, and from the stool on to the table. Squawking and flapping its wings, it knocked over the jar, which fell on a stoneware pot and smashed. Xiaohong didn't notice the gleaming golden grains, but the hen's sharp eyes spotted them and it plopped down to peck one up. Mmmm! Tasted good. It proceeded to peck up the rest.

Just then who should come in but Zhang. His first words were, 'Where's that jar of mine, Xiaohong?'

'It got knocked over and smashed.'

Zhang looked down and saw the hen pecking up the sixth and last grain. He bounded forward and caught it by the neck.

[1] A period of fifteen days in late April and early May.

What could be done? There was a pair of scissors on the table. He snatched them up and cut the hen's throat.

'Don't kill my hen, grandad!' begged Xiaohong. 'Don't kill my hen!'

But it was too late. The hen had breathed its last. The little girl's crying brought in her grandmother.

'Granny!' sobbed Xiaohong. 'Grandad's killed my hen.'

The old woman gasped—this seemed to her so senseless. 'Mercy on us, old man!' she cried. 'Are you off your head? Killing this hen is worse than smashing a whole jar of eggs.'

Then she saw him do something that struck her as even more senseless. A hen is always plucked before it's cleaned, but without stopping to pluck it he slit it open and fished about in its crop till he found two yellow grains, which he placed on the table. Since there were no more there he cut open the gullet and retrieved the four other seeds. Now his wife understood. Their squabble just before New Year had been over these rice seeds, and they were the reason today why he'd killed the hen. She knew they were precious seeds.

But Xiaohong, not to be comforted, was sobbing, 'My hen, grandad! I want my hen!'

'Don't cry, child,' said Zhang Yougu. 'Come here. I'll tell you a story.'

At that Xiaohong dried her eyes and sat down on a stool.

'It happened twenty years ago, Xiaohong,' began her grandfather. 'There was a man in our village who was cruelly ground down and fleeced by the landlord. In those days the peasants who tilled a *mu* of his land had to pay one picul and eight pecks of rice as rent. Well, this fellow sweated his guts out year after year to produce some high-yield rice seeds called "yellow paddy," which yielded 750 catties a *mu*.[1] The poor peasants from near by all came asking to exchange seeds with him. But that landlord Zhang Boren was a vicious schemer. When he got wind of this he thought: You paupers want to stand on your own feet. If you produce more rice you'll stop borrowing from me at eighty per cent interest. He arrested that peasant on a flimsy pretext, strung him up and

---

[1] This would probably have been $2\frac{1}{2}$ to 3 tons per acre.

beat him for one whole day and night, while his thugs went and ransacked the peasant's home. They smashed his vats and took away all his grain. Not a seed of that "yellow paddy" did they leave him. When at last they untied the peasant, the landlord kicked him in the back. "So a worm like you, crawling through the mud, wants to produce high-yield rice," he sneered. "Bah, you're dreaming! A clodhopper setting up as an agricultural expert!" After that, Xiaohong, the peasant gave up all hope of raising high yielding rice.'

Xiaohong had caught on. Wiping her eyes she said, 'You needn't go on, grandad. I understand.'

'Just think it over, Xiaohong. Since Liberation, we poor people have stood up and become our own masters. The Party's called on us to raise our output of rice by choosing good seeds. Do you think I should sow these six seeds or not?'

'Of course you should!' she said.

As Zhang put this question to the child, he gave the same decided answer in his own mind.

Zhang was too busy thinking to sleep much that night. In order not to let the Party down, he would have to find a good place to sow the seeds. He got up before dawn to select a suitable plot and fixed on a small pond with a rich muddy bed. One by one he sowed his six seeds in the mud. After that he went back every day to see if they had sprouted. Three days later one seed came up. Zhang's jubilation gave him fresh energy. In another three days three more sprouted. But a whole week later the other two had still failed to germinate. When Zhang uncovered them, they had turned black. Of course, he thought, those two seeds in the hen's crop must have been spoiled. So there were only four seedlings, instead of six, and these he tended with the utmost care. He went to look at them first thing every morning, and again before going to the fields; he took his rice bowl to that plot during meal times, and went back there straight after work.

The four seedlings grew taller and greener day by day. But then two of them were trampled down by some sheep, leaving only two precious plants! Zhang redoubled his vigilance.

Time flashed by until it was autumn again. When he reaped

his two rice plants, the ears weighed 4.3 ounces.[1] The commune Party committee took Zhang's experiment very seriously. The next year they gave him a small patch on which to sow these seeds, and this time he reaped 33 catties of grain. The third year he sowed two *mu*, which yielded 1,051 catties each. By 1963, the whole commune was using these new seeds, while quite a few people were coming from other communes in the county and elsewhere to learn from their experience.

One day in the winter of 1963 the commune leadership sent someone to ask Zhang Yougu to attend a meeting of advanced agricultural workers in the county town the next day, telling him that he would be expected to speak. The cadre bringing the message produced a letter from the Shanghai Scientific and Technical Association inviting Zhang to become a member. He was too happy to sleep that night. He tossed about in bed, turning over six times a minute! If I keep this up, he thought, in eight hours I shall have turned over 2,880 times and that will ruin the bed. So instead he sat up and thought of everything—whole cratefuls and sackfuls of words—that he wanted to say at the meeting.

The next day Zhang went to the meeting in the town. When he was referred to as a farming expert, scene after scene flashed through his mind like a film. He recalled how he had been ground down by the landlord, and his back started aching again where he had been kicked. A bitter-sweet sensation flooded his heart, as if a jar of mixed spices had been emptied into it. When his turn came to speak, the words stuck in his throat like a dumpling in a teapot. It took him three minutes to calm down enough to shout, 'Long live Chairman Mao! Long, long live Chairman Mao!'

Truly:

> When peasants lived in utter destitution
> They had no means of growing better seeds;
> But farming now is for the revolution,
> Success must follow where the Party leads.

---

[1] About 7 English ounces.

LIST OF SOURCES

Titles are given in Chinese characters as well as roman letters.

TWO NIAN STORIES
Gao Yuanxun: 'Er Laoyuan' (Liu Eryuan)
Guo Tongde: 'Qiganzhen' (The Flagpoles)
　　from *Nianjun gushi ji*, ed. Anhui-sheng Fouyang zhuanqu
　　　wenxue-yishu gongzuozhe lianhehui (1962)

高元勋　　《二老渊》

郭同德　　《旗杆阵》

安徽省阜阳专区文学艺术工作者联合会编　　捻军故事集

Lu Xun: 'Kong Yiji' and 'Guxiang' (The New-Year Sacrifice)
　　from *Lu Xun quan ji* (1957 ed.), vol. I
　　　　'Zhufu' (My Old Home)
　　from *Lu Xun quan ji* (1957 ed.), vol. II

鲁迅　　《孔乙己》，《故乡》　　鲁迅全集 1

　　　　《祝福》　　　　　　鲁迅全集 2

Rou Shi: 'Wei nulid muqin' (Slaves' Mother)
　　from *Shierjia*, ed. Gao Lei (1955)

柔石　　《为奴隶的母亲》　　高垒编　　十二家

Guo Moruo: 'Shuanghuang' (Double Performance)
　　from *Moruo xuan ji*, vol. V

郭沫若　　《双簧》　　沫若选集 5

Mao Dun: 'Chuanshang' (On the Boat)
　　from *Mao Dun wen ji*, vol. VIII (1966)

茅盾　　《船上》　　茅盾文集

Lao She: 'Kai shi daji' (A Brilliant Beginning)
　　from *Lao She xiaoshuo xuan*, n.d. (? reprint of 1947 ed.)

老舍　　《开市大吉》　　老舍小说选

Ye Zi: 'Tou lian' (Stealing Lotuses)
from *Ye Zi chuangzuo ji* (1955)

叶紫　　《偷莲》　　叶紫创作集

Zhang Tianyi: 'Duliang' (Generosity)
from *Zhui* (2nd ed., 1941)

张天翼　　《度量》　　追

Ai Wu: 'Haidao shang' (On the Island)
from *Nan xing ji* (1964 ed.)

艾芜　　《海岛上》　　南行记

Zhao Shuli: 'Meng Xiangying fanshen' (Meng Xiangying
Stands Up)
from *Li Youcai banhua* (2nd ed., 1958)

赵树理　　《孟祥英翻身》　　李有才板话

Gao Langting: 'Huaiyiwan'
from Kong Que and others, *Yige nüren fanshend gushi* (1949)

高朗亭　　《怀义湾》　　孔厥等　　一个女人翻身的故事

Sun Li: *Tie mu qian zhuan* (The Blacksmith and the Carpenter)
(1959)

孙犁　　《铁木前传》

He Guyan: 'Feng' (Maple Leaves)
from *Duanpian xiaoshuo xuan*, ed. Zhongguo Zuojia Xiehui
(1956)

和谷岩　　《枫》　　中国作家协会编　　短篇小说选

Fang Shumin: 'Shuang chen yue' (The Moon on a Frosty
Morning)
from *Xue da deng* (1964)

房树民　　《霜晨月》　　雪打灯

Wang Xingyuan: 'Tiebi yushi' (The Iron Inspector)
from *Xinren xiaoshuo xuan* (1965)

王杏元　　《铁笔御史》　　新人小说选

TWO MODERN STORYTELLERS' STORIES

Tang Gengliang: 'Qiong bangz banshe' (The Paupers' Co-op)
   from *Shengchan douzheng he kexue shiyan gushi ji* (Shanghai,
   1965)

Xu Daosheng and Chen Wencai: 'Liangge dao suitou' (Two
   Ears of Rice)
   from *Gongnongbing gushihui xuan*, 2nd series (Peking, 1965)

唐耿良　　《穷棒子办社》　　生产斗争和科学试验故事集

徐道生　陈文彩　　《两个稻穗头》　　工农兵故事会选第二集